GRAHAM HUTTON was born and brought up in Essex, where most of the novel is based. He was educated at the local school before being enrolled by his parents at a boys' boarding school in Surrey. Graham spent most of his life working as an accountant, employed in the health service. A serious traffic accident in 1996 left him disabled and partially sighted. The doctor's prognosis was that he would never walk again and be confined to bed. With the help of members of his family and friends, Graham learnt to walk short distances. This enabled him to begin putting his life together again after many years of inactivity. On a holiday in Tenerife he met an authoress, who persuaded him that it might be good therapy to spend his mornings writing a novel, and even advised him on the elements of successful writing.

Gloworm: In the Beginning is the first book in a trilogy about the adventures of George Earlswood. Since the purpose of writing was purely as therapy, no action was taken to get the work published, until one day a friend asked to read it. Her opinion was that it was the type of book that you did not want to put down and she said how much she was looking forward to reading the second book. Since then several friends have read the book and offered similar comments. Inspired by this enthusiasm Graham has finished writing his second story, called the *Gloworm Chronicles*, and is currently working on the last book if the trilogy, titled *Gloworm: At the End of the Day*.

GLOWORM

In the Beginning

GLOWORM

In the Beginning

GRAHAM HUTTON

ATHENA PRESS
LONDON

GLOWORM

In the Beginning

ISBN 978 1 84748 588 5

First published 2009 by
ATHENA PRESS
Queen's House, 2 Holly Road
Twickenham TW1 4EG
United Kingdom

Printed for Athena Press

This book is dedicated to all the hospital staff who treated me following my accident, and to the many relatives, friends and neighbours who have supported me since, but especially to my wife, Christine, without whose support and encouragement this book might never have been written.

From Small Beginnings

The story of 'Gloworm' begins on a hot, airless, sunny summer's day in July 1969. I had made an early start in order to make the journey from my red-brick university town to my parents' home in Essex. This would be the first time I had been home, after informing my parents' that I had gained a first-class honours degree in management studies as well as completing my accountancy examinations, the results of which would not be known until the middle of August.

Lily (the name I had given to my dark blue Ford Anglia) was purring away to the sounds of Jerry Keller's 'Here Comes Summer'. I too was in a restful state of mind, having completed my studies, and was now looking forward to a long and relaxing holiday. I had decided that I would not be beginning my career in the family firm until after my twenty-first birthday the following September. That meant two whole months of rest and total relaxation.

Looking back, I can still remember the overwhelming sense of excitement, pride and tranquillity that I felt as I turned in through the large wrought-iron gates leading to Alswell Manor. I suppose that this feeling was akin to the feelings enjoyed by a conquering hero home in triumph after a long battle.

I drove right up to the front steps of the manor, switched off the ignition and just sat, taking in the sheer splendour of the manor and its grounds. Hawkins (Ted), the family butler, having heard my arrival, was hurrying down the stone steps to greet me. Resplendent in his sparkling white shirt, regimental tie, grey pinstripe trousers and black frock coat, he extended his hand in greeting as I climbed out of the car. 'Welcome home, young sir, and many congratulations on your educational success. Mary [his wife, and housekeeper to the manor] and I were so pleased when your mother imparted to us your good news.'

'Thank you, Hawkins,' I replied, 'and how is Mary?'

'Very well and at this moment cooking your favourite meal of roast beef with all the trimmings followed by raspberry pie and clotted cream.'

Forgetting that I was no longer plain George Earlswood but rather the eldest son of the household, I opened the back passenger door and began unloading the two suitcases that lay on the back seat. Hawkins immediately eased me aside, taking charge of my luggage, and said politely, 'Let me, sir, I will take them to your room and Mary or I will unpack for you after luncheon.'

Realising my previous error, I replied, 'Thank you, Hawkins and, by the way, you will find several boxes containing crockery, cutlery and bedding which I took with me at the start of the year when I moved off campus.'

Ted smiled and said, 'I will put them downstairs until Mary has time to sort through them.'

Smiling I said I had better go to find Mother. 'I expect she is in the library.'

'Yes, she is, sir, but your father has left strict instructions that you are to meet him in his study, just as soon as you arrive.'

I climbed the stone steps leading to the front door and went into the cool, panelled hall. Turning to the left, I went down a further corridor which led to my father's study. I knocked once and went straight in. I suddenly had a strange feeling of foreboding, brought on by the immediacy of my summoning, what I had learnt from Hawkins, and the worried look on my father's face. He glanced up from the papers he was reading and started to rise from his leather captain's chair. He was stood ramrod straight, his six-foot-two figure still slim but with a thickening around the waist. Looking into his face, I was aghast at the change that had taken place over the three months since I had last been home. His face had a strange pallor. There were bags under his eyes and his well-groomed hair showed touches of grey.

'Welcome home, my boy,' he said extending his hand in greeting, 'and many congratulations on your academic achievement.'

I smiled and replied, 'Thank you, Father.'

He beckoned me to sit in the chair immediately in front of his large Victorian partner's desk, and then sank down in his chair.

He replaced his glasses, looked again at the papers in front of him, cleared his throat and began. 'I know that it is the custom in this family for the eldest son to join the family firm as soon as he has finished his education. Your Uncle Edward and I were therefore expecting you to join us in the company following your twenty-first birthday. I know that you will be shocked to learn that this custom is to be abandoned in your case. Your Uncle Cecil, at a recent board meeting, stated that as Managing Director he felt that your appointment, on the grounds of rank and privilege, was not in the best interests of the company. He declared that in future all new and replacement managerial positions would be filled on the basis of proven ability, not through family influence.'

He paused and then went on to say, 'Therefore, my boy, you will not be joining the company in September as planned. Your Uncle Edward was of the opinion that as majority shareholders we should call an immediate Special General Meeting and vote out your Uncle Cecil and the other traitorous directors, and replace them with directors faithful to the family. However, after much discussion, we have concluded that the threat of either a public boardroom split or the wholesale sacking of key directors would seriously jeopardise the stability of the company. In the circumstances your Uncle Edward and I had to bow to a majority board decision. I am sorry, son, and, believe me, your Uncle Cecil has not heard the last of this matter.

'Since then, your Uncle Edward and I, together with other business contacts, have been able to put together a package that we feel will provide a managerial challenge as well as an opportunity to enhance your reputation as a businessman. Your Uncle Edward and I, as majority trustees of a fund set up for you when you were born, have purchased on your behalf the entire interest in a long-established and well-regarded company in the restoration trade, called G Lowe and Company, based in Harwich, for the sum of £14,000. We have also authorised the bank to place a further £5,000 into the firm's account, in the way of additional working capital. Additionally we have purchased on your behalf sixteen pre-war maisonettes situated in Colchester. Eight of these are in superb structural and decorative condition, and currently rented out to the university for £2,000 per annum. The other eight, while being structurally sound, have unfortunately been neglected and currently stand empty. The entire package cost £22,000 and we have authorised a further £6,000 to cover refurbishment and repairs.

'This money is an advance on the £170,000 trust fund that matures on your twenty-first birthday. Additionally I can tell you that on that auspicious occasion your allowance will rise from the current figure of £10,000 per annum to £15,000.' I looked up, slightly numbed by all the news, and went to speak, but my father raised his hand, saying, 'Don't try to thank me, as this compromise is less than I would have wished for. I think you had better cut along to the library, where your mother is waiting to discuss your twenty-first birthday bash.'

I rose from my chair, shook hands again with my father and collected the bundle of papers he handed to me. On my way to the library, I passed Hawkins in the hallway. He said, 'I was just about to bring you some coffee. I presume that you will be in the library with your mother?'

'Thank you, Hawkins, that will be fine, but please ask Mary to make it strong as I have had a nasty shock,' I exclaimed.

Walking into the library, I found Mother at her desk writing. 'There you are at last, George,' she said, raising her face to receive a kiss. 'I am adjusting the guest list for your party. We have decided to hold it in London, at the Connaught Rooms, for about 250 people. Can you look at this list and tell me if I have missed anyone off, like a girlfriend from university, for instance.'

I glanced down at the four sheets of paper and replied, 'I am sure you have not missed anybody out.'

'I hope not,' she said, 'but your Uncle Cecil and his family have already declined and have said that his London home will be full to bursting with influential business guests. I really don't know what things are coming to when my brother, your uncle, forgets important family dates.'

At that moment Hawkins knocked at the door and entered with a laden coffee tray. He put it on the table and poured out two cups which he handed to us both, and began to make his exit. However, before he could do so, my mother called him back. 'Hawkins, his lordship and I have decided to replace that machine,' pointing to Lily, 'and give my son something more befitting his status. I was at the Rover dealers the other day having my car light bulb replaced and in their showroom was a new blue saloon car with leather upholstery. Tomorrow will you drive into Colchester and tell them to do whatever they have to, in time for George's birthday?'

'Yes, madam,' Hawkins replied, before being dismissed by a wave of my mother's hand.

She suddenly looked up and said, 'Surely, George, you have not driven down from your university in your gardening clothes.' She looked at my loafers, jeans and sweatshirt (the normal attire of a student). 'I do hope that you intend to change before luncheon into something befitting the future heir of this estate.'

'Yes, Mother, I will go now,' I replied as I finished the rest of my coffee, grabbed my papers and left.

Luncheon was a long, dragging affair, even with Mary having cooked some of my favourite dishes. Refusing coffee, I made my apologies and left for my rooms saying that I was tired after such a long drive in such weather.

Back to the Beginning

When I entered my private sitting room, it was with the intention of working on the papers my father had given me earlier in the day. I soon realised that my concentration was anywhere other than on those papers, so I gave up and walked into my adjoining bedroom. I lay on the large four-poster bed and gazed into the canopy above. Why, I wondered, had Uncle Cecil turned against me and the family? It had been my father and Uncle Edward who had caused his appointment, following the death of my grandfather and the subsequent retirement of grandfather's friend and confidant, Harry Martin, the family firm's long-standing managing director. His appointment had come about only by the pleadings of his two sisters, my mother and Auntie Flossie (Lady Bun). How had my father allowed my Uncle Cecil to rob him of his influence, while he controlled the majority shareholding, reducing his role to that of a roving ambassador? More importantly, what was it that my uncle did not want me to find out, had I joined the firm? True, I had studied the firm's accounts while at college, but I had seen nothing but a fast growing successful company. Perhaps, before the next annual general meeting in March, I would investigate the family firm in depth.

Most of all I was cross with myself for not having been at home more, and not being at my father's side during what had been a worrying and disturbing time. Finally, I did not understand my Uncle Cecil's threat that a boardroom split would do untold damage to the company, as the family firm was a private company, not quoted on the stock exchange, and bearing in mind that my Uncle Edward and my father controlled seventy-one per cent of the shares. Nothing seemed to make sense.

My mind flashed back to the conversation I had had with my father earlier in the day. I was now owner of a small family firm with people relying on me for their livings. True, I had excellent academic qualifications, but my practical experience of running a company and of man management was extremely limited. My Uncle Edward and my father obviously had faith in me, and I would do my best to succeed, but when it came to the crunch, who was I, and what personal skills could I offer the world of business?

I entered the world on a damp, dreary September day in 1948. Having decided to arrive three weeks earlier then planned, I was small, red, and wrinkly, having little or no hair. My mother told me years later that when my grandmother first saw me she declared that I was the ugliest baby she had ever laid eyes on, an omen as to how the opposite sex would view me, at least for the early part of my life.

Arriving home, I was immediately placed in the care of Nanny Roberts, a short cockney nurse who, having survived two divorces, had by her own efforts gained the reputation of being a first-class nanny and a tough disciplinarian in the nursery, something I soon learnt. Tantrums and bad behaviour were put down with a firm hand, usually aimed at my little posterior.

I was christened George Edward Horatio Earlswood, heir to the future Lord and Lady Earlswood. During the first five years of my life I saw little of my father, who for a large part of the time was away with his regiment. I did however see my mother, usually when she visited the nursery at tea time, or when Nanny took me downstairs to say goodnight. Other than that I saw very few people except Nanny, of course, and my cousin Robert, the son of my mother's sister, and Charlotte, the daughter of her brother, when they visited the house. Nanny did not approve of my mixing with the village children and therefore for the most part I led a very lonely life.

When I was five years old I was enrolled in a private all-boys preparatory school to be educated sufficiently to pass the entrance examinations of a number of public boarding schools, which were popular with the upper class during the fifties. While I enjoyed the company of boys of my own age, mixing was frowned upon, and few boys came home to tea. The discipline at the school was as harsh as it was in the nursery and slothfulness, inattention and bad behaviour had painful consequences. Nanny was a full-time supporter of my education and made sure that the homework for that evening was completed before I could do anything else.

The only other people I saw during the first ten years of my life were my father when he came home on leave or my paternal grandfather when I went to stay with him. What a wonderful man my grandfather was, generous, wise and yet able to communicate at my level. I will never forget the last time I saw him alive. It was in the summer of 1958. We had been out for the day to the London Zoo at Regent's Park, and during our ride home we had passed a man begging in the street. I later asked my grandfather, 'Why was that man asking for money? Surely everyone has enough money.'

My grandfather sat me down and quietly said, 'George, not everyone is as fortunate as you, and many people are extremely poor through no fault of their own. One day you will become Lord Earlswood and take your seat in parliament. You will then have the duty to rule the country for all men, and you must exercise your power and wealth wisely. Even more important, George, is that you do all in your power to prevent war. It is a bad and beastly thing, killing hundreds of men and maiming many others.'

I turned questioningly and said, 'but Grandpa, you were a great soldier, as is Father. You both went to war and yet both of you are still here.'

He smiled thoughtfully and said, 'George, my boy, in the Great War I was one of the lucky ones who came back. I saw some pretty gruesome things which I will tell you about when you are older. Your father on the other hand had to go to war to protect the weak and oppressed. Like all wars, it was started by some mad man, hungry for power. His actions killed many thousands of people, George, and produced a bomb which one day may destroy the whole world.'

My grandfather died in December 1958 aged seventy-eight. During that fateful year I was sent to a private boarding school, which many of my forefathers had attended with varying levels of success. During that time such schools were largely staffed either by older men or by newly trained staff, who had been given crash courses at the end of the war. The Cold War was very much on everyone's minds, and all the staff believed that another world war was just around the corner.

The school's emphasis was to ensure that the sons of gentlemen were prepared for the officer ranks of the future with heavy concentration on discipline, leadership and self-sufficiency. I was fortunate in so far as the discipline was less than in the nursery and prep school and therefore not a problem. My father, then a serving officer, had always taught me essential leadership skills and Nanny had taught me self-sufficiency, like making my own bed, cleaning my shoes and being polite to my elders. Additionally I found I had natural hand and eye co-ordination skills and within a year played for the school's under-fourteen hockey team and cricket eleven.

In addition to the normal curriculum, all boys had to attend interest clubs two afternoons a week. I chose Music Appreciation, mainly because it was run by our hockey coach, and the Young Businessman's Club, as I knew one day I would head the family firm. I went to these clubs for all five years of my time at school, ending up with eight good O Levels as well as an understanding of a wide range of music from traditional jazz to rock and roll. Though the school did have a sixth form where boys could go on to A level, it did not offer the subjects I needed for my chosen career and I therefore left the school shortly before my sixteenth birthday.

I was then enrolled into the local technical college to study A levels in accountancy, economics, economic history, principles of English law and statistics. While I found that my education had equipped me well for the subjects I had selected, I soon discovered that what I had not been taught was how to make lasting relationships, especially with the opposite sex. During my first year I found myself nervous and hesitant when in a girl's company and, though I took a few girls to the cinema, after one date, they did not want to see me again.

In my second year, I plucked up the courage to ask a girl in my class to the Valentine Dance. Dressed to the nines, I met her outside the hall and accompanied her inside. All night we danced, drank and talked. As the evening drew on the lights were lowered and the music slowed. We held each other tight, and she smiled when I let my hand fall to stroke her bottom. We then began kissing passionately and she smiled again as my eyes fell on the tops of her breasts which showed above her ball gown. This, I thought, was to be the night I would break my duck (as the other boys termed it). Escorting her to the door of the ladies' cloakroom, I waited for her to retrieve her coat, fingering nervously the packet of condoms in my inside jacket pocket. Then she reappeared, smiled at me, and went into the arms of a much older man. She brought him to meet me and introduced him as her father. He thanked me for taking good care of his daughter. She bent forward and kissed me and then they were gone. Here endeth the first lesson in love.

I did however stay on friendly terms with her, and on another date we kissed and cuddled in the back row of the cinema, but I suppose that we were both too occupied with our forthcoming examinations to spend much time courting. This lack of social activity obviously paid dividends as in the following August I was informed that I had gained three ones and two twos at A level, more then enough to allow me to take up my university place.

What a summer I had that year. 1966 was warm and dry, and I was able to take a rest from my studies. My Uncle Edward used his considerable influence to obtain three World Cup Final tickets, and took me and his son Robert to the match. Uncle Edward may have been a peer of the realm, but he cheered and sang as loud as anybody in the stadium. My mother and father took me for two weeks to Scotland, to, as father said, learn the skills of a gentleman, that is fishing and shooting.

October soon rolled round and found me entering university. The first two years of my course were to be spent in residence. I was allocated a bedroom in an all-male cluster (four bedrooms with shared lounge, kitchen and facilities). The other three of my fellow students were a mixed bunch, but we got on well enough. Mary's instruction in the art of basic cooking stood me in good stead and was certainly appreciated by the others.

While the academic work went well during the first two years, my utter failure with women continued. I joined various social groups like the debating society, music appreciation and even the college rowing team as I thought that a well-toned body and brawny legs in tight shorts would enhance my appeal to the girls, but to no avail. I did take one or two girls out on dates, but somehow we did not connect either mentally, socially or in any other way.

Then came the start of the final year. During the summer holidays, Ted took me to a car auction just outside Colchester, where I bought Lily. The weeks that followed saw Ted stripping down the engine, repairing and replacing any worn parts. I worked beside him, both learning about car mechanics and attending to Lily's bodywork. Mary in the meantime had been busy getting together all the things I would need if I were to live off-campus, plus supplies, enough to feed a regiment.

I therefore set off for my final year in good spirits, believing that a young man with his own transport was bound to succeed in the world of women. I had joined three other students in renting a private house, which we all thought would rid us of petty campus restrictions. The four of us seemed to get on readily, and my life was filled with study, social events and parties.

We decided to hold a Christmas party. You know the kind of thing, bring a bottle, all welcome and we will provide the food. The event got off to a roaring success with everybody in the party mood. I found myself in a dark corner with a fellow student named Liz. Liz and I had been in the same social circle and we seemed to gel right away. By ten thirty that evening I had coaxed Liz into my bedroom with the door locked and me brimming with expectation. The kissing got hotter and I had already removed her blouse and bra. Nuzzling her breasts, I let my hands stray on to her shapely buttocks. This is it! I thought as she sighed and smiled at my ministrations. Suddenly, without warning, she slid down my zipper and her fingers delved for my manhood like a ferret after a rabbit. Freeing it from my Y-fronts, she seemed to groan inwardly as she took stock. Now, I thought, but before I could finally secure my quarry, I came unexpectedly, right down her skirt and over her hands.

She glared at me, saying I was a filthy beast, a pervert and many other names I will not repeat, grabbed her clothes and disappeared along the landing to the bathroom. I waited a few minutes, cleaned myself up, and rejoined the party, hoping to see

Liz and apologise. I asked her friend whether she had seen Liz and was told that she had left.

I was absolutely mortified. Apart from attending lectures, I hid myself away in my room, convinced that every girl on campus would be aware of my abject failure.

Christmas that year was spent in London with my Uncle Edward, my Auntie Flossie and their son Robert. Things got off to a poor start when Robert came in from a party blind drunk, and was then physically sick on the lounge carpet, right in front of my mother and father, to the utter horror of my uncle and aunt. While Uncle Edward took his son up to bed, Aunt Flossie said that he had got in with the wrong crowd, and was drinking to excess. The next morning, Robert was up early and I found him in the library with half a bottle of vodka, which he was drinking with gay abandon. He insisted on relating tales of wild parties, gambling and wenching, the last making me feel worse about my own inadequacies.

Returning after the Christmas holidays, I set to with my studies, realising that the time before my finals was dwindling at an alarming rate. When not at lectures, I again hid in my room, using the excuse to my other flat mates that I was finding my academic work difficult.

Then on a cold February morning, I met Billie-Jo, a mature American student, whom I had spoken to at a social function the previous term.

'Hi,' she said. 'I have not seen you around lately.'

'No,' I replied, 'I have been working hard, and I guess I have not felt very sociable of late.'

'The course getting you down or is it sheer panic?' she enquired.

'Something like that,' I said as we took our seats in the lecture theatre. When the lecture had finished, we all trooped out into the corridor. 'Fancy a quick coffee before the next lecture?' I asked.

'Thank you, I would love one,' she agreed. We made our way to the refectory, where I bought her a coffee and grabbed a table in the corner. 'Cheer up,' she said, 'Anyone would think you were going to a funeral.'

I grimaced and responded, 'Perhaps I am, my own probably.'

‘Bad as that?’ she remarked. ‘Want to tell me about it?’

‘No,’ I replied. ‘And even if I did you probably would not understand.’

She smiled back and said, ‘When I was at Kansas State, people told me I was a wonderful listener. Tell you what, it’s Friday night, so why not take some time off from your books and meet me at the Dog and Duck for a drink. And you can tell me what is keeping you from our social set. Eight o’clock, all right? Sorry, I must fly.’ And with that she left.

I found her at the Dog and Duck as arranged and bought her a drink. We took our drinks to an empty table at the end of the bar and sat down. The conversation began on mundane college gossip, until she finally said, ‘I hear all that, but what is worrying you?’

I began the story of my life, Nanny Roberts, the boy’s prep school, boarding school and my failure to make relationships at the technical college. I told her that the problem had now followed me to university, and even about that disastrous Christmas party episode. ‘So you see, I am a complete failure in the love stakes, and will probably go to my grave still a virgin,’ I moaned, thereby ending my sad tale. I then noticed that our drinks needed filling and went to the bar to refresh them. When I returned and sat down, she was looking thoughtful.

‘Now, I am no professional counsellor, and what I am about to say may not help, but anyway here goes,’ she said. ‘Now, there are several things I have never understood about the British upper class, and from your description you do come from it. You send your boys to a boarding school, not because it is the right thing for the child, but because it is the correct thing to do and is very often a family custom. You do not seem to take into account either the child’s needs, his temperament, or his wishes. The opinion seems to be, “I will make a man of him”. True, that this does work in the majority of cases but can destroy for life those children of a quiet or nervous disposition.

‘The second thing is the notion in such educational establishments that it is not manly to cry, no matter how badly you feel or are hurt. I think it is called the British stiff upper lip. Lastly, without proper training or advice, boys consider that their sole purpose in life is to inseminate every female they come across and they get downhearted when rebuffed. In such circumstances, boys take such rebuffs as an insult to their manhood. In your case you got off to a bad start, with a woman who dominated your early life. This was followed up by a further period of domination in an all-male preserve. When they did at last let you join the rest of mankind, you neither felt comfortable nor knew the rules. Nevertheless, driven on by other playground tales of seduction and conquest, you tried to follow suit and surprise, surprise, did not succeed. Then, rather than talk to someone regarding your fears and worries, you bottled it up and displayed to the world the typical British stiff upper lip. Believe me, I do know a little about how you feel, and I sympathise.'

She looked me straight in the face and continued, 'I was brought up in a middle-class family in a poor farming community. My father was the bank manager of the only bank in town and therefore held life and death over the farmers' heads. Being the bank manager's daughter I had to be whiter then white, or I would catch hell from my mother. When I was fourteen I finally rebelled – you know the sort of thing, hanging round the soda bars, staying out late, etc. I also had a passion for modern records, clothes and make-up far exceeding my modest allowance. I therefore began taking the odd dollar bill from my father's wallet when he took a nap, leaving his jacket in his den.

'One day he caught me in the act, and said he was going to paddle my butt. I foolishly told him I was too old to be spanked, whereupon he took off his belt, bared my ass, and skinned me alive. Boy I screamed so much that they must have heard me in the next county. Believe me I neither displayed that stiff upper lip, nor bottled up my discomfort or shame thereafter, not that anybody cared.

'No matter what disciplinary measures were introduced into our house, I continued to rebel, hanging around street corners and listening to other girls' tales of romance and surrender. Unfortunately, everyone in our community respected and feared my father's position and none of the local boys dared to dally with me. I too felt like a freak and finally surrendered my cherry to a high school history master in the back of his Dodge. I didn't enjoy the experience and worried for weeks after in case I was pregnant. I foolishly left home as soon as I had finished college, marrying at twenty and divorced three years later, when I found that my best friend was carrying my husband's child. Since the girl came from a well-heeled and respected family, a quickie divorce was arranged in Reno, so that the child would be born with a father.

'Fortunately, I then found myself with more money then I had ever dreamed of, and the following year hightailed it to England to begin a new life. Therefore, buddy, I can tell you, you're not as badly off as you feel, and sometimes better times are round the corner.'

I listened carefully and said, 'Thank you, I can see what you are saying but my problems, as you have guessed, stem from the fact that I am caught in two separate worlds – one as plain George Earlswood, student, and George Earlswood, only son of Lord and Lady Earlswood, heir to their titles, lands and fortunes.'

She held up her drink, looked deep into her glass and said quietly, 'As I found out, you cannot make a life permanently shrouded by your father's powers and influence.' She then looked at her watch and said, 'Gee, is that the time? Have to go now, as I have a basketball practice session in the morning.'

'I know the feeling, I am due on the towpath for rowing practice at eight,' I commented.

She rose from the table, turned and said, 'How about joining me for brunch at twelve o'clock in the cafe next to the river?' I smiled back and said, 'That's a date.'

The next day, I met her at twelve o'clock, outside the cafe. We both went in, selected a table and sat down. The cafe, though clean, had little in the way of refinements. Wooden tables were covered in a patterned oilcloth and the wooden folding chairs were each fitted with a padded cushion covered in a material that matched the curtains. However, the food was good and the portions generous, considering the prices charged. We both feasted on eggs, bacon, sausages, baked beans and fried bread, all washed down with mugfuls of steaming coffee. Once we had finished our meal and I had paid the bill, we decided to go for a walk along the riverbank. The weather was seasonal for a

February day, cold and damp. We walked and talked for the best part of an hour, each telling the other of our hopes and dreams, once our finals were finished.

When we reached the road, she guided me across a turning and into the garden of what was a large Edwardian house. She led the way up the path and, using her key, opened the large imposing wooden front door. Inside was a tiled hallway, containing a staircase in the middle and doors either side. We walked up to a door marked '1', and again using her key she opened the door to her apartment. She ushered me inside and shut the door behind her.

There was a small hallway with a kitchen on one side and a bedroom on the other. Next to the bedroom was a bathroom and a toilet and next to that another bedroom. The rest of the apartment was open with a table and chairs at one end and a three-piece suite, television and coffee table at the other. There was a large fireplace with an imitation log fire, which was fuelled by gas and very modern. In front of the fire was a large rug, patterned with colourful designs. Billie-Jo immediately bent down and ignited the log fire. 'Well, this is home,' she said, looking round. 'I know it's not a palace but I feel comfortable in it.'

'It's very nice,' I said.

'Sit yourself down on the couch,' she said, 'and I will go and make us some tea. Do not worry, I will warm the pot first.'

'You are learning our ways quickly,' I said, 'and will make someone a wonderful wife.'

Minutes later she entered the lounge with two steaming mugs of tea and handed me one before seating herself on the couch beside me.

We laughed and talked while we drank our tea, matching quip for quip as though we had been friends for years. Then we suddenly and unexpectedly found ourselves embracing and kissing each other. However, not having been in this situation before, I grabbed her, and holding her firmly, began kissing her lips frantically as I had read was expected from a real man. When I tried to insert my tongue roughly into her mouth, she suddenly stopped and said, 'Hold on, tiger, there is no big hurry and it is not a race.' I apologised and we began gently kissing once more. During the next hour she showed me how to caress and coax her, gently allowing me to undress her, while she undressed me. When we were both naked, she suddenly got up, pausing for a moment while I took her in her absolute loveliness. My mind raced. Here was I with five-foot-five of sheer animal beauty. Her hair, which was champagne blonde, hung loose down her back; her breasts were small and pointed and the nipples seem to be blinking at the light. She was not fat but was well covered with flesh, with a flat stomach beneath which was a bush of strawberry blonde curls. Her legs were well formed and muscular, probably due to her various sporting activities.

She smiled as she watched me scan her body and said, 'I hope you like what you see?'

'You are just beautiful,' I replied.

'Thank you, kind sir,' she said smiling, 'but I am getting cold and need to go to bed.' I followed her into her bedroom like a faithful dog. She quickly rolled back the bedclothes and got in, beckoning me to follow.

During the next hour, she taught me to stroke her, caress her and to kiss her in all the places that brought her pleasure. 'You see,' she said, 'making love to a woman should be slow, languid and totally unhurried. Treat your women as though they are precious porcelain, taking in their curves, touch and shape.' Then she looked into my eyes and softly said, 'I think it is time, don't you?' as she gently rolled on her back, pulling me on top of her. Expertly she guided me into her steamy body. I began thrusting into her roughly and with increasing speed, but again she stopped me. 'Slow down, there is no race. Remember that a girl likes slow, even strokes, at least to begin with. Make it last.'

In the next few minutes I finally experienced the joy and satisfaction of tender lovemaking. We lay in each others arms, both totally spent and happy. She cuddled down in my arms and said quietly, 'If you are a total failure at lovemaking, I hope I never meet a real success. Man, you were just wonderful.'

Sleep overtook us and it was well after seven when we awoke. She turned to me and said, 'After that performance you must be hungry. I know that I am.' Then she got out of bed, slipped on a robe and left the bedroom.

I emerged some minutes later dressed in my underpants and shirt, and found her in the kitchen, making scrambled eggs on toast and strong coffee. Once we had finished the meal, I helped her clear away and wash up. We sat in front of the television and watched the late news, followed by *Match of the Day*. She sighed and said, 'Would you like a nightcap or shall we go straight to bed?' You can guess my reply and we went back into the bedroom where we made the most delightful love one could imagine. We both awoke during the night and made tender love again before falling into a deep and blissful sleep.

The clock on the wall was well past nine when I awoke and found her raised on one elbow looking down at me. 'Morning, you,' I said.

'Morning, you,' she replied. I gave her lips a tender kiss, letting my hands wander gently over her breasts. By the time I had found her and reawakened her body, she was stroking my back and arching her spine to meet me.

'Now,' she gasped, 'do it now,' and do you know, I was more than happy to oblige.

The clock showed after twelve when we finally arose, bathed and dressed. We both felt lazy and so we walked up the road, stopping at another cafe, which seemed to be always open for business, and breakfasted on a large, traditional English fry-up.

I walked her back to her house, where we kissed on the door-step. I then said I had some work that had to be finished for the next day, kissed her again and left for my house, whistling a tune and feeling like a man reborn.

We spent many happy hours together that term, a period in my life that I will never forget.

During the following term we saw less of each other as we battled with revision and final examinations. The day I had finished my last exam, I found a note in my pigeonhole saying, 'I must see you tonight, my place at eight.' When I arrived there were cases in the hall and the apartment was all neat and tidy. Billie-Jo ran into my arms saying that her dad had had a serious stroke and she was returning to the States later that night.

'I will miss you,' I said.

'I will miss you, too, you are the nicest man I have ever met.'

Then we kissed passionately until she pulled away and said, 'Go now, George, please, as I hate goodbyes.' I turned around, left the apartment and sadly never saw Billie-Jo again.

Suddenly, I was back to the here and now, knowing exactly what I had to do. Here was I, twenty years of age, in good health, well qualified, and the owner of my own company, a man of property with additional working capital to back up any decisions I might wish to make. There were good people reliant on me for their living and a father and uncle who believed in me. I would show my Uncle Cecil that I could be a successful businessman, well able to take over from my father when the time came. I would also ascertain what Uncle Cecil was trying to stop me finding out, but that would have to wait until I had Lowe and Company back into profitability.

Lowe and Company

I excused myself after dinner that evening, pleading pressure of work, much to the annoyance of my mother, who was intent on discussing the merits of several eligible young ladies. I entered my private sitting room and went straight to my desk, where the papers I had been given by my father earlier in the day still lay.

The first paper gave a brief history of the company to date:

> Lowe and Orm was started in 1770 by a Mr Lowe, master saddler and upholsterer, and a wheelwright named Mr Orm. The firm was based in Liverpool not far from the docks. The principal business was the repair, maintenance and renewal of horse-drawn carriages. The business must have thrived because in 1893 Mr Orm was crushed to death under an unsupported coach he was mending and Mr Lowe bought out the widow.
>
> Nothing much is known about the business at this time, apart from its creating a reputation for workmanship and reliability. In 1916 Mr Lowe was killed in action in France and the business was continued by his widow until 1920, when the son, born in 1904, was able to succeed his father. Records are not very helpful but old archives seem to show that just before and during the war the company had contracts for the refurbishment of state rooms on the growing fleet of liners that docked in Liverpool for refits. Under the late Mr Lowe's father the business seemed to diversify during the late twenties and thirties into refurbishment of small hotels, coach houses and work in a few stately homes. In 1940 the Lowe business premises was totally destroyed during a raid on Liverpool docks, while the late Mr Lowe was on active service, killing his mother and father.
>
> The late Mr Lowe was finally demobbed in Colchester in 1946, and together with several army colleagues set up G Lowe and Company in Harwich. The firm soon regained its reputation for workmanship and reliability in the field of maintenance, repair and renewal of small hotels, boarding houses and at two nearby holiday camps. The business continued to thrive under the late Mr Lowe, who had built up many trade contacts,

handling sales himself. In February 1969, Mr Lowe suffered a heart attack at work and died aged only fifty.

The next paper had been prepared by an accountant at White Gull, the family firm and read as follows:

> The company turnover for the year ended 31 December 1968 was £75,000. Wages were £47,000, other costs £20,000 and profit was £8,000 (including £2,000 commission from plumbing and electrical subcontractors). Land and buildings are valued at £4,000 for the Parkston site and £6,000 for the Harwich site. Other assets: work in progress £6,000, materials £2,000, and recoverable debtors £1,500, a total of £9,500. Creditors for materials £2,500, and tax and National Insurance £1,500 and retentions £500.
>
> Buildings are structurally sound but dilapidated. The business is currently being managed by a Miss Maureen O'Shea, twenty-three years of age, who has worked for the firm since leaving school at sixteen.
>
> Order book is full till December and there are several that which have been submitted and are awaiting evaluation.

I jotted down certain facts I would want to know the answers to. Turning over the financial summary, I found a note in my father's handwriting, noting that an appointment had been made for me to meet Miss O'Shea at ten thirty the next day, and an appointment for eleven thirty on Tuesday to meet G Lowe's bank manager and as it happened mine too. The note also confirmed the bank manager was a Masonic brother of my father's and would take me to lunch following our meeting.

The next day I drove down to Harwich, in Lily, to survey my new acquisition. Following the map kindly left by the accountant, I turned down a lane not far from the Parkston Road and found two industrial buildings on my right. My spirits suddenly fell as I passed a yard and building boarded up and with a For Sale sign that had obviously been there years. I then turned into a gateway which had a hand-painted sign saying G Lowe and Company. I immediately noticed that the perimeter wire was badly in need of repair, as were the gates, one hanging on its hinges while the other was so encrusted with weeds that it had not been used for years. The large car park was full of potholes with large clumps of weeds growing from them. I parked my car in front of the building and surveyed the sight that met my eyes. The building was approximately forty-eight feet long and I would guess approximately twenty-four feet wide. To the left of the main double doors was a steel staircase, which gave external access to the second floor. The guttering and paintwork was in urgent need of attention and several of the ground floor windows were cracked.

I alighted from the car, crossed a short path and started to climb the iron staircase, following a sign that simply read 'Office'. Reaching the top, I knocked at the door and walked in. A young girl rose from her desk and slowly walked towards me. 'Yes?' she said, not even bothering to smile.

'I am Mr Earlswood and have an appointment to see Miss O'Shea.'

She turned and disappeared into an office on the far side of the building, emerging quickly with a young woman in tow. 'Mr Earlswood, how nice to meet you,' Miss O'Shea said brightly. 'Please come this way.' She led the way into her office. 'Would you like some coffee?' she asked. I replied that I would, whereupon she put her head around the door, asking the girl to make it. 'Please sit down,' she said, pointing to a chair placed in front of her desk, while she sat down opposite to me. 'You found us all right?' she said.

'Yes, thank you,' I replied.

While we waited for coffee; I glanced round her office. The paint was peeling off the walls, and the floor covering of brown lino was patched in several places. The desk was something out of the ark, and the filing cabinet was rusty down the side.

She saw me looking and said, 'The late Mr Lowe did not believe in what he called "staff fripperies".'

'I can see that for myself,' I commented, and smiled.

She added 'It was not Mr Lowe's fault. He had a spendthrift wife who withdrew the profits as soon as the cash flow allowed. Are you married?'

I told her I was too young to settle down, an answer which seemed to please her. The girl bustled in with the coffee and set it down on the desk. She was about sixteen, short and dumpy with oily hair and a face covered in acne. 'This is Mildred,' Miss O'Shea said brightly as the girl nodded and left the room. 'Forgive Mildred,' she said as she poured the coffee, 'she is a temporary copy typist, and will return to secretarial college in September. Poor cow,' she said, 'she would be happier working in a shop, but her parents think she will be a secretary one day, although I doubt it. It is sometimes difficult to tell your parents that you cannot fulfil their dream.'

After we had drunk our coffee, we got down to business. Miss O'Shea produced several ledgers which she placed in front of me one by one. 'This is the purchases book, now the wages book, the debtors' ledger and the creditors' ledger.' She then produced a rolled-up scroll, which she unrolled and pinned to the table. 'This shows each trade and their allocated work. There are, you see, the occasional free days, which can be used to catch up delays or to fit in small jobs. The current programme goes up to December, but this is not necessarily a bad thing as many requests for work will not be placed till the end of the season in September.'

I then asked her what role she thought I could play in the future of the company. She thought for a moment and said, 'I do not know what strengths or weaknesses you have, or what the new owners had in mind when they bought the company and hired you. Since Mr Lowe died, I have been left to run the company all on my own, and for the most part have enjoyed it. I am not sure how I will get on, having tasted the power. Certainly we need to increase sales in what is becoming a very competitive market. I have done my best and only time will tell if I have succeeded. I would therefore like you to take over the management role, freeing me to increase the sales effort.'

I thought for a minute about all she had said, and also about her obvious strengths and need for assistance in running a company she loved. She was not a big girl, about five-foot-four or five. She had a pleasant face, decent body, neither too fat nor too thin. Her crowning glory was her rich red hair and beautiful green eyes. I had wondered when I had first met her that morning why she was neither engaged nor married. Then, studying her closely, having realised she had a speech impediment, I saw from her mouth that she had a cleft palate. Was this the reason she was still unattached, and if so would this prey on her mind as she grew older?

I paused and said, 'I will speak to the owner and having surveyed the company for myself, try to arrive at an effective management structure.'

She smiled, stood up and said, 'Let me show you around.' She told me that the late Mr Lowe had disapproved of any expenditure on staff comforts and that, as a result, the building was in her opinion down at heel.

Leaving the offices, we entered a long room dominated by a large boardroom table and about twenty leather chairs, all past their best to put it mildly. The table top was covered in curtain and carpet pattern books, paint charts and upholstery swatches. Both sides of the table were flanked with rolled-up carpeting, the remnants from jobs. At the far end were two tea chests bulging with ends of curtain materials, again remnants of work carried out. Miss O'Shea saw my horror at the total chaos and said, 'The late Mr Lowe would not let returns from jobs be destroyed on the basis that we might be able to use them on small jobs.'

We then went through a door and found ourselves on a large landing with a toilet in the corner. The landing was also covered with carpet rolls, the only empty space being a lane to access the toilet and another access to the stairs. We went down the stairs into the very large workroom. Like the upstairs, everything appeared to be in chaos. There were obviously areas set aside for carpentry, upholstery, French polishing, carpets and curtain making, but the whole area displayed an air of confusion.

Miss O'Shea introduced me to a mature lady working at a sewing machine making curtains, who she said was called Kathleen. Her young assistant then arrived, bearing two cups of coffee. Maureen introduced her as Carol, an apprentice learning how to make curtains, tie-backs and pelmet coverings. When I asked where the rest of the staff were, I was told that they were all working at customers' premises.

We then went back to the office, where I offered to buy Miss O'Shea lunch if she would show me the other premises. We had a pleasant lunch at the Ship, a public house down near the port, where I discovered that Miss O'Shea's name was Maureen (Mo to her friends).

Leaving my car in the public house car park, we walked to our depot. The premises were two run-down buildings, the first being an old brick chandler's shop, with a large metal Nissen hut in the centre of the very large yard. The chaos was as bad in the workroom, with electrical and plumbing pieces stacked on every surface of the old shop. 'Mr Lowe always kept any returns from our two subcontractors after every job.' We then went into the Nissen hut which was stacked high with pieces of furniture, some awaiting refurbishment, others already refurbished awaiting delivery to the customers' premises (these items being covered in plastic sheeting), and other furniture bought from the auction and again ready for refurbishment. I noticed a desk and chair in the corner, covered in magazines and a kettle. 'That is where Pete and Arthur go when they are not working.'

We went back to the office and at four thirty went down to the workroom to meet the other staff. They were a varied group of people, but seemed to get on well with each other and also had respect and love for Maureen, who had steered them through the uncertainties following Mr Lowe's death. I sensed an atmosphere of unease, so I made a short speech telling them that I had been sent to help Maureen run the company and to protect all their jobs. I admitted to them that, as a new boy to the company, I had a steep learning curve and hoped that they would be patient with me if I asked silly questions. We then left the workroom and went back to the office.

I asked Maureen what reaction my little talk would have on the staff. She told me that there had been so much uncertainty that the staff were suspicious of the new owners and what plans they might have for the company. However, she assured me that they would give me the benefit of the doubt and watch to see how I performed over the next few months. I left the office just after half past five, telling Maureen that I had various business calls to make the next day, including the company's bank manager, but that I would be in early on the Wednesday morning and hoped her diary would be clear for a meeting. I drove home with a mixture of fear and excitement at the task that lay ahead.

That evening, over dinner, I discussed my day with my mother and father. Mother was alarmed at my description of both the buildings and management of the new company that my Uncle Edward and my father had purchased for me out of my trust fund. She was certain that the whole venture was doomed from the start, and she could not understand why I was not taking my rightful place alongside my father at the family firm. My father explained to her again the difficulties that her brother Cecil had created, so as to prevent me from joining the company. Her reply was simply that she no longer understood her brother, who never contacted her or joined in with family celebrations.

My father then asked me whether he could be of assistance in what seemed to be a bigger job than either my Uncle Edward or he had foreseen. I told him that what I planned to do was to get the whole organisation on one site, and that to do this I needed three second-hand containers as storage. He told me that White Gull had a large depot in East London, where damaged containers were stored until they could either be repaired or cut up, and he was sure that he could arrange for me to have one or two, suitable for storage. I asked him if he could enquire as to the availability of three such containers, their cost and the costs of transport to Harwich. Father seemed pleased to be able to contribute to the project and promised to have a word with the transport manager of White Gull the very next morning.

Once dinner had ended, I excused myself and made my way up to my private sitting room to prepare for my meeting with the bank manager the next morning.

I began by summarising my total financial position as follows:

Trust Fund
Total Value £170,000
Amount Advanced on G Lowe Ltd £19,000
Amount Advanced property fund £28,000
Amount Due End of Sept £123,000

Personal Finances
Current Account Balance £3,500
Deposit Account Bal £20,000
Total Personal Bal £23,500

I calculated that I had enough funds in my current account to see me through till the end of September. My allowance would increase to £15,000 from the end of September, enough to keep me in the manner my mother would wish. That meant that I could live comfortably off my allowance until my two new companies could support an additional salary. I also decided that I would transfer a further £5,000 to G Lowe and Co to finance my planned capital development, and a further £10,000 to my new property company to allow further purchases. Once my trust fund matured I would transfer a further £100,000 to my property company, enough to buy another thirty properties. This I concluded would realise an annual rental for the property company alone, a sum of at least £15,000, enough to pay me a salary.

Getting Down to Business

The next morning I was up early, and I breakfasted before my parents had risen. I dressed in style that I thought a budding property developer would wear, and set out to take a first glance at my newly purchased properties in Colchester.

The first twelve flats I looked at all seemed neat and tidy, well maintained, and in the morning sunlight looked grander than they really were. The second group of flats were entirely a different story. The outside paintwork was peeling and the guttering looked in a poor state. The front gardens were overgrown, and the steps up to the ground-floor flats were cracked and chipped. The rear of the flats were even worse, with old furniture, beds and bits of old cars lying everywhere I looked. The interiors of the flats were even more terrible, with peeling wallpaper, chipped and dirty paintwork, and stained sanitary fittings. The carpets that remained were dirty, torn and had obviously been abused by previous tenants. I visited four of the twelve flats and found they were all similar in condition. Walking down the driveway of two of the flats, I wondered whether the £6,000 set aside for the total refurbishment would be enough to do the whole job.

While I was walking towards my car, I was suddenly confronted by an elderly man who introduced himself as Mr Crow. He told me that he lived in the house opposite, and that in his opinion the properties I had just visited were a disgrace, and that something should be done about the state of them. I told him that I represented the new owners, and that I had come to inspect their condition for myself. I agreed with his assessment. This seemed to please him, and he offered me coffee at his house across the street. I thanked him for his offer, but said I had an urgent appointment in town. I promised to return with an assessor within the next few days to decide exactly what would be required. He shook my hand warmly and then turned and went into his house.

I parked my car at the rear of William's and Griffin's and walked through the store, crossed the road and entered the bank. I went to a desk marked 'Enquiries', identified myself and told the assistant that I had an appointment with the manager at eleven thirty. She smiled and reached for the phone, advising the person at the other end of my arrival. She told me that Mr Pocock was still with a client and asked if I would wait in the waiting area just across from her desk. I do not know what it is about bank managers in general, but waiting for an audience is in my opinion akin to waiting outside the headmaster's office following some terrible breach of the rules.

I did not have to wait long, and was soon being ushered into the great man's office. He rose from his chair as I approached his desk, extending his hand in greeting. He was a stout man in his early fifties, with a round, jovial face. He was dressed in a smart dark three-piece suit, with a gold chain hanging across his waistcoat. 'Welcome,' he said, indicating a chair.

He sat down and began to study a file that lay before him on his desk. He then looked up and smiled, telling me of a meeting he had had with my father at the lodge two weeks earlier, when my father had proudly told him of my success at university. He offered his own congratulations before asking me how he could be of assistance. I briefly told him of my change in career plans and of my purchase of G Lowe and Company, who luckily banked at this branch. He asked me to excuse him, and quickly made a phone call to ask his secretary to trace and bring the G Lowe file to him. Two minutes later she appeared in the office and placed the file in front of him. He opened the file and quickly glanced at it.

Looking up, he smiled and said that the company had been long established, as well as being loyal customers for a number of years. They had never requested a loan, or had become overdrawn, although their average cash balance was around £100. I then told him that I was increasing the company's cash flow by £5,000, and passed over the cheque, drawn on my trust fund. I also requested that he transfer an additional £5,000 from my own personal deposit account to finance capital improvements. I explained my plans to him and he nodded his agreement.

He then asked me whether, in view of my increased investment, I had thought of gaining limited status. I told him that was a good idea and that I would make the necessary enquiries. He told me that the bank had a department that could do this for me at a small charge. I thanked him for his advice and asked him to put the change into train.

He next asked me whether there was anything else he could do for me. I thought for a moment and told him that I wished to become a cheque signatory of the firm, and he nodded. Secondly I told him of my plans for advertising, and my need for a competent photographer. He leaned back in his chair and considered the question. 'I recently opened an account for a young photographer named Suzie Sermon,' he said. 'She operates a small business called Focus on the Future from a small office in the Hythe district of the town. She showed me her portfolio when she saw me, and though I am no expert she seemed very competent. I tell you what, if you are free, after lunch, I will phone for an appointment for you.'

I then said, 'I will also need a small printer, one who can print letterheads, business cards, etc.' He smiled again and told me that he knew just the firm, 'Printing Galore,' he said, 'funny name for a firm but the person running it is a James Bond fan and named it after some character or other.'

'Pussy Galore,' I volunteered, which brought a smile to his face. The bank manager told me that he did not have the printer's address to hand, but I could find it in the telephone directory.

I then broached the subject of forming a property company. He told me the bank could do this for me and asked if I had chosen a name. I thought for a moment and said, 'Lily Estates.' I passed over the deeds of the twenty-four flats together with the £6,000 cheque for the refurbishments. I also asked him to transfer £10,000 from my personal deposit account into the company as working capital. He glanced at the notes he had made previously and warned me that my decisions would reduce my deposit account to only £5,000. I told him that at the end of September I would receive the balance of my trust fund totalling some £123,000, of which I intended to transfer £100,000 to Lily Estates, and the rest to my deposit account. I told him that at the same time my allowance would increase to £15,000 per annum. He nodded and told me that he and his wife were looking forward to my twenty-first birthday party, but did not know of my inheritance. He then promised to do all I asked and send me new cheque books, etc, to my home. Looking at his watch, he remarked it was nearly twelve thirty and time for lunch. He rose from his chair and I followed him through the door into his secretary's office, where he stopped to tell her he would be back in time for his two fifteen appointment.

We left the bank, crossed the road and went straight to a tobacconist's shop. I naturally thought that he was stopping to buy his favourite brand of cigarettes or tobacco, and was surprised when he began climbing some wooden stairs on the left as you entered the shop. Reaching the top, I found a small lobby with a cashier's office at its centre. My bank manager stopped and informed the cashier of our arrival. We were soon joined by a tall man, who was introduced to me as the restaurant manager. He showed us through into a wooden-panelled dining room and to a table at the corner of the room. Once the waitress had taken our order, the bank manager leaned towards me and asked me whether I had ever considered joining my father in the lodge – if so he would be happy to sponsor me.

I thanked him for his kind offer, and told him that at present I thought I should devote my energies to setting up and running my two businesses. He nodded and told me that that was probably a wise thought, but that should I wish to take him up on his offer, I had only to ask.

Looking around the room, I also noticed a large sign which told the world that the Rotary Club met there each month. My companion noticed me looking and told me that that was another organisation I should consider joining, as there were very useful business contacts to be gained. 'There is a club in Harwich, you know,' he explained. 'I occasionally go there to lunch, as we have a sub-branch in the town, and I could take you with me, once you have settled in.'

The lunch was very good and the service excellent, and by two o'clock we had finished lunch. The bank manager excused himself, paid the bill and left.

I followed him out and went into William's and Griffin's, where I bought a dark blue and green striped summer jacket that I had spotted on my way to meet the bank manager. I then collected my car and drove to the Hythe to meet Suzie Sermon of Focus on the Future.

Following the directions given to me by the bank manager, I soon found the building that housed the offices of Focus on the Future. I quickly made my way up the staircase, where on the first floor I found a door with a neat and attractive sign on it announcing the name of the firm and proprietor. I knocked and entered. The room was plain and painted in a shade of magnolia. The floor was covered in plastic flooring in a coloured pebble design. In the corner was a desk and chair, and behind the desk sat a young woman. She rose to welcome me, and extended her slim hand in formal greeting.

I shook the hand as she commented that I must be Mr Earlswood. I told her that that was correct and that she must be Miss Sermon. She invited me to sit down, and once I was settled asked me what she could do for me.

I described the business of G Lowe and company the best I could and its need for some advertising material. I told her I was looking for a talented photographer to take the pictures for my new brochure and that she had come highly recommended. She smiled and commented that it would make a nice change from portrait and wedding photography which currently made up most of her business. She then picked up a piece of A3 paper and folded it in four. 'This,' she explained, 'will be the size of your brochure, with eight panels showing the various products that you offer together with a short statement of the improvements you can provide for a wide variety of private and business premises.' I told her that I thought that was a brilliant suggestion, with her taking the photographs and Miss O'Shea writing the captions. I of course would be allowed to edit the document before it was submitted to the printers.

I then began describing my idea for the production of a large book showing projects before and after refurbishment, which could be carried by my sales manager when she visited customers' premises. Suzie nodded enthusiastically, agreeing that in the long term such a book might prove invaluable. She then glanced at her watch and, seeing the time, apologised for the lack of beverages. She explained that since the majority of her time was spent either out of the office or in the darkroom she seldom had time to make tea. I told her that I had noticed a small cafe a few doors up the street, and that, provided she had the time, I would willingly buy her a cup of tea. She thanked me and readily accepted my offer.

The cafe was small and very basic but convenient. I asked what she would like and she told me tea. I asked her whether she wanted any food with it. She paused and told me that she had been busy in her darkroom and had skipped lunch, so could she possibly have a hamburger.

'With chips?' I asked, to which she nodded.

When the tea and food arrived, she asked why I was not eating too. I explained I had only just come from having lunch with the bank manager. We must have spent an hour talking and the more we talked, the more I took to this young woman. She was about five-foot-eight tall, slim, wearing jeans and a baggy T-shirt, telling the world of her love of Noddy. She was obviously an outdoor girl as both her face and arms sported a healthy tan. The features that really attracted me were her piercing blue eyes, which sparkled as she talked and laughed.

When her meal was finished and we had had our second lot of tea, she remembered a four thirty appointment and had to go, but she promised to ring the next day and fix up a meeting. I asked her if she was free on the following Thursday for lunch at the George, where she could meet Miss O'Shea. She smiled and told me that for lunch at the George she would make herself free and we arranged to meet at one o'clock.

During dinner that evening I shared the events of the day with my father and mother. My mother said very little, other then her usual comment of, 'That's nice, dear.' My father, on the other hand, took in every word, nodding in agreement at the various arrangements I had made. Once I had finished, he asked me whether Mr Pocock had mentioned anything about the lodge, and I replied that he had offered to sponsor me, should I be interested in joining. I then told Father that while I might be interested in becoming a mason, in the next few months I needed to concentrate all my efforts in running my two new businesses. Father nodded and smiled, telling me there was no hurry, and of course I was right to devote all my energies to running these two enterprises.

Once dinner had ended, Mother went off to the library to finish some letters, while Father made for his study. I gave him several minutes to settle before I knocked at his study door and entered. He looked up, smiled, and asked me what I wanted. I took a seat before his desk and began to tell him of the new problems I faced in running my two new companies. 'You see, Father,' I told him, 'I intend to buy run-down properties for my property company, and then refurbish them using my repair company, but at present I do not want the staff at G Lowe to know I also own Lily Estates. I want them to feel that they win contracts from me by the strength of their tenders, rather then because of me. Eventually, I will have to tell at least Miss O'Shea who I really am, in case it leaks out, and therefore I cannot use the manor as my business address.'

My father thought for a moment and then told me that he often visited White Gull's solicitors, in his position as company chairman and majority shareholder. On the ground floor by reception, he had noticed a large board bearing the names of many companies. He told me that, for a small fee, the solicitors allowed their address to be used as the head office of companies, redirecting the mail. He told me that as he would be in London the next day he would enquire as to the cost of registration and if it was reasonable he would register Lily Estates Ltd with them redirecting the mail to the manor. I thanked him warmly and made ready to leave, when he told me that he had had a word with the Transport Manager of White Gull regarding containers. The manager had said that he had two damaged containers in his yard taking up space. The damage was at the corners and down the sides which made them unsuitable for future use, but both were still fully weatherproof and suitable for static storage. They would both need a coat of paint of course, but that would not be too expensive. The manager confirmed that he needed the space they occupied and that I could have them for nothing, but there would be a charge of £20 per container for delivery to my site.

I told Father that I accepted the deal and if the Transport Manager phoned me the following day, I would arrange a suitable date. My father added that damaged containers were often received and I would be informed as soon as another container became available. I thanked Father again and left his study.

I then sought out Mary and Ted, whom I found in the kitchen having a cup of coffee. I went in and joined them, saying I needed a favour. They both agreed that if they were able they would be glad to help. I explained my problem that arose from running two companies, without one knowing the identity of the other, and that I needed two people whose names were not directly connected to the Earlswood family. I therefore wanted to make them company directors of Lily Estates Limited. I would naturally do all the work, and all they had to do was to be signatories on letters and cheques. Mary, I suggested, would become Company Secretary and Ted Commercial Director. Naturally, I told them that there would be a small director's fee, which they both refused. I did however persuade them to join me twice a year, on their day off, for a good lunch on the company.

I went to bed that night extremely happy at the progress I had made during the day.

The following morning I was in the office early. I immediately rang the agents of the building next door and enquired about the price, telling them of the dilapidated state of it, and that I only wanted it as storage. The agent told me that the building had been on the market for several years, originally at a price of £3,000. I told him that in its current state the figure quoted was far too expensive, and I offered £2,000. The agent took my name and number and promised to ring me back as soon as he had spoken to the owner. I did not have to wait long before the agent called me back to say that the owners would not accept a penny less than £2,500, and that they, the agents, were authorised to proceed on that basis. I agreed the price and told the agents I would have a formal offer and the details of my solicitor in the post that night.

I heard Maureen arrive. Once she had settled she was knocking at my office door, notebook in hand. I invited her to come in and take a seat. Then I told her that, since my first visit to the company, I had had a meeting with both the owners and the bank. 'The owners were glad to hear of the expertise, loyalty and long service of the workforce and in particular your efforts in continuing to run the business following the death of Mr Lowe. They were, however, unhappy with my report on the organisation, use of resources and building maintenance that I had found. They have therefore instructed me to put in hand all necessary repairs and decoration without delay. They have also taken the decision to site the business on only one site, thereby increasing efficiency and effectiveness. They have therefore arranged for the delivery of two secondhand containers to be delivered next week to act as electrical and plumbing stores, with two further containers to be delivered as soon as possible to act as paint and furniture stores. All the containers will need a coat of paint and shelving inside. I have decided that the first two containers will be sited at the ends of this building, with a passageway between. Siting of the other two containers can be decided later. Internal and external decorations should be put in hand as soon as possible. In readiness for our centralisation project, I have this morning bought the land and building next door for £2,500. Naturally the building, car park and perimeter fence will need to be attended to and, once they are weatherproofed, you can begin drawing up plans for a corporate office on the first floor. The owners realise that these improvements will cost money and yesterday transferred the sum of £5,000 in capital funding into our account.

'Looking to the future, the owners have decided that turnover can and must be increased. One of the key elements of our expansion will be an investment in advertising, with cash to provide for the additional working capital that will be required. The owners have therefore transferred an additional sum of £5,000 to make such plans possible. Accordingly, I have arranged for us both to meet a talented photographer named Suzie Sermon at the George for lunch tomorrow. She will assist us in organising a suitable advertising campaign.'

Maureen was busy scribbling down notes in her notebook, before looking up. She asked if there was anything else. 'Yes,' I told her. 'Due to the increased investment, arrangements are being made to make G Lowe a limited private company.' She rose from her seat and began to make for the door, when I called her back, and told her that the previous day the bank manager had introduced me to a property developer from an outfit called Lily Estates Ltd, and he had asked me whether we would like to quote for the refurbishment of twelve flats the company had recently purchased in Colchester. 'They have been neglected for a long time and he felt that they would need some extensive work doing. I thought we could go and look at them tomorrow morning on our way to lunch. He has generously given me the keys, which I can hold on to for a week.'

I then asked Maureen to obtain estimates for the painting of the outsides of each building, the refencing of the compound, clearance of weeds from the car park, the filling of holes and a new top covering of asphalt. I also asked her to get the jobbing builder to check both roofs for leaks, repair broken windows and attend to the guttering. I, in the meantime, contacted a local solicitor to act for the company, and local accountants to give the company specialised tax advice and to take over the payroll from 1 September.

Later I went next door to tell Maureen about the conversations I had conducted that morning. I asked her to phone the accountants I had appointed to set up a meeting to transfer the payroll records.

I noticed a worried look on her face, and asked her what the matter was. She told me that things were moving ahead so fast, she was finding difficulty in keeping up. I sat down in front of her desk, and told her not to worry, and explained my theory that after four years of austerity under a Labour government, people were getting fed up and would soon wish to change the government. 'That,' I concluded, 'will lead to a boom in people wishing to rent or buy property, and they will be demanding a much higher level of facilities and decoration than would their parents. That being so there will be, at least in the short term, much work for us to go after, and we have to be ready. Changing the subject, I said, 'We should start advertising for an office manager-cum-secretary, and in the meantime get on to the local agency and get a competent shorthand typist here from tomorrow. I cannot afford to have my new sales manager doing her own typing.'

I went down to the workshop and found Lou the carpet fitter and Kathleen having coffee together. I asked them both to measure the offices for curtains and carpets and to see whether a good job could be done using the remnants of past jobs, which seemed to be everywhere I looked. I then went in search of Irwin the upholster and Fred the French polisher, who were both working hard on customers' furniture required to be finished on a job ending the following Friday. I apologised for interrupting their work, but I needed some advice. They both looked at each other, smiled and asked how they could help me. I began by saying that, in my opinion, we needed to improve our appearance, so our clients could one day visit us. That being so, we needed to smarten up the offices. The furniture either needed replacing or if worthwhile reupholstering and repolishing, and at that they were the experts. I also asked them to look at the boardroom table and chairs and for them to estimate how much it would cost to put the things in saleable condition. The painters were both out, as was Peter the driver, so I left a message for them to come up and see me as soon as they returned, Paul to estimate time and cost of painting the top floor, and Peter using his reported skills at the auction to obtain a good desk and chair, a side table and several secondhand filing cabinets.

I suddenly began to notice the atmosphere in both the workshop and in the office change, like someone opening the window and reviving the tired workers. Maureen and I had a sandwich sent in. By the time I had left the office, I felt that not only had I arrived but had begun to make my mark.

The rest of that week flew past as did the first two weeks in August, with activity all around the place. I had agreed during a conversation in the workroom to allow music, a thing that my predecessor had felt was not in the best interests of productivity and positively sinful.

On the Friday, we closed for the two-week works' holiday. Maureen reported that £500 had been received from a long-outstanding debtor, and that, with the £500 saved on the purchase, would enable all the work to begin as soon as required.

I wished all the staff a pleasant holiday and left to drive home on a very clement summer evening.

The summer break simply flew by, as I helped my mother to arrange my twenty-first birthday in London. I was also asked to actually go to London, by my mother, to check personally the arrangements. I combined this trip with a visit to a property auction, courtesy of Arthur Welsh, an old friend of my father's, and property manager of White Gull Enterprises.

Anyone who has never been to an auction cannot imagine the immediate intoxication of the atmosphere, and people's excitement. Arthur bought two properties on behalf of White Gull, and was ready to leave, when four flats in East Colchester came up for auction. The guide price in the catalogue was £8,000, and I waited for the bidding to begin in earnest. However, this being the last lot of the morning, many bidders had left. The auctioneer tried to start the bidding at the guide price, but with no success. Unable to contain myself, I raised my hand and bid £5,000, not expecting much reward. No other bids being forthcoming, Lily Estates had purchased its first property at auction. Arthur was both perplexed and amused at my action, but admitted after lunch that he too had bid on a property he had not planned to bid for. He told me that perhaps I had my grandfather's nose for a bargain.

During lunch, Arthur told me how unhappy he and other managers were at White Gull. When I asked why, he told me that Uncle Cecil was constantly overriding their managerial decisions. He then told me that, in his case, he had been ordered to buy a country mansion in Surrey, way above the market price. White Gull was spending thousands of pounds restoring it to its eighteenth-century glory. Arthur then frowned and declared that, in commercial terms, the project was sheer lunacy. I took in all that was said, and set myself the task of doing some research as soon as White Gull's annual report was issued in late May.

The other project, during my two weeks' holiday, was to go with Ted into the garage at Colchester to make final arrangements for my new car to be delivered on the Monday after my party in London. On the way home I told Ted that the papers I had just signed made no allowance for part exchange of my beloved Lily. Ted told me he had been meaning to talk to me about Lily, and that he wanted to buy Lily from me, to give to his son the following Christmas. I told him that I could not possibly sell Lily to him, but I would give him the car as my contribution to their family Christmas. Initially he would not hear of such a suggestion, but by the time we reached home he had agreed.

Gloworm Comes to Stay

I was in the office early on my first day back, only to find Mo already working. She told me that during our closure more work had come in, including the entire refurbishment of a ten-bed hotel in Constable country, which was due to begin on 6 January. She confessed to being worried whether we could meet the ever-increasing order book without at least one additional painter and decorator. I told her that she should talk to Paul, who was in charge of the painting, to arrange some more staff.

There then came a knock on the office door, and there stood Suzie, with a smile that would brighten the dullest day. Mo stood up, went round the desk, and the two women embraced each other, like long-lost friends, rather than people who had met only briefly just before the summer shutdown. Suzie was three inches taller than Mo, with much lighter hair. She was also much slimmer then Mo, with a body that stood testament to her healthy lifestyle. I imagined that their bond, which had already formed, was due to the similar position they found themselves in, both twenty-three, both unmarried, and both living under the influence of their mothers. Mo was still under the spell of her late mother and Suzie was still living at home with her widowed mother. Neither of the girls had a man in tow, and both were attempting to carve out a career for themselves in what at that time was a male-dominated world.

Suzie was eager to begin the meeting, so after getting our secretary to provide some coffee we proceeded to get down to work. Suzie produced seven layouts, each one depicting a facet of our business. Each one had a photograph of our tradesmen working, together with a short analysis of what we could achieve in the way of repair, refurbishment and restoration.

I told the girls that I was impressed both with the content and quality of the proposed brochure pages, especially after so short a period. We then agreed a series of small alterations to the text before moving on to the proposed front cover. This contained the name of the company, details of how long it had been established, our address and telephone number. The artwork was very good and, just as I was proposing to adopt it, Suzie interrupted. She said that although the company could trace its origins back over many many years, and had a fine reputation, 'G Lowe and Company' did not inspire her. What she thought needed doing was for the company to have a new, up-to-date image. She had therefore been working on an idea she had got from the company history I had given her on our first meeting. She then produced a new draft front page containing a golden insect on a black background, enclosed in an oval. Underneath, it had the name 'Gloworm Ltd', and under that, in smaller script, the phrase, 'Those nice people with the bright ideas'. At the foot of the draft page was the usual information, with a short phrase, 'Established for over two-hundred years.'

Mo and I were lost for words as we took in what was being proposed. After what seemed an age, Suzie said, 'Well?'

I looked over at Mo's face and could sense a feeling of excitement. 'Well,' I said, 'the name of the new company will be Gloworm.' I thanked Suzie for her inspiration, while both women hugged each other.

Suzie then produced some draft letterheads to go on various pieces of stationery. Suzie said that she was glad we approved her suggestion, as she had already paid a friend £25 for art work, as well as her fee. I told her that Mo would sort out payment.

Once the meeting was concluded, I suggested an early lunch to celebrate the launch of our new name, which we agreed would be early in January, as G Lowe and Company always closed its books on 31 December. The three of us agreed, and we took off in Lily down to the local hotel, where we enjoyed an excellent lunch. We decided to take coffee in the lounge and I found a table in the far corner. Once the coffee had been served I told them I had a confession to make. This was greeted by the two women with alarm and apprehension. I began by saying that while I was currently plain George Earlswood, I would, on my father's demise, become Lord Earlswood. That, I said, would not be for many years to come. The business had been bought by my trustees, who would maintain a watching brief till I was twenty-five, when I would inherit a second trust fund that had been set up by my grandfather when I was born. I also told them that I would soon be twenty-one, and would be enjoying a family celebration. However I would like to have a small party for the staff on the preceding Wednesday, both to mark my birthday and to announce the new plans for the company. Mo and Suzie promised to organise things for me, and I thanked them both.

Mo then said, 'We both thought that there was more to you than you had let on. The news should not affect either the company or our relationship, but nevertheless we are grateful that you told us.' We agreed that my association with both my parents and my father's business would remain a secret between the three of us.

The next three weeks flew by, with more and more work coming in each day. On the Monday before my birthday, I completed the purchase of our new building, and told Mo to get the various contractors to start the painting, car parks, windows, guttering, and to order two new pull-up metal doors, with a small door in each, one to replace the current wooden double doors and the second one to be placed in an enlarged entrance at the other end. I also told Mo and Suzie to put down any ideas they had for the new office layout.

I was therefore able to announce to the staff at my birthday get-together that we would be moving into the building next door, vacating the Harwich site, in order to get the business on one site, and that from the first of January the company would be known as Gloworm Ltd. This was greeted with a genuine air of happiness and enthusiasm. Once the party had broken up I retired with Mo and Suzie to my office. Suzie gave me a great big kiss, wishing me a wonderful birthday. Mo followed Suzie's lead, coming into my arms and giving me the same. I was embarrassed when both girls gave me a large gift-wrapped parcel, telling me not to open it till my birthday, and that they both hoped I liked it.

On the Friday night we had a family dinner with Uncle Edward, Aunt Flossie, my cousin Robert and his girlfriend, Angela. The nine of us enjoyed a very splendid meal, my parents reminiscing about my early life. During the meal, however, my eyes were drawn to Angela's, no matter how much I tried to resist her gaze. At the end of the dinner I said goodbye to my guests, shaking hands with the men and kissing the ladies. When it came to Angela's turn, she seemed to melt into my arms, snuggling in close, as I gently kissed her cheek. Long after I had retired, I could not get her out of my mind: her mid-brown long hair, her lovely five-foot-four body, and those captivating brown eyes. I told myself not to be so foolish; after all she was my cousin's girlfriend and I should put her out of my mind.

The party went like clockwork, as did everything my mother organised. She had an amazing eye for detail and left nothing to chance.

The evening started with all the guests being marshalled into dinner, via a receiving line. My mother was in her element, proudly introducing me to all her socialite friends, particularly those with eligible daughters. While there were no missing guests, my mother was disappointed that her brother and family had not changed their plans so as to enable them to attend.

During the ball that followed, my mother made certain that I danced with every eligible female, in the hope that Eros might shoot his arrow, but that was not to be the case. Towards the end of the evening I spotted Angela sitting alone and looking miserable. I walked over and asked her to dance, taking her hand and leading her to the dance floor. I asked her where my cousin had disappeared to. She responded, 'He is in the bar, getting tanked up, and will then probably make a scene or go off with a willing female and try and make a conquest.' I told her I was sorry. If he treated her so badly, why did she stay? She told me that she had initially stayed because Lord and Lady Bun had asked her to keep an eye on their errant son, and then she had fallen in love. Lately though, his drinking, gambling and wenching were gradually killing that love.

During that first dance she told me how she had been brought up in a series of orphanages and foster homes until, at the age of sixteen, she had been thrown out to fend for herself. She had ended up in a hostel, but luckily also found a junior clerk's position in Bun Industries. For those three initial years she had spent every evening at night school, as well as most of her spare time, learning shorthand, typing and accountancy. Gradually she had made her way up through the ranks to the point that she was one of Lord Bun's personal assistants. The Buns meant everything to her, and she felt it would be ungracious to leave their son, in spite of the present difficulties.

I in turn told her of Gloworm and my ambitions to make my own way in the world.

When the dance finished, we both stood stock still until the next dance began, and we both melted into each others arms. Angela seemed to merge into my body, the thin material of her long, tight dress outlining every curve. I started to find her so enticing that a lower part of my anatomy decided to make its presence felt. She obviously knew of my predicament, and while I tried to apologise, she just looked into my eyes and smiled. 'Don't apologise, please,' she said, 'I am very flattered. Perhaps it is fortunate that we are in the middle of a crowded dance floor, or who knows where things might go?'

When the dance ended I returned her to Lord and Lady Bun. Taking Uncle Edward aside, I said, 'Robert is in the bar, in a very sorry state. I think you need to get him home before he causes a scene.' He thanked me and went off in search of his son. Mother later told me that they had apologised for having to leave early, but Cousin Robert could no longer stand or walk, on account of excessive drinking.

Driving to work on the following Tuesday in my new blue Rover, I wondered what people would say, especially those who did not know my parentage. But I need not have worried, as Mo had spread it about that my parents had given me the car as a twenty-first birthday present.

The next few weeks passed quickly, while our new building was being planned and altered. Work kept on coming in and in mid-October Arthur, acting on my instructions, wrote to say that Lily Estates had accepted our tender for the restoration of the twelve maisonettes. The letter also asked for an estimate to restore the four flats I had bought at the August auction. In October, I purchased twelve terraced houses, in three blocks of four, for

£20,000. They were in an appalling condition, having been let to the army, and had had little or no money spent on them. However, they were structurally sound, and I was sure that Gloworm could bring them back to a really high standard. That was the first purchase from the remainder of my trust fund, which had been passed to me just after my twenty-first birthday.

I attended the December property auction, buying six more properties for £20,000. Three of these were in Colchester, two at nearby Wivenhoe, and the last was a three-bedroomed house in Copford. Most of the properties were in reasonable condition and would probably only need a coat of paint to restore them to their former glory.

I was just about to leave the auction to meet Angela for lunch, when a large house in Lexden Road came up for sale. Currently, according to the auction particulars, it had been converted into four flats. These were now classed as being inhabitable as both the electrics and gas supply needed replacement. However there was a large garden making the property a good long-term investment. The guide price was £8,000 to £10,000 and I was bemused at no bids being made. The auctioneer asked for opening bids, first at £7,000 and then at £6,000, waiting for the stakes to be raised. I was therefore surprised when, after a long pause, the lot was knocked down to me at £6,000.

In the taxi to the city, where I was to meet Angela, I pondered my purchase, realising, perhaps for the first time, that I wanted a fine residence near to Harwich to take my bride to when I found her, and a place to raise my children.

Angela was already at the restaurant when I arrived and I apologised for being late. We quickly ordered, and I began to tell her both of my new acquisitions and of my dreams for the Lexden Road property. She smiled and sounded so happy at such a madcap but maybe profitable bid, saying she really did think dreams could come true. I asked her how things were between her and my cousin and she told me they were still together, but she did not know for how long. His drinking, gambling and wenching were even worse, and now he was experimenting with drugs. She told me that she was worried at his constant mood changes, and begged me to have another word with my Uncle Edward.

The meal soon came to an end and we found ourselves outside in the street. Once again she melted into my arms, this time kissing me passionately. My body responded as before, and she smiled and said, 'I think that the future honourable member has just come alive.' I returned her kisses enthusiastically, but fighting with myself at the thought of taking my cousin's woman from him. I then pulled away, as if to leave, but remembered the Christmas present I had stowed in my overcoat pocket. The present consisted of two pairs of Harrods' best silk knickers, bought for me by Mary. She thanked me and then we kissed again, oblivious to the world around us. Then she hailed a taxi and was gone, leaving me standing lonely on the pavement. Why, I thought, was I always the one to make the sacrifice, merely to accord with my code of chivalry? But there again, that was how I was.

Christmas fell on a Thursday that year and on Christmas Eve I gathered with the rest of the staff for the traditional Christmas lunchtime drink, organised by Mo and Suzie. When the staff had gone, Mo and Suzie accompanied me back to the office. I handed them each a Harrods' gift-wrapped parcel containing a silver business card holder, wishing them both a happy Christmas. The girls then told me of their plans for Christmas, Mo spending Christmas Day with an elderly aunt and Boxing Day with her best friend and neighbour, Nancy, her husband and two children. Suzie, on the other hand would be spending a quiet Christmas with her mother. I told them of my plans to go to the local village pub on Christmas Eve followed by Midnight Mass, and to attend a luncheon the following day.

We then wished each other a happy Christmas, as I kissed each lady in turn. I drove home in a pensive mood, wondering what Angela would be doing, and whether she would ever leave my cousin, allowing me to pick up the pieces.

Christmas and Sylvia

The old manor house looked lonely and deserted as I drove up to the front steps on that cold, dark Christmas Eve. The reason for the house being in complete darkness was that Ted and Mary had left the previous day to spend Christmas with their son and family, and my parents had left for Scotland the previous week and would not be returning until after New Year.

Mary had been worried when I had announced that I would be staying at home on my own for the festive season. Mary had only been appeased by my agreeing to attend the village Christmas Eve supper, and lunch the next day, down in the village pub. In addition Mary had laid in enough festive food to feed an army, including two packets of the new powdered potato, so as to relieve me from having to cook on Boxing Day.

I ran up the stone steps, opened the door, and immediately switched on all the downstairs lights, including the fairy lights round the windows and the lights that were on the large Christmas tree in the front hall. I went straight to the library, and switched on the gas log fire, as well as switching on and tuning the portable radio that my mother used to listen to the news. The room was immediately bathed in light, as well as being filled with seasonal music.

Sitting down in the big library armchair listening to Bing Crosby singing 'White Christmas', the Salvation Army Band playing 'Silent Night' and Rolf Harris singing the number-one Christmas hit for the year, 'Two Little Boys,' I began to feel more seasonal. The heat, gentle light and the music must have had an effect on me and I dozed off, dreaming of Christmases to come, spent with Angela. I suddenly awoke from sleep to find that I had only enough time to shave, wash and dress for the village Christmas Eve supper.

Promptly at nine thirty I arrived at the pub and went in. The pub was not as full as I had remembered from previous suppers, and I asked George, the publican, why. He told me he had had several cancellations due to people going down with flu, and others cancelling after hearing the Chief Medical Officer asking people to avoid large gatherings. However George was confident that both the supper and lunch the next day would be a roaring success.

The bell behind the bar rang at ten thirty and we all made our way to the pub's large dining room. The tables were laid out in two rows, with villagers sitting either side. I found myself sitting next to Doris and Alf Clark. I had met Doris when she had helped Mary with my parents' entertaining, and had met Alf the previous summer when he had helped Ted to repair the sit-on motor mower. I exchanged greetings, and was then introduced to a lady sitting on my right, who was the niece of Doris. I extended my hand in greeting, and started to introduce myself, but Sylvia stopped me in mid flight by telling me that everyone in the pub knew who I was.

Sylvia, I judged, was in her late twenties or early thirties, petite with jet black hair and deep brown eyes. During the meal we talked at length and she told me she was a professional artist, but was currently writing a book. She explained that she had been widowed less than twelve months before and that this would be her first Christmas since losing her beloved husband. Later in our conversation it emerged that most of her commissions were to immortalise historic buildings and churches. I told her that perhaps when she had finished her book, my parents, or indeed I, might wish to commission her to do an oil painting of the manor house. She agreed that she had been impressed by the house when she had seen it from the road earlier that day, and would welcome the opportunity to record it on canvas for posterity. I told her that perhaps one day, when she was next visiting her aunt, I might have the pleasure of showing her around the manor.

The bell behind the bar rang again at eleven thirty and the majority of the villagers left the pub to make the short walk to the village church for midnight service. There is something warm and welcoming about our small village church, especially on Christmas Eve, when the only light is from candles. I immediately made my way to the family pew (Grandfather had endowed it when he first bought the manor) and sat down. The vicar, who had been standing by the vestry door, hurried over to greet me, expressing his gratitude that someone from the big house had found time to join the villagers at this special service. The service always gets to me, especially the carols, even if the vicar drones on for nearly twenty minutes about hope for the future and justice for all. The service over, I took leave and drove back to the manor, which this time was all lit up.

The next morning I was awake early, not because it was Christmas Day, but because my body clock thought it was a normal working day. I had a breakfast of toast and Marmite and coffee, and then made my way to the library. Passing the big Christmas tree, where presents from my parents and Ted and Mary had been left, I noticed a brown paper package addressed in Angela's handwriting. I immediately picked it up and carried it to the library. The package contained another gift-wrapped parcel, which I hastily undid. Inside was a hard-backed copy of the first edition of *Lady Chatterley's Lover*. I opened the book, and inside the cover was a brief note saying, 'I wanted to buy you something which you would not buy yourself. Have a lovely Christmas and I will see you at the opening ceremony.' Angela was referring to the forthcoming event at Gloworm and I was delighted to learn that she would be there. I carefully placed the book on the table next to my chair, then sat back and daydreamed about Angela, who I hoped would one day be mine.

At just before one I returned to the pub for Christmas lunch. The dining room had been set up with tables in groups rather then in a long row, as had been the case the previous evening. The table plan had been placed on a blackboard by the door, and as I studied it I saw Doris out of the corner of my eye, waving frantically. I walked across to the table where the three were already seated, and offered warm Christmas greetings. I was then told by Doris that I had been placed on their table, and would share Christmas lunch with them. I leaned forward to speak to Sylvia, and was greeted by a big smile, which seemed to make the dining room light up.

The Christmas dinner was, as usual, extremely good, but rather filling. During the meal I had learnt that before Doris and

Alf had known that Sylvia was spending Christmas with them, they had accepted an invitation to join other pensioners at a Boxing Day bash in Ipswich. Sylvia, who had declined the offer of joining them, would consequently be on her own the next day. A gentleman to the end, I suggested that she visit the manor, and I would give her the grand tour. This she accepted graciously and would arrive at eleven o'clock if that was in order.

That night in the library I reread Angela's note wondering what she was doing and whether she was happy. I also remembered Billie-Jo's advice that faint heart never won a fair lady, and I resolved to tell Angela how I felt when she attended the opening ceremony. I also found myself thinking of Billie-Jo and our wonderful lovemaking. And then found myself comparing Sylvia to her.

The next day I was again awake early, probably because it was Friday and normally a working day. I quickly washed and dressed, and then tidied my room and made the bed, ready for the grand tour later that day.

Sylvia arrived promptly at eleven o'clock and I welcomed her into the manor. Having taken her coat, I ushered her into the library, where the log fire was burning brightly. She wore a plain black dress and long black boots, looking stunning. We both had coffee, which I prepared, while we exchanged local gossip.

Coffee finished, I began to tell her the history of the manor, the people who had lived in it and the changes that had been made to suit various generations. Sylvia was surprisingly knowledgeable about architecture, saying that it was not unusual for house like ours to have several different styles, especially when successive occupants, influenced by the fashion, had added bits, like the balconies that graced the two floors at the rear of the house. 'Obviously Italian,' she said. 'Someone had certainly done the Grand Tour, so fashionable during the seventeenth century.'

Lunchtime had arrived and I asked her whether she would like to join me, and we could do the tour of the house later. She agreed, and we both went to the kitchen, where every corner of the fridge and every cupboard was stacked full of seasonal delights. After lunch I showed her around the house and she marvelled at various pieces of antique furniture, especially the four four-poster beds that graced the four suites on the first floor. She told me that her parents once took her to Woburn Abbey, where she had seen her first four-poster bed, and she had subsequently dreamed of sleeping in one.

When the tour had finished we went back into the library, where we spoke about the new book she was writing. Due to the terrible treatment she had experienced when she was first widowed, she had decided to write a handbook for widows. The book would have chapters dealing with registering the death, organising the funeral, finance and benefits, retraining, employment interviews, creating a new social life, and how to deal with unwanted advances from men. I told her that I was surprised that any gentleman would do that sort of thing, especially soon after the loss of a loved one. 'Believe me,' she said, 'there are many men who think a lonely young widow will drop her knickers for the first man she comes across.' I asked her whether she herself had suffered unwelcome advances and she told me she had. She then looked me square in the face and told me she had not been tempted.

'While we are on the subject of men,' she said, 'why were you, a wealthy, handsome male, alone at Christmas?' I started to tell her that it was by choice, but ended up telling her of my sexual difficulties and Billie-Jo. I then told her about Angela and my love for her. She asked if it was the same Angela as had sent me the book lying on the table by the side of my chair, with the note lying on top. I told her that it was, to which she replied, 'In that case, I think that you are in with a chance.' Sylvia stayed for supper, not only to keep me company, but also to do justice to the large amount of seasonal feast laid in by Mary.

The meal over and Mary's kitchen returned to its tidy self, we drifted into the library with our coffee. Sylvia then told me that she had enjoyed her day more then she had thought possible. She complimented me on my knowledge of the history of the house and my professionalism as a tour guide. She then told me she thought that I was an extremely nice person, who deserved better from the female sex. She concluded that I was trying too hard at the beginning of a relationship and frightening the lucky lady away. She told me she wished me well in my quest for Angela, but warned me that I might get hurt. Surprisingly she remarked that she might have fallen for my charm, and commented on the fact that during a long day I had not made a pass at her, for which she was grateful. It was all too soon as she was still mourning for her husband, and she hoped I would understand. Sylvia left at eleven o'clock, kissing me goodbye.

Ted and Mary returned the next day with stories about what a wonderful Christmas that they had had, especially when they had handed Lily over to their excited son. I told Mary about Sylvia's visit, and she told me that she was glad I had invited her as this was the first Christmas since her husband had died. Later that day Ted handed me a handwritten note from Sylvia simply saying good luck and thanks.

The next day being Saturday, I spent all my time calculating the 1970 budget for the company. The turnover for 1969 was estimated at £90,000. The success we had had since the previous July led me to the conclusion that we could achieve £115,000 for the new year. The savings we were expecting to make from a single-site operation made it possible for me to include within the figures an extra week's bonus for all the staff.

I then began looking at the various documents that I had received from Companies House following our change of name. The first file required the company's Memorandum and Articles of Association. I had among my university papers a model of both a Company Memorandum and Articles of Association that I would use as a blueprint for Gloworm. The other folders consisted of a register of shares, which I could easily fill in, there being only one shareholder. The last binder was for official minutes of board meetings. That would be more difficult to comply with as the company had no directors, other than me, and no board. I therefore resolved to restructure the company as soon as possible.

On Wednesday, 31 December I received a letter enclosing an advertisement offering a small property and leasing company for sale by private tender. The article was attached to a White Gull compliments slip, to which had been added, 'I think that this might be in your line of country. Best wishes, Arthur.' I immediately telephoned the number given on the advert, and found it to be a firm of solicitors in Colchester. The solicitor I spoke to promised to send me full details in the post that day.

I spent New Year's Eve down at the local, which again was not as crowded as usual. When midnight came we all toasted the new year, with a hope of prosperity for all. The full details of the property sale arrived. The company owned thirteen properties, all of them structurally sound, but requiring substantial investment. The company also owned the lease of small premises in the centre of town, where it collected rents both for its own properties and forty other properties privately owned. The letter went on to state that due to poor management and insufficient investment on maintenance, rental income was poor, and the leasing company was running at a loss. The report concluded that this would be an ideal investment for people with the right management skills and capital.

I spent the next day driving round and seeing twelve of the properties. There were six two-bedroomed flats all in Colchester, two two-bedroomed houses in Wivenhoe and four three-bedroomed houses in and around Colchester. All properties were in a poor state of repair, and four of the flats were empty and boarded up.

The last house was in Upper Dovercourt, a three-bedroomed detached property which, according to the surveyor's report, needed an entire makeover. I valued the entire package at about £27,000 with repair costs of at least £12,000.

New Year Challenges

The first thing that I did when I arrived at the office was to ring the solicitors and make an offer of £26,000, just slightly less than the value I had placed on the properties. The person I spoke to told me that she would ring the seller to get his opinion of the offer, and would phone me back later that day.

Gloworm held its first management meeting that morning. I began by presenting the 1970 budget. I stated that the initial figures for 1969 indicated a turnover of £90,000. Since the volume of orders was up for the first quarter, I had fixed the annual budget at £115,000, which allowing for inflation was twenty per cent. Mo said that the figure was ambitious but if orders continued to flow as they had over the past few weeks then anything was possible.

I then told them that my estimates included one additional week's pay for all members of staff, payable on the first week of December. This was agreed. I then went on to tell my colleagues that Suzie was now working three days a week for the firm, and I felt that it was time for her to join the firm on a part-time contract of three days per week. Suzie smiled at Mo, then accepted the offer.

I then reminded them that from 1 January, Gloworm was a private limited company, and as such had to keep statutory records. One of these was records of board meetings. Trouble was that we did not have a board of directors to hold such a meeting. I therefore proposed that from 1 January, Mo would become Sales Director, and Suzie Promotions Director. I would for the time being carry both the roles as Finance Director and Managing Director until we were big enough to have our own financial person. This was agreed.

I then told them of the West German management initiative, whereby the workforce elected one of their number to serve on the board. This was only an idea and Mo and Suzie were asked to go away and think about it. I also announced that all directors would receive an extra £50 a year, being director's fees. This was also agreed.

Mo then reported that the new building would be finished in time for the grand opening, and plans for the event were going well. I thanked Mo for her hard work and I looked forward to moving into my new office. Mo then reported that she had already received cancellations for the opening, due to flu. She asked whether we should draw up contingency plans if the flu epidemic grew worse. Suzie thought that things should stay as they were, at least till nearer the event. This was also agreed. Mo then presented her plan and costings for a rationalisation of the original building when we moved out. This she said would bring the total cost of the project, including acquisition, to £4,000. The project and costings were approved.

When the meeting finished, I returned to my office, having only just sat down when the phone rang. The solicitors had contacted their client, who although disappointed by the offer had decided to accept. He thought that the necessary paperwork could be completed within the month. I told him my offer in writing would reach him the next day. I then told him that I wanted to get estimates in respect of the repairs and would need the keys. He thought that would be in order and would alert Miss Flowers at the letting shop of the sale and instruct her to let me borrow the keys when necessary.

I then rang Angela to ask her to write a letter on Lily Estates headed paper confirming our offer, and to include the twelve properties that I would also be sending on her quotation list, which was to be given to Mo on the day of the grand opening, when the award of a contract for the repair and renewal of twelve terraced houses would also be announced. I then asked her how her Christmas had been, to which she replied, 'Miserable'. I told her that I had been lonely too, and that I could not wait to see her again, especially after reading the first few chapters of her Christmas present. She laughed and said, down boy, it can make you blind. She added that she looked forward to seeing me at the opening, and we could talk then.

The day of the grand opening started bright but cold. I stood in my new office watching guests arrive, until I saw Angela's bright red mini enter the gates, and I went downstairs to meet her. Angela was out of her car and walking towards me when we met. I pulled her into my arms, and immediately knew something was wrong. Not only had she winced when I pulled her to me, but her eyes were puffy with crying, and heavy make-up tried to cover a bruise on her cheek. I asked her what was wrong, but all she said was, 'Not now, I will explain later.'

The opening ceremony went off well, with several impromptu speeches by guests wishing Gloworm well. Angela announced the awarding of a tender for the repair of twelve terraced houses, and said that she hoped that the contract would be the first of many.

When the guests had left, I quickly pushed Angela into my office and invited her to sit down, which I could see caused her pain. She then told me that my cousin was now a drug addict, and liable to be violent. She then stood up, unbuttoned her jacket and rolled up her sweater. I gasped as I saw a mass of blue, green and yellow bruises from the bottom of her bra to the top of her skirt. She said that her back, bottom and legs were the same. I told her firmly that she should not go back to London, and must stay with me where I could protect her. She smiled and said, 'You are very kind, as I knew you would be, but I am in the middle of an important project for your uncle and cannot bring myself to let him down, however tempting your offer.' She came forward, took me in her arms and kissed me with pure thoughts of two lovers alone together after a long absence. She then told me she planned to leave Robert as soon as the project finished in the second week in February, and at that time might take up my offer. We kissed again and then she left to return to London.

When she had left, I asked Mo to come and see me to discuss the ceremony. Mo was ecstatic, as not only had there been a rush of orders, but many requests for estimates, including one for Lily Estates for the refurbishment of eighteen properties.

During the next few weeks, both Mo and Suzie were out of the office on estimating visits. I took time to go and see Miss Flowers, the lady in the letting shop. She was in her late twenties, early thirties, getting over a painful estrangement. She was doing a part-time management course at the local tech – the office being closed on Mondays and Thursdays suited the study programme. I told her I would be taking over the lettings shop from 1 February, but I did wish her to stay on. I also told her that a lady named Suzie would visit her one morning to discuss both the upgrading of the shop as well as how future photography needs would be met. I told her that any requests for urgent repairs were to be passed to Miss O'Shea at Gloworm. We parted on exceptionally good terms, especially as I told her in conversation that I was not married.

Valentine's Day fell on a Saturday in 1970, and I arranged for flowers to be delivered to Mo, Suzie and Angela.

Toil and Tribulation

The telephone rang in my private sitting room, next to my bedroom. I sprang out of bed to answer it, noting that it was only six forty-five on a Sunday morning. I lifted the receiver to hear a muffled voice crying for me to help her and I instinctively knew it was Angela. Once the phone went dead and I obtained a ringing tone, I dialled Uncle Edward's number. The phone was answered by Uncle Edward himself, and I quickly told him of the phone call and my worry for his assistant's life. He promised to go straight round to the flat, and said he would be round there in fifteen minutes. I told him I would drive to London immediately if he thought that was needed. He promised to ring me back as soon as he could. Within ten minutes I had washed, dressed and was having breakfast downstairs. The phone rang again and I snatched it up. Uncle Edward's voice came over the phone telling me that things were really bad and asking if I could come straight away.

I was just opening the front door when I met Mary and Ted coming in. I hastily told them what had occurred and that I was off to London. Ted told me he knew London like the back of his hand and it would be quicker if he drove.

We drew up outside Robert and Angela's flat, and I hurried to the door, which was already open. The place looked as if a bomb had hit it, and in the hall stood Uncle Edward, pale with tears running down his cheeks. I asked him where Robert and Angela were and he told me Robert was in a drugged coma in the downstairs bedroom and Angela was in the lounge. I went to open the lounge door but was stopped by Uncle Edward. 'The doctor and nurse are in there, but things look very bad.' I asked him whether he had called an ambulance and the police, to which he shook his head. 'I will do it now,' I said, but again he stopped me. 'George, you have to understand that it seems Robert attacked Angela, and if I call the police they will almost certainly charge him with grievous bodily harm or even attempted murder. I have rung my lawyer, who has advised me to do nothing until he arrives.'

The lounge door suddenly opened and a nurse dressed in a blue sister's uniform emerged. She was a tall lady, I guessed in her middle fifties, and judging from her accent was of Cornish descent. Uncle Edward introduced her as Sister Jennifer Stern, who was his Manager of Occupational Health in Bun Industries. She asked if I was George and said that her patient, though very ill, wanted to see me. I went to enter the lounge when Sister Stern said, 'Prepare yourself for a bad shock. She is not a pretty sight, and do not tire her.'

Angela was lying on her side at the end of the lounge, covered by a blanket. I kneeled down beside her, and spoke softly to her. Her pretty face was no longer, with both eyes swollen shut, dried blood from her was all around her mouth and her lips badly bruised and swollen. She seemed to come to for an instant and mumbled, 'You're here, I knew you would come.' She then said, 'Do not let them take me to hospital,' and then fell back.

I looked at the anxious face of the doctor, who shrugged and said, 'I know her wishes, but I may not have any choice but to send for an ambulance.' Sister Stern then re-entered the room and signalled for me to leave.

Ted was by this time attempting to clean up the glass and pottery shards that littered the kitchen floor. He told us that the upstairs flat had also been wrecked but that he had made the upstairs lounge comfortable, and would it be better if we waited there. However, as we were preparing to go upstairs, the doorbell rang and two gentlemen in white coats carrying a stretcher entered. Uncle Edward took them to the bedroom, where his son was lying. Five minutes later, the men reappeared with Robert covered in a red blanket and well strapped in. After they had left, Uncle Edward told me that Robert was in a bad way and probably wouldn't wake up for many hours. The hospital would ring Lord Bun's house when they had any news.

The men had not been gone five minutes, when the doorbell sounded again, and another nurse entered, dressed in a blue sister's uniform. Asking for Sister Stern, she identified herself as

Sister Joan Brown, a colleague of Sister Stern, and was promptly shown into the lounge.

Uncle Edward was beginning to look ill and Ted took him upstairs to sit him down and make some tea, while I waited in the hall. Ten minutes later, his lawyer arrived and I showed him to the upstairs lounge.

I had only just gone back downstairs when I was collared by Sister Stern. 'George, I hope you don't mind, but I have asked Ted to help me clean up the floor, throw away the debris and most of the bedding as it is foul and needs to be burnt. I would like you to go upstairs to the girl's bedroom and find some clean sheets, pillowcases and duvet. Can you also look in her cupboards and drawers for a clean nightdress and knickers.'

By the time I had located everything and taken them downstairs, the room had been tidied and the bed stripped. Sister Stern then instructed Ted and me in how she wanted the bed made, and when we were done, she folded back the bedclothes and laid a large rubber sheet over a large area of the bed. She told us that when the doctor agreed we would transfer the girl to the bedroom where Sister Brown and she would wash her and tend to some of her wounds, in order to make her feel more comfortable. She then told us that we could return upstairs and she would call us when required.

Uncle Edward was sitting in the upstairs lounge with his lawyer. I asked if I was interrupting their conversation and I was told no. Within ten minutes the doctor appeared, looking grim faced. We all asked how Angela was, and he merely shook his head. 'The girl,' he told us, 'has suffered a sexual assault and a horrific beating, the worst I have ever seen in twenty years of practice. However she appears – and it is still early to be certain – not to have sustained either fractures or internal organ damage. I cannot however comment on her psychiatric state. That will only become clearer with the passage of time.

'The problem is that if we do not send her to hospital, which would be my preferred option, where can she go where she can receive proper treatment by qualified staff?'

Uncle Edward offered his London House and to employ round-the-clock nursing, using agency staff, but the doctor said no. 'While that is a most generous offer, what would you do if next week your son was discharged into your care? Furthermore, at this moment your son and wife will require your undivided attention.'

I then offered the manor as an ideal sanctuary, as it was well hidden in the country, with a single drive for access. Security, if felt necessary, would be easy to maintain. The doctor thought for a moment, and told us all that, though it was a very generous and practical offer, it would mean bringing another doctor into the equation. I told him that our local doctor had treated the family for many years, and could be trusted to keep a confidence. I then gave the doctor the name and home telephone number of Dr Foster, and he disappeared downstairs.

Sister Stern was next to appear, and stood in the middle of the room. She stared down at Uncle Edward and told him that, though he employed her, and she respected him, there were certain facts that she had to impart. She went on to say that in her opinion his son was a monster and should be locked up. He had not only beaten the girl half to death, she continued, but also had raped her both vaginally and anally. The girl might well be damaged mentally for life.

The doctor reappeared, and said that he had spoken to Dr Foster, who had agreed to take over the care of Angela, as long as it was understood that if her condition worsened, he would send her straight to hospital. 'He also knows a nursing agency that can be relied upon to keep a confidence as well as providing a top nursing service. I have told my colleague that someone will ring up when a decision is made, to authorise him to make all the necessary arrangements.'

The lawyer, who until that time had remained silent, told us all that if I undertook the care of the girl, and complications arose requiring hospital treatment, they would almost certainly report her injuries to the police. That could mean a charge being brought against us all for a possible attempt to pervert the course of justice.

I then said that that was a risk; 'However the girl cannot stay here, does not wish to go to hospital, I guess through a sense of loyalty, and is advised not to go to Lord Bun's house. What other course of action is open to me? And in any case, this is also a case of family loyalty, and I will not shrink from my duty.'

Uncle Edward left the room in order to phone Dr Foster and authorise the employment of nursing care. The remainder of us got down to sorting out the way Angela was to be transferred. Sister Stern told us that after suturing three deep wounds to her buttocks, she had given her a strong sedative, and she would sleep for the next two hours. Therefore we should try to book a private ambulance for, say, two thirty. 'I will go with the patient and familiarise her with the case. I will then return with the ambulance to London.'

I told Sister Stern that I knew she would also wish to hand over her patient to Dr Foster. Would it not be better if she stayed the night? Ted would drive her back to London the next day. Sister Stern nodded in agreement. I went to the kitchen and found Ted sitting and drinking a cup of tea. I quickly told him what the plans were, and asked if he could go and phone Mary to make the necessary arrangements.

At four thirty that afternoon our convoy consisting of my car and the ambulance arrived at Alswell Manor. The agency nurse was there to welcome her new patient. Sister Stern then organised the ambulancemen on how she wanted them to transfer Angela from the ambulance to her first-floor bedroom. Once that was done, I took the two ambulancemen down to the kitchen, where Mary had laid on tea and hot buttered crumpets.

Sister Stern did not emerge from upstairs for over an hour. I took her to the kitchen to meet Mary, have tea, and be shown her room.

Mary set dinner for four in the small family dining room, so that we could make Jennifer more at ease. Mary had made a Sunday roast with all the trimmings, followed by jam roly poly and custard.

Ted and Mary then cleared away while I took Jennifer on a whistle-stop tour of the house. She told me that her suite was simply grand, but if she moved in permanently, with Mary's cooking, she would need a bigger uniform. We both laughed at such a suggestion. Suddenly she became serious, and told me that what I had done that day was extremely noble and that my Uncle

Edward was lucky to have my support. Nevertheless, she had meant what she had said earlier in the day – that Robert was a monster and deserved locking up.

I excused myself, went into Father's study and rang Mo at home. I quickly explained what had happened and asked her to go with Ted and Jennifer, the next day, to assess the damage and find local firms to do the work. The flats were to be sold, so all the furniture, cutlery and crockery could be disposed of. I would get Peter to take his big lorry up, clear everything, saving what items of cutlery, crockery, and kitchen utensils could be used later in another flat.

Mo instantly got my gist: 'You want the evidence removed as quickly as possible. Who knows, this might be the forerunner of a London base in the future.'

Mo arrived next morning at eight o'clock and helped Ted put several cases in the boot of the Rolls Royce, in which he was going to bring home Angela's clothes and belongings. The party left at eight thirty, with Mo and Jennifer sitting in the back seat practising their royal wave.

I went upstairs and spoke to the nurse, who told me that Angela had had a restless night, waking up twice screaming. She said that she would report this to the doctor when he came later in the day, to see if Angela needed a sedative at night. I peeked into the bedroom and saw a pale-faced girl with a badly misshapen face, sleeping.

Two days later, my parents arrived home from America. Luckily Ted had told them what had occurred, so when I greeted them at the door I had no uncomfortable explanation to give. Mother went immediately to Angela's room, emerging half an hour later looking stern and worried. Why, she asked, had her nephew turned into an animal? And how was her sister coping with the situation? She then asked Mary to bring tea into the library while she telephoned her sister.

Dinner conversation that night was all about their trip, and of course the trouble with Robert. Apparently Robert was still very ill and had been transferred to a drug rehabilitation centre. 'Flossie is worried that there may be permanent brain damage,' said Mother, 'but it is still too early to know. She is furious with

Cecil, who she has rung to warn him of possible adverse publicity. He had not inquired about Robert, merely saying that it was wrong for the rich to be able to buy themselves out of situations in which normal people would end up in jail.'

My father said little, but invited me to join him in his study for coffee. Once coffee was served, I naturally asked how his business trip had gone. He leaned back in his chair and told me that America was about to erupt both over the Vietnamese War and the bussing of black children to white schools. While he was there, he had seen on television scenes of grown men stoning school buses, and of anti-war riots on college campuses. I told him that there had been angry demonstrations in London, and that there were plans for a large demonstration to march on Downing Street, next month, to protest at Mr Wilson's plans to visit Washington in April.

My father said that the Prime Minister was gambling his future, and that the war in Asia could tip the balance. 'Then we would have that raving European Heath. He promises to take us into the Common Market, however much it costs, and cost it will. You mark my words, George, a super giveaway budget and a snap election might lead to five more years of socialism or result in Europeanism, both scenarios the country cannot afford.'

He then began a conversation about Robert, and said, 'Yesterday you had a difficult call to make, and although you took a terrible gamble, which will hopefully pay off, I think you did the right thing. Congratulations. I would have probably done the same thing, had I been in your shoes.'

I then asked Father whether there was a family feud between the two sisters and their brother. My father asked what made me think that such a feud existed. I told him that, 'First, my uncle blocks my joining of the family firm, then he refuses Mother's invitation to my twenty-first birthday party, not even bothering to send a birthday card. Then, when I was here at Christmas, I noticed that Cecil had not even taken the trouble to send his own sister a greeting of any sort. Now he has upset and refused to help his other sister in her hour of need, and instead condemns our action to save his nephew.

'Over the past seven years he has not only filled the board

with his own cronies but has reduced the Chairman's role to that of a roving ambassador. He is now trying to reduce any authority you might still have by defeating you on any vote he chooses, and yet you and Uncle Edward allow him to get away with it, and I wonder why. Now he has started to overrule managers on items clearly in their domain, causing unrest among many of your loyal staff. You could get rid of him and his cronies at the next annual general meeting, if you wished, but choose not to.'

Father grimaced and then said, 'I am totally committed to my ambassador role, and to my duties in their Lordship's House. Edward is likewise engaged in running Bun Industries and his duties in parliament also. I am afraid that both of us have lost touch with the affairs of White Gull Enterprises, and therefore have to accept the conclusions your Uncle Cecil makes as Managing Director. Having said that, the firm continues to prosper under his stewardship and it might be hard to remove him from office.'

I could see that this conversation was upsetting my father and so I dropped the subject.

Every night for the following two weeks I sat by Angela's bedside, both before leaving for work and again during the evening. While her face was healing fast, she lay motionless, starring into space. The doctor reduced the nursing cover to sixteen hours a day shortly before the end of March, increasing the strength of her sleeping pills, but I was often woken by her screams during the night.

During the last two days of March, Mo reported that the ten-bed hotel project was ready for handover, on time and on budget. I therefore travelled into Constable country, to hand over the project to the new manager. When I arrived I was shown into the manager's office, and by his expression knew something was wrong. I told him that I presumed he was satisfied with our workmanship, to which he replied in the affirmative. The grounds and gardens and the outside painting also looked good, even though the work had been carried out by other contractors.

Eventually he leaned forward and told me that although ninety per cent of the work had been finished on time to a high standard, the opening ceremony, planned for two days hence, would have to be postponed. The problem was that Environmental Health Officer had refused a certificate on the kitchen. The main reason was that the kitchen machinery installers had created so much damage to the floor tiles, splashback tiles and walls.

The manager showed me the problem and I was amazed at such shoddy workmanship.

In a moment of madness, I said that Gloworm would come to his aid. I then rang Mo in the office and told her the facts, asking her to send all our painters over the next day as well as the tiling contractor we had often used on kitchen projects. To my surprise, she agreed that we should try to help, to show that the company could rise to an emergency.

Imagine my pride when at eight thirty on the day of the opening, the Environmental Health Officer granted the all-important certificate. The manager was simply overjoyed that he had not had to cancel the opening, to which one of his directors had been invited to make a speech of welcome.

The event went well, and I allowed Mo to talk to the press and bathe in the glory, as Gloworm's part in the refurbishment was gradually unfurled.

The next day in the office, Mo appeared with ten copies of the *Eastern Daily News*, showing everybody the kind comments made and of course her picture. She was like a dog with two tails that day, and found concentration on other projects hard.

Angela did not emerge from her room till the middle of April. When she did, she was thin and pale with wild eyes that seemed constantly to be looking around the room. During the following two weeks, a combination of Mary's good cooking and my mother involving Angela in her social and charity work saw a physical transformation. However, everybody noticed that she flinched at even the slightest bodily contact, even from my mother.

In early May, my parents left for a trip to Europe, leaving Angela alone in the house with Mary, Ted and I. One night after Ted and Mary had locked up and gone to their bungalow, leaving us alone in the library, Angela suddenly began what was the first real conversation she had had since the traumatic events of the previous February. She told me that the whole household had been like a family to her over the past weeks, especially me, who had watched over her during the worst times. However, she felt that she could not stay indefinitely, and needed to rebuild her life.

I told her there was no hurry and she could stay for ever if she became my wife. She smiled at me and took hold of my hand, and told me how flattered she was by my proposal, something my mother had told her would be forthcoming. However, she could not marry me, at least for the present, as in her current state she could neither return my love nor give me the heir my mother and she suspected that I also wanted. I told her that I would wait till things improved, but she told me, that I might wait for ever and that would not be fair either for me or my family, whom she loved like a daughter.

'Your uncle has kept my job open, and I will leave next week. I gather my flat has been sold, and until he can find me a suitable flat from within his portfolio, he will pay for me to stay in a small hotel, near to the office.' She ended by saying that her decision, she felt, was the best for everybody, and she hoped I would understand. Three days later, she was collected by a van belonging to Bun Industries and returned to London.

Returned to Life

The next two months were especially painful for me, as I believed that I had lost Angela for good. Mo was particularly understanding, and tried to make life at Gloworm as pleasant as possible. One day at the beginning of May she took me out and showed me the refurbished two-bedroomed flats I had bought the previous August. The workmanship within the flats was, as I knew it would be, of the highest quality. She also told me that the work on the eight maisonettes would be completed by the end of the month.

On the way home to the office we stopped for lunch at a little pub. During lunch, Mo told me she had a confession to make, and she hoped I would not be angry with her. She then told me that ten days before Angela had left the hall, Lord Bun had rung her to ask if Gloworm could work its magic on a two-bedroomed flat in the city. She told me that she had been very busy at the time and so had despatched Suzie to estimate the work required, and when the go-ahead was received to get the work done in the quickest time possible but to the highest standard. Suzie had spent three days in London, estimating, getting agreement and putting the work in hand, using Gloworm staff as well as local contractors. Last Friday, Mo said, Suzie had handed the flat over to Lord Bun and Angela, who had both been overwhelmed by Suzie's creation. Lord Bun had since written to the firm, praising the work and the timeliness of the project well as enclosing his cheque for the agreed amount. The letter had also said that he had told the Bun Industries property department to use only Gloworm in the future for all major refurbishments.

Mo also told me that it had not been necessary to use the various contingency sums contained in the estimate and that, as a consequence, Gloworm had made an additional £100 profit.

When we returned to the office, I arranged for our secretary cashier to draw two £50 cheques, one for Mo and one for Suzie. I then called in Mo, told her that I was proud at the way she had dealt with the Lord Bun commission and handed her a cheque for £50 (two and a half times the average weekly wage). Initially she did not want to accept it, but eventually smiled and told me I was very generous.

I then called Suzie in, telling her to shut the door behind her and to sit down. I sat opposite her, perching on the front of the large desk. Suzie obviously did not know why I had requested her presence, and had the expression on her face of a naughty schoolgirl summoned to the headmaster's office to answer for crimes unknown. I started by telling her I wished to speak to her about the Bun project. Suzie, without waiting, began to apologise for keeping me in the dark, but Mo and she had thought it for the best. I told her I did understand their reasoning and was gratified I had two such friends, and how proud I was of her and her work.

I then asked her whether she had seen Angela, and how she was. Suzie told me that she looked well, but when she went to greet her, as friends do, Angela had pushed her away. 'George, her eyes were full of terror, and her whole body went tense. I know it is early days, but I feel the girl needs professional help.'

I regained my composure and handed Suzie the cheque, as a special bonus, telling her she had earned every penny. Suzie, without warning, threw herself into my arms, pressing her body into mine. I looked down into her eyes and saw a mixture of deep loneliness and expectation. 'Hold me,' she whispered, and I did so. She then pulled my hands down to rest on her bottom, and planted a gentle kiss on my lips. Throwing caution to the wind, I returned her kiss, and gently fondled her twin globes. When we drew apart, she smiled and said simply, 'Thank you.' I told her that if ever she needed a cuddle, not to be afraid to ask.

That night I dreamed of Suzie standing naked in front of me, beckoning me to come to her, and of finding myself unable to do so through respect, and common business sense of propriety, as well as fear of entanglement with a friend I did not truly love.

I confided in Mo, the next day, who said that she had wondered why Suzie had left my office like a cat with two tails. The dream she dismissed as quite normal for a young man in need of female love and affection, and told me not to worry.

The following week, a general election was announced. As we had had a giveaway budget the previous March, the opinion polls predicted an overwhelming victory for Labour.

At the end of the month, Mo took me to see the finished eight maisonettes, which were so impressive that I gave Mo a great big hug for being such a clever girl.

The following week the lettings man from the university came and snapped up both the maisonettes and the four flats, paying £5 per week for all the twenty dwellings they had agreed to rent. The terms of the lease were fifty per cent of the annual rent on the first day of July and the remaining fifty per cent at the finish of the contract in June.

The next week, against all predictions, the Tories were swept to power, and all the newspapers forecasted a big boost to the economy. I was relieved at the result, because a rise in the economy would almost certainly mean a rise in both properties' prices and rents.

My thoughts then turned to Lily Estates, which in a few weeks would end its first year's trading showing a book loss. However by the end of the next twelve months it would begin showing a modest profit, with above average returns in year three. The workload would increase as more properties came on stream to be rented, yet I could no longer rely on Angela. The only solution seemed to be better use of Pauline Flowers' time.

I therefore invited her to lunch during the third week of June, when she had finished her examinations and had no college. I took her to my favourite restaurant, Jacklin's in the High Street, where I knew both the wooden polished walls and good service were bound to impress her.

Over lunch I began telling her of Lily Estates, which I said were temporarily in the custody of trustees. I then proceeded to tell her who and what I was.' I then told her of my plans to let her keep the day-to-day books of the company, a task I had calculated could be performed during her existing four days when the letting shop was open. I would also increase her salary from £16 per week to £20 a week, which was at that time the average weekly wage. I told her that Thursday, from now on, could be considered as day release. She immediately accepted my proposal and thanked me generously.

During the remaining part of lunch she told me she was married but separated. Following a whirlwind romance, she had expected a blissful married life. However once they were married she had found him to be selfish, domineering and hopeless with money. He had expected her to take over from his mother, even to the point of cleaning his shoes every morning. The final straw came when he insisted she turn over the deeds to her flat to him, as he was man of the house. This she refused to do, and he had gone back to his mother. She had met him on a couple of occasions to try mediation, but soon came to realise that such visits were when he wanted a free meal and access to the marital bed. They had been separated for two years and she planned to sue for divorce when she completed her studies.

When lunch was over, I drove Pauline back to her flat. She leaned over and kissed me as the car came to a stop, thanking me for a wonderful lunch. Without any real intention, I found myself watching her lovely bottom as it swayed under her tight skirt as she climbed the stairs to her flat.

I was deeply shocked at what I had done, reminding myself that not only was she a married woman but also an employee.

That night the same dream returned, but this time it was Pauline who was standing before me, her seductive eyes that promised paradise to any man who could capture her heart, her small, pert breasts straining against the top she was wearing, and that alluring mouth, which seem to call me to her. However, as in previous dreams, I could not go to her, as I was being held fast by the bonds of honour and respectability.

The next morning I awoke with a headache and felt pretty grim, and I resolved to find another outlet for the energies that were fuelling such dreams.

The following Monday we held an emergency meeting to discuss the looming dock strike. Mo reported that all materials required for ongoing jobs and those planned for later that year had already been ordered or were sitting in our store. We concluded that provided the dock strike did not last too long we should be able to survive. I reported that turnover in the first six months had been over £65,000, and if it continued it would be more than enough to reach our target.

We then went on to discuss the forthcoming trade exhibition, which was to be held in the lower castle grounds. Suzie reported our having booked the large marquee, and that the publicity material was also well in hand. She had talked to the staff who had agreed to take part in the event. There was to be a demonstration of French polishing and carpentry on day one, followed by demonstrations of upholstery and curtain making on the second and last day. Suzie asked whether Mo and I would also be available both days, as the event was a prestigious one, with many visitors expected. We both agreed, and went to our diaries to ensure we were all free for the exhibition.

The show was a complete success, with many visitors, especially in the large marquee. Our stand and demonstrations were also well received with many bookings to go to price work, as well as enquiries which we would follow up.

The following Monday morning, Mo declared that the number of jobs to be priced would keep her and Suzie busy for months, and we would still be left with many enquiries to follow up. Suzie reported that the following the government's State of Emergency, the dockers had agreed to accept a revised pay offer, and would be returning to work in August.

When the meeting broke up, I asked Mo to come and see me in my office. I told her I could see the concern she was having, regarding workloads. Since I had made no firm plans for the holiday, perhaps I could come in for two days a week to follow up on some of the enquiries. Mo said that my offer was very generous, and that as she also had no plans for the August break, perhaps we could work together.

The two weeks of our annual shutdown were, for me, exceptionally enjoyable, as between the two working days we both agreed to do, Mo and I went for days out to places such as Clacton, Yarmouth, Norwich and Chelmsford. We also took in various shows at the local theatre, Clacton, Yarmouth and Southend. We found we had much in common, liking the same things and just being together. Those two weeks simply flew by and on the last Saturday night, as I sat with Mo in the car outside her house, we agreed that we would try to find times in our busy schedules to simply indulge ourselves in pure fun.

The first day back was one of mixed emotions. During the holiday break, four transatlantic airliners had been hijacked by extremists, who had taken the passengers off one aircraft and then blown it up. Reports were also being carried out by the news media about the rapidly deteriorating situation in Northern Ireland. In the main, however, Gloworm staff, refreshed by their holiday, seemed to be bright and cheerful as ever, seemingly ignoring what was going on in the wider world.

Later that week, I asked Mo to pick me up from home, so that we could look at a special project in Colchester. I directed her to the Lexden property and on to the circular drive in front of the house. Mo took the keys and opened the magnificent front door, the porch being supported by two stone pillars. We decided to survey the top floor first. The layout comprised six large rooms and four bathrooms, two at either end of the house. On the left-hand side of the stairs were two large rooms opposite each other. In both rooms a stud partition had been erected to give a living and sleeping area. The bathrooms serving the two flats were both in a terrible condition. The other side of the staircase was not much better. True, there were no stud walls, but in one room the ceiling boards had come down, and in the other the wallpaper was falling off. The other two bathrooms were also in an advanced state of decay, revealing years of neglect.

The downstairs was a little better, and virtually everything would need replacing. The large kitchen had probably been equipped in the thirties for large-scale food production. Mo drew my attention to a small storage space under the stairs that had been left open and which, like the rest of the house, smelt fusty. We were just about to leave when Mo spotted a sheet of hardboard coming away from the wall opposite the cupboard. She pulled at the board to see what it was hiding and then declared that she could see the outline of a door. She excused herself, and went out of the front door, soon returning with a large screwdriver and torch. Ten minutes later, the sheet of hardboard was down and Mo was trying one of the many keys in the rusted lock.

At last she found the correct key and unlocked the door. She surveyed the darkness with her torch, exclaiming, 'As I suspected, a basement.' I offered to go down first to survey the area, but she only said, 'You stay there. If these steps are not safe I will need you to call an ambulance.' She was gone for a good twenty minutes before she reappeared, triumphant.

She told me that the area of the basement was huge, and spread below all six rooms. There was little space to walk, however, as the whole area was littered with old magazines, books, old furniture and many sealed boxes. Mo believed that the last time a person had gone down to the basement was in 1946, judging from the dates of the top newspapers. Mo then relocked the cellar door and replaced the hardboard cover, before going to the front door where we left locking the large front door.

We next went round to the back of the house, where Mo bent down to see what was covering the basement windows, and found it was earth from the overgrown garden. The large lawn and flowerbeds were totally overgrown. At the end of the garden stood a lightweight building which we discovered had been used as a workshop and for the garaging of an old car, judging by the amount of oil on the floor. The area of the workshop still had an abandoned wood-turning lathe, as well as ten or so rusted chisels. We relocked the garage, walking up the garden to Mo's parked car.

Once we were settled in the car I asked Mo what she thought. She told me that she thought the house was magnificent, but would cost thousands to put right. She then asked who the owner was, and was dumbstruck when I told her it was me. I explained that I had decided to leave home and fend for myself, and had chosen this house as a suitable home in which to bring up children. 'I know it will be a very lengthy and expensive project, and I am going to give you and Suzie a free hand in its renovation. In this respect, I shall be a normal customer of Gloworm.'

As we drove, Mo was considering the project, and when we stopped the car she threw her arms around my neck and told me she accepted the challenge.

We stopped on the way at the Upper Dovercourt property. Mo got out of the car, and said that the property had been empty for years while lawyers tried to track down lost relatives. The whole house had had not been touched since it was built in the early thirties. Mo told me that everything needed replacement, central heating installed, a new kitchen and bathroom. She thought that the final estimate would be in the region of £3,000. I told her that the property now belonged to Lily Estates, and as soon as a proper estimate had been prepared I would get it approved. I told her to assume that she had brought the place and was refurbishing it to the highest standard, stamping her mark on the place.

Several days later, Mo handed me two detailed estimates, one for the Dovercourt house amounting to £2,900, and for the Colchester property, £6,200, plus an additional £800 for furniture. I immediately accepted the one for my Lexden property, and confirmed that for the Upper Dovercourt property two days later.

During the next three months the country seemed to lurch from crisis to crisis, as group after group of unhappy workers flexed their muscles against the new Tory government. Gloworm, however, seemed to go on from strength to strength, with orders and enquiries coming in daily, ensuring that the order book was virtually full for three months ahead.

In October, Mr Watts, the older director of the electrical contractors that we had used so much since I arrived so much so that they were nearly full time on our various projects, told me that he was planning to retire sometime after Christmas, and would therefore not be able to accept any more work from us. He and his son would honour the contracts already placed with them. I asked him what had precipitated his decision to retire early, and he told me that it was due to changed family circumstances. He went on to say that his mother-in-law had suffered a bad fall, and was currently in the Norfolk and Norwich hospital. Although she would not be released for several weeks, when she was discharged she would need constant care. Since his wife was the only female in the family, that care fell upon her.

The previous weekend they had arranged to visit his mother-in-law in hospital. During that visit they had been asked to collect some things from her house, and on the way back to the hospital had spotted a new development of small bungalows, only five minutes from his mother-in-law's bungalow. They had stopped and visited the show house, and after some discussion decided that the easiest thing to do was to relocate to Norfolk. I asked him how much the house was and was told £2,500. I asked him whether he had found a buyer for his house and yard, to which he replied, 'I am just on my way to the estate agents.' I asked him how much he thought his property was worth, and he told me that a valuer had estimated between £4,000 and £4,500.

I then asked him if he would be so kind as to step outside while I made a telephone call. When I invited him in, I told him that a firm called Lily Estates would buy the property for £4,250. His face burst into happiness as he shook my hand and said he accepted the offer.

I asked him what would be happening to his son once the property was sold. He told me that as a fully qualified electrician he would probably get a job in the port. 'The situation is however very delicate, as my son plans to move into his girlfriend's flat as soon as we move. I am sure you will understand my missus is a bit upset that they will be living in sin, so to speak.' I nodded wisely, before suggesting that perhaps his son would like to join Gloworm as a full-time employee, when the contract work finished. He smiled again, and said, 'I am sure he would like that, and I will talk to him this evening.' This he did, and the next day we agreed that he would begin his new job at Gloworm straight after Christmas.

When at our November meeting I informed my colleagues that I intended purchasing Mr Watt's house and the workshop that stood in the large garden, they were at first extremely hesitant. I then explained that I had noticed a strong growth in kitchen sales. I had also noticed how many samples were needed for every sales visit, of taps, plugs, door handles, worktops, etc. 'What I have in mind is to open a kitchen centre. As you know,' I told them, 'the premises are just off the main town centre, and according to the deeds and records have planning permission for retail use. Apparently when the business changed from electrical retail to electrical repairs nobody applied for a change of use, and the Planning Officer of the council has told me we only need building regulations when refitting the showroom. I paid £2,000 for the workshop, large car park and yard as well as the right of way down the road at the side of the existing house.'

Mo was the first to speak, and said, 'Having heard the proposal

I am impressed, not only by the project, but also by the forward thinking. Presumably you are investing part of the proceeds of our former Harwich depot?'

I told her that my estimate for refurbishing the building, the installation of a large window, and an illuminated sign would be approximately £1,000, bringing the total cost of the project to £3,000, less than half the capital return on our former depot. Suzie then told us that, although she was in favour of the project, she was concerned at the continual growth of the company, and wondered whether we had the staffing resources to keep expanding. I told her I knew things were tight, and when I came to revise the budget in December, I would be looking at both workloads and future staffing. The vote was unanimous and Gloworm Kitchens was born.

When the meeting finished, I told the girls that my mother had invited them both to dinner on the following Friday evening, and I hoped it would be convenient. They both told me that they were free and would be happy to accept my mother's kind invitation. Mo asked whether the dinner was a special occasion and, if so, ought they to bring anything? I told them, just themselves. Later in the day, I took Suzie on one side, and told her that my mother wished to commission some family portraits, and she should bring the necessary equipment with her. When Mo asked later in the day what the dinner was really for, I told her that as mother had met both her and Suzie, during the Angela business, and had subsequently heard me praise their various talents. Mother had decided to look again at her son's two fillies to judge whether they would make good breeding stock. Mo simply nodded and smiled.

The following Friday, Mo and Suzie arrived at the house, dressed to the nines. During pre-dinner drinks, mother quizzed the girls on their work, ambitions and families. Dinner was served by Ted and Mary in the large dining room, with father and me dressed in full evening attire, as ordered by my mother. Once dinner was over, my mother announced that we would all be having our pictures taken. The reason for this was that she was putting together a special album for Angela, picturing all the people Angela had met while a guest at the manor. Each of us would be given a card, on which should be written greetings and a wish for a speedy recovery. Each card would be displayed beside the picture of the writer.

One by one, we went to the library to let Suzie photograph us. I was last in and after careful instruction took Suzie's picture.

The evening was a complete success, and after the weekend both girls were anxious to learn what my mother had thought of them. I told Suzie, that mother had been impressed by her, but thought her hips to be too small to make a good breeding mare. Mo laughed, telling Suzie she must put on some weight before her next outing. Suzie then said, 'What did your mother think of Mo, then?'

'She was very impressed with her, but felt that she was a bit frisky for her own good and could do with a firm hand and touch of the whip to bring her into line.' Mo blushed, while Suzie fell about laughing, telling Mo that she should practise bending over her master's desk.

During the first week of December, Mary and Ted made their annual visit to Harrods, both to do their own Christmas shopping and that of the families as well. Family presents were left to their discretion and Mary had to go away and buy presents for Ted, and Ted set off to pick up something suitable for Mary. Mother always ensured that not only did they have sufficient money for presents, but also for a slap-up lunch in Harrods' famous top-floor restaurant. I was feeling particularly generous and gave Mary sufficient money to buy something really feminine for the three girls and a nice briefcase for Pauline, who was maturing into a first-class businesswoman.

During that week, Suzie delivered the photographs to Mother, and was soundly scolded for refusing to accept any money for her work. Over tea that afternoon my mother had told Suzie that when Angela left the house it had been like losing a daughter. Suzie told me the next day that my mother's insistence on making her eat three pieces of Mary's sponge led her to believe that she was still in the frame of runners and riders.

That first week in December, Mo presented the payment of the annual bonus, and one could feel the sense of achievement and happiness coming from the workplace.

During that week I had lunch with the bank manager, who was full of praise for the joint achievements of both Lily Estates and Gloworm. We discussed the future of both enterprises, as well as reinvestment of profits in existing and new ventures.

Leaving the restaurant that day, I turned right, passing the displays of the large department store that stood in the High Street. I saw in one display a statue of a woman attired in a black baby-doll nightie, which was trimmed in red lace. My first thought was how scandalous was the display, and then I suddenly saw the funny side of things. The name that suddenly came into mind was the black widow spider, not the sort of widow portrayed in Sylvia's book. Sylvia, of course, might or might not be staying with her Auntie Doris this year, but if she was, and they met, it would be a fun thing to give her. I nervously entered the shop and was soon greeted by a young lady assistant. When I told her what I wished to buy for my wife, she became very understanding, offering to wrap the present herself.

The week before Christmas was a torrid time for the new government, who had become so annoyed about the sheer volume of wildcat strikes that they had published an Industrial Relations Bill for consultation that, if passed, would severely contain the power to launch such strikes.

On the Thursday we held our Christmas Eve party for the workers. That year seemed special for some reason, as I was to find out when, after my usual thanks and good wishes, I was presented with a framed picture of the Gloworm works, signed by every member of staff. I found this not only to be very touching, but it also brought a feeling of really being accepted by all, as a fellow worker.

Once the party was over, I retired to my office with Mo, Suzie and Pauline. I handed each of them their presents and hoped that they would all have a nice Christmas. Mo was spending Christmas with her next door neighbour, Suzie with her mum and family and Pauline with her parents. I kissed them all in turn, and then left for the short drive home.

Christmas Surprise and New Year Sadness

I felt that I had been here before as I entered the dark driveway that led to the manor. Here was I, a successful businessman and eligible bachelor, spending yet another Christmas on his own. I resolved, as I stopped at the bottom steps leading to the hall, that this would be the last Christmas I would spend alone, even if I had to pay a young lady to keep me company. The Christmas Eve supper at the pub was as usual a happy occasion, and better supported than in the previous year. Alf and Doris were already seated at a corner table with Sylvia as I entered the pub. During supper, Doris told me that Sylvia's book had been published to great critical acclaim, and that she was so much in demand she could not stay for Boxing Day. The Christmas Service was as beautiful as ever, and as usual made me glad that Christmas was upon us. Once the service ended, I noticed Sylvia hanging back, and I quickly went to join her. She told me that she had brought my mother a signed first edition of her book, in gratitude for the foreword my mother had written for. She wondered if she could deliver it on Boxing Day, and I immediately invited her for lunch, which she readily accepted.

The Christmas lunch was again well attended, giving me time to meet with old friends and neighbours. Conversation between Sylvia and me was confined to everyday, mundane matters. This was designed not to give away our secret luncheon the next day.

Sylvia arrived promptly at eleven o'clock. I took her coat to reveal a plain blue jumper and blue plaid skirt. She followed me into the library, where the fire was burning brightly and the coffee brewing.

Once Sylvia had finished her coffee she began to relate the highlights of the past year, the successful launch of her book, the wide interest it had created and the interviews she had had with both radio and television. She then told me of a second book she had been commissioned to write, about surviving a broken marriage, and how her research was coming on. By the time she had finished it was time for lunch. We dined well, thanks to Mary's usual Christmas delights provision, which I am sure was enough to feed an army. Once we had eaten and cleared away we took our coffee, plus a bottle of brandy, into the library. Sylvia then produced two packages from out of her briefcase and handed me one. This, she explained, was the book for my mother. I placed it on a side table to await Mother's return. Handing me a second parcel, Sylvia told me it was for me, something she thought I would not buy for myself. I unwrapped the package, and was surprised to find a *Playboy* calendar. I began thumbing through the pages and admiring the various bunnies of the month. Sylvia smiled and told me she had remembered my difficulty with the opposite sex, and thought the calendar would comfort me during long, lonely nights. Attached to the calendar was a notice, telling me I had subscribed for a year. I thanked her for her generosity, but said that I did not know how my parents would react to such a magazine landing on the doormat, to which she responded, 'It may give your father a new lease of life.'

I then retrieved a package I had placed behind my chair and gave it to Sylvia, telling her that I too had remembered our last year's conversation. Once she had unwrapped the present, and taken the garments out of the box, she smiled before bursting into laughter. I then told her that if she ever became the evil sex-starved widow, I thought she should dress the part.

The rest of the afternoon flew by as I told her about Lily Estates, Gloworm and then Angela. She listened carefully to all I had to say, and at the end of my story, merely said, 'Poor girl and poor you.' I told her that, since the incident, I had proposed to Angela, a proposal that had been turned down, because of Angela's lasting revulsion to anyone's touch. Looking at me, Sylvia said, 'Is the girl getting professional help, and is it working?' I told her yes to the first question and definitely no to the second. Sylvia thought for a moment, and then told me she thought I was still carrying a torch for the girl, and that it might well be in vain.

I looked at my watch and noticed it was after seven. Outside the wind had got up and there was an icy rain falling. 'When do you have to be in London?' I asked.

'Ideally for tonight,' she told me.

I told her I thought the roads would be bad. Why didn't she stay in the guest room tonight and go first thing in the morning? She smiled and told me that to have her car outside the manor all night might ruin my reputation. 'In that case,' I told her, 'let's go and put your car in the garage, there is plenty of room.' And that's what we did.

We then went to the kitchen and rustled up a meal, and took it into the television room. While we ate, we watched the Boxing Night film about some disaster. When the film ended, I proposed to lock up and then go to bed. She knew where the guest room was, and I would take up her case for her. She told me that she was tired and wanted an early start.

I had showered and changed into my silk pyjama trousers, and stood by the bed setting the alarm clock, when I heard a soft knock on my sitting room door, followed by the sound of feet on the carpet. I looked up and there Sylvia stood, dressed only in the baby-doll outfit. She smiled and said, 'I thought that you would like to see how well they fit.' I opened up my arms to her and very soon my pyjama trousers were lying on the floor with her nightdress and knickers, while in the big bed above two very lonely people were finding warmth and solace in each other's bodies.

When I awoke next morning, Sylvia was already awake, propped up on one elbow and looking down at me. 'Morning, lover,' she whispered, to which I responded, 'Good morning to you – and how are you?'

'Well,' she replied. 'I woke up this morning in a four-poster bed, just like my childhood dreams, and wondering whether the second part of my dream will also come true.'

'What is that?' I asked.

She moved towards me, pulled me on top of her and proceeded to show me.

It was after ten when we both came to the surface, and I had the delight of watching her glorious bottom as she went through to the bathroom. I then got up and, using the guest room, quickly showered and changed. As I entered my bedroom, Sylvia was just coming out of the bathroom, clad only in a towel. Seeing me looking at her, she smiled, dropped the towel and did a twirl. 'Is everything to sir's satisfaction?' she growled.

We had a quick breakfast of toast and coffee, as she wanted to be on her way. As we got to the door, and as I helped her on with her coat, I begged her to stay. She then told me I had been a really good lover, but now was the time to say goodbye, at least for the present. With that I followed her to the garage, opened the door and stood watching as her car quickly went out of sight.

When Ted and Mary came home everything was as they had left it, with no trace of Sylvia. I told them Sylvia had called in with a present for Mother, and had stayed for a meal on her way back to London. Mary remarked that Doris had told her that her niece was now famous and her visit was only fleeting.

The next few days I spent on the Gloworm budget, which I set at £160,000, which included provision for a ten per cent increase in wages, additional staff, and an increase in the company's prices of 9.9 per cent. I then looked at the affairs of Lily Estates, who were some six months into their financial year. The twenty premises let to the university would yield a further £2,600 in January. Ten additional properties were now ready for letting, and would contribute approximately £1,200, with ten more properties following in February and March, probably yielding a further £2,000. That being so, I should be looking at a profit of between £4,000 and £5,000. Owing to the heavy investment during the year, there would not be a substantial tax bill, nor expensive repairs.

The next day I took time to examine all the Christmas cards received, which were hung on strings in the library, and again found no greetings from my mother's brother and his family.

On New Year's Eve I again accompanied Mary and Ted to the local pub, where this year's toast was for health, wealth and for increased prosperity for all.

The first morning back after the break was a busy one. We held our first board meeting of the year, and were joined by Peter, the driver, who had been elected by the staff to represent their views. I welcomed him to the board before we began discussing the agenda. Our meeting was dominated by two main items, the forthcoming national postage strike, and our progress towards decimalisation, planned for the end of February.

Mo reported that from a supply point of view, the company should not be unduly affected. Where we would be affected was in the sending out of invoices and the collection of cheques from customers. The company might also see a slowdown in the receipt of new orders, but it was hoped that our telex system would be used by customers wishing to place new orders, or to make enquiries. However, the order book was surprisingly full and the cash flow extremely healthy and, even if there was a slowdown, the company could ride the storm.

Peter, who had listened intently to the report, asked if he could make a suggestion, and this was welcomed by all. He then told us that his young assistant had passed his motor cycle proficiency. He was sure that he could make his assistant available once a day to deliver and collect mail from our customers, who were for the most part near at hand. Peter went on to say that, if this suggestion was acceptable, he knew where he could purchase a second set of panniers. I thanked Peter for his suggestion, which was immediately accepted.

Suzie presented her report on the company's progress on the decimalisation changeover, predicting few or no problems. Peter told the meeting that some of the staff did not fully understand the changeover, and there might be queries on the first pay day following the change. However, it was thought that the change-over would be satisfactory.

I then introduced the budget for the year, which was approved as being very achievable. I explained that an across-the-board increase of ten per cent would be paid in the first week in August, and that the annual bonus would continue to be paid on the first week in December.

Following the meeting Suzie came to see me, to thank me for my Christmas present. She went on to tell me that she had unwrapped in front of her mother, who had immediately accused her of having a secret fancy man, and told her what happened to girls who allowed liberties before they were married. I told her that I hoped she had put her mother straight on the issue, to which she just winked and said, 'What do you think?'

Later, Mo came to see me to discuss the meeting. We began by recounting what we had been doing at Christmas, and how much we had enjoyed the holiday. Mo told me that my present to her was one of the best Christmas presents she had ever been given, then stood up and kissed me.

I then explained that my plans included the appointment of our own plumber to deal with both kitchen fitting and odd jobs coming from the letting agency. I also shared with her that, when finished, the kitchen centre would be self-sufficient with its own fitting, electrical and plumbing staff. We also agreed that we would need to find another electrical contractor who could undertake the bigger jobs. My last point, caught her by surprise, when I told her I wanted her to appoint an assistant sales person, whom she would train up, not only on the kitchen pricing (the department where he or she would be based), but over all our products. Mo agreed it would be helpful, provided that she could find the right person.

Everything seemed to be going smoothly at both companies. The staff were happy and most not even in unions, so the threat of national strikes in protest at the government's industrial relations bill seemed not to affect us. Admittedly, the increasing number of wildcat strikes, and the declaration by Rolls-Royce that they were bankrupt, did little to improve business confidence. We were coping well with the postal strike, and had seen a slight increase in orders. Decimalisation came and went, with no problems.

Mother and Father returned from their Christmas holiday in mid-January. Mother handed me a note of appreciation from Angela to everybody who had taken the time to assist with her special album. She said in her letter that reading the many good wishes contained in the book certainly made her feel she was among friends. I told Mother I would show the letter to Mo and Suzie the very next day.

My mother then handed me a sealed letter from Angela, and addressed in her own fair hand. I immediately took the letter upstairs to my room and hastily opened it. The letter began with

'My dearest George', and went on to say how beautiful and thoughtful my Christmas gift had been. She was still undergoing psychiatric treatment and, though her therapist was pleased with her progress, she still reeled when anybody touched her. She concluded that my mother was concerned at my disinterest in other girls, and longed for an heir. Angela then said, 'Please do not wait for me, as I may never regain my former health.' The letter finished 'Your dearest friend'.

On the following Valentine's Day, I sent flowers for Mo, Suzie and Pauline, and for Angela, twelve red roses.

The world at that time seemed to me perfect, but little did I suspect that trouble was on the horizon and ready to pounce. The first major event happened on a dark, wet night in late February. I was sitting in the library reading some mail, when I heard strange noises coming from the hall. I was just rising, to investigate the disturbance, when Ted entered the library. He told me that Miss Maureen was in the hall, in a terrible state, and I should come immediately. I followed him into the hall only to find Mo sobbing in Mary's arms. I waited for the sobs to subside, before gently taking her into my arms. I asked her whatever had happened, but this only gave rise to more sobbing. Waiting till she calmed down, I continued to hold her, gently leading her into the library. Mary then appeared with a tray of tea, and poured Mo a cup, adding plenty of sugar. Mo took a couple of sips of the tea, then sank into her chair. Gradually, she became calmer to the point where she could tell us the reason for her distress.

Apparently she had had a telephone call that morning, informing her that her best friend and next door neighbour was in hospital, and was asking to see her. Mo had therefore travelled to the hospital in Colchester, straight after work. When she had arrived, she found that she was too early for visiting, but when she told the staff nurse who she was visiting, she was immediately taken to a single side ward were her friend was being treated. Mo was horrified at seeing her friend looking so ill, and enquired how she was doing. Her friend told her she was suffering terminal cancer of the liver. Her friend then explained the reason for her call that morning. 'When the time comes, will you help Philip, my husband, arrange the funeral? He is a dear, but was never good at organising anything. The children, along with their dad, will be moving to his mother's in Dovercourt. They will obviously wish to take some things from the house, and what is left will require disposing of.' Her friend asked Mo if she might organise the move. 'Finally, before Philip hands back the key to the landlord, can you make sure that the whole place is clean? I would not wish anyone to think I was a dirty bitch who didn't care.' Having made her requests, and being totally exhausted, her friend had closed her eyes as if in sleep. Mo, being alarmed at this, called a nurse, only to be told that her friend was on heavy painkilling medication, and had bouts of activity and bouts of sleep.

Having been told her friend might sleep for some time, she gave the nurse the flowers she had taken in with her and left. Mo told us that she had managed to remain composed until she reached her car, and then had broken down in grief. She had tried to drive home, but her constant tears and periods of distress had made her driving erratic and dangerous, and she had barely made it to the hall.

Once Mo had finished her story she collapsed into tears, and was comforted by Mary. Once the tears had subsided, Mary began on the practicalities of the situation. She asked Mo when she had last eaten, and when told lunchtime, told Mo she needed to eat and that a plate of scrambled eggs on toast would make her feel better. Ted was despatched to put Mo's car in the garage. Ten minutes later Mo was presented with a plate of food and fresh tea, which she was told by Mary to eat. Mary then said, 'As soon as you have finished, I will take you up to bed in the guest room,' and promised Mo that things would look very different in the morning.

The next morning Mo was more like her old self, but her eyes were red from crying, and she looked washed out. Mary tried to get her to stay, but Mo wanted to go home, so I escorted her there before going into the office. When I arrived, I explained to Suzie what had happened and asked her to keep an eye on Mo when she returned to work. This Suzie did for the following ten days, until the phone call that Mo was dreading came. Suzie took Mo home, staying by her side until the funeral, several days later. Suzie returned to the office, and said that Mo was arranging for Peter to carry out the removal and dispose of the unwanted furniture. Suzie, knowing Mo's poor state, had arranged for a team of contract cleaners to go into the house. Suzie told me that she hoped I didn't mind, but the bill would come to Gloworm. I hugged Suzie to me, and told her she was a treasure, and that I was very proud of her.

The next four weeks flew by, and saw an end to the postmen's strike in April, allowing things in the office to return to normal. Mo threw herself into her work, particularly her two pet projects. More wildcat strikes at one time threatened our supplies, but these disputes were usually short-lived.

One morning in the middle of May, Mo took me to see the progress on her projects. My house in Colchester had had a coat of paint, new windows, and the gutters had been repaired and painted. The grounds and gardens had been flattened and returfed, making the whole house seem more lived in. Inside, the new electrics, plumbing and ceilings had all been finished. Upstairs, the false walls had been taken down. Downstairs, the old kitchen had been completely ripped out and a big empty space was left. In the basement, two false walls and a new staircase had been erected, to make two staff flats. However, there still seemed so much to do, and I began to worry if the project would ever be finished. I shared this thought with Mo, who told me that according to her progress chart all the work would be completed by the first week in December. I then suggested we went into town for lunch, to which she happily agreed. Once seated in a corner table at Jacklin's, we began to talk about Gloworm, its growth and future potential.

Mo then began to tell me that she had wanted to have a serious conversation with me for several weeks, but the opportunity had not arisen. She then told me that since her best friend's death she had been re-evaluating her life. Her only aunt had recently been taken into a nursing home, and had lost the house she had rented for years. She had little in the way of savings, and was now reliant on her old age pension. Mo said that she had made up her mind not only to save more, but one day buy her own house. 'Assuming that Gloworm continues to go from strength to strength, in a few years I will not only have my house but will be looking forward to a good pension.' I told her that I thought she was right, and that in a few years everybody would have to provide for their old age.

Mo then paused, and said, 'George, we are very good friends. We like the same things in life and going to the same places. I know that I would never be considered as a possible wife by your mother, nor do I think that I am the one you are searching for. I also know that the Angela saga hurt you badly, and that you still hope that she will get better. When my friend died, she was my age, still a young lady, and yet in her short life had managed to marry, have children and run the family home, in fact all the things we had expected from life when we were both growing up. I have now faced the fact that I have never attracted a single male and may never do so. However, I still want to experience of being loved and cherished, even if that relationship is short. George, I know you are lonely, in the same way as I am lonely, and I therefore wondered if we could become lovers, until we find what we are searching for.'

I told her I was flattered and honoured by her proposal. However, I felt she was still grieving for her friend, and it would neither be honourable nor gentlemanly to take advantage at this time. Seeing a tear roll down her face, I quickly added that if she still felt the same in two months' time, and assuming both of us were still single, then we could arrange a suitable time and place to take a holiday together. She immediately took my hand and squeezed it.

On the way back to the office, we stopped at the Dovercourt property, which seemed to be at the same state as the Lexden property. 'This will be completed by the end of November,' said Mo. 'I shall miss this place, as I often come here, dreaming that I have won the football pools, and that when finished it will be mine.' I told Mo that everybody needed their dreams, and she should hold on to that dream as long as possible.

At the June board meeting I was able to announce that the final accounts had now been completed by our accountants. The year had been a good one, with 1970 registering a turnover of £130,000, with a profit before tax of £15,000. I told the board that

I had discussed the matter with my trustees, and it had been decided to reinvest the net profit after tax into the company. I then turned to Peter, and asked him how he was adapting to his new role. He told us that he was enjoying it, but there seemed so much to learn. I suggested that, as a director, he might like to take on a study into the company's present and future transport needs. I further suggested an investment from the previous year's profits of £2,500. Peter, who by this time was beaming with delight, promised to have a report ready for our September meeting.

In the third week in June, I had an urgent telephone call from Pauline, regarding the letting business, and asking whether I would be free later that day. I agreed to meet her outside my favourite restaurant at one o'clock. When I arrived she was already waiting for me dressed in a nice summer dress. Once we were seated I noticed, as any man would, the low cleavage of her dress, and I saw her dark eyes shine as my gaze drifted down to her ripe breasts. Trying to remember that she was an employee, and we were there for a business discussion, was difficult, but I did manage to bring up the reason for the meeting. She told me that a Mr Rich, for whom we managed ten properties, had died. The only son had visited the office the previous Saturday, to advise her of his father's death. He had already visited his father's rented properties, and was angry at the state of them. She went on to tell him that, because of the bad state of repair, eight were currently empty and the last two would be empty at the end of June. 'He asked me what they were worth in their current state. I told him £15,000 to £20,000, if he sold them one by one privately, but that might take months. He told me, as soon as the funeral was over and he had emptied his father's house and put it on the market; he was planning to return to his home in Canada. He then asked me whether I knew of anyone who might be prepared to buy all the properties in one deal. I told him that the state of the properties, and the work required before they were in any state to relet, would probably discourage most developers or future landlords. However, I would try a firm who were already in the letting market, and who had available financial resources. I then told him that I could not contact the firm that day, but that I would contact them first thing on Monday morning.'

Straight after lunch we went back to the letting office and picked up the keys to eight of the ten properties. In every case they were worse than I feared, and not fit for human habitation. I told Pauline to ring the son and tell him that I had found the properties unattractive as a viable letting proposal, but I was prepared to offer him £14,000 for the lot.

We returned to the letting office. Pauline unlocked the door and we both went in. Pauline immediately rang Mr Rich's son, and told him of my offer, which he immediately accepted. He then gave Maureen the name and address of his solicitors, to whom all correspondence should be addressed. I then told Pauline that she had been a clever girl, and would turn out to be a superb business woman.

Pauline went through to the back to make some coffee. When she returned, I asked whether the four three-bedroomed properties had been rented out. She told me that the photographs had not arrived until the previous Friday, and she still had to finish the specification. I told her to change the document from 'to let' to 'for sale', advertising them at £4,250. I also asked her to order six estate agent's boards for delivery as soon as possible. I could see a look of concern on her face and I asked her why. She told me that she thought I was trying to build up a large portfolio of properties yet here I was selling some. I explained that that day's dealings had cleared out the company's cash reserves, and therefore we could not continue to invest in such deals. 'Selling four properties and probably the two two-bedroomed cottages we bought today will repay the capital we expended. This means in the long term we will gain an extra four properties for virtually no cost.' Her face brightened, and she told me she hadn't thought of the effect capital might have on the growing of the business. She suddenly threw her arms around me, telling me that no woman could resist such a thoughtful, caring yet dynamic man. I then asked her how she was getting on with her man, to which she replied that the divorce papers had been served two weeks previously, and that she hoped to be free of him in the new year.

Driving home that night I began to worry at the new effects I was having on women, and how I would deal with the situation if Mo did not change her mind.

My Uncle, Mother and Mo

Early in July I had an appointment in London during the morning. I had travelled up to town with my father. He told me that I should go to his office at about twelve thirty to collect him, so we could walk to Uncle Edward's club, where we were meeting for lunch.

Therefore at twelve thirty I found myself in the main foyer of Gull Industries. I told the uniformed security guard that I had an appointment with Lord Earlswood. He pushed the visitor's book towards me, and told me that I should fill it in before going to my father's office on the top floor. Once I had finished filling in the book, the security guard turned it towards him and read the entry. He then opened his desk drawer and took out a bundle of memos, and started fingering through them. His expression then changed, and in a commanding voice he ordered me out of the building.

I began to protest, telling him that I was Lord Earlswood's son, to which he replied, 'I know who you are, and if you refuse to leave, I will ring the police.' I told him that he should do it, but perhaps he should ring my father first. He was obviously not sure what to do, so I told him that I would stand outside in the street if he telephoned my father. This he agreed to do.

I had not been waiting more than two minutes when my father's secretary appeared, beckoning me back into the building. However the security guard suddenly appeared and thrust the young lady aside roughly. I then turned and faced him and warned him that if he did not apologise to the young lady I would teach him his manners. Backing off, he told me he was an old soldier who had served his country during the war and had been wounded. However, it was more than his job was worth to ignore one of the Managing Director's orders.

Suddenly, my father's voice boomed out from the open lift he was leaving. He asked the guard why he had manhandled his secretary, and why he had got his son's jacket lapels in his hand. The man, by this time white-faced and worried, tried to say he was merely carrying out orders. My father, being an old soldier himself, demanded to be shown those orders. The security man stumbled over to his table and returned with the memo he had waved at me as he had ordered me out. My father read the piece of paper before tearing it into little pieces, telling the man that his orders had been overwritten. Then, taking the man by the scruff of the neck, he told him that if ever he manhandled a woman again, my father would kick his backside out of the building.

Lunch was somewhat quiet as the two White Gull directors chewed over the problem of how to get rid of my Uncle Cecil. I told them to do nothing until I had time to get to the bottom of things. However, I asked Father and Uncle Edward to return with me to Bun Industries' offices to make a phone call. Father gave me Uncle Cecil's private line number and before I dialled it I switched on the speakerphone so Father and Uncle Edward could hear Cecil's reply. The phone was soon answered by my uncle, and I began.

'Hello, Uncle,' I said, 'long time since we met.' My uncle responded by asking me who I was, how I had got his number, and what was it that I wanted. 'Come, come, Uncle,' I said, 'surely you haven't forgotten your favourite nephew, George? The reason I am phoning is to get an explanation of why I was forced out of the building by your security guard, when all I wanted was to meet my father for lunch.'

I heard him make a snarling noise before he replied. 'I will tell you why I will not tolerate you being in my building, and the reason is simple. I already have to put up with that no-good father of yours constantly wanting to question my orders. He may well have been a good soldier, but has no place in modern business. I could not stomach the possibility of another Earlswood in the business, and I not only blocked your appointment, but have made sure you cannot enter my building, talk to my people or have any influence over my company.'

'Uncle,' I said, 'is that not short-sighted? For while I agree that I have little practical business experience, I think that my qualifications far exceed yours.'

'You impudent puppy!' he screamed. 'You are as bad as the rest of youth, thinking that because you have had the opportunity to go to college and get a qualification, you know it all, and you don't. That is why I will not have any young know-alls recruited into my company, as all they want to do is challenge for my job. I am king here, and will remain so until I retire.'

I then played my trump card, telling my uncle that, come the next June, I would be asking some searching questions at the annual shareholders' meeting, to which he screamed, 'You won't, you wouldn't, and in any case I will make sure you are not let into the hall!' and then slammed down the phone. There was complete silence before I told them that Uncle Cecil's preventing me from joining the company was not necessarily personal, but applied to any other bright young manager who applied for a job. Furthermore, his present attitude might well mean that the company, although profitable, might actually be underperforming. What I could not understand was his fury regarding my attending the annual shareholders meeting, when he knew that I did not hold any shares. My father and uncle merely nodded, but then asked that I leave the office, to enable them to talk business.

Angela was at her desk, looking to me as radiant as ever. She gave me a big smile and asked whether I had had a good lunch. During the next fifteen minutes we caught up on all our news and I had the opportunity to ask her how the treatment was going. She told me that the treatment was fine, and that she now walked alone to and from the office. She did tell me, however, that she still suffered violent flashbacks, and still could not bear anyone at all to touch her.

I really felt elated at Angela's progress, and believed that there was still a chance for me. I detoured to some shops I had spotted earlier, went in and bought a new umbrella. The man behind the counter told me that business had really started to boom following the government's relaxation of purchase tax.

On the night before Gloworm was due to close for its summer break, when seemingly everyone had gone home, Mo suddenly appeared at my office door. She said that she was about to make a cup of coffee and asked if I would like one. When the coffee came and Mo was settled on the chair in front of me, we began to talk. During our discussion, Mo suddenly said, 'George, we have to talk.' Mo then recalled our conversation of two months before, and my promise to review our relationship should she not change her mind. She went on to say that, after a great deal of thought, she had not changed her mind. She looked so nervous, just like a puppy dog having been caught doing something he shouldn't.

I gently rose from my desk, went round to the other side, and cuddled her to me. Then very gently I told her that a promise was a promise and, if she was sure, we would arrange to spend some time away together. I asked her when it would be a good time for her, and she blushingly told me the end of the next week. I returned to my desk, opened the drawer and took out an AA handbook. I flicked through the pages until I found the appropriate entry, and then wrote down the details. I handed the piece of paper to Mo, and told her it was the number of the Angel Hotel in Bury St Edmunds and that she should ring them to find out if they had a nice double-bedded room for the nights of Friday, Saturday and Sunday, and to ask them if they could book two tickets for the local theatre on Saturday evening.

Mo went back to her office to make the call, returning fifteen minutes later to confirm that the necessary arrangements had been made. The atmosphere suddenly seemed explosive and, without warning, we were in each other's arms kissing and cuddling like a pair of love-struck teenagers.

The next week passed quickly as Mo and I combined work and play during the first week of the shutdown. On the Thursday evening, just before locking up, Mo asked about being picked up the following day. I told her that unless she had changed her mind, I would collect her from her house, promptly at ten o'clock.

The next day was a warm summer's day, with not a cloud in the sky. I arrived as promised at ten o'clock, only to find Mo outside her house waiting for my arrival. I got out of the car and put her case into the boot, while she made herself comfortable in the front passenger seat. Once we had started off towards Colchester I asked her how she was, only to be told that she felt tired, as she had not slept well the previous night. Just outside

Colchester, I turned off towards Sudbury, which was on our route for Long Melford, where I planned to visit one or two antique shops before taking Mo to the Bull for lunch. I soon found a present I had intended to get for my mother (a piece of Georgian silver) and then drove to the Bull. We each had a light pub meal, as neither of us was hungry, returning to the car about two. Mo did not say anything on the journey to Bury St Edmunds, where we arrived outside the hotel just before three in the afternoon. I turned off the engine, turned to Mo and told her there was still time to change her mind, and that if she did I would understand. She assured me that she had not changed her mind, but was feeling very nervous. I got the cases out of the boot, then opened her door for her. She got out of the car and insisted that she carry her own case. I asked why, and she told me that a friend of hers had told her that they always knew whether a couple was married by who carried the cases.

Walking through the main doors, we found reception to our right and a small sitting area to the left. I invited Mo to sit with the luggage while I dealt with the formalities. The theatre seats had been confirmed and we were asked if we would wish to have dinner in the hotel that night. I made a table booking for eight thirty, then made my way back to Mo. A porter suddenly appeared to take our cases, and we followed him up the old staircase to our room on the second floor. He opened the door and put the cases inside, turned and handed me the key. I tipped him well, and watched as he sauntered back down the stairs. I ushered Mo inside and followed her in, remembering to turn the sign hanging on the door to 'Do Not Disturb'. And finally I locked the door behind us.

Our room was a large one, dominated by a large bed. The far side of the room boasted a settee and two chairs, complemented with a small coffee table. On a compact bureau stood a portable television. The drive had been warm, and we had both carried our jackets over our arms, and these Mo was hanging up in the wardrobe. She then excused herself and went to try out the facilities. When she returned, she found me standing by the bed. Seeing her distress, I quietly pulled her into my arms, and began softly kissing and cuddling her. Using all the advice and technique learnt from Billie-Jo, I gently began undressing Mo and encouraged her to reciprocate. When we were both fully undressed, I stepped back a pace in order to study Mo's naked body. She was even more beautiful than I had imagined, with small, firm breasts, flat stomach, and a lush triangle of red hair. When she saw I was taking in the sight standing before me, she became coy and, in a manner only Mo could bring off, bent down to pick up our discarded clothes and begin folding them neatly and placing them on the sofa. I moved to the side of the bed and began pulling back the bedclothes. Mo responded by going to the opposite side of the bed, helping me to neatly turn down the bed. She watched me climb on to the bed, then followed suit. I took her into my arms and began kissing, cuddling and fondling her glorious body.

Judging that we where fast approaching the time for me to begin our physical lovemaking, I reached over my shoulder and picked up a condom that I had strategically placed on the bedside table. Looking up, I saw Mo watching me as I applied the condom. She then whispered that she had never had any real sex education, learning what she could from the playground. Sure, she had heard about boys buying a packet of three before a heavy night out, but had never actually seen one.

Slowly we approached the point of penetration, and I was concerned I might hurt her. However, once Mo felt I was not proceeding very quickly, she suddenly arched her back, pushed forward and the deed was done. Remembering Billie-Jo's instruction I began with slow long strokes, gradually bringing Mo forth with gasps and uncontrolled convulsions. Fate was with us, and we both reached our climax together.

We lay panting for a moment, savouring the ecstatic feeling which follows good sex. I asked her how it was for her, and she told me that it had not been as painful as she had been told it would be, and after the initial discomfort she had really enjoyed it. Watching me remove the used condom, she held it up, inspected the contents and asked whether that was what made babies. We cuddled and fondled each other until sleep overtook us.

In fact it was nearly seven o'clock, before Mo awoke, and

realising the time, woke me also. She then slid out of bed and padded across the floor, naked, on her way to the bathroom. Half an hour later. Mo reappeared, completely covered by an enormous white towel, and began searching for the hair dryer, which was kept in the bureau. I then jumped out of bed and made my way to the bathroom and a hot shower.

When I came out of the bathroom, Mo was sitting in front of a large mirror with her back towards me. Her shoulders were bare, except for the red tresses of hair that hung down to the middle of her back. I crept up behind her, and kissed her neck, allowing my hands to cup one of her breasts. She stroked my hand, and simply said, 'Later.'

The meal in the dining room was superb, and I noticed that Mo had regained her appetite. She looked absolutely radiant and very happy. Once we had finished the meal, we took our coffee into the lounge. I had hardly finished my coffee, when Mo said, 'Husband, I think we should have an early night, as there are many wifely duties to perform.'

I soon found out that Mo was a fast learner, always wanting to know more.

After breakfast the following morning, we walked the short distance into the town centre. There was a small market in the square, and we spent much time looking at the stalls and discussing the merchandise. We had lunch in a small pub, and afterwards started walking down a side street towards the hotel. On the way we passed a ladieswear shop, and noticed in the window a jade trouser suit. Mo immediately exclaimed that it was probably not her size, and in any case would be too expensive. However, with little coaxing from me, we soon found ourselves entering the shop. The lady assistant confirmed that the suit was in Mo's size, and took her to a changing room. Five minutes later Mo appeared dressed in the suit that not only fitted her superbly but looked a million dollars. Mo then disappeared to change. The assistant soon returned with the suit and began to fold it. I went up to the counter and used my credit card to pay. Once the packing was completed, Mo appeared, wallet in hand. The assistant then told her not to worry as her husband had already paid. Mo held my hand as we left the shop, whispering that I was naughty to have spoilt her, but she thanked me all the same, and she kept on thanking me all that afternoon – so much so that we were nearly late for the theatre.

Those of you who have never been to the theatre in Bury St Edmunds have missed a treat, for the theatre is still just as it was 200 years ago. Everything looks, smells and feels like a theatre, and we much enjoyed the production of *The Winslow Boy*.

When we arrived back at our hotel and collected our key, the receptionist informed us that a cold buffet had only just been delivered to our room. Cold chicken, sparkling wine, and a gentle, generous lady is a combination I can really recommend, especially to lonely bachelors.

As we lay in bed the next morning, in each other's arms, Mo told me that the previous day had been one of the happiest days of her life, not only for the lovemaking, but just having someone to go shopping with, to have lunch with, and to feel needed. However, the highlight was when the shop assistant had told her her husband had paid the bill. It was, she told me, like being admitted to the world of couples.

The rest of the time was spent sightseeing, shopping, eating and making love. When I dropped her off at her house on the Monday afternoon, we both knew we had both found love.

When we returned to the office after the holiday, we were both careful to hide our affection for each other, plunging ourselves into the mountains of work that had come in since we closed down for our summer break. Mo behaved as though nothing had happened, never slacking in her work. The only time she mentioned our little adventure was after work, when we were sure to be alone.

A Hunt for the Truth

The September board meeting had a very crowded agenda indeed. Mo presented her report on the progress of the new kitchen centre. She told us that orders had been placed for the exterior cladding renovation and the fitting of the new large window, now that building regs and drawings had been approved by the council. Mo was currently in discussion with an outside contractor concerning the re-laying of the car park. She predicted that the showroom would open for business on 1 April 1972.

Suzie then outlined the appointment of a sales representative chosen by Mo and her. The lady they had appointed was called Mrs Black, aged forty, and a widow. She was moving early in January in order to be near her mother. Suzie also outlined the lady's previous experience, which included sales work in soft furnishings, electrical, furniture and kitchens.

Peter reported on the transport situation, and proposed that the original sales van, bought in 1969 and widely used by Suzie and Mo on trips to customers, had now become expensive, in terms of both time and cost. His second priority was for a transit van to deal with an increasing demand for local small deliveries. His third recommendation was to replace his large lorry with one with a tail lift. This was occasioned by an increasing demand from the kitchen department for the delivery of cookers, fridges and washing machines. Peter was thanked for his detailed report, which was then approved.

Mo told the board that kitchen sales to ordinary homes had increased substantially, in spite of the reported downturn in the economy. Sales were also increasing for upholstery work, as people decided to have their strongly made furniture re-covered instead of buying new. Sales of our traditional services continued to increase. However, she reminded the board of a lull in the order book till the end of March, any additional work requiring contractors or part-time employees. The board, having discussed the matter, agreed to continue our sales promotions and to deal with problems when they arose.

September raced by, and I suddenly found myself a year older, and richer, thanks to the continuation of my £15,000 allowance. However, the next year would see me leaving home, and for the first time responsible for the running costs of my own house. Nevertheless, I still put away, in a capital account, a further £5,000, giving me a total of £10,000 to invest in personal projects.

My father was the subject of controversy in early October for his outspoken remarks on the increasing wave of violence, particularly in Northern Ireland. This followed a bomb blast in Belfast in September, killing and maiming many innocent bystanders, and the shooting by a sniper of an eighteen-month-old baby. He told his fellow lords that there were many people in England who were using political upheaval to justify their lust for violence and crime. Whether in Northern Ireland or on a picket line, these were not political protesters but common criminals, who should be treated as such, and he welcomed the news that the government would be sending more troops to the province, in order to restore peace and the rule of law. My father, as a result, received many letters, either of support or containing threats to his life.

I, however, on a more mundane level, was trying to put a business plan together for the years 1972 to 1975, and I still did not know what important event was to happen in 1973. I had asked repeatedly for my father to tell me all the facts, but had been totally rebuffed. I therefore decided to go and see the family solicitor, Mr Tubby of Tubby and Short. I rang his chambers, making an appointment for early November.

I arrived at Mr Tubby's chambers slightly early for my appointment, and had to wait twenty minutes for an audience. When I was shown in to the solicitor's office, it was like stepping back to the nineteenth century. All the furniture was obviously Victorian, and had not been looked after. On the floor were piles of papers, files and briefs, noticeable by their pink ribbons. Mr Tubby could also have been a typical Victorian solicitor, with his frock coat, silver waistcoat and pinstriped trousers. He reminded me that he had last seen me at the age of six, when I had accompanied my grandfather to these very chambers. He then enquired about the health of my mother and father, before asking me what I wanted.

I briefly told him of the secret hanging over me and the difficulty I was having planning my business affairs over the succeeding three years. He then nodded, muttering the words, 'Quite so, my boy,' and he opened a dusty file in front of him. He quickly read some papers from the file before sitting back in his chair. He then began to explain that although there was no mention of secrecy in the will, there had been various letters from my trustees urging the need for complete confidentiality. Looking up at me, he smiled and told me that since I had now reached my majority, he could see no legal reason why I should not know about the parts of my grandfather's will that affected me.

He began by telling me what an honourable person my grandfather had been. He then told me that, during the last war, while on active service, people did not always act in a manner becoming of their position. 'In 1946 your grandfather was called upon to settle his son's enormous gambling debts, which he did, as a matter of honour. However he never forgave your father for what he saw as a weakness. When you were born, your grandfather changed his will, both to protect the family's wealth and to ensure a sound financial future for you. He therefore left both the manor and the London house to you in trust, till you were twenty-five. The trust documents, however, allow your mother and father to reside in the manor for the duration of their lives. The London house could have been used by your parents or let on a lease, which would expire on your twenty-fifth birthday. In order that neither property would deteriorate, your grandfather left twenty-five per cent of the stock of White Gull, the voting rights being retained by your father. Dividends and any bonuses were to be paid into a separate account, with the first call being upon the structural repair and maintenance of the two buildings. Secondly, from the age of eighteen you were to receive £5,000 per annum, rising to £15,000 per annum upon your reaching your maturity. Money not expended on these two items was to be invested in your name, in trust till you reached the age of twenty-five. In this way, your grandfather ensured that you would take your proper place in society.'

I asked whether Mr Tubby had any idea as to how much had accrued in my trust fund, to which he replied, 'No, but the auditors of the fund, being White Gull's auditors, might furnish you with a copy of the accounts, which incidentally are delivered annually to each of the trustees.'

I thanked Mr Tubby for his help and left his chambers. I walked for a while from Chancery Lane to St Paul's, where in Paternoster Square I found a small cafe. I then ordered lunch and, while I ate it, pondered on all that I had been told.

Things were falling into place, probably for the first time. Uncle Cecil was terrified that his authority would be challenged by a younger man, even to the point where he might be removed from his job. While he had managed to block any managerial post being offered to me, time was running out, as it would be difficult to keep a major shareholder off the board. I then thought that I had never even mentioned challenging his position, and therefore he might well have given me the benefit of the doubt. I also realised that the London house would no longer be available to White Gull Enterprises, and my uncle and family might well lose their company's grace and favour residence.

Finishing lunch I walked across the square and headed towards St Paul's Underground station. I found the platform for Liverpool Street and stood waiting for the next train. My attention was drawn to other passengers waiting for the train. Suddenly the city gent standing next to me was hurling himself towards the edge of the platform and almost instant death. Luckily my reactions were quicker than my brain, and I found myself holding on to him, and being dragged towards certain oblivion myself. I managed to clutch hold of him as his feet dangled over the platform, and if a train had arrived that moment he would surely have lost both legs. A soldier in the crowd came forward and between us we hauled the man back on to the platform. His eyes were rolling and I could see beads of sweat on his forehead. I removed my overcoat and laid it over him, while the soldier moved his kitbag to make a pillow. A lady alighting from the next train stopped and offered help, as she told us she was a nurse. She then took his pulse and felt his forehead, telling us it might well be a heart attack. Another passenger, seeing the scene, went and found a member of the station staff, asking him to call an ambulance.

We seemed to be waiting an age, although it was only minutes, before a London Transport policeman arrived. The nurse told him that the man might well have suffered a heart attack, and would, according to eyewitnesses, have fallen under the train were it not for the quick thinking of 'these two gentleman'. Then the London ambulanceman arrived and with the nurse made him comfortable on a stretcher. Once they had departed, the policeman told us he was satisfied that the man's actions were a result of sudden illness, but that he would take our names and addresses as a formality.

I rang Ted from Liverpool Street station, telling him what train I was on, and asking if he could meet me. The soldier and I then caught the next train bound for Colchester. During our journey, the young sergeant told me that he had just returned from a posting in Germany, and had six weeks' leave before returning to his regiment and a posting in Northern Ireland. He was therefore spending Christmas with his parents and fiancé.

Ted met the train, and I soon discovered the young soldier was from Ted's old regiment. Ted asked him where he was going in Colchester, and he told us his parents lived in Lexden Straight Road. We loaded his kitbag into the boot of the Rolls, and then took the young man to his destination. When we arrived, and after Ted had unloaded his kitbag, we shook hands, wished each other a merry Christmas and a prosperous new year, before making the journey back to the manor. I told Ted about how we had met at St Paul's Underground station, and of the man who according to the nurse had suffered a heart attack.

During the first week in December, Mo asked me to meet her at the Lexden property at eleven thirty in the morning. When I arrived, she was already there, and she invited me in. The whole place had been transformed, and she proudly led me around the ground floor and servants' basement flats, stopping at the room she referred to as 'sir's den'. A gas log fire was burning, showing off the highly polished wooden Victorian desk, and on the other side of the fireplace an enormous stuffed couch and chair. She then took me upstairs and showed me the three staterooms, all picked out in a pastel colour, with matching upholstery, curtains and bedspreads. The fourth room, she told me, was the master bedroom, and had been decked out in shades of gold, even to the gold coloured taps in the en suite bathroom. I said that I could not believe the transformation, and told her how clever I thought she was. She smiled and said it did not come cheap and that she had spent every penny of the £8,000 I had given her.

She suddenly turned to a table that had been placed by the bed, and removed a cloth, revealing an ice bucket containing champagne, as well as a plate of chicken sandwiches and two stem glasses. Smiling, she told me she thought we should have a little bed-warming ceremony, and was surprised when I shook my head. I told her that it was not because I didn't want her, but that I had come unprepared for lovemaking. She smiled and said, 'Is that all?' I nodded, and was surprised when she told me not to worry. She then explained that following our little holiday she had realised that it would not be long before she wanted to make love without those rubber things. 'I therefore went to see my doctor, and have been on the Pill for at least two months.' I stood there trying to take in all that she had said, but was interrupted by her saying, 'Last one in bed is a sissy.'

The time was after six when we emerged from my new house into the cold, dark December evening. We found our cars and in convoy drove to the Siege House, where we both knew we could get an early evening meal. Over dinner that night, I asked Mo what her plans were for the holiday, to which she replied she had no firm plans as her auntie was now in a home, and her best friend gone. She told me that she had had an invitation to spend Christmas with a distant cousin in Hull, but had not decided. I then invited her to spend Christmas with me at the manor. I told her Ted and Mary would be away for Christmas, and we would need to fend for ourselves. She told me that she would love to, even if it spoilt both our reputations.

During that week I met Angela, at our secret place, for our pre-Christmas lunch. She told me that she would be spending Christmas in Scotland with my mother and father, Uncle Edward and Aunt Flossie, whom she now regarded as mother and father. I asked her about Robert, and she told me he was still in the sanatorium, but that nobody ever told her how he was doing. She then asked me what my plans were, and I told her of the demise of Mo's friend and her subsequent loneliness, and my invitation to spend Christmas at the manor. She commented that, as usual, I was still a white knight coming to a lady's distress. We then went on to talk about her treatment which, although proceeding well, still precluded any physical touching.

When lunch was finished, I escorted Angela to a taxi and opened the door. As she went to get in to the taxi, she turned towards me, smiled and gently brushed her lips over my cheek. Watching the taxi as it turned into Giltspur Street I was struck by Angela's actions and the courage that it must have taken in her then state of health.

On Monday, 20 December I arrived in the office later than usual. On my desk were two messages, one from Pauline asking me to contact her as soon as possible, and the second from an Inspector Steer, also asking me to contact him urgently. I rang the letting agency, and got no reply; of course, it was Monday, and the agency would be closed. I then rang Inspector Steer, who thanked me for returning his call. I asked him if something was wrong, to which he replied, 'Yes and no'. He was reluctant to speak over the phone, so I agreed to meet him that afternoon at the police station.

I attended to various pieces of work, dictated a couple of letters, had coffee, and then left, telling my secretary I would be out for the rest of the day. Driving towards Colchester, I decided to call at Pauline's flat, to enquire what was so urgent that it could not wait another day. Luckily, Pauline was home and invited me in. She showed me into a pleasant and well-ordered lounge. She then apologised for not waiting till Tuesday to consult me, but she had been at a party the previous Saturday night, and had been introduced to a local builder. He had told her that he would shortly be commencing the building of a small development of twenty houses. When, through conversation, he had learnt of her involvement with Lily Estates and the agency office in Colchester, he had asked her whether we would be interested in marketing the houses. He had said that he could offer us £150 for each house sold. Unfortunately, he wanted an answer by the next day as he was finalising the site board with his commercial artists.

I told her I liked the idea and asked her to proceed. I then got up, ready to leave, when she asked me whether I had time to discuss other pressing items. I sat down, and told her I could give her another hour. She began by telling me that all four houses that we had put up for sale were all sold subject to contract, and should be finalised by February or March. She went on to confirm that the target of 150 private letting agreements had been reached. Owing to the large increase in rents being paid at the office, she was beginning to worry about security, and asked for permission to install a small safe.

Her next worry was in coping with the large increase in workload, while managing all the other administrative duties that I had assigned to her. In such circumstances, she wondered if it was time to think about employing a junior assistant, which could be afforded by the new income. I told her I thought that it was a good idea, and said she could go ahead with the recruiting. I then told her to try the local Labour Exchange for her needs, especially as Anthony Barber, the minister responsible, had recently announced new funds to offset the growing number of people out of work, which had been caused by the continued shrinkage of manufacturing industry. I then suggested there might even be training and other grants we could claim.

That being all the business she had wanted to discuss, I rose from my chair, making towards the door. She then asked me whether she could show me over her flat, to which I agreed. The flat was well appointed and well maintained. There was a small kitchen, bathroom, and large dining room-cum-lounge. The small second bedroom appeared very cramped, as Pauline had put in a double bed, but nicely furnished. She then showed me her bedroom, which was furnished in delicate shades of pink, and smelled of perfume and soap. She escorted me to the door, ensuring that she went in front of me, as she wriggled that lovely bottom of hers, knowing the effect she was causing.

I drove back into Colchester, parked the car and went into the Red Lion for a bar snack and a lager. I then had coffee before leaving the pub. Having some time to spare before my appointment with Inspector Steer, I did a little extra Christmas shopping, mostly small, silly things for Mo.

When I arrived at the police station later that afternoon, I was immediately shown to a small interview room. Inspector Steer soon joined me, seating himself on the opposite side of a small table. He began by thanking me for coming so promptly. I asked him what actually was wrong, and asked how it involved me. He opened the file in front of him and read the front sheet before looking up at me. 'I understand,' he said, 'that you were involved in an incident in St Paul's Underground station last month.' I confirmed that I had been, and that all that happened was that a man had suffered a heart attack, and I had rendered help until a nurse appeared on the scene and taken charge. He told me that, according to an official report, my explanation was, to say the least, modest. He told me that, several days later, the man had been interviewed, claiming that he had not stumbled but had been pushed to the edge of the platform, and only suffered a heart attack when he was hanging from the platform, awaiting his demise. He asked me if I had witnessed anything unusual or suspicious while waiting for the train. I explained that I had been to a particularly traumatic meeting that morning, and was probably deep in thought while waiting for the train. 'In fact,' I told him, 'I am far from being a hero, as what I did to save the man was pure instinct and reaction.'

'This case,' he told me, 'would normally be routine. However, considering who you are and who your father is has raised a possible theory – that the man you saved was an innocent victim, and it was you who was the real target. We are, of course, aware of the speech your father made last month decrying the IRA as well as many other terrorist groups. The bombing of the GPO Tower last month proves that there are active cells living within the capital, and one may be plotting to punish your father by killing you.'

I told him that he had been reading too many spy stories, and his theory was based on an ill man's testimony. Nevertheless. I thanked him for his warning, and said I would be extra vigilant from now on. I wished him merry Christmas, and was shown out.

Over dinner that night, I relayed the story of my trip to the police station and their theories as to my future safety. Ted said that, hopefully, the police were wrong, but in the meantime we all needed to be security minded.

The Christmas celebrations at the office were in full swing when Pauline asked whether she could have a quiet word with me in my office. Once she was seated, she told me that there were one or two things that she had forgotten to mention at our last meeting. The first thing was that she had been invited to have a pitch at a forthcoming Homemakers' Fair, to be held on the second weekend in March. She had said that Lily Estates would almost certainly be interested in taking part. She had also found out that there were still a few spaces for companies engaged in homes in general, and had immediately thought of Gloworm. She handed me a piece of paper with the organiser's number written on it.

Her second item was that the local college was holding a ten-week course on housing management. She said that the course was primarily aimed at local authority staff and others in the housing sector. The course was to be held one day a week, on a Wednesday, and now she had completed her business studies, at least for the time being, the course would improve her knowledge of housing laws and regulations, as well as allowing her to make useful contacts. I told her that she could attend, and that the fees would be paid by the firm, but that work must not suffer. She thanked me, turned and walked out of the office, waddling her bottom in the most provocative way.

Mo followed her into my office, shut the door and asked what Pauline had wanted. When I told her, she said that that could have waited till we came back after Christmas holiday. Mo then told me that, in her opinion, Pauline was looking for her next husband, and was trying to get her claws in me.

Once the party had ended, and only the girls and I were left, I had them come to my office to receive the gifts I had organised Mary to buy on my behalf. Suzie, she had learnt, was desperate to have two large books on interior design, and Mary had obtained them for her. For Pauline she had bought a nightdress and negligee set, for Angela a gold bracelet, and lastly for Mo a leather weekend case, matching bag and purse. Having completed our celebrations, I left the building, knowing that Mo would be following in an hour's time.

Dreams Do Sometimes Come True

Even though the manor was in complete darkness as I drove up the drive that Christmas afternoon, my heart was lighter with the thought that, for the first time for many years, I wasn't spending Christmas alone.

Mo however did not arrive till after six. She parked at the bottom of the stone steps leading to the front door. I ran down the steps to greet her, taking her into my arms and kissing her. When we had finishing embracing each other, Mo asked me to help her unload her little Morris Minor car, which seemed to be full to the gunnels. She first handed me a large cardboard box containing wrapped Christmas presents, followed by a further large cardboard box containing Christmas goodies of all kinds. I told her that I had said to just bring 'you and your clothes, and nothing else', but she merely smiled. I helped her with her case and a large suit carrier, which we took straight up to the guest room.

The night had turned cold, and I suggested that we should put her car in the garage as we would be using mine to go into the village later on. We took the box of goodies into the kitchen, where Mo attempted to put them away. However she found this to be a difficult task as every corner of the store cupboards was stuffed full, as was the fridge. Mo was not to be beaten, however, and using her organising skills soon rearranged cupboards and the fridge to contain everything. When she had finished, she turned to me and asked whether we were eating out over the holiday and, if so, why so much food. I laughed and told her that Mary always left the manor at Christmas ready to receive any passing brigade of soldiers, hungry and down on their luck.

Mo then set to toasting muffins, which she served with melted butter and honey, accompanied by large mugs of tea. We ate in the breakfast room, clearing away before we made for the library, where the curtains were drawn and the fire well alight. We both sank into the two easy chairs, well fed and happy.

About eight thirty, Mo said that she would go up, have a bath and change for supper. I had shaved, washed and showered before she had arrived, and therefore was allowed to stay in the library and dream of a very happy Christmas.

Mo appeared just after nine thirty, dressed in a smart light green dress. I got up to greet her, and told her how lovely she was, at which she smiled, leaning forward to kiss me. I then reached for a long box I had placed earlier on the library shelf and handed it to her. The box contained a necklace in gold, decorated with small emerald green stones, with matching earrings. Mo's eyes lit up as she gazed at the sparkling necklace. She told me that I had to stop spoiling her, but obediently turned her back to allow me to fasten the clasp of the necklace. She then changed her earrings, stopping to admire herself in the library mirror.

The village supper was as usual well attended. As we pushed our way through the crowded bar I spotted Doris and Alf sitting alone at a corner table. I took Mo over to them, made an introduction and asked them to look after her while I got drinks for us all. I asked Doris where her niece was this Christmas, and was told that she preferred to spend the holiday in California, where she was cowriting a screenplay. The bell soon announced supper, and we all tramped into the dining room. The supper as usual was a happy occasion and was followed by a wonderful midnight mass. Mo joined me in the family pew and was warmly greeted by the vicar.

Later in bed that night, Mo said how much she had enjoyed the evening, but said she had also felt like a prize breeding mare at the county show, receiving knowing glances and nods, particularly from the men. I told her that the villagers were just interested in any one from the manor.

The next morning we spent together, opening presents, laughing and making love, so much so that we were nearly late for lunch. Mo again seemed to be the centre of interest, owing to Doris telling everyone that Mo had suffered a bereavement earlier in the year, and was spending her first Christmas since at the manor.

We did not arrive home till after four, both filled to bursting, and in Mo's case after a lot to drink. We both crashed out in the chairs in the library, and after some joyful banter fell asleep. I was awakened by the sound of Mo creeping off to the kitchen, returning with a plate of chicken sandwiches, home-made sponge and a large jug of coffee. Once we had finished supper it was getting late, and I knew it was now or never for me to have a serious chat with my beloved Mo.

I began by telling her that the police thought an attempt had been made on my life by the IRA following my father's speech in the House. The attempt had failed, but the police felt that they would try again. I was now being vigilant and hoped to avoid any further attempts on my life. However, according to the police, these were dangerous men and would stop at nothing to further their cause. I then told her that in the event that they were successful, all my wealth would go back to my parents in line with the terms of the trust, which theoretically owned both Lily Estates and Gloworm. Nevertheless, I wanted to make some lasting provision for not only my best friend but my lover, and I hoped that she would accept the gift I was about to give her. Before she could react, I handed her a package wrapped in Christmas paper. 'What is it?' she asked. I told her to unwrap it and see, which she did. 'What do these documents mean?' she said, looking at the bundle of deeds tied up with pink ribbon. I told her that they were the deeds to her dream house, and in her name. Her first reaction seemed one of anger, as she threw the deeds on the table. This was followed by a tirade about not believing my story of danger, or accepting any gift that attempted to buy her in the long term. She then fled from the room, and I heard her slamming the guest room door. I hesitated, not knowing quite what to do – to leave her or to go to her – and decided on the former course of action. Later on when she had not reappeared, I locked up and went to bed.

I was just getting ready for bed, when a gentle knock came at my sitting room door. I called for her to enter and was greeted by a tear-stained face. She apologised for her behaviour, and told me that she had behaved like an ungrateful and badly spoilt child, but what I had said and done had come as a complete surprise. She then produced a parcel wrapped in Christmas paper and handed it to me. She said that she had brought it as a joke, after what my mother had said, but now, perhaps, my mother was right after all. I unwrapped the parcel and found it to contain a riding crop. I swished it through the air, and said that perhaps Mother was right, and that I always did as my mother wished. Then without warning, Mo went to the bed, bent over it, lifting her thin nightdress to reveal her lovely backside. I stepped forward and swished the crop in the air, before gently bestowing a kiss on both cheeks. I then smacked her bottom lightly and told her to take of her silly nightie so we could make up properly, and we did.

Mo was awake early the next morning, but had resisted the urge to wake me up. Sensing her movement, I opened my eyes and looked at my watch, to find it was not yet seven. Turning to Mo I said, 'Good morning, darling, and what makes you so awake so early?'

She told me that she could not sleep, as there was much on her mind. We talked about many things, her dreams for the future, what she felt about the murder attempt, and how difficult it would be to go on living without me. Having convinced her I had no plans to go anywhere in the foreseeable future, and that I did not want her to worry, I told her that we should make the best of life while we could, as there were no certainties in the future. I pulled her gently into my arms and tried to calm her fears and show her how much I cared.

Mo was still on edge at eight o'clock, and I asked what was on her mind. She told me that although she knew that Suzie and her mum were coming to tea in the afternoon, if we were quick, we could go and see her new house. Seeing the anticipation on her face, I agreed to her wish and by ten o'clock that morning we were standing at the door of the detached, three-bedroomed house. Luckily, Mo had the keys in her car and, unlocking the door, invited me in. The next hour was spent going from room to room, with her describing how she intended to furnish her little house. When we reached the room that was to be her bedroom, she told me her plans for a new bed and bedroom furniture. 'Then we can have a proper house warming, but this time I will let you buy the champagne.'

On the way home, Mo asked how I thought she could explain her owning the house. I told her to tell people that a distant relative had left her a legacy, which she had used to buy the house. She laughed and said, 'First you make a dishonest woman of me, and now you want me to tell lies,' but she said how brilliant my suggestion was. I then told her that I had not mentioned my house to others, or my intention to leave the nest. I therefore asked her to keep the whole project a secret, at least for the present.

Suzie and her mother arrived at three o'clock and stayed till after ten. During the visit, at Suzie's mother's request, I told her the history of the house, and found her very knowledgeable about architecture and history. This was followed by a conducted tour of the house, including the dilapidated below-stairs area.

The next day, Mary and Ted were due back from their holiday. They arrived mid-afternoon. Mo then walked over to their bungalow, saying that they must be tired after their long journey, and asking if they would like to have a cup of tea with her. Mary was hesitant, but Ted just laughed, steering his wife towards the manor. Tea over, Mo told Mary that she had prepared an enormous cottage pie, using her mother's secret recipe, and that dinner would be at seven.

That meal set the tone for the rest of the holiday, with the two girls visiting Mo's new house, as well as going to the sales to select her bedroom furniture. Ted had serviced Mo's car, and he showed her how to cut the paint and bring the car back to its former glory.

On New Year's Eve I found myself working on several papers in the library, when Mary appeared with coffee. I asked her where Ted and Mo were, to be told that they had gone to Colchester to buy some special chrome cleaner and leather restorer for the car. Mary sat in the chair opposite, and told me that over the past few days Ted had seemed to be younger, both in mind and energy. She put this down to the influence of Mo. She told me that Ted had always wanted a daughter and, now that he had someone who welcomed his interest and help, Mo had become the daughter she and Ted had never had. She then asked me whether I loved her, and if so what would she tell my mother when she returned later in January. I told her we were currently living life to the full, and as yet had not discussed the long-term future. She then surprised me by telling me that there was no need for Mo to scramble out of bed and to go into the guest room when she heard Ted and Mary arriving for work.

New Year's Eve was spent in the pub, where Ted introduced me to a local farmer. The conversation naturally turned to farming, and the difficult life farmers were having. The farmer said that the government needed to support the farmers, not sell them down the river. He also feared that 'that Heath fellow' was secretly negotiating with the French and Germans over Britain's entry into the Common Market, even though, according to an opinion poll he had read, the majority of people in Britain wanted no such union. He then told me that he was disposing of two farm workers' cottages that were so poor and derelict that he could not afford to repair them and, in any case, fewer and fewer people wanted to work on the land. I told him that I was always willing to look at any proposition, and asked if I could meet him the next day to inspect the cottages for myself.

The next day, Ted and I visited the cottages as arranged. They were two semi-detached, two-bedroomed cottages. The thatch had long since failed to keep out the elements and all the walls were suffering from damp and rot infestation. There was no sewerage to the site, and the only toilets were out at the back of the yard. The properties came with a large garden, and I estimated that including the pathway to the road, the plot was in excess of half an acre. I asked the farmer what price he was looking for, and he told me £3,500. Ted was astounded at the price and told his friend so, but after a period of haggling I bought the site, cottages and all, for £3,000.

On the way home, Ted asked me why I had bought the property. I told him that one day I might wish to settle down and have children. In that case a nice five-bedroomed house, with a small stable and a paddock, might be perfect, especially as the site was near to the manor, and I could keep an eye on my parents as they grew older. Ted nodded and told me that, put like that the proposition did seem sensible, but he thought the price paid was more than the property was worth.

Mo left the manor on the Sunday after lunch and, having said her goodbyes to Ted and Mary, turned to me and said, 'Goodbye, my darling. I will see you in the office on Tuesday, but how I keep my hands off you, I don't know.'

On the Tuesday morning we had our January board meeting, where I proposed a budget of £210,000. This included a price increase of ten per cent, with only a small increase in sales. This was because I felt we needed time for the conciliation of the business. This was agreed and, there being no other business, the meeting was soon over.

For the next ten days, Mo and I examined pricing structures, workloads and future probable orders. We found ourselves more relaxed in each other's company, and spent many hours locked in my office.

On 22 January 1972, I was driving to work as usual. The weather, though cold, was bright. Ahead of me was a growing stream of traffic, mostly lorries heading for the port. I therefore tried to brake gently, and was concerned when nothing happened. Thanks to Ted's instruction while I was learning to drive, I did not panic, easing the car down by use of the gears. Once I had reduced my car to a crawl, I looked for a place to get off the road. Luckily, a farmer's field entrance came into view, and I was able to drive on to it, stopping myself by turning off the ignition and using my handbrake.

I soon managed to flag down a passing car, whose driver kindly took me to the nearest village. There I found a telephone box and rang Ted, telling him what had transpired, where I had left the car and where to find the call box, saying that I would wait there seeing as it was a cold morning. Ted arrived to pick me up twenty minutes later, to drive me home. On the journey, he told me that Mary was going to ring the garage to have the car recovered, as well as informing Mo what had happened and telling her that I would work from home until the car was repaired.

When we reached the manor I had a quick cup of coffee before going up to my private sitting room to work. I heard the phone ring several times, calls that were dealt with by either Mary or Ted. I went down to lunch about one, and was surprised to find Ted and Mary whispering to each other. I asked if anything was wrong, only to be reassured that all was well. I then took my coffee into the library, where I intended to do some research into a problem facing Gloworm.

Later that afternoon Ted announced that an Inspector Steer was waiting to see me. I told Ted to show him in and to ask Mary to kindly make some tea for us. Inspector Steer began by asking me about the breakdown that morning – had I seen anyone, near the garage, when I was backing out? I told him no. He then told me the reason he was now talking to me was that the garage who had recovered the car that morning had found that the brake fluid pipe had been deliberately cut. I asked him whether he was sure – was there no indication of wear and tear? He told me that as soon as he had heard of the incident he had despatched a police engineer to confirm the garage's suspicions.

Ted was just bringing the tea in as the inspector told me that they were treating this incident as yet another attempt on my life. Ted served the tea, expressing little emotion. After we had finished tea, and Ted had shown the inspector out, I sought Ted out to ask him why he had shown no surprise. He told me that the garage had first rung the manor, and that it was he who had alerted the police. He then asked me what I intended to do, now that the police were sure that someone wanted me dead. Luckily my parents were staying with the Buns in London, and were now under the protection of the Metropolitan Police, for which I was thankful. I told him that I did not know, and was going upstairs to consider my options.

I then rang Mo and told her everything. Judging by the tone of her voice, I could tell that she was very worried, and was desperately seeking reassurance. I then asked her who else knew that the Lexden property was finished and ready for occupation, to which she replied that, unless I had told anybody, it was only the two of us. I then told her I had decided to go into hiding, at least for a time, in order that the police could catch whoever was responsible. I told her that in the following morning's post she would receive a packet containing instructions and money. She would need to take Peter into her confidence, explaining that any careless talk might cost me my life.

Peter should follow precisely my instructions delivering the goods to the house, in the new unmarked transit van, on the

Thursday morning. 'No one will take any notice of a delivery van arriving at a house under refurbishment.' I carefully packed a case with the clothes, books and other essentials required for my enforced period of hiding. I then went downstairs and told Mary and Ted that I was going into hiding for a couple of weeks till things died down. I told Ted that the following day he would receive a call from Mo, asking him to meet her at some lonely spot, where my suitcase could be transferred to her car.

Ted then told me that he had just heard on the news details of another bomb atrocity, this time involving women and children. 'They have to be insane to wage war on the innocent, but that only proves how dedicated they are to removing anybody and anything that stands in the way of the cause.' I told him that we were partially to blame as, in spite of universal requests from politicians from both sides of the border, the government was yet to announce a formal enquiry into Bloody Sunday. We then both agreed that that knowledge would not help in the present situation, and we would all need to be on our guard.

On Thursday morning Ted took me to the station to catch a train to London. I bought a ticket and waited for the train to arrive from Ipswich. When it pulled in, I merely joined the crowds who came daily to work and shop in Colchester. I caught a bus going down Lexden Road, alighting at the first stop away from the house. I then simply walked down the service road, through the back garden, and in through the back door.

I had chosen, as my enforced prison, one of the basement servants' flats. The flat contained a modestly sized but well-equipped kitchen and a small dining area with a sideboard, table and four chairs. The lounge was of medium size, with a comfortable three-piece suite, coffee table and bookcase. The bedroom was furnished with a double bed, wardrobe, chest of drawers and single wardrobe, the room being next to an en suite bath, toilet and shower. The advantage of using the basement accommodation was that the house from the outside would remain looking unoccupied; even if one opened the door at the head of the basement stairs and looked down, all that would be visible was a small area, with two doors, hopefully indicating just storage areas.

I went through to the kitchen, boiled a kettle, and made

myself a hot chocolate, using a sachet I had been given at a recent stay in a London hotel.

Peter arrived about eleven o'clock that morning, and I stayed hidden, until all the boxes had been placed in the front hall, and I heard the door close. Peter appeared to be relieved to see me as I suddenly appeared from beside the staircase. We exchanged greetings, and I began helping him to take the boxes downstairs. Everything that I had listed on my note was there, including a Calor gas stove and spare gas bottle, a number of appliances we routinely kept in the stores, which were used when work was being carried out in empty houses during the winter. Peter then told me he had brought two extra things. He had obtained from a contact in the electrical trade a small chest freezer and one very new microwave, brown and extremely bulky, which he set up on the kitchen worktop.

We both unpacked the various boxes, carefully filling the various cupboards. He then asked me where I wanted the large case put, as it seemed to weigh a ton. I ushered him down to the bedroom, where we continued our conversation while I unpacked and put away the contents, books on shelves, clothes in either the wardrobe or drawers, until the task was almost completed. The bottom of the case seemed to be filled with old clothes, jeans, heavy pullovers, thick socks and sneakers. However, I amazed Peter when I removed from within a sweater a wooden butt and trigger unit from a shotgun, from the jeans the barrels, and from the socks the central holding clip.

I hastily put the gun together, moving the last remaining garment from the case, receiving a box of cartridges. Peter remarked that I had obviously taken the threats to heart, and he could not blame me, as clearly, from the reports given over the radio of terrorist atrocities in Northern Ireland, I was dealing with some very dangerous people.

We went back to the kitchen and made coffee, taking it into the lounge. Peter then began to voice his fears about the depressing industrial news, especially the threatened miners' strike, as well as other strikes aimed at wrecking the new Industrial Relations Act. Peter thought that, whatever the rights or wrongs of the various cases were, strike action, affecting the ordinary man, was bound to end in heartbreak and recriminations. We finished our coffee, and I helped Peter to carry the empty boxes upstairs.

Once Peter had gone, I returned to my basement flat and looked around, feeling a bit like Robinson Crusoe, happy that I had most of the necessities of life, but wishing I had someone to share it with.

Mo arrived on Friday night. After we had finished eating and had cleared away, we took our coffee into the lounge. She then told me all the news from the office, including a particularly large order to be carried out in the summer. We then began to speculate how long a miners' strike might last and the possible consequences. I knew that the government had already warned that they would take emergency powers if needed, as they had done in the previous year over the dockers' strike, but this had only inflamed an already explosive situation. I told Mo that the next day we would sit down and draw up contingency plans, based on several different scenarios, in order to be ready, whatever the situation.

Mo was horrified to find the gun next to the bed, and asked me to put it in the wardrobe. Our lovemaking that night was extremely tender, as both of us tried to shut out the danger and give each other strength.

The next day we spent working on our contingency plans. When we had finally completed them, late on Saturday evening, we were both tired but elated. On Sunday morning Mo put on a headscarf, and continued to wear an overall she used when cooking. When I asked her where she was going, she told me to get the Sunday papers. She then told me that, if stopped by a neighbour, she would tell them she was a cleaner looking after the house until the new owners returned from abroad later in the year.

Half an hour later she returned with an armful of newspapers, which she said would provide additional reading.

Mo left on Sunday night in order to be in the office as usual on Monday morning. She told me that Peter would deliver further supplies on Wednesday morning, as well as to pick up the rubbish bag and any dirty laundry. Holding each other tight, we kissed goodbye. I promised to ring her each evening at five, and she promised to return the following Friday evening.

That routine lasted for the following six weeks, all through the miners' strike, the three-day week, and ASLEF's keeping restrictions going even after the strike had been settled by refusing to let their members transport blacklisted coal, or to cross former picket lines. During that time, Gloworm had kept working at full pitch by simply adjusting work schedules to fit in with any closure days.

During my third weekend in hiding, I was surprised when Mo, having told me that schedules of work were being maintained, and that completion dates would all be met, suddenly began to moan about Pauline. Mo had kept all her customers informed of progress, and in the main they had not only been very understanding but had also offered to do anything to make the situation easier. However, when Mo had announced a late start date of the ten Lily properties, Pauline had not only been difficult and rude, but had threatened Mo with dismissal, saying that, as soon as I returned to work and heard of her concerns, Mo would be in real trouble. She then told Mo she thought that I was secretly in love with her, Pauline, and that he would begin to ask her out as soon as her divorce came through.

Mo believed me when I said that I had not given Pauline any indication of my feelings, and had never made a pass at her. Mo smiled and told me she knew of my fidelity, but warned me that Pauline was a gold-digger, and smelt wealth and a better life. Mo was of the opinion that Pauline was getting too big for her boots, and I needed to bring her to heel. I told Mo that as soon as things returned to normality, I would raise the matter with Pauline. Mo smiled, and remarked that, provided that was all I wanted to raise, then so be it.

On the following Friday I decided that I badly needed some fresh air. Unshaven, and dressed in old jeans, a sweater and a pair of sneakers and a cap pulled down over my face, I left the house, making my way to the main road. I walked down Lexden Road until I reached the town centre. I soon found my way to the letting shop, pausing outside while I made sure that Pauline was on her own and not with a customer. I opened the door and went in, and to my surprise was greeted by Pauline asking me if she could be of assistance. When I drew nearer to her and called her by name, she instantly recognised me and ushered me into the back room. Precisely at one o'clock, Pauline shut up the shop and joined me in the back room. She immediately wanted to know what was going on, and why was I wearing such awful clothes. I stopped her midstream, gave her some money and told her to go and buy us some lunch, and said I would explain as much as I could.

She returned quickly with hot meat pies and a bottle of fizzy orange. While we ate I told her that, owing to circumstances I could not at present explain, it had been necessary for me to go into hiding. I then asked her what the problem was with Mo, to which she answered that, since I had disappeared, Mo seemed to wish to take everything under her control, and that she, Pauline, would not be talked down to. I told her that Mo was only carrying out my orders, and in future Pauline should do what she was told, or I would personally deal with her. Licking her lips, and smiling, she then reminded me of my Christmas present to her, and that she could not wait to model it for me. I reminded her that, in law, she was still married, and that neither of us could afford to take any risks. This seemed to satisfy her, and I left before reopening time for the long walk home.

By the second week in April, and in spite of Mo's regular visits, incarceration was really getting to me. Therefore, after lunch, I went into the bedroom to pack my case. Mo asked what I was doing, and I told her going home. Together we tidied up the flat, leaving it in its former pristine condition. We did, however, leave food that would not spoil, in case we were in town and needed a quick bite.

Mo dropped me at the hall, just after six on that April evening. Hearing the car, Ted hurried down the steps to meet us. Mo went into the hall carrying a box of fresh food, which she hoped Mary could use. However, Mo turned down the offer of dinner, and left just after seven.

Dinner that night was a very happy and welcoming event, as I realised how much I had missed Mary's home cooking, as well as having real friends around to talk to. Ted, who thought that I had been in semi-isolation for the previous five weeks, regaled me with stories of how the village had lived through the worst of the power cuts and how a real Dunkirk spirit had been shown in dealing with the problems of the three-day week. People generally believed that, in a democratic land, it was the people rather than the unions who should change a government. Having said that, with many other unions queuing up to take on the government over the Industrial Relations Bill, it was difficult to see the government surviving. This was made more difficult by Edward Heath's signing our entry into the Common Market, which most people, when asked, did not want to join. Ted's view was that thousands of people had died in the last war to keep Britain free, now we were going cap in hand to France and Germany to ask to be admitted to their club on their terms. He said that in his opinion it would all end in disaster.

New Possibilities – New Dangers

The next two days I spent working from home, attempting to get up to speed with all the information, figures and reports that Mo had given me the previous Friday evening.

The Homemakers' Fair had gone ahead at the end of March, in spite of continuing restrictions. There had been many enquiries and firm orders at the fair and on the whole it had been very worthwhile. Looking through the content of enquiries, I was struck by the increase in kitchen and upholstery work in ordinary homes. There had been one large enquiry at the fair that Mo had marked as an excellent possibility. Pauline had reported a growing interest in houses both to buy and rent, with the greatest interest being shown in well-maintained property.

I slowly started to realise that our market was changing fast and that we needed to adjust our position in the marketplace. One reason for the change was due to the increasing number of people taking their holidays abroad. Clarksons, Cosmos and other holiday firms were pioneering the package holiday at prices below the traditional British seaside holiday, with the additional benefit of guaranteed good weather. I realised that if the trend continued, many small and medium boarding house and hotel companies would go out of business, thereby curtailing a major part of our trade.

The problem in my mind was how to respond to this new business situation. There seemed no point in sitting and waiting for any decline, but instead an incentive to plan and institute a new strategy.

Gloworm Kitchens was set to open at the end of April, and I decided that rather than exposing myself to further danger I would let the other directors take centre stage. I felt sure this new facility would create vital new business.

I then turned my attention to a problem that had worried me for several months, ever since my visit to the family solicitor's in

London: how would I cope with my new responsibilities and fortune after September the next year, without letting Gloworm and Lily Estates down. I knew I needed to make changes in the organisation by September 1972 in order to let any changes settle in before September 1973. I made a note to talk to Mo in the near future.

The attempts on my life were foremost in my thoughts, and I wondered how I was going to increase my personal security while returning to my normal routine. But little in the way of positive improvements came to mind.

April drifted into May, and by this time I had gone back to a normal daily routine, telling myself that through a combination of my extended absence and the power troubles my would-be assassins had probably given up on me. Looking back, I can now see that my assumptions were based more upon hope than evidence. One day in the middle of May will always stick in my mind as the moment that someone in the great unknown decided to extend my life. I had risen early, had had breakfast and was walking towards the garages where my car was parked. The morning, although bright, was still chilly and I had put on my car coat and gloves before leaving the manor. I took my keys from my pocket so as to unlock the security panel recently installed to prevent any unauthorised entry to our cars. The door of the security case opened easily, giving access to the switches that controlled the electric doors. I reached out and pressed the lift button, but the next thing I remember was lying on the apron of the garage cradled in Ted's arms. I remember that his voice sounded far off as he told me to relax and not try to move, as help was on the way.

The local doctor, who had been alerted by Mary, arrived first, followed by a police car, also alerted by Mary. Dr Foster gently began examining me but found it difficult because of my frequent blackouts. He asked Ted to call an ambulance, but this command became unnecessary, as the police had already made such a call. Ted told me some days later that by the time I had been seen in Accident and Emergency, the place was crawling with police and forensic scientists. Mary had insisted on travelling in the ambulance with me, telling Ted that she would ring him as soon as she was given more news about my condition. Once in Accident and Emergency, I soon became part of a huge system of care, which eventually led to my being admitted to the ward for observation.

Mo came to visit me that evening, having been told of my accident by Mary. I could see that Mo had been crying and was extremely pale. Through more tears, she asked me what we could do to protect ourselves, as next time they might succeed in their bid to kill me. The only words that came into my mind were that I was 'sick of running, sick of hiding and no longer prepared to let a bunch of terrorists dictate my life'. Like many before me, I had to stand and fight – but against whom?

Two days later I was discharged and told to go home and rest for at least a week. I was also given a letter for my doctor, advising him of my condition and the need to have the burns to my left hand dressed every two days. The other document I was handed was an appointment to go back to the hospital two weeks later.

My parents, having been told of the incident, decided to stay in London where the police were providing round-the-clock security, and consequently they would not be home to greet me when I returned from hospital. I knew, however, that whatever I was about to do in terms of added security, I needed to take Ted and Mary into my confidence. Therefore, after dinner one night, I asked them to postpone the clearing away until we had had a little talk.

I began by stating that I knew that they were both worried about the threats on my life, and the almost permanent absence of my parents. My understanding of the situation was that London was more convenient for both the House of Lords and Mother's ever-increasing national charity work, as well as for airports. I therefore had decided to take over Mother and Father's local responsibilities and live in the manor as lord in waiting. Therefore Ted and Mary's positions were not in doubt. There would however need to be some changes to the routine of the manor while the risk of assassination remained. I would work from the manor three days per week, travelling to Harwich the other two. On those days Ted would drive me. I confessed to having another secret. I told them that three years ago, when I had received my inheritance, and Mother and Father were living permanently in the manor, I had decided that the time had come to leave the nest. I had bought a large but very dilapidated property, and had since spent many thousands of pounds restoring and furnishing it. Even though things had changed, I still found it difficult to sell it. That being so I needed someone to keep it clean, aired and dusted until I decided what to do, and I thought that, since Mary had less work to do in the house, she might undertake the chore herself.

The next day I went with both of them to see the house, and immediately they entered the front door I knew they were impressed. When the tour of the house was complete and we were drinking our coffee, Mary said that she would be pleased to become its part-time housekeeper, and what needed doing could easily be fitted into their present workloads. I also told them that they could change their days off to being free the whole weekend. On Friday night to Sunday night I would use the Lexden House, allowing them to have Friday night to Monday lunchtime free.

Three days later, one week after the incident, I had a visit from Inspector Steer. He told me that a man had been arrested and charged with my attempted murder. The man, in rearranging the circuits at the garage, must have removed his gloves, and had left a print on the circuit board. The man was well known to Scotland Yard as an 'enforcer' (someone who collects outstanding gambling debts, usually by force), consequently his fingerprints were on record. During his detention the police had raided the man's flat, and among other things had found evidence linking him to me. Faced with such overwhelming evidence, the man had confessed to three attempts of attempted murder. Inspector Steer then handed me a photograph of the man they had in custody, but the face meant nothing to me. I asked him who the man was and was, told he was a dangerous criminal, but that his aspiring to become a hit man was puzzling to the police.

Inspector Steer then produced a photograph of me that had been found in the man's flat. I told him that it was a press photograph taken at my twenty-first birthday. He asked me whether I still had a guest list, to which I answered no, but that I was sure my mother would have kept such a document. I rang for Ted and asked him to contact our local part-time secretary to see whether she knew the whereabouts of the guest list. Ted revealed that he held a spare key to Mother's filing cabinet and he would go and see if he could find it. The inspector told me that the man had made a statement to the effect that he had been hired to kill me by a lady, probably young, with a cultured accent. She had offered him £1,500 to do the job, half down and half when the murder was done. 'When the documents arrived they were in a manila envelope, and addressed in type. However, whoever it was had left a fingerprint on the paper giving details of your normal movements. The paper, which had been typed, had at some time been leaned on, and police scientists have been able to lift a sample of the handwriting.'

The inspector went on to say that what they had was a fingerprint, a specimen of handwriting, an envelope posted in central London, and the description of the lady's voice. I asked him whether the IRA was responsible, only to be told that the police were keeping an open mind.

Ted then returned with the party list and handed it to the inspector, who shook his head at the number of names the list contained. 'I shall also need a list of all employees, both past and present, any that were sacked or who left under a cloud,' he told me. Finally he said, 'Can you think of anyone who would want you dead, anyone with a grudge or possibly suffering from mental illness?' My mind automatically reminded me that Angela was still undergoing psychiatric treatment but, no, it just could not be her.

Inspector Steer spotted my mood change and asked the reason. I then told him the whole story: the cover-up, Roberts's detention under the Mental Health Act and Angela's struggle to regain her life. Inspector Steer thanked me for telling him the whole story and said that when he interviewed Angela he would be as gentle as he could.

A week later, the inspector phoned to say that he had interviewed Angela that morning and had now excluded her from their enquiries. I had only just put the phone down when it rang again, and I found the caller to be Angela herself. She told me that she had been interviewed that morning by the police, who had told her that they were investigating the attempted murder of George Earlswood. I briefly told her what had transpired, and how we had decided not to tell anyone while police enquiries were proceeding. Angela was very shocked when I told her that someone wanted me dead and was still at large.

Inspector Steer called to see me at the end of June to tell me that they had interviewed everybody on my lists and had eliminated all from his enquiries. He then said that it was not unusual for terrorists to bring people with no previous police records in to operational groups, so as to allay any suspicion. While the police's enquiries would continue, he felt that there was little chance of an early breakthrough, and that I would need to continue to be vigilant.

June was a pleasant month, both in terms of weather and in terms of continuing success in both companies. One morning, while working at home, I needed an urgent letter typed. I knew that my parents' secretary was working in my father's study answering letters, replying to invitations. I asked her if she could type my short letter, and she agreed to, placing a clean piece of paper in her typewriter. While I stood and waited, I began glancing through a pile of documents put out for filing. Among the documents was a smart blue binder, with a label on the front stating it contained the annual accounts for the George Earlswood Trust, for the year ended 31 December 1971. Flicking through the pages, I found that the trust had grown for the year by £260,000, and that the investment in the Special FF Trust, now stood at £1,850,000. I was also relieved that the firm of auditors used by the family firm for years had certified the investment holding.

I had revisited my theories on the effect that package holidays abroad would have on our core business, especially by the news in May of Thomas Cook being denationalised. I knew I would have to act, and soon, and turned my attention to future cash flow, funding and disposals, sufficient to increase Lily Estates' portfolio of properties.

That weekend Mo came to stay at the Manor, and I broached the subject of future change within the company. While she agreed that no business can afford to stand still, Gloworm was doing so well that we did not need any upheaval. I did not want to upset Mo so soon after my accident and the worry it had caused my dear friend. Perhaps the changes I had outlined would wait till the August break, when I planned to take Mo on a well-deserved holiday.

I also found myself, increasingly handicapped by not using my own car to travel to and from Harwich. Ted had many other duties apart from driving me to and fro, and my use of his services had begun to become a fixed timetable, the last thing that someone with personal security worries should allow to happen. I discussed this with Ted, and we both felt that security would be better served if sometimes I drove myself.

A Search for the Truth

My July diary was extremely full, even before the month started. I had made appointments with my architect to finalise the plans for the rebuilding and renovation of the two farm cottages I had bought the previous New Year's Day. I had also promised Pauline that I would take her, as part of her training, to a London property auction, where there were four Colchester properties up for sale. This would involve visiting all four properties and assessing their individual potential, as well as fixing a maximum price I would be ready to go to. The eight flats I had purchased last year were due to be completed in the second week in July (too late for letting to the university) and I would need to visit them to decide whether to sell them or let them.

On the first Sunday morning in July, Mo and I were lounging in bed, both of us glad we did not have to get up until we wanted to. I asked Mo what she had planned for her holiday, to which she replied that that was what she was going to ask me. I asked her if her passport was in date, to which she replied, 'What passport? I do not even have a copy of my birth certificate.' I told her that that put an end to my surprise of taking her abroad for a holiday. She said she was sorry to spoil my plans, and perhaps we could go next year. I told her that what I planned to do was take her to London for a week, where we could see some theatre, art galleries, museums and perhaps do some shopping. She told me that sounded wonderful. I then remarked that I thought we should have a second honeymoon in a certain hotel in Bury St Edmunds; she greeted the idea with both enthusiasm and humour.

The following Wednesday, I had my meeting with my bank manager, agreeing a £30,000 loan using Lily properties as security. This meant that, with what I already had in the bank, I could buy £60,000 worth of new properties.

The following week I met with my architect to discuss the dilapidated cottages. He produced designs and drawings that outlined a three-bedroomed house, the four upstairs bedrooms being made into three bedrooms, with a family bathroom and en suite facilities for the master bedroom. Downstairs, the original four rooms would form a dining room, family workroom or office, and a very spacious lounge, created by knocking two rooms into one. The old sculleries at each end of the house would be enlarged to make a family kitchen at one end and at the other a WC and shower. At the back of the house he suggested building on a granny or teenage flat consisting of a bedroom, bathroom, lounge and kitchen diner. He did not think that this would cause planning problems as the back of the cottage faced open fields. The old cart shed would be rebuilt to provide a garage and workroom. I asked him why no stable or paddock, to which he replied that, after making various investigations, he had determined there was insufficient room to support even one horse.

Following our meeting we went to the local pub for lunch. During our lunch, we discussed the Poulson case, which seemed to dominate both the newspapers and politics, causing the resignation of a cabinet minister. My friend told me that taking bribes was in his opinion an isolated case, and said that the whole of his profession should not be damned as crooks.

On the third Monday in July we found ourselves at an emergency meeting to discuss the threatened dockers' strike, set for the end of the month. Mo reported that supplies for current work were in the main already in stock, but that if the strike lasted for months, jobs planned for November and December might well be affected. We took the view that we would order as much of what we needed for later in the year, where such materials were in stock, and hope for the best. The board was able to do this because of additional working capital caused by my decision not to withdraw profits. I reminded them that although excessive and unused working capital was in most cases bad management practice, in times of growing industrial unrest, spare capital might prove essential.

Towards the end of July I took Pauline to the London property auction. There were four properties in the Colchester area, and I gave Pauline my notes of them to read on the train. When we arrived at the auction, I told her she had a total of

£20,000 to spend including reinstatement costs. Pauline took to the task like a duck to water, buying three properties for £11,000, with refurbishment costs estimated at £4,000.

Over lunch I told her how pleased I had been at her performance, and said that in future I would let her attend auctions on her own. Her dark eyes sparkled at my praise. She said that her divorce had come through and in a few weeks would become absolute. She said that she could then date whom she wanted and do whatever she liked. Then she smiled and told me she could not wait to model the Christmas present I had bought for her. Not knowing how to respond, I changed the subject back to work, telling her to let all eight flats and to sell the two cottages.

On the way home I found it difficult to stop her talking about what we would do as soon as she was free, and realised that this was a problem waiting and ready to burst. The next day I told Mo of the situation, and asked how I should resolve it. She told me that it would be difficult, assuming I still wanted to employ Pauline after I had made it clear that her advances were unwanted, but Mo was sure I would find a way.

Our week in London was heaven for both of us, visiting art galleries and museums during the day, going to shows and plays in the evening. The second week in Bury St Edmunds was far more relaxed, as we took the opportunity to unwind. We both managed to forget the threats on my life or the changes that would befall both of us in the coming months. On the last night, while we lay in bed, Mo told me she felt the luckiest girl in the world.

When we arrived home at the manor on the last Saturday of our holiday, I naturally thought that Mo would be staying at least till the Sunday afternoon. I was surprised, therefore, when instead of letting me take her bags inside, she asked me to take them to the car. When I asked why she was not staying, she laughed and told me that, while I might still have plenty of energy, she needed to go to bed, her bed, if she was to be in any state to face work the following Monday. I pleaded with her to stay just one more night, to finish our holiday in style. She thought about my pleas but still said no, on the basis that she knew all about style, and if we had stayed in Bury St Edmunds another week she would probably go bow-legged. We both laughed while we packed her car, and she was soon gone. Entering the empty manor made me realise how much I needed human and loving company, like that of Mo, and before long I would need to make our relationship more permanent.

The rest of the morning was spent unpacking and sorting out my laundry. I then became aware of the shotgun standing beside the bed, and realised that for two weeks I had given no thought either to my security or the attempts on my life.

Once I had finished lunch. I went upstairs to put the finishing touches to the plan I had agreed with Mo and would put to the board at our September meeting.

Then another thought crossed my mind: if terrorists were going to end my life before the end of the year, then I would go out with a bang, and celebrate my next birthday at the end of September with a formal dinner party.

On the first day back there was a lot of work to catch up on and I needed to begin the early stages of my reorganisation. During the morning I spoke to Mo about the rising tide of public concern over bribery and corruption following the Poulson case. I told her that, while I trusted everyone in the firm always to act honestly, as we grew and placed more and more orders for kitchens, carpets and soft fabrics representatives who visited us would try to influence us to bring their products to a position of favour. I therefore asked Mo, as Sales Director, to prepare a paper setting out simple rules as to what to accept and what not to accept from representatives. We also discussed the dock strike, which had ended while we were on holiday, and decided that any effect either now or in the future would be negligible.

That night over dinner I consulted Mary and Ted about my plans for a formal dinner party to mark my birthday, a plan which they both greeted with enthusiasm. I told them that there was one proviso, and that was that Mary arranged for staff from the village to cook, serve and clear away the meal, in order that Ted and Mary could attend the dinner party as both guests and family.

The next day I contacted Mother, told her of my plans for a family dinner, and asked her if she and Father would be free. Since the day I had chosen was a Friday night, and there were no weekend engagements in the diary, they would arrange to spend the weekend at the manor, a nice change from London. I next rang Angela to see if my aunt and uncle were free that weekend, and she told me she would find out and ring me back. I asked her if she was free also, as I always looked forward to being in her company, and she said she would love to come for the weekend. I then raised the subject of my trust, and told her that the monies were invested in a special FF trust. I told her I had been unsuccessful in finding out about the trust, what it invested its money in, and who ran it. She told me she now had contacts in the city, and would track the trust down.

September came, with the terrible news of the massacre at the Olympic Games. Everyone in the country was not only grief-stricken over the deaths of so many young people but also full of incomprehension that such a thing could happen at all. The Olympic Games stood for understanding, harmony and playing fair; was this ideal now being devalued to a point where the Games would never be the same?

The September board meeting had only four items on the agenda: a review of the business, its turnover, order book and any large orders possibly in the pipeline. Mo then presented her paper on bribery and corruption, setting out the new guidelines that must be followed by every member of staff. I next turned to my paper, which set out the background and necessity for change. We discussed the increase of board members, to be put into place in July 1973, together with the concept of shadowing the existing post holder. Peter told the board that, in his opinion, there was much merit in the paper, and he thought that the staff would be pleased that I had nominated Mo as the future Managing Director rather than throwing it open to competition.

Retiring to my office, I discussed the events of the morning with Mo. She felt that things had gone well, but she was still finding it difficult to imagine that in less than a year she would be Gloworm's Managing Director. I told her that before then she needed to shadow me closely, really closely. She smiled and said that seemed a very interesting concept.

The next day news broke to the effect that an Israeli diplomat had been assassinated, by means of a letter bomb. Fears I thought

I had put behind me over the attempts on my life came flooding back. I told myself I was being silly, but if a diplomat could not be protected, then what chance did I stand against a determined killer? Thinking over the precautions I had started to take since returning from holiday, I felt more secure, but the thought of any of my friends being blown up by a letter bomb meant for me filled me with concern.

The day of my birthday dinner arrived, and all was in place. Mary had, as asked, recruited many ladies she knew from the village who could be trusted to help run such an event, but she still spent much of the day ensuring everything would go smoothly. I had asked Pauline and Tiny (our new sales lady) to arrive early, as I wanted to tell them some good news. When they arrived, I took them up to my private sitting room, and sat them both down. I quickly told them of the plans for the future of the company, agreed by the board at its last meeting, offering them both directorships from the following July, before which time training would be provided. My offer was taken up by both women with enthusiasm, and we then rejoined the other guests for dinner. There were thirteen guests all decked out in their fineries, making a very pleasant scene. After dinner we all withdrew to the large lounge where coffee was to be served. Angela came and whispered that I was needed in my father's study immediately. Mother had obviously been forewarned and immediately took over as hostess.

Arriving in my father's study, I discovered that Uncle Edward was there too. I was immediately struck with a feeling of foreboding, similar to the feeling I had had, in this same office, in July 1969. My father began by telling me that, as trustees of my trust fund, they had found out that the investments they had authorised might not be as safe as one might wish. Uncle Edward then remarked that they were both extremely sorry and had already commissioned a firm of accountants to look further into the matter. Their report would be available by the end of September. Uncle Edward asked what dates I would be available in early October. Angela would let me know the date in a few days.

We all then rejoined the other guests. Ted had been given the job of taking Tiny, Pauline and Peter on a tour of the house, while mother and Auntie Flossie quizzed Suzie and Mary about my progress in finding a suitable bride. When the tour party arrived back in the lounge, they were all in good spirits, particularly Pauline, whose coal-black eyes shone like a beacon.

Two weeks later I arrived at Bun Industries' offices, in the centre of the city. Everyone was already there seated round the boardroom table. I apologised if I kept any of them waiting, but explained I was reliant on the trains. Lord Bun had decided to chair the meeting himself, and began by introducing a Mr Godsbody, who was a forensic accountant working for one of the bigger accounting firms. Mr Godsbody outlined the task agreed between him and Lord Bun, saying that the report he was about to table was a preliminary one.

He then outlined the steps he had taken to track the special FF fund down. The fund was in fact the Fawcet Family Trust, controlled on a single signatory by Earl Fawcet. Investigations and enquiries had shown that currently only £80,000 was left in the account and that at the rate of current spending the money would last only till January, when the next dividend cheque was due from White Gull. Earl Fawcet appeared to have no other assets except a five per cent holding in White Gull, valued at approximately £1,000,300.

Therefore, even if a restitution order was obtained from the court for the entire shareholding, the fund would probably be short by approximately £700,000. He went on to highlight other assets that could be seized. The London house had been extended by the addition of two new wings. The whole house had then been completely redecorated, and now boasted one of the finest collections of antique furniture, rugs, pictures and porcelain. The new building and antiques were valued at over £250,000. Additionally Earl Fawcet had bought the freehold of the large house that backed on to his garden, both as servants' quarters and an opportunity to enlarge the garden of the London house. The value of this house was currently £50,000. He therefore concluded that the best result would leave a shortfall of about £400,000 and at worse over a million.

My father then got up, and started towards the phone. Uncle

Edward told him to sit down, as they were not yet finished. Mr Godsbody then resumed his analysis of the situation.

'Under trust law you, Lord Bun, and you, Lord Earlswood, together with Earl Fawcet, are jointly and severally liable for all and any losses caused to the funds entrusted to you to meet the remainder of the loss. Should one party be unable to meet his share of the loss, then it might well fall to the other trustees to make up any losses in full. Additionally, it may be that you both failed in your duties as trustees to the trust, in which case there may be a case for criminal charges to be brought on the basis that you failed to discharge your legal duties. I have asked on your behalf for a professional legal opinion, based upon the facts in this case, and have received this advice. On the information available, it is likely that the trustees not involved with the planned deception might not be criminally liable, if they pleaded that they were able to rely upon the information they were provided with as trustees – especially if such information is backed up, as by an audit certification. That being so, the trustees not involved in the deception might be able to sue the auditors for breaches of professional competence, given that the audit was carried out by a professional firm of auditors. Losses caused to a client by poor auditing are normally covered by the audit firm's professional indemnity insurance.

'Should you wish, in the event of uncovered losses, to pursue a claim against the auditors, you would need to prove that the audit was not carried out to normal accounting standards, and this is sometimes difficult to prove.

'The case most cited is the Kingston Cotton Mills case. The case was brought by some of the company shareholders, who found that the accounts, as provided by the directors, did not show a true and fair view of the state of the company. The shareholders claimed that the auditors had not fully protected them by the annual audit. In this case Lord Justice Lopes stated that an auditor is a watchdog, not a bloodhound, and that provided the audit was carried out in a diligent and professional manner by qualified staff, then the directors, rather than the auditors, would be liable for any losses sustained. Therefore if auditors carried out a full professional audit, yet did not identify a clever fraud, then the auditor might escape a charge of negligence. However, in this case, the degree of negligence in certifying something that clearly did not exist might well be deemed as reckless.

'The next thing you two gentleman must look at is that Mr Penn, the auditor who erroneously signed off the trust accounts, is the same gentleman who signed off White Gull Accounts for at least the past five years. Therefore, if there was collusion between Earl Fawcet and Mr Penn, and I am not saying there was, then the accuracy of White Gull accounts comes into question, with all its many ramifications.'

There was dead silence as my father and Uncle Edward tried to take on board the situation that they now found themselves in. Angela, who had been silent throughout the meeting, suddenly spoke, asking Mr Godsbody how we should proceed. Mr Godsbody thought for a moment and said, 'Whatever we do, we must not alert either Earl Fawcet or Mr Penn as to our suspicions. This will mean total confidentiality from all within this room. Secondly, we have to talk to the senior partner of the accountancy firm, Sir Donald Ebit, show him my report, again in confidence, and then arrange a meeting with all interested parties to decide our next move.' This was agreed, and after a vote of thanks to Mr Godsbody for all his work he took his leave. The atmosphere in the board room was very tense, and Angela suggested sandwiches and coffee would be in order.

Over lunch, my father and my uncle discussed not only the fragile state of the British economy, caused by the terrible industrial relations, but also the way in which the pound was losing ground against the dollar. Luckily, the accountants had foreseen the problem and had bought dollars while the pound was strong, and we would not suffer the worst effects of the falling pound. This being so, there were nonetheless gathering storm clouds over America that could be far more damaging than short-term currency fluctuations – the Watergate saga was unfolding. Two presidential aides had already been charged on a number of offences relating to the Watergate cover up, and every day there were more revelations.

I left Bun Industries' offices with a feeling of total uncertainty, of being a millionaire one day and a pauper the next. Never mind, I told myself, what you never had, you never miss.

The next day I made one of my periodic visits to the leasing shop and found a hive of industry. Pauline greeted me enthusiastically, telling me that all eight flats had been snapped up for rental, and the two terraced cottages were under offer at the full asking price. Leaving her young assistant in charge, Pauline took me out to the back room. She told me how she had enjoyed the dinner party and how impressed she had been with the manor. She then gave me one of her special looks, and said she looked forward to trying out my four-poster bed. I told her that we would have to wait and see.

I spent a sleepless night, trying to sort out my love life. I knew that my body wanted to feast on those dark eyes, feel the creamy softness of her breasts and hold those delicious buttocks. But in my mind was a determination not to cheat on Mo. In my dream, I would tell Pauline that I was already spoken for, and that I would be announcing my engagement in the new year. Did that mean I was going to ask Mo for her hand in marriage after all? My mind then drifted to the consequences: what would Mother say regarding my choice of bride, and how would people in Gloworm react when it became public knowledge that I had carried on a secret affair with a colleague for over a year? Finally I decided to tell Mo of both my predicament and my dream.

The beginning of November was very cold, with frost on car windscreens most mornings. The shops were filled with festive goods, and carols seem to confront you in every shop you went in. I was at this time a bit depressed, as daily news about IRA actions filled both the newspapers and television screens. Avoiding unnecessary accidents and taking care of one's health is one thing, but waiting for someone to attempt to kill you is another. I had rung Inspector Steer to check on progress, only to find that no progress had been achieved.

Working at home one morning I received a telephone call from Tiny, asking for a meeting, which would be attended by both Pauline and herself. I instantly agreed and told her I would fix a time and place for the meeting in a few days.

This turn of events was strange, as for some time I had been thinking how I could tell my two new shadow directors about my house in Colchester, without them feeling that I had not trusted them previously. I therefore decided to arrange the meeting at the house the following Friday.

On that Friday, having settled the two women down in my study and served them coffee, I began to tell them about the house. I reminded them of the attempts on my life, and the necessity for keeping this house a secret, and stressed that my safety might well rely on this stipulation. I then asked them to explain the reason for the meeting, whereupon Tiny placed a large report in front of me. I thanked her for the report, but said that it might save time if she outlined the main facts contained within it. Tiny nodded and began to explain that, at present, Gloworm Kitchens carried a vast range of brochures and samples covering virtually all the current kitchen manufacturers and suppliers. This practice of using many suppliers had its roots in the former company; the late Mr Lowe had insisted that his customers could choose whatever material they liked, and this policy had been carried on to the new company. Many of the goods contained in all the brochures were practically the same. This meant that duplication was made over a wide range of samples, all of which were transported to people's homes in order to assist them in choosing the style and shape of their new kitchen. Gloworm consequently ordered goods from many suppliers in quantities that did not command the best discounts. She therefore proposed to narrow to two the range of manufacturers we regularly bought from. She had discussed this with the largest of her suppliers, who had promised sales support for either a sole or duplicate agency. Tiny also maintained that cutting down on the choices offered to customers actually made their selection easier. In addition, her report had suggested that instead of just offering a fitted kitchen we should offer a complete service, i.e. floor covering, painting, tiling and window coverings. Tiny also proposed that a similar complete service could be extended to bathrooms.

I told Pauline and Tiny that the idea could move the company into a whole new market, a direction I had already seen as essential. Pauline then remarked that the house adjacent to the yard was still empty and had not yet been refurbished. I told them that I had not forgotten the property and that refurbishment would soon take place. Tiny said that if she could have use of the building, as a show house, she could provide displays of kitchen, bathroom and bedroom items so that customers could see a finished design. The lounge and dining room could also be used to display reconditioned furniture from our own factory. I asked how much this would cost, and was told all costings were set out in the report.

Finally, Pauline asked whether the policy of buying up property to refurbish for sale or rent was likely to remain for at least the next three years. I asked why that was important to the subject under discussion. Tiny told me that manufacturers let agents have display kitchens, bathrooms, etc at below cost price, and with six months' free credit. When colours and styles change, retailers normally get their money back by having a sale, but in our case we would divert the material to a refurbishing, thereby reducing the cost of the job. There would probably be six unit changes per annum. I told them to present the paper to the December board meeting.

I then, at their request, gave them a tour of the house, knowing that they would be impressed. Tiny asked who had carried out the design work, and was genuinely surprised when I told her it was Mo. When we came to my suite, Pauline gasped in astonishment, not only at the luxury of the materials used, but also at the large four poster bed. When they had gone, I re-read the paper and thought that both of them would make first-class directors. This brought to mind a special piece of advice given to me by one of the professors at the university. He told me that managerial success did not flow simply because of the talent, foresight and ingenuity of a single individual, but often when that individual had a team of talented and reliable people, and let those people have the space to develop their talents and skills in achieving a set corporate target.

Success and Disaster

The second week of November saw the second meeting of those people investigating the suspected theft of my trust monies. This was held at Bun Industries' offices, was to sort out our next moves.

Uncle Edward, in opening the meeting, introduced Sir Donald Ebit, chairman of the accounting firm, responsible for both the audit of my trust fund and the audit of White Gull Enterprises. Sir Donald, a tall man, straight as a ramrod, slim with receding fair hair, opened his address by saying how much he regretted the current situation, and commented that if his worst fears were realised it would be a black day for the whole accounting profession. He had read Mr Godsbody's report, and had concluded that there was sufficient evidence for the auditors to carry out a spot audit to review the conduct of previous audits over the past five years. Since serious liability would fall on his firm if current suspicions were correct, his firm was prepared to pay not only the costs of his own staff and expenses, but also those of Mr Godsbody's team, who would take part in the proposed exercise.

He then asked whether there was any period when the managing director of White Gull Enterprises would be away from his desk, and therefore unable to interfere in any way with the proceedings. My father told the meeting, that Earl Fawcet was planning to visit their American operation on 12 December, his visit lasting ten days. On 23 December he would be joined by his wife and daughter, and they would all spend Christmas and New Year with friends in New England. His first day back would be Monday, 8 January.

Sir Donald told the meeting that the timescale suggested by the Managing Director's plans was ideal. He then said that on Sunday, the 10th he would bring a team of auditors down to London from their Birmingham office. 'None of the team will know, or will have worked with, Mr Penn, and therefore will be completely independent. They will not be briefed until 0900 hours on Monday morning, and will arrive at Gull Industries at 1100 hours precisely. Mr Penn will be invited to a routine meeting at our headquarters at 0930 hours, and will be detained till 1800 hours, during which time certain facts will be put to him.

'You, Lord Earlswood, will be in your office, please, at 1000 hours, to ensure that nobody is allowed to take any documentation out of the building during the course of the audit, and to settle any questions from management and staff over our activities. The audit, we estimate, will take ten days, but there is no reason why any staff functions cannot go ahead as planned. I already know that you and Lord Bun are leaving for Scotland on the weekend of the seventeenth, by which time our audit should nearly be completed. The report on the audit will be available on the second of January, and I will telex you a copy in Scotland.'

He then turned to me, and told the meeting that I seemed to be the principal loser in this case, and he thanked me for not closing in on Earl Fawcet immediately facts had come to light. However, he was aware that the next dividend payment was due to the account from White Gull on 10 January, and this would need to be directed to a new account controlled by the remaining trustees. Additionally, the company secretary of White Gull should suspend any transfer of Earl Fawcet's shares until such time as an action for restitution could be made.

Sir Donald and Mr Godsbody then left the meeting. My father was first to speak after they had left and the boardroom door was firmly shut. 'I gather the fellow served in the Guards as an officer.' Lord Bun concurred and noted that, once introduced, he had taken over the meeting, and given everyone their orders. My father agreed with the sentiment and said he was afraid that the chap would require full military dress at the start of the operation. Angela suggested more coffee would be in order, and then a good lunch, an idea accepted by all present.

Over lunch we all discussed the implementation of the new Race Relations Act, which was just coming into law. Uncle Edward said it would hardly affect his business, and father admitted the same, just as long as the law was not extended to the

United States, which would only serve to stir up an already fragile situation.

I managed to arrange a pre-Christmas lunch with Angela before she left, with the Buns, for Scotland in the second week in December.

The last two weeks in November I spent with Mo, visiting new, possible, and established customers, in an effort both to gauge their future requirements and to see whether we could rearrange our services, to better meet their requirements. Local authorities were plainly telling us that, with falling allocations, price was more important than quality. However, this did not apply to the Health Service, where there were lucrative contracts being issued from April 1973 in respect of refurbishment of offices for the new health authorities that would come into being in April 1974. There was also a general agreement among our core business clients, those in the seaside holiday trade, that business was declining, and that within a few years many of them would be out of business if the growth in overseas travel continued. This trend, however, did not seem to apply to hotels away from the sea, especially those situated in picturesque places, where tourism was up, particularly from overseas visitors.

We spent the last weekend at my Lexden house and, although we did the same things as usual, I noticed that Mo's mood was one of trepidation. During the weekend I asked what the matter was and was told that she feared another attempt on my life; how would she manage a changing business without me to help and guide her? I told her that I had no intention of getting killed, and that as chairman of Gloworm I would be behind her for years to come.

In the first week in December I had my usual discussion with Mary regarding Christmas shopping. I told her that on my last trip to London I had ordered from a well-known jeweller six silver business card holders, each monographed, and asked if she would go to pick them up. I still needed her to do the rest of my Christmas shopping, including extra gifts for Mo, who had agreed to spend Christmas with me.

The December board meeting was held and Tiny's paper received. Her proposals agreed, subject to full consultation with the staff involved. Peter asked if, just before our Christmas celebrations began, his wife could address all the staff on the importance of carrying one of the new kidney donor cards, to which we agreed. We also invited his wife to stay and take part in the celebrations.

During the week of the spot audit I met Angela at our favourite restaurant. I asked her why Mo was fast changing her moods, and what I had done wrong. Angela smiled and told me that basically I did not understand, and never had understood, women. Seeing that I looked totally mystified, she continued: 'When you first met Maureen, she had been left, totally unexpectedly, with trying to hold on to a dying company. You came along and, with additional capital and managerial expertise, helped her turn things around. Since that time, while allowing her freedom to manage, you have always been there in the background to take responsibility for anything that went wrong. Then there were three attempts on your life, which might have left Maureen back in total charge, something she may not have wanted. Then, just when the danger seemed to have subsided, you then told her that, from next July, she would once again find herself in total control. You did consult her before telling her of your plans?'

I replied that I had not consulted her, as I had assumed that she had aspired to the top job right from the start. Angela then said, 'Not everybody aspires to the top job, and many are happy to be the number-one deputy. It may be that Maureen is feeling terrified at the prospect of having to run things on her own, with all her friends' livelihoods in her hands.' I told Angela, that I had always been there for Mo and had given her whatever I thought she wanted, but apparently that was wrong also. I then told Angela about the previous year's Boxing Night escapade, when Mo had actually wanted me to punish her. Angela laughed, 'Poor George,' she remarked, 'that must have made you sit up on your heels, especially as gentleman like you, could never lift a hand to a lady. But you must see that, for decent females, the last thing they want is all their own way. They need boundaries and a knowledge that their menfolk will enforce such boundaries in a truly masculine way.'

I quickly changed the subject, knowing I could not win, and

asked her how things were for her. She told me that things were going well at work and that she was enjoying life once more. Her treatment, however, was not so good, and her recovery, according to her therapist, had slowed down. 'I have begun getting nightmares about that terrible night, and it not only frightens me but upsets my sleep pattern.' I told her I was very sorry and said if there was anything I could do to help her, she only had to ask. She thanked me and squeezed my hand.

Then she said, 'I nearly forgot to tell you – your Uncle Cecil has never paid rent for the London house since he moved in ten years ago. This means he has no tenancy rights and, that being so, your Uncle Edward, acting in his capacity as trustee, is getting our legal department to draw up a notice to quit.'

When lunch was finished I started to say goodbye to Angela, handing her my Christmas gift. She thanked me, and then passed me a small, neatly wrapped parcel, which had been concealed in her handbag. We hugged, wishing each other a very happy Christmas, and then she was gone.

I thought a lot about what Angela had said, and was determined to make Christmas for Mo as happy as I could. Arriving home, I consulted Mary as to whether she knew of any ladies living in the village, who would be willing to prepare, serve and help at a Christmas tea I was planning to hold. She said that she would make enquiries the very next day.

The next day in the office was full of excitement. Mo announced that we had received an order to totally refurbish a ten-bedded hotel near Frinton. The hotel would close for business after the New Year, and hoped to reopen for Easter. Mo said that this filled many of the gaps in her work schedules and meant a full order book till May.

The following week brought news of the spot audit, by way of a telex that informed me that the audit was completed, but that various serious irregularities had come to light involving not only the Managing Director, but also the Chief Accountant and several directors. The full report would be telexed to me after Christmas. I showed the telex to Mo, who remarked that it sounded very serious and asked what I thought my father would do. 'Sack the lot, I suppose, but it may mean running the firm on his own for a time.'

Profits and Losses

For the first time in four years I drove up the driveway of the manor on Christmas Eve feeling happy and expectant. Mary had obviously accepted that I would soon announce my engagement to Mo, and that the manor would soon echo to the sound of little pattering feet. Mo seemed to be happy, and had shaken off her worries as to the future. The next big hurdle I knew I would have to cross, in the New Year, was to reconcile my mother to my forthcoming plans. I knew that Mother would be disappointed in my choice, although she and Mo did get on well. I only hoped that that friendship would overcome any misgivings or prejudices Mother might still hold. That, I told myself, was next year, and for the present I could enjoy Christmas.

Mo arrived just after seven, as usual weighed down with boxes, baskets and wrapped gifts. This year her suitcase seemed to be heavier than ever. When I mentioned the fact I was told that it was important for a girl to look her best.

The Christmas supper was as well attended as ever, and when I arrived with Mo on my arm the bar was very crowded. Suddenly, Mr Sparrow, chairman of the parish council, had a table cleared for us, greeting Mo with a ceremonial kiss on the hand. Blast, I thought, had Mary let out the secret of our relationship, or was it just good manners on Mr Sparrow's part? This hope was soon dispelled as more and more of the villages came over to greet Mo. When we entered the dining room, tables had been rearranged to make a top table, where Mo and I had seats, together with other village worthies.

The same thing happened as we entered the church, only to find the vicar and a churchwarden ready to show us to the family pew. Even the sermon seemed to be aimed towards Mo, when the vicar told all the importance of a new baby not only to the world, but to individual families all over the globe. Once the service was ended, people waited in their pews until we had made the journey to the door, only to find a smiling vicar wishing us both a lovely Christmas, and saying how much he and his lady wife were looking forward to the Boxing Day tea.

When we arrived home and were lying in bed, Mo asked me whether there was something I had forgotten to tell her, as three times that night someone had addressed her as 'your ladyship', and the chairwoman of the WI had asked her if she would be taking over from Lady Earlswood as president of the local club. I told her that, since this was the second year she had attended functions with me, they had obviously put two and two together and made five. This seemed to satisfy her, and both of us were soon in a deep slumber.

We were both awake early that Christmas morning. Mo was excited, just like a child, as she tore open the many parcels I had placed in a pillow case at the end of the bed. Most of the presents were the small, silly things couples often exchange between themselves, like favourite music cassettes, books, scanty underwear and chocolates. Mo gave me a funny look when she unwrapped two tubes of chocolate body paint, saying, 'Down boy.' Mo had reciprocated with socks, ties, books, magazines and sweets, and a large *Playboy* calendar. She had also managed to get a friend of hers, who worked on the boats, a Scandinavian magazine picturing naughty girls being put over various men's knees. Mo smiled and told me that it was a handbook for future use. When I said it was all in a foreign language, she merely told me I would have to guess what was going on.

Once we finished breakfast, and made ready to go out, I took her into the library and there handed her a velvet case. When she opened it she found a gold watch, which I put on for her. She surprised me with a similar-sized box, which contained cufflinks and a tie pin, that she had had specially made, using the Gloworm motif.

The Christmas lunch was as enjoyable as ever, with Mo and I being extended all the courtesy and respect normally offered to my mother and father. When we arrived home and were sitting down having tea in the library, Mo told me with a giggle that next year she would wear her tiara.

Later in bed that night, Mo confessed to feeling a fraud,

allowing all those nice people to think that we would soon be announcing our engagement. I told her not to worry, as it was often good for people to have something to look forward to.

We were both late up on Boxing Day morning, after I had demonstrated the artwork that could be attempted using her chocolate body paint. She squirmed as I licked off the paint, saving the best bits to last.

Mo began to panic when she saw how late it was, but I told her that she had plenty of time. She then told me that she would take a hot bath, in case any body paint remained. Later, after she had washed and dressed, she came down to find a brunch breakfast, cooked by yours truly. She told me that I could do that any day I chose, although she did feel a little guilty.

Sharp at one the two ladies arrived, carrying large wicker baskets containing various tea-time treats that would not fit in to Mary's fridge or larder. I went into the large dining room to check on the heating and to arrange the large table against the wall, where the buffet would be placed.

The two ladies, now dressed in black dresses, white aprons and frilly white caps (uniforms purchased by Mary for her regular helpers), busied themselves in the kitchen. Precisely at three o'clock, the first guests arrived at the door, and were shown by one of the maids to the large drawing room, where Mo and I waited to greet them. Mo was dressed in a smart jade dress and was wearing the jewellery I had given her the previous Christmas, and she really looked the part of Lady of the Manor. Her daily experience of meeting customers gave her an ease in conversation that put strangers at their ease, and I was more than confident that she would turn out to be a treasure at this particular function.

The first guests to arrive were Suzie and her mum, quickly followed by Tiny and her mum. By three thirty, everyone had arrived, and all were busy getting to know each other. Mo, well used to making conversation with new clients, circulated, introducing guests to each other and indulging in small talk. I tried to do the same but, wherever I seemed to be in the room, there was Pauline, smiling at my every word and gesture. I then saw one of our ladies, quietly go over to Mo and whisper in her ear. Mo smiled, clapped her hands and announced that tea would now be served in the dining room next door. Mo escorted the chairman of the parish council, to the dining room, followed by the rest of the guests. I brought up the rear, with the vicar's good lady on my arm.

The buffet, planned by Mary, was superb, as I had known it would be. One lady stood behind the buffet table carving chicken, beef or ham, leaving guests to help themselves to salad, pickles or bread and butter. There were also salmon and cucumber, cheese and egg sandwiches. Further along the table were trifles, fruit and pies, leading on to cream cakes, brandy snaps and of course Christmas cake. The dining room chairs had been set out opposite the buffet table, together with card tables brought up from below stairs, and covered with crisp white linen cloths. Mo and I continued to circulate, ensuring that all guests were having a good time.

The great and the good of the village began taking their leave after six, and were all gone by seven o'clock, but the Gloworm lot stayed on till about nine o'clock, having enjoyed supper at eight. Just before nine I went to the kitchen to thank the two ladies, and was surprised to find Mary's kitchen all shipshape, and the washing-up done. I told them that the tea had gone off really well, thanks to them, giving them each a £10 note as a special bonus. One lady told me that it was time the old manor came back to life, as it had been just after the war.

In bed that night I told a very tired Mo how well I thought she had done, and how proud I was to have her by my side, helping me to entertain. She told me that she had enjoyed the function and in fact the whole of the celebrations, but that her mother would be turning in her grave if she could see her daughter putting on such airs and graces.

The next morning, as we lay in bed Mo asked me how I felt, suddenly finding myself undertaking duties to the village formerly carried out by my parents. I told her that I had always known that, one day, I would have to take on the title and its responsibilities, and the recent celebrations had given me the chance to get used to some of my future duties. Mo replied that she found much of the gossip very worrying, and I asked her why. She replied that the vicar had told her he would gladly come up to the manor when the time came, and the chairwoman of the WI had said how exciting it would be to have an active president living within the village. 'I felt like a prize mare being led round the spring sales at Newmarket.' I told her again that village people were waiting for me to install a lady at the manor, and after a two-year relationship they had decided it might well be her.

She then turned to me, looked at me seriously and said, 'What about you?' I laughed and said that maybe I should consider some New Year resolutions, including making an honest woman of her, but New Year was still a few days off. She gasped and asked me what my mother would do if I proposed such a thing. I told her that Mother would probably have her horsewhipped for seducing her baby son – then, thinking of an heir, would probably agree to my choice of bride. This, Mo told me, was like a fairy story, one she would wake up to one day and find she had married a frog.

Later that day, Mary and Ted arrived home, and for at least an hour both girls were locked in the kitchen on the pretence of brewing tea. That night at dinner, we all discussed our respective Christmas activities.

The next day, as Mo and I worked on the 1973 budget, we noticed the frequency of telephone calls taken by Mary. This, however, could not distract us from the state of Gloworm. Most businesses were facing falling orders and high inflation, with resulting high unemployment numbers. Some of the inflation was caused by demands for ever-increasing wages, in order to chase large rises in property prices. We both decided that, as business was getting increasingly difficult to come by, we would not increase sales volumes, but merely add a fifteen per cent price increase on to last year's figures. We also agreed to increase the provision for salary increases to twenty per cent, paying for some of the increase by reducing administrative overheads and profit margins.

That night at dinner, I asked what the bush telegraph was saying about Christmas and the manor. Mary smiled, looked at Mo and said, 'The current betting is on a late summer wedding. Those who know,' stated Mary, 'have decided that George's current girlfriend would make not only a very valuable but suited companion, but in time will make a very good Lady Earlswood.'

Mo flinched and said, 'Mere speculation, as neither George nor I have spoken of a long-term relationship.'

The rest of the holiday passed off splendidly, with Ted assisting Mo with her annual service and taking her everywhere, while Mary went round the house singing. New Year's Eve was as usual spent with Ted and Mary at the local pub, where Mary ensured that Mo was introduced to simply everyone. Mo left for home the day after New Year's Day, saying she needed time to prepare for the return to work.

The first day back we held the January board meeting, where we discussed not only the new budgets, but also the need to constantly review our markets and institute change where necessary. Tiny was very upbeat about her new trade initiative, and Suzie reported growing interest for quality workmanship, especially in large corporate offices and many large houses. Peter thought that there would be more than enough work to meet the new budget. The meeting therefore ended on a high note.

Once the meeting was finished, Mo followed me into my office, and sat down. She told me that my delivery of the budget was masterly, especially bearing in mind the difficult national economic situation. What would happen if the current pay and prices legislation, introduced during the previous year, was not scrapped? I told Mo that, with rising house prices, the government could not hold down pay rises for ever, and if they tried to they might well find themselves out of power. However, if they did impose part two of the freeze, both pay and prices would remain broadly in line. That would mean that Gloworm would not make its target, but that the bottom-line profit would not be affected too badly. Mo then told me that she thought that everything in the economy seemed to be getting out of hand, and that perhaps my plan for my devolution of power should be put on hold. I told her that I had every confidence in her managerial prowess, but in any case I would still be behind her backing her up.

I somehow sensed that there was something else worrying her and I asked what it was. Mo told me of a conversation she had had with Mary over the holiday. Mary had remarked that, following the Boxing Day tea, everyone in the village was looking forward to an early spring engagement and a summer wedding, especially as all had commented that Mo would make a first-class Lady of the Manor. 'George, the very thought of such a situation fills me with worry, especially as we have agreed that our current relationship is not necessarily long-term.' I told her not to worry, as it was the two of us who would decide the future together, not the village. This seemed to reduce her fears at least partially.

I later broached to Mary the subject of my conversation with Mo, and how worried she was over what she saw as pressure on her to marry Mary admitted that she was enthusiastic about what she saw as a perfect match, but she had never wanted to cause Miss Maureen any worry. However, she did not think it was right or proper for young people to deny the love that obviously existed between them. I laughed, and told Mary that, before any change in our official relationship, I needed to face my mother. That seemed to end the conversation, at least for the time being.

The last Friday of that week was a very busy day as the government, as feared, enacted the second part of the Pay and Prices Bill, to the anger of both workers and business, who agreed that such continued legislation would be unworkable. I convened a hasty meeting of the board to break the news, telling them we would give staff such rises as were allowed under the act, and for there to be no panic. The meeting finished, Mo, as usual joined me in the office, and told me I looked tired. I told her that the meeting on the following Monday morning at White Gull headquarters was keeping me awake. Whatever transpired would leave Father with managerial responsibilities he did not need at his age, and remarked how old and ill he had seemed at our last meeting. Mo told me she would be there, whenever I needed her, and to try not to worry until the worst was known. She then asked me where I was spending the weekend, and I told her at the manor house. She apologised for having an engagement that Friday night, but said she would see me at the manor on Saturday morning.

Dishonour and Disgrace

I arrived at While Gull Headquarters on that fateful morning in January. I had spent Sunday evening at a motel near to Smithfield Market, risen early, and had had a good breakfast at a cafe opposite the market itself. Entering the main entrance of White Gull's offices, I came face to face with the same doorman that I had clashed with the previous summer. This time my reception was very different and, as he asked me to sign the visitor's book, he apologised for his behaviour at our previous meeting. I told him that as far as I was concerned the matter was now forgotten. My father, Uncle Edward and Sir Donald were already there, drinking coffee and talking in low voices. They all turned to greet me, and Uncle Edward offered to pour me coffee. I thanked him and, as I took my cup, he also handed me a typed piece of paper. I looked at it and found it was an official Notice to Quit, drawn up on my behalf, by Bun and Company solicitors. Two other White Gull directors arrived, and were greeted by my father and Uncle Edward. Mr Godsbody arrived last, obviously suffering from the rush he had had to make.

Sir Donald opened the meeting by introducing everyone present. He then checked that everyone had had a copy of the audit report, and certain statements that were attached. He told the meeting that he hoped everyone had read the documents carefully, and asked whether there were any questions.

My father was next to speak. He told the meeting that he had found two resignations from directors on his desk that morning. He went on to say that in both cases unofficial loans contrary to the Companies Act had been repaid in full. My father then told the meeting that he would be accepting the resignations, and reporting the circumstances to Companies House. He said that in his opinion that would be an end to their involvement with White Gull, other than the statements they had made to the auditors. My father then went on to say that the Chief Accountant had been suspended, following his admission to the auditors of serious wrongdoing. Under the rules of employment he would be suspended on full pay until a disciplinary hearing could be arranged.

Sir Donald reported that Mr Penn, the auditor, had made a clean breast of his involvement in both frauds, and had been suspended on full pay till his firm could convene a disciplinary hearing. He went on to say that during the morning both Mr Penn and the Chief Accountant would be arrested and detained for questioning, as a result of information laid before the police the previous Friday morning. Following this meeting, officers from the City of London Fraud Squad would be waiting to arrest Earl Fawcet as he left the building.

Entering the room, he glared at my father and said, 'Earlswood, there has to be a good explanation for you being here on my first day back!' My father greeted him and asked whether he would like some coffee. Coffee having been served, my father introduced the people sitting round the table. My father then invited Sir Donald to take over.

Sir Donald explained that, as part of the audit mandate, his company was required to conduct a spot audit from time to time. This they had done in the second week of December. That spot audit revealed certain facts that, if proved to be true, would place serious doubt on the validity of the company's accounts. Therefore it was decided to conduct a fuller audit. He then pushed a copy of the audit report to Uncle Cecil. Sir Donald invited my uncle to turn to pages eleven to fifteen in the report, asking my uncle if he recognised the transactions. My uncle stated that they were special bonus payments he had awarded himself, as he thought that his salary and annual bonus did not fully reward his individual effort. He agreed that such payments should have been approved by the board, but he said that he had not asked for such approval as the majority of the board were idiots, who were not capable to judge his full worth.

Sir Donald then asked him how he had managed to hide such payments from the auditors. My uncle paused, and then said that they were probably not doing their job. My uncle was then shown a statement made by Mr Penn, alleging bribery and corruption.

My uncle told the meeting that, in his opinion, Penn was a weak character, and would say anything to save his neck.

Sir Donald then turned to the statement made by Mr Keys, the Chief Accountant, also alleging bribery and corruption, to which my uncle replied that the man was a crook, and surely his explanation as a gentleman would be accepted above that of an employee. Sir Donald turned to the loans made to directors, again pointing out the statements made by the two disgraced directors. My uncle agreed that he had been told by the Chief Accountant that such loans were against the Companies Act, but that he as the Managing Director had decided that such loans were beneficial to the company. His explanation was that one Earlswood on the board was bad enough, but to have two would have undermined his position, thereby reducing confidence in the company.

Sir Donald summarised the position, saying that the Managing Director had admitted to all the offences outlined in the report. My father, Uncle Edward, and two other directors who had been present throughout the meeting, left their seats and went to the back of the room to deliberate. Once they had returned and sat down, my father began to speak directly to his brother-in-law. 'You will be suspended on full pay until a full hearing of the board can be arranged. When this meeting is over, you will be escorted out of the building and you are not to return until the day of the hearing.'

Then the two directors left the meeting. My Uncle Cecil went to leave also, but was told to sit down again, as there were other matters to discuss. Mr Godsbody was first to speak and told my uncle that, following Mr Penn's statement, an investigation had been made into the George Earlswood Trust. According to the accounts, over £2,000,000 had been invested in a special trust fund. Since he had failed to locate the fund, he now asked my uncle to tell him where it was. My uncle then broke down, saying there was no money, and that for years he had been borrowing from the trust fund to pay for the lifestyle he thought his wife and family were entitled to. He admitted bribing Penn to cover up the fraud. He was told that approximately £2,000,000 was missing, but allowing for the additional property purchased at the rear of the London property, antique furniture, porcelain, carpets and portraits, together with vehicles and other machinery, the net fraud amounted to £1,800,000. He was then asked a question: if the missing money was merely a loan, as he had stated, how did he plan to repay it when the trust fund fell due in September? Clutching at straws, my uncle told the meeting that he would sell his White Gull shares. That accounted for approximately £1,200,000, some £600,000 short. My uncle said that his shares were all he owned.

Sir Donald took over, and told my uncle that borrowing from trust funds by trustees was against the trust law. 'But to borrow when you knew that you would be unable to pay back monies borrowed is fraud. To cover such a fraud, you were prepared to bribe the auditors, and in so doing were guilty not only of fraud but also of false accounting.'

Prompted by Uncle Edward, I stood up to speak. I told Uncle Cecil that I was sorry to find him in such a predicament, and I hoped that the consequences would not be too severe. Nevertheless, I had a duty to do all I could to protect my trust fund. 'This being so, I accept your offer of part repayment by means of your White Gull shares.' I pushed across the table a prepared document transferring the shares to the trust fund. Uncle Cecil signed it and pushed it back to me across the table. 'Additionally, I find that no rent has been paid for at least the last ten years, and therefore I have to now give you notice to quit by the end of this month. When you do so, you will take only your own personal possessions. Do you understand?'

Uncle Cecil nodded before breaking down in tears. My father rang for security, to have my uncle, now a broken man, escorted from the building. Sir Donald came over to me, patted me on the back, and told me how well I had done, especially in getting the shares assigned to me. 'I am very sorry for the trouble my firm has caused to you and your family, and take full responsibility. I will, as soon as I return to the office, ring the loss adjusters in respect of your claim against our professional indemnity policy.'

I thanked him, and he then left with Mr Godsbody. I made to get ready to leave when my father stopped me, telling me there was family business to discuss. We poured more coffee and sat in a tight huddle. My father began by reminding me how little time they spent at Alswell Manor. This was due not only to his work, but also his wish to spend more time in the House of Lords. He also told me that my mother was now involved with national charities whose offices were mainly in the capital. Therefore he had come to the conclusion that his principal residence should be in London. He recognised that the London house was mine as well as the manor. He went on therefore to suggest that his rights to live in the manor might be transferred to the London house, leaving me as local Lord of the Manor. I told him that I would give them anything, and there was no need for legal agreements, but my father insisted.

Uncle Edward was next to speak. He told me that my cousin Robert would not be making the progress hoped for, and even if he was allowed out of the mental hospital he would need twenty-four-hour care. This being so, my uncle and aunt had decided to sell their Lincolnshire estate, and were setting up a trust fund to finance Robert's care. However, some of the money raised would be used to completely refurbish their large London house. Therefore he wondered if he could secure the services of Suzie for about a year, to carry out and supervise the work. Uncle Edward also agreed to make a contribution to Gloworm, in respect of lost overheads and profit. He confirmed that much of the work would be sub-contracted to the firm. He went on to say that, while building and restoration work was going on, they, the Buns, would be staying with Mother and Father in the London house.

We then adjourned and, during lunch, agreed on dates of transfer, and how the financial liabilities would be split.

Basically Father and Mother would move in during February. I would pay all staff salaries for January and February, plus any redundancy costs of staff they decided not to employ, from the new trust account they had set up. From 1 March I would be responsible for taking over all the running expenses of the manor, and have sole rights to live there.

Walking back to the station, I was totally in a daze, trying to sort out in my mind what I now needed to do. I rang Mo from Liverpool Street station, asking her to meet me at the manor for dinner, and to bring her toothbrush.

Dinner having been cleared away, I asked that Mary and Ted join us in the family lounge for coffee. I outlined the day's events, and the agreements entered into. Mary and Ted listened intently, and as soon as I finished told me that they were thrilled that after March I would indeed become Lord of the Manor. I asked Mo to arrange a full clean of the London property at the end of January, and to pencil Peter in to help with the removal. Once the removal had taken place, I suggested a complete clean and redecoration of the rooms previously occupied by my parents. Mo said she would undertake the scheme with Mary. Mo then excused herself to go and ring Suzie and ask her to attend a meeting the next morning at the hall. I asked Ted to arrange for the spare cars at the London house to be brought down to the manor. Mary produced a bottle of wine, and we all celebrated a new life for the manor.

Later that night in bed, as we both enjoyed the afterglow of lovemaking cradled in each others arms, I asked Mo the question that I had been avoiding for some time. 'Mo,' I asked, 'if I decided to make you an honest woman, what would you say?' She told me that she loved me, and would do anything for me. She was now twenty-seven, and her body clock told her that, if she wanted children, she had better hurry up. Ideally she would like to have my children, as many as I wanted. However, the thought of one day becoming Lady Earlswood filled her with concern and worry. She told me to give her time to think about the future.

Next morning at breakfast, I could see that Mary was upset and not her normal self. I asked what was wrong, and she held up a letter she had received that morning. The letter was from her son, who was serving in Northern Ireland, and he spoke of a worsening situation, with increased sectarian hatred and terrible scenes of violence. He told her that he and his men had come under fire from a sniper, who had badly wounded one of them. Even the children had become involved in throwing stones at troops. He admitted being nervous on patrol, and prayed to God that a child would not be shot by mistake. Troops were now being armed with rubber bullets for crowd control, but these hitting the wrong part of the body could still kill or cause serious injury. He could not see where it all would end and he was glad that he had only eighteen months left before leaving the army.

I told Mary that I was sure he would be all right, and that he would soon be home on leave again. Mary said it was not only she who was very worried, but also her daughter-in-law, who was alone at home with a young child.

Suzie arrived for coffee, and was shown by Ted into the family sitting room, where Mo and I were waiting. She immediately enquired what was up and why we had needed to meet so soon. Mo handed her a cup of coffee and invited her to sit down. Leaving out the details of the previous day's meeting, I immediately told her we had been offered a commission to refurbish an elegant historic London home. The work would take about a year to complete and, during that time, the person supervising the work would be expected to stay on site. When I told her who the client was, and what was required, Suzie became more and more interested. I then asked her if she was interested, particularly as she would be away from her mother for long periods of time. She told me that the work she was doing currently in London had made looking after her mother more difficult. Happily, her mother had been able to find herself a place in a sheltered block of flats, where she would still enjoy her independence, but also be in constant touch with people of her own age. I then said that I thought that the answer was a yes. Suzie told us both that this was the opportunity she had dreamed of, which would really put Gloworm on the map.

Suzie said that she was busy and could not stay for lunch. The rest of the morning was spent planning how our sales effort needed to be employed during Suzie's absence. Mo and I came to the conclusion that the Chairman would need to retain most of the work, currently carried on by the Managing Director.

Two weeks had passed since the meeting at White Gull, a time when the economy of the country seemed to be going into free fall, with millions being wiped off of share prices. The whole concept of a pay and prices policy in a free economy was causing havoc among traders and companies, who did not know from day to day what was allowed and what was not. Even the strongest supporters of the government had to admit that the economy was in a mess, and might well prove the downfall of Edward Heath.

At the end of that week I was invited to a meeting at White

Gull headquarters to meet my father, Uncle Edward and Angela. When I arrived at my father's office, I found the others already there. My father opened the meeting by saying that after careful consideration and after discussion with other board members, the two director vacancies would be offered to Angela and me. My Uncle Cecil had resigned before he could be dismissed, as had the Chief Accountant. My father then told us that Mike Brade, the chief executive of their American companies, had accepted a three-year transfer to take up the position of Managing Director. This posting happened to coincide with his daughter's entry into Cambridge that autumn. He would be accommodated in Little Farthings in Surrey, an easy train ride into the City. In addition to my directorship, I was to be offered a two-day-a-week contract to shadow Mike, with a view to taking over from him in 1976. Mike would begin his duties in May.

Uncle Edward was next to speak, telling us of his intention to retire as Managing Director also in three years. His successor would be Angela, who had been shadowing him for some months. However, he felt in the early months of her term of office she would need some strong support. He then said that he had given Angela fifteen per cent of Bun Industries' equity, partially in gratitude for her work and support over the past two years and partially as compensation for the injury caused to her by his son, Robert. He then offered to exchange fifteen per cent of Bun stocks to me in exchange for the five per cent White Gull stocks I had recently acquired from my Uncle Cecil. In addition, if I accepted his offer, he would guarantee a seat on the board of Bun Industries. We shook hands on the deal, and I left him to arrange the paperwork.

We then turned to the subject of compensation offered by the audit insurers. With regard to my trust fund, their assessor felt that the false audit report was mainly to blame for the loss. They therefore offered a sum of £450,000, leaving the other trustees to find the remaining £150,000. I decided to accept the offer, but refused any further compensation from my father or Uncle Edward. The assessors in the case of White Gull were not so generous, only offering fifty per cent of the total loss. My father had spoken to the other directors, who had agreed to accept the offer. I then asked what had happened to Uncle Cecil and was told he had been charged with a number of offences two days after his arrest. He had appeared in court on the third day, but only for the briefest of hearings. He had since appeared again in court, and had pleaded guilty to all offences, and had been sent to the Old Bailey for sentencing during the beginning of March. Mr Penn and our chief accountant had also pleaded guilty and would stand trial shortly. My father then told us that the chief accountant's post had already been advertised. We all had lunch and I then returned to Essex.

I rang Mo when I got home telling her of developments and agreeing that I could cover my agreed duties in the three days left of my working week, plus weekends when required.

I was finishing breakfast one morning at the end of January, when Ted announced the arrival of Inspector Steer. I told Ted to show him into the library, and to offer him coffee. Five minutes later I joined him, welcoming him back to the manor. He told me that four nights previously, a car had been stopped by the traffic police, having driven through a red light. The driver had been breathalysed and found to be over the limit. The driver was taken to the police station and in a subsequent test was found to be well over the limit. The driver was then charged and, in line with normal procedures, fingerprinted. These prints were added to the national fingerprint register, and provided a match for the fingerprints found on the letter asking for me to be killed. The person was subsequently arrested and brought back to Colchester and interviewed. When faced with all the forensic evidence, a full confession had been provided. The person had been charged and had appeared at Colchester magistrates' court the previous day, and had been remanded in custody for two weeks.

I then asked the identity of the offender, and was told her name was Charlotte Caroline Fawcet. I was stunned for a second, and said nothing. Inspector Steer waited before telling me that he had conducted the interview with Charlotte. Apparently her father had told her some time in 1972 that in the following year I, her cousin, would evict them from their house and deprive her of her standing in society. 'She could not face that, and decided to have you killed.'

I began an explanation of circumstances, but Inspector Steer stopped me, telling me that what had not come out of the interview he had later found out from the fraud squad. I thanked him for taking the trouble to come and tell me himself, shook hands, and had Ted show him out.

Ted returned to the library, where I remained standing, and he asked me what was wrong. I repeated the inspector's conversation to him and saw he was very troubled by the news. He asked me whether my parents had been informed, and said if not perhaps I should ring my mother straight away. I agreed, and rang Angela to ask the whereabouts of my mother and her sister. She told me that they were in Uncle Edward's office having a terrible row. I asked her over what were they arguing, and was told that Uncle Cecil had phoned to say that they were outside Little Farthings, and someone had changed the locks. The two sisters had therefore descended on Uncle Edward in order to secure the new keys, but he told them they could not have them, as their brother no longer worked for the company and therefore had no right to live in company property. I asked Angela to bring Uncle Edward to the phone, which she did. I told him of the news I had just received, and asked him to tell my mother and his wife. My mother was first to the phone, wanting an explanation for this strange turn of events. I told her as much as I knew, and that her brother had been implicated in the plot. Mother rang off, obviously very shocked. Mary, ever ready in a crisis, appeared with a tray of tea, which we all sat down and drank, while reviewing the situation.

Changes in the Wind

February, as is often the case, began with a cold snap. I had begun my contract with White Gull, assisting my father in the day-to-day running of the business. The economic situation seemed to be getting worse each day, with the government almost daily issuing edicts aimed at controlling the situation. Unions, which seemed hellbent on destroying not only themselves but the country as well, daily threatened strikes, sometimes for the flimsiest reasons. The latest group to attempt to show its muscles was that of the gas workers, who said that they would freeze the country into submission from 13 February.

During that first week Charlotte appeared in court again, and her advocates pleaded diminished responsibility. She was remanded in custody again for medical reports. Neither her mother nor her father was in court that day, only me and her two aunts.

On Valentine's Day I changed my normal behaviour by inviting the directors of Gloworm for lunch, including Ted and Mary. I did however send flowers to Angela. All the ladies as they entered the dining room were handed flowers, while Ted and Peter were given boxes of their favourite sweets. Immediately the two ladies hired for the occasion had cleared away, we all retired to the drawing room for coffee. I then handed Mo an envelope containing the keys to my Rover car, and to Pauline and Tiny keys to smaller Rovers previously driven by Uncle Cecil's wife and daughter. I gave Suzie the keys to a nearly new Mini, bought for Uncle Cecil's secretary, being a better vehicle for Suzie's needs. Ted had had each car cleaned and valeted as well as being filled with petrol. Now the staff realised why they had either been driven to the manor by Peter or picked up by Ted in Colchester. I also informed them that I had appointed Ted as Transport Manager, and that any problems with the cars should be referred to him. Mo stayed after everyone had gone to look at the nearly new Jaguar that had also been purchased by Uncle Cecil from the proceeds of my trust fund.

We briefly discussed some urgent business before Mo departed too, anxious to get home in her new car before it became too dark.

I went into the house to read that morning's newspaper, which remained folded up on the library table. The news, it seemed, was nowadays all the same: trouble in Northern Ireland, economic gloom and more threatened strikes. Like many people, I wondered where it would all end.

In early March my father, Uncle Edward, Mo and myself were in the court to see poor Charlotte formally sent to the Crown Court for trial. She looked thin and worn as well as seeming divorced from the proceedings. My mother and aunt went down to the cells to speak to her before she was driven away, back to Holloway prison. When they returned to meet us, both aunts were visibly distressed. The fact that Charlotte was the only daughter of an earl had alerted the local press to the possibility of a good story. We became aware of this, finding several reporters and cameramen waiting at the door. We paused to let them take their photographs, but were careful not to make any comment.

Mo was very upset at finding her picture on the front page of her local newspaper with a big caption underneath that read 'Local girl to marry into aristocracy'. The story stated that people close to the couple expected the announcement of an engagement any day. There then followed a history of her life, with quotes from school friends she hadn't seen for years and hardly knew. The next day in the county newspaper there was a picture of her and me, this time with a caption 'Maureen's my darling'. The telephone did not stop ringing with friends, customers and former neighbours all wishing to pass on their good wishes. In addition, several reporters rang asking for an interview, which they all failed to get.

March saw every large and medium-sized company in the land struggling to adjust for the new VAT tax that was to be imposed from 1 April. The number of forms, special schemes and regulation meant that I spent many hours with the accountants from all the three companies I now was involved in, ensuring that we would be ready by 1 April. Mo seemed to be very put out by the government's continuous changes in direction.

Early in the month the IRA brought its murderous ways to the capital, leaving a car bomb outside the Old Bailey. Fortunately I was not in London as there was a Tube strike, and everyone whose journeys were not essential had been asked to stay away. The news bulletins that night revealed the scope and horror of the attack. The hospital nearest the scene, St Bartholomew's, and the emergency services did what they do best, responding to crisis. The next morning, and for days after, Londoners vowed to carry on with their normal lives rather than give in to a bunch of terrorists.

During all this, both Mo and I tried to keep abreast of running our various businesses. Father was doing well running Gloworm with my help, but confessed he would be glad to hand over the reins in May and get back to his work in the house. The economic situation continued to be on its way down, as union after union took a kick at the government, with a view to restoring a Labour government. The government retaliated with more and more economic rules aimed at saving the fragile economic state of the country. In addition to the pay and prices legislation at the end of March it published the Control of Inflation Bill, in a vain hope to right the ills, as they saw it, of the overall economics of the country. While the regulations became more and more severe, business spent its time and money finding ways to get round the regulations.

April saw the introduction of the new VAT tax, which we were told would gradually bring us into line with our other colleagues in the new Europe. The tax and the increasing amount of power gradually made people resist the ideals of an enlarged Europe. Enoch Powell declared that, since the majority of people did not want closer ties with Europe, the issue might well bring the government down. Business costs soared as a result of new security measures which had become necessary following the Old Bailey bomb, the inability to put up prices due to the pay and price statutes, and then the imposition of a complicated tax. My father, who had been a Tory for many years, confided to many other Lords that the current administration had lost the plot.

I continued working part-time in London and part-time locally for Gloworm. Mo appeared to be less tolerant of the arrangement, particularly as work seemed to be on the increase. The April board meeting was an unhappy one, with every director claiming they needed more and more resources to cover their commitments. Suzie told the board that she had enough furniture refurbishment contracts to keep our staff fully employed for the next nine months. The reason for this upsurge was the Bun House contract. Family pieces had been brought down from the former estate house, to be refurbished either for use with the contract or for subsequent sale. In addition, much of the furniture in the London house figured in the scheme, and that too would require refurbishment. Peter told the meeting that he was finding it difficult to manage the increasing demands for transport made by Suzie. Our administrator informed us that in spite of all the economic ills of the country, receipts for the first three months were approximately £55,000. In an attempt to calm the situation, I told them that I understood the pressure they were working under, and over the following month would see what could be done. Once the meeting was over, Mo followed me to my office, closed the door behind us and sat down. She told me she felt that the new management plans, to be introduced in July, would no longer work, as she now felt incapable of taking over. I suppose that I was expecting something like this to happen, and in my mind had formulated my answer. I then told Mo to call a meeting of directors and to thrash out a strategy that would work, and sooner rather than later. I then asked Mo whether there was anything else bothering her that I could help with, a suggestion quickly rebuffed.

I drove home that night asking myself whether I had taken on more than I could cope with, and how I could offer more support to Gloworm. The next day, I had a cheque from the insurance company for £400,000. I rang Mo and told her I needed to see her urgently, and I would meet her at the Lexden House later that morning. When she arrived and was sitting comfortably in the office, I asked her how she was. She then began crying, and I went to comfort her. I gave her more coffee, and waited for the crying to subside. She then told me she loved me, more than life itself. She added that since I had come into her life, she had never been happier, and that I was lovable, generous and thoughtful. Mo said she did not want to hurt me, but she felt unable to marry me, now, or ever. She said that if she married me, she could not take on the role as the future Lady Earlswood. Her opinion was therefore that it was better to tell me now than ruin my future life. I told that her I was very sad at her decision, but that I did understand. Hesitating, she told me that there was nobody else, and we could still spend time together, even to the extent, that if I wished, she would gladly have my baby. I told her that nothing would please me more than for her to bear my son, but my upbringing was such, I could not allow it out of wedlock. I then told her that that being so, we could just go on seeing each other as before.

The fact that she had managed to get the question of marriage off her chest seemed to put back the sparkle in her face. I then told her of the insurance money, and of my intention to purchase forty houses and have them modernised by Gloworm. I explained that a combination of increased house values and rents frozen under current government regulations, coupled with the need to keep properties up to at least a minimum standard, had forced many small landlords to throw in the towel and sell, often a below market prices. When this occurred, Lily Estates would be there to buy.

I had already decided to ring Pauline after our meeting and give her the new instructions. Mo told me that it seemed an ambitious plan, but that Gloworm could and would support it.

The meeting having finished, we took an early lunch, returning to the house to reflect on the future. That night, I told Mary and Ted about Mo's concern that she would not be up to the task of becoming my wife and Lady of the Manor. Mary thought that perhaps marriage was a step too far for Miss Maureen, and that if either of us were not sure that marriage was the right course of action, then there might be big hurdles in the future. Mary's advice was to give Mo time.

Mary then told me that she had had a telephone call from the chairman of the village fete committee, telling her that the fete may have to be cancelled. I asked why and was told that the parish council had rented the sports field where the fete was traditionally held to a local cricket club. The club had spent a lot of money laying a square and refurbishing the outfield, and had refused permission for the fete to go ahead on any part of the pitch. The rest of the field was not big enough for both the fete and car park, and the pavilion always used for the tea area was now out of bounds. Ted had suggested that the field bordering the manor gardens, and rented to the local stables for the growing of hay, would be ideal. He had spoken to Mrs Cobb, the stables owner, who told him that by August bank holiday the hay crop would have been lifted, and autumn planting not begun.

I thought for a minute, and then commented that from memory the field was uneven and full of potholes. Ted agreed, but said there was no alternative. I then told him that, when I was four or five, I remembered large tents on the big lawn in front of the house. Mary said that, while she and Ted had not been employed at the time, she remembered my mother telling her about the coronation celebrations that had been held on the lawn. I asked Ted how much damage would be done to the lawn if the fete was held on it for one day. He told me, if it was dry, none at all; if it was wet, damage would occur, but would be quick to repair. I told them that perhaps the fete committee would like to change the venue, using the adjacent field as car parking. Mary was obviously delighted with the idea, and excused herself while she phoned the chairman of the fete committee.

Fortunes Don't Buy Love

May began wonderfully, with warm weather replacing the icy blast of winter. During that first week Mike arrived from the United States to take up his post as Managing Director. My father introduced us, and from that first moment I knew that the chemistry between us was strong, and that our association was going to be successful. Later that day, Mike having been introduced to all and sundry, we finally found ourselves alone in his office. He handed me a single piece of paper, on which was written 'White Gull Enterprises, strong in capital terms but weak in management'. I nodded and told him that many of the older managers had served my grandfather and that many of the management systems stemmed from that time. He told me that we had to bring the firm into the twentieth century without delay, but to do it in such a way as to hold on to all key staff.

In the hours that followed we sketched out a rough plan of action, a predicted time span for changes, as well as a root and branch examination of every facet of the company. My first area of examination was the property portfolio, as Mike said that was where he thought my expertise lay. I made an appointment for the next day to speak to Arthur Welsh, head of property services. Ted had been a loyal friend and trusted colleague of my grandfather, and he told me that although the company had invested heavily in property over the past ten years, little or no money had been allowed for up keep and restoration. Consequently, most properties were in a poor condition and were attracting only low rental income. However, with the constant hike in property prices, capital profits made the property department better than it was. I asked Ted to work out a ten-year plan for modernisation, with full costs, and let me have it within a week.

My second port of call was the transport department. The department seemed to have no system for allocating their transport, but instead merely reacted to daily need. I found that vehicles were off the road for large amounts of time, due to age and wear. The manager had been with my grandfather for years and would be retiring in six months. I asked him to list all vehicles by age and mileage, as well as listing all journeys made during the previous month, and let me have it within a week.

The story was the same in every department, a concentration on new business, especially abroad, and little management of the bread-and-butter side of the company. By the end of June my report into the areas I had been asked to look into was complete. Looking back, the gradual break-up of my affair with Mo gave me more free time than I had given myself before, and I was fast becoming a workaholic.

Meanwhile at Gloworm, things were proceeding better than I could have hoped, with both turnover and orders coming in much as planned. Mo maintained a very professional approach while in the office, but it was obvious that the strain of our break-up was beginning to tell on both of us. My work in London and my working every weekend had meant that I had neglected Mo. I therefore suggested a weekend in my Lexden Road house, and was surprised when she refused. We went into my office, shut the door and it was then she told me she had been seeing another man, although at present their relationship was not sexual. She had therefore decided to ask me to end our personal relationship, so she could build a new social and personal life for herself. I must have looked shattered at her plea, and when I agreed she came into my arms weeping and saying how sorry she was.

On every other Saturday morning I had a meeting with Pauline, usually at Lexden Road. Lily Estates, under her leadership, was now running two offices in the town, specialising in both house sales and lettings. She reported that she was currently acting as letting agent for 200 properties for other people and seventy for Lily Estates. Rents to Lily were averaging £500 per week, with increases in the pipeline when the new properties she was buying had been renovated and came on stream. She confirmed that with the current government price restraints there were many small-scale landlords with small incomes and large outgoings on keeping properties up to scratch. Their only solution was to sell up, in a flat market. I could see from the list she presented me with that she had turned out to be a tough negotiator. I told her how well I thought she had done, which always brought a smile to her face.

Unrest in Northern Ireland continued, with everyone in the capital wondering where the bombers would strike next. The economic news was also grim, with wildcat strikes happening nearly every week, and more mass union demonstrations were planned to protest about the Industrial Relations Act, Pay and Prices laws and the Counter Inflation Bill. The whole country seemed to be in the grip of a crisis, which nobody seemed to know how to get out of.

During June I attended my first meeting of the Bun Industries' board, and was surprised how similar Bun Industries' interests were to those of White Gull, albeit on a smaller scale. Angela seemed more approachable and, when I was in London, she often accompanied me to shows and concerts, but still avoided bodily contact. I told her that my affair with Mo was at an end, and how lonely I felt, particularly weekends, to which she said, 'You poor baby.'

By the end of June, Mike and I had produced a new management plan, which we sent to all managers for consultation and comment. This came at the same time as Uncle Cecil and the others came up to the Old Bailey for sentencing. The former Chief Accountant was up first. His defence team told the judge in mitigation that, although he admitted committing a fraud against his employers some ten years previously, the Managing Director had held it over his head for all that time, unfairly holding him to account. He had lost his job and had been struck off the register of accountants. His client was truly remorseful, and wanted to pick up his life again for his family's sake.

The judge told him he had abused a position of trust by committing the original fraud, but that the subsequent pressure he had been undergoing from his employers was cruel. He therefore sentenced him to two years suspended for three years. The next up was Mr Penn, the auditor. The judge told him that he was a greedy man, who had allowed his greed to overturn his duties as an auditor. While the judge agreed with council that he too was remorseful, and would probably never be employed as an auditor again, the public needed to be protected. The judge therefore sentenced him to four years.

When my uncle was brought up to face the judge he was a shadow of his former self. His defence council in mitigation told the court that he had led a Walter Mitty existence as well as being addicted to gambling, but now saw the error of his ways. He had totally lost his position in life and his wife had left him. The judge told him that he had been a greedy, cunning individual, who had brought disgrace not only upon himself and his family title, but also on two other professionals. The number and variety of offences were so great that a long custodial sentence was necessary. He sent Uncle Cecil down for seven years. Mother and Aunt Flossie then hurried down to the cells to see their brother before he was taken away to begin a new life in prison. My father and Uncle Edward declared he had got only what he deserved, and that they were relieved it was all over.

Standing in the public gallery of Number Three Court at the Old Bailey, I tried to convince myself that the break-up of the family was nothing to do with me. Deep down I pondered that had my grandfather not made Uncle Cecil a trustee of the main trust fund, then perhaps he and his family might have stayed on the straight and narrow.

When I arrived home at the manor and told Ted and Mary the result, they said that they were not surprised in the least, but that they were sorry for my mother and aunt.

I had an early night and, lying in bed thinking of the events of the day, suddenly felt lonely, and I wept for what might have been.

My cure for my loneliness was work and more work. Weeks simply flew past, as I rattled between London, Harwich and Colchester. The beginning of June saw the publication of the White Gull strategy consultation document. While the document envisaged many changes in the company structure, it promised there would be no job losses, enforced early retirements or redundancies. The plan also promised half a million pounds a year for the next three years to tackle backlog maintenance and modernisation.

Most weekends I stayed in London, where Angela and I

became guides to Mike and his family. I found that when one is showing visitors things that have always been there and are largely taken for granted, those places of interest take on a whole new meaning. While these distractions certainly ensured that I spent less and less time on my own, I was still desperately lonely, even in a crowd.

This state of affairs was not improved when Mo announced she was going on holiday to Spain with her new boyfriend. I told her I hoped that the holiday would be a great success.

One day I accompanied the Buns on a trip to their London home, and although the place was still a builder's yard, what had been finished looked really great. Suzie seemed to be in her element and to have a close rapport with Auntie Flossie. I asked when the project would be finished, and was told that it would be at the end of January.

Then one night, while staying in my Colchester house, I found a new social activity: the talent contest in the local pub. One Sunday evening, I decided to pay the pub a visit. Entering, I quickly bought myself a drink and sat down at a vacant corner of the bar. I had arrived early and the entertainment had not started. I did not wait long, however, before the man in charge of the equipment welcomed everyone, telling them that, being Sunday, it was talent contest night. The first performer was a girl called Carole, who sang 'Sing Me an Old Fashioned Song', a Billie Jo Spears song I had always liked. I was not only surprised at how well she had sung the song, but how totally professional she was. The next singer was a young girl called Susan who sang a Skeeter Davis hit, 'The End of the World', again with great professionalism. That set the tone for the evening, with singer after singer delivering high-class performances. When the evening came to an end, I asked the landlady of the pub how often she held talent contests, and was told every Friday and Sunday.

That night as I lay awake, thinking of both the past and the future, I realised that since breaking up with Mo I had let myself sink into a state of depression, a misery to myself and probably a burden to others. Work had become mechanical, and was not giving me the buzz that it used to. I decided that perhaps I would remain a bachelor and never marry. That being the case, it was time to turn my life around and begin enjoying life again. The talent contest had shown me that even people with only a fraction of what I had could make their own entertainment, and in doing so created a warm, friendly atmosphere, even for the loneliest soul. I therefore resolved to visit the pub again.

Mary and Ted, meanwhile, had found themselves at the centre of fete preparations, and Mary seemed to gain a new sparkle. Ted told me that his wife had wanted to break into the village inner circle for years, and now found herself right in the middle. Ted, however, warned me that if I was not careful the fete would signal a new venue for many other village activities. Perhaps being the Lord of the Manor would mean spending more time at home, as of late I had neglected my duty towards Mary and Ted, by never being home, to give their jobs a fuller meaning.

Gloworm still seemed to be thriving in spite of the economic recession, and staff appeared to be happy. Relationships between Mo and me had deteriorated, although in matters concerning the business she was as professional as ever. The insurance money, paid by the auditor's insurers, fuelled an upturn in property purchases, and Mo apologised that completion dates for the renovation of such properties now stretched into the following year.

This period of my life was beginning to be affected by change, had I noticed the telltale signs.

First, in late June, we held a board meeting of Gloworm to agree formally a handover of power and to welcome two new board members. I had anticipated a happy mood at the meeting, but right from the start I could feel a positive sign of mistrust between Pauline and Mo. Pauline accused Mo of deliberately pushing her renovation work to the back of the queue. Mo denied this. Pauline then complained that the repair system she had created, not only for Lily Estates but also for other people who rented properties through the two letting offices, was in danger of falling apart owing to delays in meeting emergencies, and that that was due to Mo not giving priority to urgent repairs. Peter came to the rescue by reminding everybody that, as work had increased, perhaps the board had not made proper arrangements to accommodate such work. Since most of the 200 properties were situated in Colchester, perhaps we should open a small depot in Colchester just to look after emergency house repairs and annual maintenance. Peter told the meeting that he would undertake a feasibility study into such a depot and report back. Tiny, on the other hand, apologised to Mo for the lack of support for general sales, but since opening the show home next to the depot, sales for both kitchens and bathrooms had soared. I agreed that Mo could still carry out her sales role, and I would keep the work I had previously been doing as Managing Director as part of my role as Chairman.

As soon as the meeting finished, I told Pauline to come to my office. When she did, and had closed the door, I told her that her conduct that morning was totally unacceptable, and that if she could not work as part of the team then she might not be working at all. She apologised, and began crying. She told me that she would not have wished to upset me at all, but was finding it difficult to give up the power and independence I had allowed her before the changes. I told her that I would overlook her behaviour that morning, but any repeat would be dealt with severely.

Mo was the next person in front of my desk. I told her I was disappointed at her failure to control the meeting, and that she, in her new role, needed to embark on some team building. She also confessed that she planned to go on holiday with a boy she liked but did not love, but she was eager to finish finally her relationship with me and to begin a new social life. I told her that, whatever happened, I would always be there for her. In an attempt to be fair, I told her that I would forget that morning's performance, but if it happened again there would be serious consequences.

The second thing was that, during June and July, I joined my mother, father, Mike and his family, the Buns and, of course, Angela, at the 850-year celebrations of the City's hospital, St Bartholomew's. During the week, before the re-enactment of the Bartholomew Fair, we had seats for the William Harvey Revolutionary Circus, which was held nightly on an improvised stage, right under the Henry VIII Gate.

The show was largely written by medical students and junior doctors, who wished to highlight some significant part of the hospital's history. They chose to portray the discovery of blood circulation, by William Harvey at the hospital. However, that was as far as agreement went, and the production had to include various types of entertainment favoured by various small groups. The final production therefore embodied comedy, drama, religious plays and musicals. We all thought it was superb and said so as we drank our mulled wine at the end of the show.

On the last day of the celebrations, the Bartholomew Fair was to be held. Angela had cleverly booked a table for lunch at our favourite restaurant opposite the hospital gate, and so we were all able to witness the final preparations. After lunch we joined the crowds as they jostled to get to the front of the various stalls. The number of people joining the throng appeared to be growing, minute by minute, so much so that a brewer's dray had to be used by the organisers to get a party of Chelsea Pensioners to the stage, where they were to open the fair. Following the movement of the crowd, we were moved down the line of stalls from which we made many purchases. I bought four large pint-sized pewter mugs, bearing the hospital's coat of arms. While I was buying the mugs, striving to keep my balance despite the crowd movement, I suddenly felt Angela grasp my hand and squeeze it. I stopped and looked into her eyes, which were sparkling with happiness, and she did not relinquish her grasp till we left the fair. That was the first real physical contact I had had with Angela, since December 1969.

My father bought four limited edition Royal Worcester plates, bearing in the centre of each the Great Seal of Henry VIII, and presented them to the ladies. Seeing the stall holders' smiling faces, it was hard to remember that many of these people had witnessed the carnage of the Old Bailey bomb, less than four months previously.

That evening Uncle Edward took us all out to dinner at Maxim's. Mike and his family were overawed by the day and even more surprised when Uncle Edward recounted his experience of attending the 850th anniversary dinner held in the Great Hall. He described to Mike the feeling of walking up the great staircase, past the Hogarth mural of Christ at the Pool of Bethesda, and into the magnificent Great Hall that for the occasion had been decked out with long trestle tables and lit only by candles. Everyone there was dressed in period costume of the court of Henry VIII, and contributed to a unique occasion. A menu had been drawn up near to that which might have been eaten at the time, all washed down with mead. The occasion was further added to by the great portrait of Henry himself, gazing down on his guests.

The third thing that was gradually changing my life was my meeting with Sandy at a talent contest night. I had been back to the pub three times in less than two weeks. Sitting alone at a corner table I had had some conversation with a young lady who helped in collecting glasses when things were really busy. Through our conversation, I learnt that she was a widow who was living with her parents at the pub, following the death of her husband the previous year. The following Tuesday we had dinner together and since that time we had been out every Tuesday evening. We found that we appreciated each other's company, and doing the same things, and both of us enjoyed the times we spent together. At the end of one meeting she asked what I had planned for bank holiday, and I told her I was involved in running the village fete, but would be free in the evening. She naturally asked me what part I was providing for the fete, and I told her that I was a general dogsbody, giving my services to those who needed them. I thought afterwards that my determination to keep secret my life as the son of a lord was causing underlying difficulties and that one day I would be caught out.

On the Friday evening before the fete, Mary looked concerned and I asked her why. She told me that normally the committee had lunch in the refreshment tent before the fete opened. This year several members of the committee had suggested that Mary might arrange for them to take lunch in the dining room of the hall, and she did not like to ask.

Duty before Self

During the period that my parents were in residence at the manor they had used the August bank holiday weekend as a time for house parties.

I, not wishing to break with tradition, had invited my parents, my aunt and uncle (Lord and Lady Bun), Angela, and Mike and his wife. I had also invited Mike's daughter to join us. She was up at Cambridge. I also sent invitations to Suzie and Pauline who due to previous commitments could not join us until Sunday morning.

My guests arrived on Friday afternoon in time for tea. Mary, who had worked for my mother for many years, was keen to show that she had not forgotten the high standards of the manor, serving daintily cut cucumber sandwiches, scones with jam and cream, and various types of cake. Following tea, most of my guests retired to their rooms to unpack, rest and freshen up before dinner. My mother, however, did not go immediately to her room, but instead asked me to join her in the library. Once there she began to tell me how disappointed she was that I had still not found a lady to run my household and provide an heir. I explained that I had only recently finished a relationship with Mo which I had thought would result in marriage. My mother dismissed my explanation by remarking that although love and romance were very well in their place, my task was to find someone who had been brought up knowing how to run a house and servants.

Then she explained how she had discussed my needs with her friend, Lady Felicity Sherlock. Felicity had a seventeen-year-old daughter, who had recently been the subject of much gossip, following an illicit affair with a young married curate. This had caused her mother much worry. The girl, although young and attractive, was somewhat of a rebel but with firm handling could well become a suitable lady of the house. Her parents had indicated that should the right marriage be identified there would be a substantial settlement. My mother therefore suggested that next month I should arrange to have tea in London and meet Felicity and her daughter. I told my mother that having tea with her was always a pleasure and I looked forward to the occasion.

Dinner that night was extremely enjoyable. We were joined by Tom and Wendy, Mary's son and daughter-in-law, also Ted and Mary, as guests. Mary had arranged staff from the village to prepare and serve dinner. We had also invited the Buns' chauffeur, who always stayed with Ted and Mary when my uncle and aunt stayed at the manor.

The following day the ladies used the Buns' car to go shopping in Colchester, while Ted drove the gentlemen on a trip through the Suffolk countryside. We stopped for an early lunch at the Bull in Long Melford. Afterwards we visited Bury St Edmunds, where Mike wanted to visit the cathedral and the gardens. My father then insisted that we had afternoon tea at the Angel Hotel before returning to the manor.

During the trip, much of the talk had been about the economy and political situation in the country and the need for some resolution to the growing unrest.

On the Sunday morning my mother had persuaded all my guests to attend the village church. She had rung the vicar the previous evening to inform him that they would be attending. The vicar greeted us on our arrival telling my mother how nice it was to see the whole family at church.

Following the church service we returned to the manor for pre-lunch drinks, and we were joined by Suzie and Pauline.

At the end of lunch my mother suggested that the ladies retire to the large lounge so that they could catch up on all the news. Ted said that the men might like to go down to the village green and watch the local cricket match.

As they left the house my visitors saw the villagers preparing for the village fete which was to be held the following day at the manor. The men enjoyed the cricket match. Ted arranged chairs in front of the beer tent. We left the game at teatime to return to the ladies for tea.

The following morning I was up early to accompany Ted on

his morning walk. People were already arriving to complete the preparations for the fete which would open at 1.30 p.m.

Lunch was a busy affair, with my guests being joined by the fete committee. Mary, who was chairwoman of the committee, seemed to enjoy her status, and she introduced the various committee members to my guests. Immediately following lunch we all made our way to the lawn at the front of the manor, where my mother was to open the fete.

Once the formalities were completed, everyone followed my mother as she toured the stalls and sideshows. She stopped to talk to villagers, some she had known for many years.

Pauline, Suzie and I made an unscheduled stop at the beer tent where we were joined by Peter and his wife. Sitting at a table, everyone agreed how much Mo would be missed at dinner that evening as she was still on holiday with her boyfriend. We then continued to visit the stalls and enjoyed some time in the flower tent, which, as usual, had some spectacular displays. We all returned to the manor for tea at 4 p.m. An hour later we went back to the fete to watch my mother presenting various prizes. Dinner that night was a lively affair. My father and Mike proposed toasts to the ladies. Mother was very keen to speak to Pauline and Suzie. She wanted to know if there were any suitable ladies who might make a suitable wife for her son.

After dinner we joined the ladies and played cards until late.

All my guests left for home after breakfast the next day. As they left they thanked me for a pleasant weekend. The manor was a hive of activity as the ladies from the village, who had been employed by Mary, made beds and tidied rooms, restoring the house to its usual orderly existence.

Outside on the lawn contractors were dismantling the two large marquees, while helpers were clearing the rubbish left after the fete. By early afternoon the manor was returned to normality, and seemed very quiet. I was beginning to understand why my mother and father had enjoyed entertaining and in so doing, brought the manor back to life.

The final days of August passed quickly. Mo returned from her overseas holiday. During her time abroad she had acquired a nice tan and outwardly looked well and rested, but something in her eyes told me that the holiday had not been the success she had hoped for.

Ideas and Surprises

On the first Monday in September I decided to change my routine, and spend Monday and Tuesday in London, and the rest of the time in Harwich. I had arranged to stay at my parents' residence on the Monday night, and to invite Suzie, who had never seen the place.

The trains from Colchester that Monday morning had been delayed, and it was after nine when I arrived at White Gull headquarters. Mike was already in, and hard at work dealing with various pieces of mail that needed his attention, which had built up during the three weeks he had been away on holiday. He smiled as I entered his office, and invited me to make myself comfortable. I naturally asked him about his holiday, only to be told that everything had been terrific and apprised of all the places and sights they had seen. He asked me how things had been at the office during his absence. I told him fine, with no problems.

He then picked up my thoughts on Bun Industries, which he had obviously read, and said he could never resist an envelope which 'read for your eyes only'. I explained that at present it was only idle speculation, and might not be worth consideration. Mike told me he thought it was an excellent piece of work, and that between us we should keep the possibility of a merger at some future time very much in our management strategy.

That night I dined with Suzie, who looked well and happy. A quick tour of the house had impressed her, and she approved of all the furnishing and decoration. Over dinner I reviewed the progress on the redevelopment of the Bun project. Suzie told me that all the building work had been completed and that the redecoration and furnishing was scheduled to be finished by the end of January. A press launch of the house would take place during the middle of February, by which time the finished project could be handed over. I told her that Lady Bun was very pleased with things and that she was a clever girl. 'What are your plans after this project?' I asked. Suzie coloured up and told me that she was glad that I had brought the subject up. She went on to explain that she had loved working in London, and now that her mother was settled in a sheltered accommodation, she wanted to stay in London for the foreseeable future.

I then told her about White Gull asking us to tender for approximately £170,000 of work in London during 1974. Her eyes lit up. 'When are the tenders due?' she said, and I told her they would come out after Christmas for return by the end of March. I swore her to secrecy as I handed her a paper showing the buildings to be refurbished. Suzie then told me that after Christmas she would need to start looking both for a small office and a place to live; could Gloworm find a small amount of capital to decorate suitable offices? I told her yes.

She asked me my movements for the rest of the week, as she had a proposal in mind but had not brought the file. Since it was the weekend that she was due to see her mum, I suggested that we meet at my Colchester house, have dinner and then discuss her ideas. 'Then you are more than welcome to use one of the spare rooms for the night.' She agreed that that was a great idea, and said that she looked forward to our meeting.

The next day I spent in the White Gull offices, putting the finishing touches to a paper I was preparing on future property acquisitions. I visited Mike in his office before I left, and found him deep in thought. I apologised for disturbing him, but he said, 'I cannot get your paper off my mind and am at present trying to see how we can make money either on savings or by asset-selling over the next few years.' I wished him well and left him deep in thought as I had a train to catch.

That night I met Sandy as usual for dinner. During dinner, Sandy asked if, instead of celebrating a birthday at the hall in October, we could move the event to the fourth Saturday in November, when her parents would be celebrating their Silver Wedding Anniversary. I told her that I saw no reason why not, but that I would arrange for her to come to lunch soon in order to discuss the project with Mary. That night as I drove her home she asked me to turn into a side road and stop, which I did. Once I had stopped and turned the ignition off, I asked her if anything was wrong. She assured me that everything was fine, but told me she needed a cuddle and a real kiss, as generally she was down in the dumps. Naturally I obliged, and when she came into my arms and returned my kisses I felt elated about the future and Sandy. She insisted on walking home, leaving me with various thoughts on the drive home to the manor.

The next morning at breakfast, I sounded out Mary regarding my plans to hold a surprise Silver Wedding Party for Sandy's mum and dad in November. Mary said, 'I think that is a lovely idea and, as you say, I need to get together with Sandy soon to plan things.

On the next three days I worked at Gloworm, ensuring that all my work was up to date. Things at both Gloworm and Lily Estates appeared good, and I felt things were about to look up for me.

On the Friday evening Suzie drove down from London, arriving at about seven o'clock. Hearing the sound of her car in the drive, I went to the door to greet her. We exchanged greetings and she entered the house. Once the door closed she gave me a friendly kiss, and said, 'I have been looking forward to tonight.' I took her overnight bag and showed her upstairs to one of the two guest rooms. I asked if I could offer her any refreshment after her journey, but she told me she would like to take a shower and change ready for dinner.

When she appeared downstairs again she looked ravishing in a mandarin-style dark blue dress with a broad gold mandarin collar. I asked her if she would like a drink before leaving for the restaurant but she declined. I had booked a table at the George Hotel, where I was well known and knew I could rely on excellent service.

Over dinner Suzie outlined her plans to set up an agency office in the East End of London, where building prices and rents were far lower than in the more prosperous areas. She told me that as long as there was public transport nearby, people would visit her new offices, and that she was certain that in time property values would increase as the area became more popular. She had seen a dilapidated three-storey warehouse that she could buy and convert for approximately £70,000. The finished building would provide ground floor offices and a two-bedroomed flat on the other two floors. Once finished the offices would be worth in excess of £25,000 and the two flats at least thirty thousand. She told me she was looking for an initial investment from Gloworm of approximately £25,000 to set up a new Gloworm business, and a further £50,000, possibly from me, on which I would recoup twenty per cent interest within a year. Having sufficient monies available to me, and believing in Suzie and her talent, I agreed to fund the venture, both from my own funds and from profits from Gloworm. I ordered some champagne and toasted the project with Suzie.

When we returned to my house, I made some coffee and we retired to my study. Still excited about the project, Suzie explained that the creation of her own Gloworm outfit partially met a dream she had had of one day owning her own business. 'Once the Bun project is finished and receives the publicity it deserves, I expect people to flock to our offices, and for work to pour in,' she told me. 'When this happens, and I am confident it will, I will wish to renegotiate my contract with you, to not only give me an increased salary, but also a share of the profits.' I told her that she was going too fast for me to keep up and to slow down, but she carried on. 'I then expect to be in a position to raise a mortgage and buy the first-floor flat. I want it to be a strictly business transaction, even though we are good friends, and I do not want to be given anything, especially by you.'

Surprised, I asked her what she meant by that remark and her face coloured up. She then told me that on the Friday following my break-up with Mo, the two friends had gone out for a drink. Mo was very upset and went on a bender, so much so that Suzie had to take her home and put her to bed. During this exercise Mo had told her about the Angel Hotel, and Bury St Edmunds, about our love affair and the fact that it was me, rather than a legacy, that had purchased her dream house. I asked Suzie if she was disappointed in me for taking advantage of an employee, something I had always been brought up to believe was wrong. Suzie told me that far from being disappointed, her opinion of me had soared. Mo, she told me, had had a very special need following her best friend's death, and I as a friend had gone to Mo's rescue.

According to Mo, I was generous and gentle as well as being a perfect lover, and even after the break-up Mo loved me dearly. 'You had been the perfect gentleman, and offered to make an honest woman of her, and had been turned down.' Suzie sighed and added, 'The problem was that Mo would never have wanted to let you down, but could never be something she wasn't. That story from Mo actually enabled me to put the proposition I made tonight, knowing that if at all possible you will support your friends to the hilt.'

I looked into her eyes and said, 'The proposition you have made has two conditions and they are as follows: one that during the next twelve months you find time to remodel Alswell Manor, especially the old servants' quarters, and second you agree to my being your neighbour in the top-floor flat.' She said yes to the first proposition, but as to the second part, she asked why I wanted a flat in London. I told her that I was spending more and more time in London, staying with my parents, and a bachelor pad would in my opinion be a positive advantage. Suzie smiled, and said, 'I can see the point, and agree to the proposition wholeheartedly.'

Time was getting late and we were both tired and ready for bed after a long day. Suzie then asked me whether, in an hour of need, she could rely on me to help her through it. Surprised at her inference, I told her that if the need was as I supposed, it would be beholden on me, as a gentleman, to go to a maiden's assistance. She smiled, thanked me, and turned to go to bed. 'Sleep tight,' I told her as I gently patted her bottom. She then turned again, came into my arms and kissed me passionately.

The next morning we both rose early and breakfasted together before Suzie left to see her mother.

The following Sunday. I picked up Sandy and drove her to the manor for lunch. Having had coffee, I showed Sandy round the manor, including below stairs, describing my plans for its refurbishment. Over lunch, Sandy and Mary discussed the details of the surprise luncheon. Sally told Mary that the family had few relatives, and most of the guests would be long-term regulars at the pub. Sandy was asked to prepare a guest list of about thirty people and to ask them if they could come. Sandy turned to Ted and said, 'I hope you and Mary can come as I feel you are already good friends.' I said that that could easily be arranged.

Following lunch Sandy and I retired to my private sitting room, where we could be alone. We sat side by side on the comfortable sofa, holding hands like a teenage courting couple. She told me that my understanding and friendship were beginning to help wash away all the hurt of the past, and my generosity in holding a luncheon party for her parents had really overwhelmed her. One day, she knew not when, she hoped she could repay some of my generosity, but I told her that was a noble thought and not to worry. We gently kissed and cuddled, but when she thought things were proceeding too fast, she stopped me, saying she was not ready for such a relationship. I took her home to the pub in time to open, returning later to the talent contest.

The following two weeks flew by and my work with both White Gull and Gloworm absorbed the majority of my strength. Things internationally were deteriorating, with a falling pound and a sluggish stockmarket. The situation in Northern Ireland went from bad to worse, with increased bombings and sectarian killings. During those two weeks I had dinner with Sandy twice and spoke to Suzie on the phone on numerous occasions concerning our joint project.

On the Monday morning Angela phoned to say that all the family were home from Scotland and looking forward to the family dinner on Thursday. She reminded me of a special surprise she had arranged for the Friday, the day of my birthday.

The family dinner party was first class, as my mother's dinner parties usually were. Mother and Father presented me with a full Scottish evening attire, including a dirk and sporran. Uncle and Aunt presented me with a painting (oil on canvas) of some highland cattle grazing. Angela gave me a Fairisle sweater, and whispered she had another present for me when we dined together the following evening. The driver took Angela home, and I made my way to bed.

The next evening I met Angela as arranged and we dined in a little secluded Italian restaurant we had found earlier in the year. We left the restaurant early, and I suggested a walk by the river, but Angela shook her head saying her surprise birthday celebration was not complete. Reaching her flat, I was surprised to find a light on, and someone sitting by the fire. As we entered, a young lady of about nineteen stood up to greet us. She was wrapped in gift paper, held on by an enormous red ribbon. Angela introduced her friend as Annie, and then turned to me and instructed me to unwrap my present. I pulled the ribbon and the paper fell to the floor, revealing a cupid-type figure, not fat but extremely well proportioned. I blushed and told the girls I did not know what to say which was answered by Angela, who told me that, whatever I had lost, Annie would soon find it. Taking my hand, Annie led me to the bedroom, and shut the door. I suppose it had been some time since I had had a lady in my bed and I responded to Annie's embraces wholeheartedly, both then and twice during the night. I awoke at seven o'clock to find Annie already awake and before long we were once again wrapped in each other's bodies. I then slid off Annie and fell into a deep sleep.

When I awoke again it was nine o'clock and I could smell breakfast being cooked. I rose, putting on a dressing gown to see what and who was about. Angela stood by the stove preparing a very hearty breakfast, which she thought I would need when I awoke. I asked her if Annie had left, and was told that she had left just after eight, complaining that part of my anatomy should wear a health warning, and that she was thankful she would not be spending the whole weekend with me.

Over breakfast, Angela explained that Annie was a nice girl who often acted as a hostess for Bun Industries' overseas customers. She was not a prostitute and seldom slept with people she did not know, 'but when I explained why I could not give you what I was sure you were missing, she readily agreed to help.' I replied that it was a very thoughtful present and that, while I found it enjoyable, I would have preferred Angela in my bed. She blushed, and said, 'Who knows what will happen in the future?'

On that last Sunday of September, I again went to the talent contest at the pub, and at Carole's insistence sang 'Can't Help Falling in Love', an old Elvis Presley number, and received great applause from all the people, many of whom sang regularly every week. I left the pub feeling I had finally been accepted by the regulars for what I was and not because of my wealth and birthright.

Planning for Christmas

During the first week in October, my father, Mike and I had a meeting to discuss my report on White Gull's property portfolio. In brief, the report outlined that the policy of the company over many years had been to record only asset purchase prices in the books. No revaluation had taken place, at least since Uncle Cecil had taken the reins. Consequently, although the portfolio showed the total value as approximately £2,000,000, it was probably now nearer £4,000,000 and, with the three-year investment plan, nearer £5,000,000.

My father questioned why revaluation had not taken place, and I told him that the process was time consuming and costly, and had therefore not been seen as a priority. Following much discussion, we agreed that a third of the portfolio should be revalued every year.

We next turned to Mike's report on the company's investment portfolio. The same set of circumstances applied with no revaluation having taken place except in the cases of sales and purchases. Mike had revalued the shares from the latest stock market prices, increasing the real value of the portfolio to £5,000,000, and that did not include an initial investment in Bun Industries for ten per cent of the stock, for which grandfather had paid £50,000, and was now worth about £1,000,000. Mike told Father that what these reports indicated was a substantial undervaluation of the company, money that could be used to facilitate financial dealings.

Father thanked us both for our work and by way of a reward offered to take us both out for lunch.

The next day Mike called me into his office to talk about Bun Industries and their share capital ownership. He said that, according to his calculations, my family, including White Gull, owned forty per cent of the shares. The Buns owned forty-five per cent, and Angela Brown, the Deputy Managing Director, owned the remaining fifteen per cent of the equity.

I told him that a takeover of the company could only take place if Uncle Edward agreed, and that, at the present time, talk of a bid would be premature.

That Tuesday evening I had dinner with Sandy, and shared my thoughts about many things, including the Labour Party's alleged threat that, if they returned to power, they would place huge taxes on the rich. On the way back to the pub, we stopped at my Lexden Road house for coffee and a little privacy. By this time our kissing had become intense; although Sandy seemed to enjoy such sessions, she would not allow things to go any further.

The second week in October, not only brought bad weather but potentially bad news for Ted and Mary. One breakfast time, I noticed tears in Mary's eyes and asked what the matter was. She told me that she had received a letter from her daughter-in-law to say her father, who lived nearby, had gained a promotion and that her parents would be moving to Scotland early in December, as they had already sold their house. The problem was that her parents wanted to spend Christmas with their daughter and granddaughter, and there would not be room for Ted and Mary.

Knowing that Mary and Ted looked forward to their family Christmas, especially as their son would be on leave from duties in Northern Ireland, I was determined to find a solution. I turned to Ted and Mary and suggested that everyone might like to stay at the Manor for Christmas and New Year – 'After all, there is plenty of room.' Ted was the first to speak, and asked if I really meant it. I told them that as far as I was concerned he and Mary were family, and I would enjoy some fun and laughter round the house at Christmas. The look of relief on Mary's face was so emotional that I wanted to shed a tear too. Mary quickly bustled off, to tell her daughter-in-law of my offer to them.

Arriving at Gloworm the following morning I was met with a copy of the third part of the Pay and Prices Bill, which among other new regulations allowed rises for that financial year of seven per cent. I authorised that the Secretary to make the necessary arrangements to pay the new increased rate from 1 December, and to notify the staff of my decision.

Mo had phoned in sick, and I decided to visit her on the way home. Reaching the door of her house I was greeted by a very distressed Mo. She asked me in and, as we made our way to the lounge, she began crying. She told me that her boyfriend, Colin, had gained promotion within the bank and would be working in Yorkshire. He wanted her to sell up and move to where he would be working. After much thought she had told him she could not marry him and he had gone off to Yorkshire in a huff. I tried to comfort Mo the best that I could, telling her there were bound to be more fish in the sea, but that only seemed to distress her more. She sobbed and said, 'How can I find another man while I am still in love with you?' I cradled her neck and head, making soothing noises, till she regained her composure. We then talked for an hour on what she wanted to do with her life, and the plans I had for Gloworm. She told me that although she still loved me, she would not change her mind about marriage. She wondered whether we could resort to our earlier arrangement as lovers. I told her that now was not the time to make decisions, but we would speak about it later. I left Mo's at eight o'clock and was late home for dinner.

After dinner, I confided in Mary about my day, and asked her what I should do. Mary advised, 'Give her some space and time, then do what you think is right.'

On the last Friday of the month Suzie came to see me at my Colchester home. She announced that she had bought the warehouse for £38,000. She showed me the detailed plans for the building, which she said would be going to the local planning committee the following Tuesday evening. Assuming no problems, work would commence immediately after the Christmas and New Year break, and the showrooms and first-floor flat would be ready in mid-April. My flat would be ready at the beginning of June. I told her how impressed I was at her speed of operation and I only hoped that no one had had to be bribed, as in the current Poulson enquiry. She laughed and said that everything was strictly above board. In truth she had had the plans drawn even before she had come to see me, with estimates for the work required.

I stood and went to get myself more coffee from the coffee machine, when she suddenly said, 'George, take me to bed.' I was stopped in my tracks and said, 'What, now?' to which she replied,

'Yes, before I change my mind.' I took her hand and led her upstairs to my room. I closed the door, took her into my arms, and began kissing and caressing her, using all the skills I had first learnt from Billie-Jo. I gently undressed her, getting her to undress me. When we were both naked, I stepped back to admire her body. Leading her to the bed, I got her to climb in under the covers, quickly joining her. I began again cuddling and caressing her but, as soon as I tried to enter her, she suddenly pushed me away, leapt out of bed, picked up her clothes and ran from the room.

I gave Suzie time to recover before I got out of bed, put on a dressing gown and went in search of her. I found her lying face down on the guest bed, still naked. Her clothes lay in a heap on the floor. I sat down next to her, attempting to soothe her distress by gently stroking her back and shoulders. Eventually she sat up. Her eyes were puffy and her eyeshadow had run. She faced me and said, 'I am sorry, George, but just as we were going to, you know what, I could hear my mother saying, "Do not give yourself to a man until your wedding night," and I just couldn't go on with it. I know you must hate me for being a silly girl, but I hope you will forgive me.'

I told her that there was no reason for apologies, as I did understand. I went on to tell her that it was not the right time, the right place or the right person, and a time would come when it would be. I promised her that she was still very much a dear friend, and that I would always be there for her, no matter what. That seemed to help compose her, even though she suddenly realised that here we were sitting talking, while she was stark naked. I suggested that we both put on some clothes and continue this conversation downstairs over a cup of tea. She nodded, waiting for me to leave, and surely noticing the effect that her beautiful naked body was having on me.

Suzie left later that afternoon, with a smile back on her face. Watching her leave, I wondered whether I should have been more positive in my lovemaking, and provided that which she felt she needed. On reflection, I had been the perfect gentleman, and would never know the answer to that question.

I returned to the manor for dinner and retired early. As I lay in bed, I realised that my special birthday present had reminded me of the joy a woman can bring to a man. My thoughts then drifted to my relationship with Mo, who had made it plain that she was still there for me if I needed her. On the other hand our break-up had been very painful, and I had no wish to repeat the heartbreak, when I knew we would eventually part.

That Sunday I went to the pub, and not only enjoyed myself with my new friends, but also had ten minutes with Sandy in the car before driving home.

Revaluation, Reunion and Regret

The beginning of November was a very hectic month for White Gull Enterprises as the review of every part of the business as instituted by Mike and I continued. The leisure portfolio revealed that a string of motels in America, bought in 1951 by my grandfather, still was on the books at the original purchase price of £200,000. Mike estimated that the chain might be worth more than $4,000,000. Return from this investment was very poor, as my grandfather had negotiated a leaseback deal covering twenty-one years based on five per cent of the capital purchase price plus agreed inflation. The deal had recently come to an end but, because of the problems with my Uncle Cecil, no new deal had been negotiated. Mike therefore proposed that he should fly home with his family for Christmas and, while he was there, make an executive decision on the way forward. Two hotels bought by my father in 1970 – when Ted Heath had become prime minister, threatening to take the UK kicking and screaming into Europe – remained at their original valuation and purchase price. The return on the hotels, one in Paris and one in Brussels, remained low, as both had been leased to large hotel chains at favourable rental rates. Mike raised the suggestion that, as leisure was not part of the company's core business, the money might be used more effectively elsewhere in the business.

The next review was into our venture capital business and revealed significant weaknesses in management. The review, which had been carried out by my Uncle Edward, blamed poor judgement on the part of the previous managing director, coupled with poor control on agreements. Uncle Edward proposed that half the investment, totalling £3,000,000, should be dispensed with and switched to West Germany, where rates of return were twice that of the UK. The remaining equity holding would gradually be sold off, and the resulting cash invested in the New World, better utilising our Sydney office.

During my commuting between London and Harwich, I managed to spend quality time with both Angela and Sandy. Mo and I still had a close relationship, which now ceased at the bedroom door.

Both businesses were overshadowed by the rising tide of terrorism, and the extremely perilous state of relations between the unions and government. The latest scare was a threat from the power workers, the miners and transport unions to block Britain's power supplies, once again plunging the whole of the nation into a round of industrial power cuts. In spite of a promise from OPEC that fuel supplies would not be cut, doubts about internal distribution remained, forcing the government into new emergency legislation that, among many other many proposals, warned of an already prepared system for rationing of petrol. Such uncertainty had its effect on both the stock market and the pound, fostering an opinion within Europe that Britain was fast becoming the poor man of the Continent.

This made our international investments depressed, a feature not missed by Mike during that long November meeting.

During the middle of that month, Princess Anne married Captain Mark Phillips, which not only caught the nation's hearts but also reawakened my mother's efforts to get me married off. Mo thought it was funny, while Angela kept reminding me that my mother was right and I was not getting any younger. Sandy advised me to just enjoy the celebrations and to forget all the hassle over marriage and an heir.

During the second weekend in November I was at my Lexden home, allowing Ted and Mary to spend a long weekend in Lincolnshire with their daughter-in-law and granddaughter. I remember that it was a Saturday evening, just after ten, when I heard a knock at the door. I opened the door only to find a policeman and policewoman, supporting a very drunk Pauline. The policewoman apologised for the disturbance but said this was the only address that the young lady could remember. I thanked them, telling them I would take over, and found myself at the door holding up a very heavy young lady. Closing the door, I could see the state Pauline was in. Her favourite leather jacket was covered in mud as were her expensive leather shoes. Her skirt was soaked and she had started to shiver. I removed her shoes and leather jacket in the hall, and with great difficulty pushed her upstairs and into one of the guest rooms. We then went into the en suite bathroom, where I sat Pauline on the toilet seat, while I ran a warm bath. I had asked Pauline to start undressing, but to no avail, so I stood her up and removed her clothing. Getting her into the bath took a superhuman effort, but was eventually accomplished. The next ten minutes was spent letting out the bath water, and topping it up with hot, thereby raising her body temperature. Pauline remained like a baby while I sponged down her body and washed the mud from her hair. By the time it came to get her out of the bath, she seemed more with it, actually helping herself. I sat her again on the toilet seat which I had covered with a fluffy white towel, providing her with another fluffy white bath sheet in order that she could not only cover her modesty but begin to dry herself. Checking that she would not fall off the seat, I went to my bedroom and took a long, clean T-shirt that I thought could act as a nightdress. When I returned, Pauline was drying herself very slowly. Taking another towel, I dried most of the moisture from her hair, before wrapping her scalp in a towel headdress. Once she had the T-shirt on I manoeuvred her into the bedroom, where I had turned down the clothes. She literally fell into bed, and I propped her up with pillows.

I went back into the bathroom and cleaned the bath and floor, before taking her clothes downstairs to the utility room. I went back upstairs and found her with her head over the lavatory bowl being violently sick. When the sickness had finished, I flushed the bowl and sat her back on the toilet, while I drew a glass of water to wash her mouth out. I heard her begin to use the toilet and therefore left her to it. When she finally emerged from the bathroom she was whiter than the towels I had used, and seemed to be relieved at the feel of the soft bed. Not wishing to leave her, I got out a hairdryer from the bedside cabinet and began drying her hair. The warm air seemed to soothe her and, by the time I had finished, she was asleep still propped up by the pillows. I left the bathroom light on in case she needed to use the room, turned out the main light and went downstairs.

My first job was to sort out her clothes. I checked the labels on her skirt and top, and was relieved to find both were washable. I therefore loaded them and her underwear into the washing machine and switched it on. I then cleaned off the mud from her leather jacket and, using a clear leather polish, restored the jacket to its former glory. Her shoes were a different story as, when I cleaned off the mud, I found the front of the shoes had been badly damaged, probably as the police had dragged her in and out of the car. Still, the shoes were wearable and with a little leather polish looked reasonable. I made myself a hot drink as washing cycle came to finish. The wet towels I placed in the washing basket. Mary would send them to the laundry, with the sheets, when she came the following week. When the washing machine came to a stop, I transferred the clothes to the dryer, and when they were dry, shook them out and placed them on a hanger. To my surprise there were few creases, and the garments seemed not to have suffered any lasting damage.

The next morning, I was up, showered, shaved and dressed before I heard movement from the guest room. I was already in my study, drinking coffee, when Pauline put her head around the door. She looked dreadful, her face pale and her eyes heavy. I wished her good morning and offered her some coffee, which she refused. She told me her stomach was not too good. I took her to the kitchen and found some Alka Seltzer. She went and sat down in the breakfast room while I prepared some thick porridge which I knew would give a lining to her tummy. To my surprise, she ate all the porridge up, and told me she felt better. I then told her she could find her clothes in the utility room, and she might feel better once she had washed and dressed.

Half an hour later, she appeared downstairs, and I ushered her into the small lounge. She then told me she had only hazy recollections of the previous night, but that she knew she had caused me additional work and worry, for which she was sorry. I told her of the sequence of events, and my part in them. She blushed scarlet as I told her of the difficulty in both undressing her and getting her into the bath, both being necessary.

I then asked her the question that had been on my mind since the previous evening, and that was, why? She told me that, since her divorce, she had been lonely, seldom going out or seeing friends. The final straw was on that Saturday morning she had gone shopping with her mum as usual. However, over coffee, her mother informed her that her pastor (Pauline's mother belonged to a strict sect) had told her that marriage was for life, and that by divorcing, Pauline had broken her vows and was as a result a sinner. He had also told Pauline's mother that, as a good Christian woman, she should not have her daughter under her roof. Her mother said that, as a result, Pauline would not be welcome at the house any more. This news devastated Pauline, as she realised that without family or friends she would be alone at Christmas. She decided that night to revisit her old haunts, in search of lost friends. She had collapsed outside the pub and the landlord's wife had cared for her until the police and ambulance appeared. That was as much as she could remember. She also told me that, when she had gone to her flat following her shopping trip, she had considered suicide, but had changed her mind.

I told her that she was clever and attractive, and had a good life in front of her, so why ruin it? I also told her I regarded her, as did other members of the Gloworm board, not only as a valued colleague but also as a friend. Therefore she was not alone. I then said, 'Mo tried to be your friend, but you seemed hostile and resentful of her.' Pauline began crying, hoping that I would take her in my arms and comfort her, but I resisted that temptation. Through her tears she told me that she knew I had laid Mo and that, even though she was more attractive than Mo, I had never even made a pass at her, or taken any notice of her efforts to attract me. I was not sure how to respond, but in the end decided that truth was better than lies. I therefore told Pauline that Mo and I had had a long standing relationship, and that I had even proposed marriage. Mo had then decided to refuse my proposal, on the grounds that she could not perform, later in life, the duties as wife of a peer of the realm. I respected her decision, and we remained best of friends. Mo was therefore someone with integrity and honesty, qualities which are often hard to find in this day and age.

I reiterated that I felt that Pauline was a very important to my and Gloworm's future, on the basis that she had a good business brain. However, even though she was attractive, I did not feel attracted to her in a physical sense. I then told her that I would not let her be alone at Christmas, and if no reconciliation happened between her and her mother, she could join the family at the manor, provided she behaved herself. She then went into tears again, telling me she loved me and wanted to marry me. I told her that was not possible and that she should stop crying or I would give her something to cry about. This seemed to do the trick, and the crying stopped immediately.

When lunchtime came, I again showed off my culinary skills by making scrambled egg in the microwave, something I thought she could eat, what with her dicky tummy. She watched me prepare the toast and eggs, remarking what a good cook I was, and, when after lunch I cleared away, washed up, and put things away without her offering to give a hand, I felt myself becoming annoyed. We took our coffee into my study and began to talk. I gradually realised that Pauline was attention-seeking and used her eyes as a weapon, turning on the tears when she could not have her own way. She kept up her conversation, saying how she fancied herself as Lady of the Manor, with servants and money, and how good she could be in bed with the right man. I told her to stop, as she would never be lady of my manor. This provoked more tears.

Once she had stopped crying, she told me she had read a story where a young servant had been enticed into the study of her lord and master, and how he had bent her over his desk and taken her from behind. To my great surprise, she rose from the chair and spreadeagled herself over the desk. She then saw me rise from my seat and go round behind her. She laughed as I put her flared skirt up and over her back. She made no resistance as I pulled down her knickers, other than saying, 'Hurry up, please.' Suddenly those two gorgeous globes were naked under my gaze, and for a second, I thought of doing as she wished, but instead I placed one hand in the middle of her back, pinning her down, using the other hand to spank her, a spanking which my former governess would have applauded.

When I had finished I left the study, to let her crying subside and to get dressed. Ten minutes later she appeared at the lounge door, and came in. She told me she was sorry, and that for once her flirting had got her into trouble. I told her that nothing had changed in our friendship, other than she now knew where she stood, and any repeat of such behaviour would bring further trouble. She promised, that she would change her ways. Pauline left that afternoon a wiser and hopefully a better person.

The following Monday, Mo and I found ourselves alone in the office after everyone had gone home. Mo made coffee and came and sat in my office. I asked her how things were, and she told me that, while Gloworm would reach its target this year, things looked bleak for the future. She had recently contacted customers for whom we had carried out restoration and refurbishment work during the closed season. The answer was always the same, that business in the English holiday market was bad, and if the trend continued many of them would close down at the end of the season, next year. Consequently, they had decided to postpone work, until after next year. 'While we are still getting a flow of new orders, they are mostly for kitchens and bathrooms. Suzie, however, is brimming with confidence at the launch of the London office, and has asked me whether I can spare a couple of days a week in London assisting with the expected White Gull tender. She has found an inexpensive hotel, near to our new office, and I wondered whether you would agree the extra expenditure.'

I asked her how the Managing Director felt about the project, as she would have to make the decision, not me. 'She simply smiled and thanked me,' replied Mo. I asked how she was coping without Peter. She told me that she felt lonely at times, but she used her work to put loneliness from her mind. I told her of my Christmas plans, now that Mary's family were all coming. Mo told me she was glad Ted and Mary could enjoy Christmas with their family, especially their granddaughter. She then sighed and said that, now her aunt was in a care home, she would be spending Christmas alone. I then asked her if she would like to spend Christmas in a mad house. She looked at me and enquired whether that was an invitation, and said, if so, she would like to accept.

I told her that if Pauline was alone, and I would feel I needed to invite her as well. Mo was appalled and said, 'Surely you would not want her to spoil Christmas for the family, flirting and wiggling her backside at every eligible male?' I told Mo that I had spoken to Pauline, and I did not think she would waggle her tail at anyone, especially me. Mo did not seem convinced, and told me that someone really needed to take her in hand. I just smiled and said, 'We will have to wait and see.'

When I told Mary of the additions to the guest list, she clapped her hands and told me that it was going to be a real family Christmas, and that Miss Maureen would be more than welcome. Pauline was also very welcome, especially if she was going to be on her own.

I asked Mary to book tickets for the Christmas Eve supper, including one for her granddaughter, and also for the village Christmas dinner. 'That will enable you to play with your granddaughter on Christmas morning, without the worry of preparing lunch.' I also asked her opinion as to the holding of the Boxing Day tea. She told me plans were already in hand for the occasion and invitations would be going out at the beginning of December.

The anniversary dinner was I feel an overwhelming success. The highlight came as Ted opened the door to greet Sandy's father. The two men stood silent and then grasped each other tightly. Sandy's dad had served in the same regiment and they had been pals. As so often, one gets engaged in another hectic life, and friends can be lost touch with. The regulars and friends were impressed with the surprise that Sandy had organised for her parents. The crowd knew of my position in life, but I thought it did not change their regard for me.

Once the guests had departed, including Sandy's mum and dad, who needed to get back to the pub, Mary, Ted, Sandy and I sat in the breakfast room drinking tea. Ted wanted to know all about his long-lost pal and questioned Sandy relentlessly. Mary then said to Sandy, 'You could stay for dinner, and if you want to, return tomorrow morning in time for opening. I have already prepared the guest room.'

Dinner and most of the evening was taken up with army stories and adventures that the two pals had had together. The evening flew by and it was soon time for Ted and Mary to retire. Ted told me he had locked up and would see us both at breakfast. Alone for the first time that day, Sandy and I fell into each other's arms, kissing and cuddling. However, encouraged though I was, she suddenly stopped and pushed me away. She apologised; she was sorry. She made me promise not to tell anyone what she was about to reveal.

She told me that she had met Rob and had a whirlwind affair, resulting in an early marriage. 'We never made love till our wedding night, and that was a disaster. Rob's religious upbringing told him that sex for pleasurable purposes was wrong. Talking to the other girls at the club I soon realised that my husband was underendowed, and that was maybe the reason why lovemaking was only allowed on Friday and Saturday nights, under the bedclothes with the lights off. I did love him, and would never tarnish his memory, but one day I will have to come back to the future and begin a new love life. I know how patient you have been and I appreciate that, but the time is not right.'

I told her that she must take all the time she needed to complete her grieving process. She came into my arms again, kissing me passionately.

That night I thought deeply about Sandy, and wondered whether she was the girl I had been seeking. I decided that time would tell. Sandy left mid-morning, and was driven home by Ted, who said he might be back a little late for lunch.

November seemed to pass rapidly, owing to my constant commuting between Harwich and London.

Clouds over Christmas

Looking back, I should have realised that one day I would have to face real business problems, possibly involving a change of direction, on the basis that nothing stays the same. The national economy was again under pressure, due to the continued coal and power workers strike, and the railways not wishing to cross picket lines to transfer coal from the pithead stocks to the power stations. There was also grave concern over rising oil prices and all speed limits had been cut to fifty miles an hour, a limit hard to keep to if you're a Jaguar driver. There was also a rumour that the Government was considering imposing a three-day week after Christmas. Naturally, the country's mounting problems caused a huge loss of confidence in investors, and the stock market continued to show large losses.

In spite of this, things at the manor stayed the same. Mary and Ted had been for their annual shopping trip to London to do my Christmas shopping. 'This year,' Mary told me, 'is a time for fragrances,' and Mary had made it her business to know exactly what each person, including Peter, wore. Each director would therefore receive a large case of products in his or her favourite fragrances. Angela would receive the same but, when it came to Sandy, Ted had said, she deserved something really feminine, and he had settled on a beautiful nightdress and negligee from Harrods.

Things, however, started to go wrong when, early in that first week, a brown envelope arrived on my desk, marked 'Private and Confidential'. Inside the envelope was a letter from a well-known developer, telling me that the local planning committee had now agreed planning for houses on the two fields behind the factory. The council had made a stipulation, that access was only to be allowed down the lane, and our premises were not only preventing a wider road from being constructed, but were also blocking access to the site. The developer therefore made an offer to purchase the site at many many times its value. I immediately rang Peter at the Colchester depot, and asked him to meet me for lunch at a quiet pub situated in Straight Road, Lexden.

I arrived promptly at one o'clock and met Peter in the car park. Once we had ordered some food and had each had a drink, we settled at a table in a dark corner. Peter asked what was up, so I showed him the letter. He then asked what I intended to do. I told him I did know, but whatever I decided needed to be kept quiet until all the pieces were in place. We then discussed the options and Peter agreed to go away and consider the matter further. We agreed to meet in a week's time, when we could make a plan as to what to do next.

During the following week, Mike and I discussed what needed to be decided before he left for America. He offered to postpone his trip, on the basis with my father would be leaving for Scotland the next week. I told him that I could manage. We then discussed the economic crises and what White Gull would need to do if all the measures that the Government threatened came into force at the same time. We agreed to close down White Gull from Christmas Eve till January the second. All managers would be on call, and a recorded message would be placed on the switchboard telling clients and customers the phone numbers to ring in case of emergency. I then produced a bottle of whisky, a Dimple bottle in fact, and wished him a good trip and holiday. He thanked me, and I left his office to go to do some work.

The following week I saw Angela, and gave her the present Mary had bought and wrapped on my behalf. She told me that a present would arrive in the post for me, as she had not known whether we would meet before she left, with my parents and the Buns, for their traditional Christmas and New Year break. I told Angela of my plans for Christmas, and she seemed to be pleased, telling me that Christmas with a child in the house made things better all round. Angela then smiled and said, 'By the way, Annie sends her regards. You seem to have made a deep impression on that particular lady.' She gave me some money to buy a gift for Katy, from Auntie Angela.

Mike and Father both left in that second week of December, leaving me in sole charge of what was a very large company indeed. I arranged to go into the office every other day, till the Christmas closure, leaving two days to attend to the problems of Gloworm. During those two weeks I had taken Sandy to dinner, always ending up with a kiss and cuddle, which Sandy seemed to enjoy, although I continued to play the gentleman, instead of the red-blooded male that I was, which was causing increasing frustration. I think she knew how I felt. She maintained her insistence that we did not make love, at least not at the present.

Later that week I met Peter as arranged. He confirmed that the painters could be accommodated within the Colchester depot, and that the planning officer had no objections to the paint store being put in the yard. The corner shop was for let, but only on a five-year lease. 'The building is structurally good, but the place needs a complete clean and a new coat of paint,' he said. I told him that the shop and two-bedded flat in Colchester needed a complete makeover. I informed him of my decision to move the offices to the manor, using the main hall facilities to entertain important clients. He thought for a moment, and then said that it was a brilliant idea, but asked whether I was sure I wanted to have such an operation where I lived. Having settled the details, I agreed to write a paper to put to an emergency meeting before Christmas.

When I returned to the office I asked that Mo join me. I began by reminding her that from 20 December to 3 January, firms could only use one week's power. I then asked her how it would affect our work schedules, if like many other companies we closed from Christmas Eve till 2 January. She said that she had already been asked by several customers to review schedules as they would be closed, so she did not think that it would be a problem. I asked her to notify all staff as soon as possible.

We went on to discuss contingency plans in the event of another three-day week. We concluded that we should wait till it happened but, after hearing Mr Heath on the radio, she had made some plans. She went on to say how disappointed she was that, apart from Christmas, all stations would close down at ten thirty in the evening. We also discussed the plans by Anthony Barber, the Chancellor of the Exchequer, for raising taxes, but concluded that they would in the main hit the very big companies. Mo then told me that she had already secured all the materials needed to fulfil all the contracts on the book. I told her that that was a good idea, especially as we did not know which other unions might join the strike.

I then showed Mo the letter from the developer. Her reaction was one of shock rather than surprise. 'I see that you have known for several days, and have worried yourself considerably,' she said.

'I wanted to think,' I replied, 'and consider, if we accepted the offer, how we would cope.' But before I tell you of my conclusions, I would like your opinion.'

She said that the offer was too good to turn down, but asked where we would go. I gave her my suggestions and we agreed on most. Mo, however, thought like Peter: did I really want the job on my doorstep? I told her that I had discussed the matter with Mary and Ted, who were both happy to have more life breathed into the house. 'I have already begun drafting a paper for an emergency meeting that I am calling. Can you ring Suzie and the other members of the board, telling them I will be making an important announcement affecting Gloworm's future?'

On the Friday before Christmas, I attended White Gull's staff Christmas party, which was held in a large hotel. Having been told that the party would not finish till after midnight, I booked a room at the hotel. A large number of the senior managers had worked for my grandfather and welcomed me as a long-lost son. Many of the younger managers I had met during the consultation period, and I felt at ease. After the supper, which was lavish to say the least, I rose from my seat and asked for quiet. I began by thanking each and every one for their hard work during the year. I also said a brief word on the current state of the country, and said that, if the company were forced to make changes, I hoped that all of them would play their part. I finished by wishing them a very happy Christmas and a prosperous new year. I sat down to be greeted with loud applause.

Tables were cleared away and the dancing started, and I spent the rest of the evening dancing with as many female staff as possible. I thought that might further build morale, which had already risen considerably since Mike's arrival.

The weekend was spent catching up on my work and

preparing for the board meeting that I had decided to hold on Christmas Eve before the traditional lunchtime celebrations.

On the Sunday evening before Christmas, I went to the talent contest as usual, and had a really good night out. Once the customers had gone I met Sandy at the car, and we both got in. After a good kiss and cuddle, Sandy told me she had decided to have a few days off after the New Year, to visit the sales in London. However there was a problem which she needed to sort. I asked if I could help and was told yes. She told me that she planned to stay in London on the nights Thursday to Saturday, but did not yet know if her lover could get the time off. 'Where would you plan to stay, assuming that your lover could get the time off?' I asked. She replied that, as her lover worked in London, he would know a suitable hotel and make the necessary arrangements. I told Sandy that I would ask her lover to arrange the trip and I would confirm things when we met at the Boxing Day tea.

On the Monday, once everyone was settled with coffee, the meeting began. Mo, as Managing Director, gave a short summary on the new government regulations, confirming that they were the sole reason for the long Christmas and New Year break. Peter said that the idea of closing was a good one and gave them all a chance to charge their batteries. Pauline then presented a short report on Lily estates, including her revised office opening hours. Pauline was thanked for her work.

I turned to the main item on the agenda, that of the future of Gloworm. Mo began by reading out the letter which, she reminded everyone, was still a close-kept secret. Peter followed with the contingency plans for the carpenters, painters and furnishing operation, if the board accepted the offer on the table. I then put forward my suggestion for the soft furnishing operation, saying that, in the event of the board agreeing, Gloworm would buy the flat and shop from Lily Estates, as well as funding the new London office with money to spare. I next turned to the question of where best to place the management and administrative operation, again putting forward my suggestion of using the manor as offices, and using the main floor of the hall for receptions and entertaining.

Peter was first to speak, giving the plan his approval. Suzie said that she thought the idea exciting, especially as, after the Bun House opening, Gloworm would be attracting more upmarket customers than before. Pauline said she had no objections and congratulated all involved at reaching what she thought was the right decision.

Mo then took over presenting all attendees with a timetable of work and the tasks that each would undertake. The meeting closed well in time for the Christmas party.

Once the meeting had finished, I asked Mo why Tiny had not appeared, and was told she had rung in sick. 'That's bad luck just before Christmas,' I said, 'perhaps you can drop her present off on your way to the Manor. Mo smiled and said that she was looking forward to a real family Christmas.

The lunchtime get-together was as usual a great success. I made my normal Christmas address, thanking all for their efforts during the year. I also told them the reason for the long holiday, and everyone laughed when I suggested thanking Mr Heath for bringing about the current conditions. I told them of the decisions made earlier in the day and the reasons for those decisions, and about the opening of the new London office. I commented that the future looked bright for the company, and I looked forward to seeing them all again next Christmas in our new headquarters. Finally I wished them all a very merry Christmas and a prosperous new year.

Peter then stood in the middle of the assembly and told everyone that I had discussed the moves at the first opportunity and that the moves were made with the staffs' interest paramount. These were changing times and we all had to be ready to meet those changes. He finished by proposing a toast to Gloworm.

Once the staff had departed, the directors met in my office for a final drink and to receive their presents. I told Pauline and Mo that their presents were beside their beds, ready for Christmas morning. The directors left one by one, until only Mo and I were left. Mo said that she thought that my speech gave hope to the staff, but unless orders were received quickly, we could run out of work by late summer. I told her I had the greatest confidence in the future and I did not want her worrying over the holiday. I then asked her whether she had told Father Christmas what she wanted for Christmas, to which she replied, 'Yes.'

Leaving the office that afternoon, I too wondered how the company would fair if the national economy kept going down, and what sort of party we would have at the end of 1974.

A True Family Christmas

The lights at the manor were all ablaze as I motored up the drive that Christmas Eve afternoon. Mary's son, Tom, his wife, Wendy, and their daughter, Katy, together with Wendy's mum and dad, arrived in convoy, about three o'clock. By the time I arrived, at four o'clock, all the family were gathered in the breakfast room drinking tea and eating Mary's speciality scones with jam and cream. I entered the room, wishing all welcome, shaking Tom's hand warmly. We had been childhood friends, and the fact that I had not seen him for several years made our reunion more pleasing.

Pauline arrived at about five o'clock, laden with her luggage and a large bag of presents, which she placed by the tree, which stood in the entrance hall. Ted took Pauline's case to her room, while Mary bustled around making more tea. Mo was the last to arrive, also burdened not only with her luggage and parcels but a big wicker basket filled with goodies which Tom carried into the kitchen. Mary gave Mo a big hug, and told her how good it was to see her again, a greeting Mo returned. Now Mary, being a real country girl, felt that all guests were not happy unless continually fed. She therefore announced that a light tea would be served in the large dining room at seven. Promptly at seven we all filed into the dining room, only to find the buffet table groaning under the weight of enough food to feed a regiment, including sandwiches, pork pie, sausage rolls and pasties, with fruit and cream as well as a plate of fancy cakes. The atmosphere was one of joviality, anticipation and excitement, with several conversations going on at once. Once we had finished, all the girls helped Mary to clear away and wash up.

We all congregated at the front door shortly before ten. Ted drove his son, daughter-in-law, Katy and his son's parents down to the village in the Rolls. I followed with the remaining two girls in the Jaguar. Ted had organised parking to be provided for both cars in the drive of a nearby house. When we entered the pub there was a notable hush in proceedings, as Ted, along with mine host, ushered us to a table in the dining room, and then took our orders. Ever since the holding of the fete in the manor's grounds, I had been accepted as the rightful Lord of the Manor.

Instead of the normal rows of tables, this year a top table had been provided for my party. Once the bell in the bar had sounded for supper, people began drifting in to the dining room, coming up to our table and greeting Mary, Ted, Tom, myself and Mo, much to the astonishment of Pauline, who sat on my left-hand side. I quickly explained that Mo had accompanied me for the past two years and was now considered to be the Lady of the Manor. Pauline replied that, if they thought that and I eventually found a wife, wouldn't the village folk feel disappointed? I told her that I would deal with the situation when and if it arose.

At the end of the meal I was asked to say a few words before the church service. I briefly introduced my party, particularly Katy, who seemed to have boundless energy. I told them I looked forward to this occasion every year and hoped they all had a very merry Christmas and a prosperous new year, ending my short speech with a toast to the village. This was greeted with sincere applause, making me really feel part of my community.

When the pub bell rang again, it was the signal that it was time for those people attending midnight mass to make their way across the road to the village church. When we all arrived at the church, there was insufficient room for us all in the family pew and Mary and family filed into the pews immediately behind us. The vicar, at seeing our arrival, hurried over to greet us, saying how pleased he was to see so many people from the manor attending his service. He warmly took Mo's hand, and told her he had expected her and her intended to have made their way to his door, but he supposed that like many young couples we had decided to wait till we were sure. Pauline let out a breath and looked at me. I in turn introduced Pauline to the vicar, who welcomed her to his church. The service, to me, was as special as ever, and upon leaving I had a feeling that Christmas had really began.

By the time we all got back to the manor, it was well after one o'clock, but Mary still insisted that we all had a hot cup of chocolate before retiring, except of course Katy, who wanted to be asleep so that Father Christmas could deliver her presents. Everyone agreed that the evening had been very enjoyable. Mary told everyone that at long last the village really believed that they had a Lord of the Manor who really cared. Pauline then asked how I could allow the village to believe I was to marry Mo, when clearly that was not the case. Ted told her that Miss Maureen had attended the Christmas functions for the past three years and had won the hearts of the villages, who hoped and prayed that the Lord of the Manor would at last find a lady for both the manor and the village. This seemed to stifle conversation and one by one people finished their hot chocolate and made for bed.

The time was after two when I climbed into bed and immediately drifted off to sleep. The next thing I remember was being woken up by the warm feel of another body and hands doing their best to remove my pyjama trousers. I knew instinctively that the person in my bed was Mo and that she was stark naked. I went to say something, but stopped when she placed a finger against my mouth. She then whispered that Father Christmas had been and told her that if she popped into bed with me she could have what she most wanted for Christmas, and so here she was. While my brain told me that my break-up with Mo had been very painful and I should not restart our affair, my body had a different view, one I shared as I gently rolled Mo on to her back.

Afterwards, as we lay side by side with her head cradled into my shoulder, Mo told me that she had missed me and our lovemaking, and that now she felt whole again. I told her I had missed her too and, judging by the welcome she had received from the village, they had missed her too. She then told me that nothing had changed and that she could never marry me, but would like to be my mistress until I found a bride. We talked about many things until we both dozed off to sleep, but later, just as the sun was beginning to rise, we both woke to enjoy each other's bodies.

When I awoke again it was well after seven, and Mo was nowhere to be seen. I immediately got up, showered, shaved and dressed, arriving downstairs shortly before eight.

On reaching downstairs, I could hear life from the small lounge and went in. Katy was playing with a new farmyard she had been given, while Mary looked down, happy and content. For the first time ever, I noticed that Mary was still in her housecoat and presumably her nightdress. I looked at her sympathetically and said, 'What time?' She smiled and said, 'About five thirty.' Mary then suggested that I keep Katy amused while she made some tea. I agreed and, just as Mary got to the door, Pauline arrived, dressed seasonally in a tight white top and red trousers. Mary told her she was just going to make some tea.

When Mary returned Katy was on Pauline's lap busily talking but, by the time we had finished our tea, Katy was deep in sleep with her head against Pauline's breast. Looking up, Pauline told Mary in a whisper that she would look after Katy, until Mary had time to go up and wash and dress. Shortly after Mary had gone up to change, Tom appeared in the doorway, surprised to see his daughter fast asleep on Christmas morning. Pauline quietly explained that Katy had been very late to bed the previous night, had probably not slept much through excitement, had been up since five o'clock, and had simply run out of energy. We both left Pauline and Katy alone as we went into the kitchen to search for some fresh tea. Mary soon joined us, after checking on her granddaughter, and remarked that Pauline was obviously very fond of children and would make a wonderful mother.

The rest of the guests appeared one by one in the breakfast room where Mary was serving cereals, hot buttered muffins and coffee. Pauline was relieved by Katy's mum, who gently laid the sleeping child on the sofa and covered her with a blanket. After breakfast people either went to their rooms or congregated in small groups to talk. I crept away to my study to try to sort out in my mind my problem of what to do about Mo.

I was deep in thought when there was a knock at the door, and Mo came in closing the door behind her. She asked me how I had slept last night, and I told her that I had imagined that a beautiful naked girl had come into my bed and had her evil way with me, but it must have been a dream, because when I awoke she was no where to be seen. Mo smiled and said that she thought it was a clandestine visit by one of Father Christmas's little helpers. Mo then said that I looked tired and still had time for a rest before we all left for lunch.

Mary rang the dinner gong in the large dining room to summon all to a session of present opening. Ted had brought all the presents from round the tree into the dining room, and little Katy was sorting out who they all belonged to. There was no mistaking who had the biggest pile, as Katy amassed gift after gift. Wendy told her daughter not to open them all now, so that she would have more surprises later on in the day. While Pauline and Mo had brought their presents down from their room, I noticed that the baby doll nightdress I had bought for Mo had strategically been left upstairs by her bed. Watching Katy excitedly opening her presents, and the laughter that greeted each new surprise, reinforced my wish to settle down and have a family. Mo looked on as well, and then looked back at me, and I swear at that moment she could read my thoughts.

At twelve thirty we all piled into cars for the short drive to the village pub. Inside the dining room the top table stood laid ready for lunch. While Ted and Tom organised drinks for everyone, George, our host at the pub, took me to one side and asked me to make a very special announcement during lunch, which I readily agreed to do. Therefore, just as the remains of the starters were being removed, I tapped my spoon on the table and asked for quiet. I began by wishing everyone a very happy day, especially happy for a couple in the room who had now agreed to announce their engagement. There was at this a notable hush, especially from my guests. I went on to say that it gave me great pleasure to let everyone in the room know of the engagement of Roger and Lynn on table six. The couple, urged on by me, stood to huge applause, during which time they were presented with a bottle of champagne. I sat down, hearing Mo under her breath call me a most unkind name.

Lunch went on for some hours and it was at least four thirty before we all arrived back at the hall. Mary announced that a traditional Christmas Day tea would be served at eight o'clock. Virtually everyone headed for their rooms, except Tom and Wendy, who announced that they were going for a walk. Pauline asked if she could join them, and they all left the hall together. I went up to my room for a rest, and was surprised to find Mo following me. When we were both in my private sitting room and the door was closed, I asked Mo what was wrong. She smiled and said, 'You know what is wrong – that speech you made at lunch. I nearly passed out when I started to think what you were about to announce, and I was not the only one.'

'Really,' I said, 'all I was doing was announcing a long-awaited engagement in the village, and what can be wrong with that?'

She clenched her fists and said, 'I will deal with you later,' and left the room to recharge her batteries. I then tried to take a nap, but was constantly bothered by Mo's advances and my forthcoming tryst with Sandy. I also knew that I would need to be gentle with Mo who, although she was still refusing to marry me, was becoming more and more in love with me.

The traditional Christmas Day supper laid out in the dining room would have fed a regiment, and consisted of cold meats, salad and pickles, followed by fruit and cream, sherry trifle or raspberry pie and custard, after which one was expected to have a big slice of either Christmas cake or chocolate gateau. Needless to say after the enormous lunch we had all had at the pub only hours before, appetites for more food were poor. Once everyone had finished, the girls helped Mary to clear away.

The men all retired to the lounge, where Ted produced several crates of beer together with pint tankards. For the next two hours, we talked about life, the economic situation of the country and our individual hopes for the future, while at the same time consuming a lot of beer. Tom and Ted were both seasoned beer drinkers and did not seem affected at all, but Tom's father-in-law started to say the most incredible things in a slurred voice, and was taken up to bed by Tom and Ted. Hearing the sound of loud voices, Mo appeared to see what the matter was. I told her that Wendy's father had had too much to drink and had been taken to bed. Mo looked at me and told me how tired and old I looked, and said that maybe I should call it a day. I agreed that I did feel exhausted and had done for some time, and perhaps she was right. I rose from my chair and unsteadily made towards the stairs, closely followed by Mo. When we got into my bedroom, Mo helped me to undress and get into bed, wishing me a good night and turning off the light.

I must have slept well, because the next thing I remembered was Mo's voice telling me it was nearly eight o'clock and time for breakfast. I swung my legs over the bed and made my way to the bathroom. Once showered and shaved, I returned to the bedroom to find Mo still sitting on the bed. As I dressed she told me that she was concerned about my health, and about overwork. She told me that, during the night, she had climbed into my bed and cuddled up to me with her naked body, but in spite of her pleas nothing would wake me from my deep sleep. I apologised to Mo for being so disappointing, and said I would make it up to her. She said that it was not my fault as I had obviously needed that sleep.

We both went down to breakfast to find only Mary, Pauline, Wendy and Katy there. Mary explained that Tom and Ted had risen early and had decided to join a Boxing Day shoot at a nearby farm. Wendy's father had been taken ill overnight and his wife was upstairs tending to him.

Mary told us all that the extra staff I had hired to assist Mary with the Boxing Day tea would arrive at one o'clock, and that lunch would be served at twelve o'clock.

Mo suggested that, since there were no plans for the morning, she would make a start on estimates for the new offices below stairs. Pauline asked if she could help and so all three of us disappeared down the stairs that led to the old servants' quarters. Mo had decided that the best site for the offices would be the four rooms furthest from the kitchen. With Pauline's help, they measured walls, floors and ceilings, Mo noting carefully the various measurements and details of work required. Mo suggested that instead of trying to extend the current heating system, which was connected only upstairs, we should go for slimline electric fires fastened to the walls, connected to a new, separate meter. The dark room with no natural light was chosen as the filing room, where strong fluorescent lights would be fitted. The old staff toilets would be refitted, and a more pleasant colour scheme used.

Mo then excused herself in order to get some carpet samples, colour charts and curtain samples. While she was gone, Pauline asked me whether I was really all right, as the other women had noticed my tiredness. I assured her that after a good night's sleep I was recovered.

Mo returned with the samples, and for half an hour discussed the colour schemes to be employed, finally settling on oatmeal-colour carpets throughout and magnolia for the walls, complemented with bright curtains. The work was interrupted by Wendy, who had suddenly appeared downstairs, reminding us that it was time for lunch. We therefore all trooped upstairs to the dining room, to find steak and kidney pie and fresh vegetables followed by syrup pudding and cream. Pauline remarked that, if she lived at the manor permanently, she would be the size of a house. Wendy agreed, and told us that she had already had to loosen her skirt. Mary asked whether it was the good food that had put on the weight or whether there was another reason, at which everyone laughed.

Once everything was put away after lunch, most people went to their rooms to get ready for the afternoon tea party. Having changed and gone down to the study, I was suddenly aware of Mary standing at the doorway. I asked her to come in and tell me what was wrong. She said there was no problem, to the contrary, and she told me that I had made her the luckiest person in the world by having her family for Christmas. I told her that I had enjoyed Christmas as well, and that I considered Tom, Wendy and especially Katy as my family. I told her that she and Ted had in many ways been my mum and dad during my early years and both of them would always remain very important to me. Mary then excused herself, telling me the early guests would soon be arriving.

By two thirty the main dining room and lounge were filled with people talking in small groups. Sandy and her mum and dad arrived just before three, and were greeted by Ted as long-lost family, hugging each other and all looking very happy. Sandy circulated until we found ourselves alone in the corner of the room. 'All set for Thursday?' I asked, and she nodded. I then told her I would meet the ten o'clock train from Colchester at Liverpool Street.

Sandy blushed when I asked her if she was still sure, to which she replied, 'As sure as I can be.' I then took her to meet Mo and

Pauline, and was glad I had told Sandy of my relationship with Mo and how she had turned down my proposal before splitting up, and of Pauline's crush on me. The girls seemed to get on like a house on fire and I left them together while I continued to circulate. Prompt at four, Mary rang the gong, telling everyone it was time to eat. Sandy and her parents were first to leave the party at five o'clock, in order to get home in time to open the pub. The rest of the great and good of the village made their goodbyes shortly after and were all gone by six o'clock.

That left my guests and the Gloworm crowd to continue partying. Suzie and her mother were in deep discussion with Mo, and Pauline was talking to Peter and his wife. Ted, Wendy and Tom were sitting in the corner each taking it in turns to play with Katy. Suddenly I heard Peter's voice behind me asking for a quiet word. I suggested we went to my study, where it would be quieter.

Once we were comfortably settled, Peter came right to the point. Lily Estates had recently redecorated a small three-bedroomed semi-detached house not far from the Colchester depot. According to Pauline, the house would be put up for sale after Christmas, and he would like to buy it. I asked him how much Pauline was asking for the property to which Peter replied, 'Ten grand.' He went on to explain that his wife's aunt had recently died, leaving her £5,000. He told me that over the years he had ducked and dived, dealing with all sorts of commodities. As a result he had amassed £3,500 in cash, which for various reasons had not been declared for tax. In the circumstances he did not want to go for a mortgage in case they asked him where he got his money. Trying to shorten what was becoming an embarrassing tale for him, I simply said, 'So you need a loan of fifteen hundred pounds?'

'Yes.' he replied.

'For how long?' I asked, to which he replied that he could manage £50 per month. I then shook his hand and told him he had just bought himself a house. He thanked me, and said he would go and tell his wife that they finally owned their own place.

As he left, I asked him to send Pauline in. When I told her of the deal, she simply smiled and said that I was playing fairy godmother again in order to make Peter's dream come true, and what a lovely late Christmas present it was. She then told me she was leaving after lunch the next day, as on Friday she was manning one of the offices, but that she would return on New Year's Eve. However, before she left she wanted to thank me for one of the best Christmas's she had had for years. She also told me that since our little talk on that fateful November weekend, life had got better, and people responded to her more positively. She said, 'I did need a short sharp shock, and will always remember it.'

I told her that I was not the only one to notice the change in her and that I was now proud of her. She thanked me again and left. That night at dinner I proposed a toast to Peter and his wife and their new home.

Later that night in bed, as Mo lay in my arms, she started to tell me how much she had enjoyed Christmas with me. She told me, however, that watching me as I played with Katy told her that one day I would settle down and have a family of my own, and that as a consequence she would lose me. I told her that, after watching the two sets of grandparents watching their grandchild growing up, I had a better insight to how my mother was feeling at my failure to find a suitable wife. I then told Mo that there was an easy answer to both her and my mother's worries, and that was to marry me. Mo hung on tight and told me that, if only that were possible, she would be the happiest girl in the world, but that it just wasn't to be.

The next morning, after breakfast, Mo and Pauline took Ted below stairs to get his approval to the refurbishment of both the gun and box rooms, and the fitting of new stairs down to the wine cellar. They all appeared at lunch looking proud of themselves, having reached total agreement over the alterations. Pauline left after lunch, but not before arranging to meet Mo at the new shop in Colchester to arrange the necessary work. Watching Pauline as she drove away, Mo commented on the change that had come over her. Pauline told Mo that I had had a big hand in bringing about the change, but did not say what. I smiled and said that Pauline did have a problem, but that I had helped her get to the bottom of it. Mo begged to know all the facts but I told her no, as when she had too much to drink she could not keep a secret. She went red and asked me how I had found out. When I told her what both Suzie and Pauline had related, she nearly burst into tears and asked to be forgiven.

New Year's Eve was a real family occasion, with two girls from the village helping Mary to lay on a superb dinner. Toasts were proposed to me as host, to Mary for the food, and to the New Year. Since my visitors would all be leaving the following day, my final toast at midnight was for a safe journey to all.

I travelled to London on that New Year's Day, having said farewell to my guests. I had told Ted and Mary that I would not be home till Sunday evening, and that they should take some time off to recharge their batteries after the onslaught of the family. Mo said that once she had put the house back to rights they both would have a few days' rest. Mo took me to the station and, as we sat in the car in the station car park, Mo leaned over and kissed me. She told me that she had had a wonderful Christmas and would miss me terribly. I told her I would see her on the following Monday, and maybe we would have lunch together.

I spent that night at my parents' home to ensure that everything was ready for their return from Scotland the following weekend. I asked the chauffeur to take me and my case to the office and so arrived early.

Mike was already at his desk, looking through the notes and papers I had set aside for him while he was away. 'Morning, Mike,' I said, and he looked up, rose from his chair and greeted me as a long-lost brother. I asked him how things were in the USA, to which he replied, 'Fine,' and then as an afterthought remarked that his mum and dad appeared to have aged. I told him that, if you do not see someone on a regular basis, when you do see them you notice any change.

He told me of his visit to our American office and how worried the business world was at the state of the British economy. 'Problem is, they are worried that the loss of confidence in the British stock market will transfer to the USA.'

'I can see that,' I replied, 'but the worst may still be to come, now that the railway unions are threatening to disrupt not only the lines from the pithead, but the whole network.'

Mike shook his head and said, 'What do they hope to gain? They got rid of the Labour government in 1970, and now want to destroy the Conservative administration. At least in the States we all know that our unions are run by the Mafia, whose only interest is money and power.'

The phone rang in Mike's office and he picked it up and listened. He then handed me the phone telling me it was a Miss Maureen O'Shea, needing an urgent word. From the start of the conversation it was apparent that Mo was distressed and spitting blood. I told her to slow down and tell me what was wrong. She replied that, in the post that morning, there had been a letter offering a substantial amount for our kitchen and bathroom division. 'The letter makes it clear that Tiny has had a hand in the bid – the treacherous mare, that's why she did not come to any of the Christmas functions. I am now going to ring her up, get her down here and sack her.'

I asked her who else had seen the letter and she told me no one. I told her that was good and to keep it that way. 'I think you should do nothing at present, while I have time to think.' I then instructed her to ring me at twelve o'clock.

I put the phone down, and Mike asked, 'Trouble?' 'Nothing I cannot handle,' I replied. Then Mike brought me up to speed on his trip. He had put the word out that White Gull was thinking of selling its large motel chain when the current rental agreement ended in March. Before he had left the States he had received a tentative offer of £3,000,000 in cash and twenty-four freehold sites in cities around the UK, the remnants of an attempt to set up a chain of American theme restaurants that had gone belly up. I told him that, depending upon their worth, it might be worth considering, and advised him to send the list of sites to Arthur Welsh for investigation and valuing.

Mike was obviously buoyed up by the potential sale as being a sizeable chunk in his plans to take over Bun Industries. I reminded him that, before we revealed our hand, I would get a chance to sound out my Uncle Edward. Mike said, 'I remember, but that is some months away.' He then asked me when my father would return to his office, so that he could update my father on possible changes before my mum and dad began their goodwill trip in mid-February. Mike also informed me of the probable purchase of a firm dealing in futures in New York for $1,000,000.

Mo rang back at midday and appeared to be more composed. I

suggested that she asked Tiny to her office to find out what she knew about the offer. I asked her to stay calm and to ask Tiny to prepare a paper for an emergency board meeting to be held the following Monday. Mo then asked how we would manage future contracts without the division. I told her that we would buy direct from wholesalers or the increasing number of DIY outlets, and do as Mr Lowe had been doing before I arrived, using trusted subcontractors. 'I suggest you ring Peter and take him into your confidence and by Monday have a list of possible discounts and subcontractors ready for the meeting on Monday. Then, as Managing Director, ring the writer of the letter, thank him for his offer, which will be discussed at a special meeting of the board on Monday. Alert the other directors and, if Suzie cannot make it, tell her you understand.' Mo thanked me for my advice and told me she was so happy that I was always there for her.

I spent the afternoon setting out the steps and timetable for a takeover, noting that we would need to put a paper to the board in April, and then our secret would be out. The driver picked me up from the office at five thirty as requested and took me back to my parents' home. I had an early dinner and then retired to ponder on the day's surprises.

I rose early the next morning, and had had breakfast by seven thirty. The driver took me and my suitcase to the office arriving just after eight. I went to my office, where the day's mail was already waiting. I sorted through, and either attached notes to myself or dictated replies into the Dictaphone which sat on a table next to my desk. I then went to see Mike, who was surprised to see me, as he thought I was on holiday. I explained that my friend's train did not arrive till eleven thirty and therefore I had had time to deal with my morning mail. 'Anything special to tell me?' He replied in the negative, just the usual. I had a cup of coffee with him before leaving for the station.

The train from Colchester arrived on time, and from the gate I saw Sandy struggling up the platform with her suitcase. She was dressed in a dark blue suit with a loose tweed coat. Once through the gate, she came into my arms as we exchanged kisses. I asked her if she had had a good journey, to which she replied the train was fine, but there was no restaurant car, 'So I could kill a cup of coffee.' I guided her to a small pub that stood by the Bishopgate entrance, where I knew they served coffee. When we had finished our coffee, I guided Sandy to the taxi rank and on to Brown's Hotel.

I think Sandy was surprised when the taxi stopped and the door was opened by a doorman, in a long coat and top hat, who helped her out. I soon followed, by which time the taxi driver had brought the luggage from the compartment next to his seat. I paid off the taxi and then Sandy and I followed the doorman, who carried our cases, to reception. Sandy sat on a chair looking extremely nervous while I completed the formalities. I then turned to her and told her that our room was not quite ready and that the clerk would arrange for our luggage to be taken to our room and the key delivered to our table in the dining room. Neither of us seemed to have much appetite and therefore both chose light meals. The clerk, true to his word, delivered the key to our table just as we were served coffee.

After lunch I guided Sandy to the lift and up to our room. The room was spacious with a large bed and two comfortable chairs and a television. Once the door was closed, I drew Sandy into my arms and began kissing her. She looked into my eyes and asked me to wait until bedtime before starting to make love. I told her to take as much time as she needed. We hastily unpacked and then caught a taxi to Bond Street, where we spent three happy hours window shopping and browsing. We arrived back at the hotel about half past five, and went straight to our room. Sandy made some coffee while I removed my shoes and trousers, before stretching out on the bed. To my surprise I was soon joined by Sandy, who had also removed her shoes and skirt. Later on, we both washed and dressed and made our way to a little Italian restaurant, not five minutes walk from the hotel and highly recommended by our taxi driver.

It was ten thirty before we arrived back in our room, where I waited for Sandy to make the first advance. Instead of coming into my arms as expected, she turned and told me she was going to get ready for bed and promptly disappeared into the bathroom. When she reappeared she was wearing the nightdress and negligee that I had given her for Christmas, and she asked if I approved. I told her she looked lovely, and she smiled, slowly removing the negligee and climbing into bed. Trying not to alarm her, I went and also changed in the bathroom, appearing in silk pyjama bottoms. I put my clothes on one of the chairs and climbed into bed next to her. As I gently pulled her towards me, she asked me if I minded switching the light out before I started making love to her. Sandy was very tense and nervous at first, but many minutes of caressing, cuddling and kissing, as well as utilising techniques taught to me all those years ago by Billie-Jo, brought its rewards. Her nightdress soon joined my pyjama bottoms on the floor by the bed, while her body welcomed me as its new lover.

Later, as we lay naked in each other's arms, I asked if she was all right, to which she replied, 'Extremely happy. I did not know it could be such a wonderful experience.' Gradually, we both drifted off to sleep. The next morning I awoke as usual at seven o'clock, crept out of bed and made for the bathroom. When I returned, Sandy was awake and sitting up in bed, her lovely breasts peeking above the bedclothes. I asked whether she had slept well, and how she was. She smiled and replied, 'In a minute, darling, but now I need to go to the bathroom.' She slipped naked out of bed, and made her way to the bathroom while I admired her sheer beauty. When she returned, she got back into bed, begging me to resume where we had left off the previous night.

The next two days were spent merely enjoying each other's company, and learning how much we had in common. On the Sunday morning, the last day of our holiday, as we lay in each others arms, Sandy told me that before the past three days she had felt empty inside and unable to think about the future. Now, because of me, she felt she could look at life afresh, able to face the future with both help and expectation.

After breakfast we travelled back to Colchester, arriving just after midday. I asked her what she wanted to do for lunch, and she told me, 'Go back to your house, find a snack from the freezer, and then spend the rest of the afternoon in bed until I have to go home before six.' And that's what we did.

I was at the Gloworm offices early, hoping to have a word with Mo before the meeting. However, when I arrived Suzie was in deep conversation with Mo, and I did not wish to interrupt. The meeting started promptly at nine, with Mo taking the chair. She outlined the purpose of the meeting and invited Tiny, as the director responsible, to outline the advantages and disadvantages, as she saw it, of accepting the offer. Tiny began by outlining the reason behind the bid, and the possibility that, if we did not accept the offer, we might face the firm making the bid setting up in Harwich as direct competition. Should this happen, we could not compete with the prices a manufacturer could offer selling direct to the public. The bid therefore offered Gloworm the chance to sell the business at a vast profit, which would not be the case if we closed later as a result of competition.

Peter asked why Harwich and not Colchester or Chelmsford – after all, Harwich was a relatively small market. Tiny explained that they had liked our operation, the speed at which the business had grown and its profitability. Pauline asked on what they had based their figures on, as no major company would have gone into a new enterprise blind. Tiny started to cry, as Mo accused her of treachery and dishonesty to the company. Tiny then broke down altogether, blubbering that she only had a few years left to work before she would need to look after her mum full time, and that she had to take every opportunity to advance her prospects as best she could. Mo continued her tirade, accusing Tiny of being in bed with the firm.

I then stepped in and asked what Tiny had been offered as an inducement to betray the company. She told the meeting that she had been offered an area manager's job, and would be setting up similar outlets in Ipswich, Colchester and Chelmsford. All the existing staff had also been offered three-year rolling contracts, which she had urged them all to accept.

I asked Tiny to wait in my office while we made a decision. I began by reminding everybody that, before I had arrived on the scene, the company had worked quite successfully with sub-contractors providing the plumbing and electrical services, and in my opinion, if necessary, could do so again. Mo told the meeting that she had already identified two such companies willing to team up with us. Peter then reported on his investigations regarding suppliers and the level of discounts that might be expected. I summed up the options that appeared to be open to us: either stay and fight, probably losing our staff to the new competitor, or accept what was after all a generous offer, providing customers with kitchen and bathroom services, albeit in a slightly different way.

Mo then asked for a vote on the matter and found a unanimous vote to accept the offer. I called Tiny in and told her of the decision to sell. She could stay till the takeover of the business, but could not stay as a director. She whispered her thanks and left.

Suzie took the opportunity to tell the board about the White Gull invitation to tender the work needing to be done and the timescale. She asked the board if Mo could be released from her duties for two days a week over the next two months or so. I agreed that my two days at Gloworm would coincide in future with Mo's absences. Peter and Pauline both offered to cover the office should the need arise. Mo updated the directors of the progress towards the various moves made necessary by the sale of the factory, with a promise that everything would be ready by the third week in March.

Following the meeting, Suzie and Mo came into my office to discuss expenses in respect of the tender, mainly concerning accommodation in London for both Suzie and Mo until Suzie's flat was completed early in April. Suzie had found a comfortable and inexpensive hotel which I agreed they could both use while preparing the White Gull tender. Just as they were leaving, I asked Mo whether the launch of the Bun project to the press was still set for the third week in January, and was told yes. 'Since I and two of my directors will be there, I do hope that they will present a first-class image,' I said.

Suzie said, 'In what way?'

I smiled and said, 'I think that a shopping trip on the company might be a good idea.' This suggestion was taken up without argument.

On the Tuesday evening, Sandy arrived at my Colchester house, clutching a bag of fish and chips, telling me that she did not intend to waste a minute of our precious time together.

However, she had not yet confided in her parents about her new affair, and therefore would not stay the night.

The next three days I spent working at the offices of White Gull, in an attempt to learn as much about the company as possible while at the same time learning the skills of top management from Mike, who had already been in post twenty-five per cent of his secondment period. I kept asking myself whether, when the time came, I would be ready to take over from Mike, and just what sort of Chief Executive I would make. My reputation up to then had been of a lucky, well-meaning manager, always ready to put his staff before himself, but did I have the hardness or force of character to head up one of Britain's biggest companies? The answer, I concluded, would come in the fullness of time, but what if I failed? I was also worried about Gloworm, and although I had confidence in Mo, she had lost the plot over the kitchen and bathroom sale, letting her feelings interfere with her judgement. Would she be ready when I had to leave her in sole charge?

That night and the following two nights I spent in the company of my extended family. They all told me of the fun and happiness shared by them all during their stay in Scotland. I in turn told them of my family Christmas with Mary and her family, particularly little Katy. My mother was clearly pleased that Mary and Ted had been able to provide a venue at the hall, where they all could come together. I also told them of the whole family's enjoyment at taking part in the various village celebrations. Uncle Edward remarked that it was good that in such a short time I had obviously established myself in the eyes of the village as Lord of the Manor.

After dinner on that first night Uncle Edward, my father and I had withdrawn to my father's study both to take coffee and talk. Uncle Edward was becoming increasingly alarmed by the economic state of the country and feared it could even get worse. I told him that, while I agreed with him, there were some advantages for him, like going to see the Arsenal on Sunday afternoon, owing to the power emergency. My father remarked that Mike had told him that, together, we were forging a deal that would not only improve profitability in the long run but also increase our core business in the States. I told them that the deals were still in the course of negotiation and it was too early to reveal the full facts of our forward planning. My father went on to say that, in his discussions that morning, Mike had said that I was now an important member of White Gull senior management.

I spent the weekend at the manor, working on the moves and policies required by Gloworm to protect its future. Monday and Tuesday I spent checking our progress on all our jobs and preparing a tender for another local contract, from figures prepared the previous week by Mo. Tuesday night I spent with Sandy, making love and discussing the future.

The day of the big Bun residence launch was a clear, cold but fine day. In keeping with my father and Uncle Edward, I wore a grey morning suit to give an air of aristocratic well-being. When we arrived, we were not surprised at the number of press and photographers, but had not expected several television outfits. The house itself had been redecorated superbly and Auntie Flossie was enjoying centre stage. Suzie was taking small groups round the house while Mo fielded questions on Gloworm. When we entered the main hall, we found ourselves drawing an audience, Lord Bun as the owner, my father and mother as leading lights in the social world, and me as chairman of Gloworm.

Lunch was served by the caterers at one o'clock and the press fell on the food like a pack of locusts. Once the food was finished along with the wine, the press and other distinguished guests seemed to fade away until, by three o'clock, our party were the only ones left. Suzie and Mo were ensuring that the caterers cleared away properly and that the room was returned to its previous condition.

That night Lady Bun hosted dinner at my parents' house to which both Mo and Suzie were invited. The whole day was judged to have been a complete success, with all the main magazines and periodicals being represented. Suzie remarked that we had done all we could and it was time now for the critics to pass judgement. Mo had not been to the London house before and so after dinner I gave her the grand tour. She remarked how exquisite everything was, and how lucky my parents were to be living in such a house, but her mood soon changed when we reached my bedroom and she had closed the door. 'George,' she told me, coming into my arms, 'you are a naughty boy for not coming to see your mistress.' I told her I was sorry, but that she knew how difficult things had been lately, with her in London while I was in Harwich and vice versa. 'I miss you so much,' she replied, 'and must see you soon. How about staying at mine the weekend after next?' – a suggestion I said I would comply with.

The following weekend I went to the talent contest at the pub on the Sunday, arranging to meet Sandy the following Tuesday, as usual. I must admit that I was more than a little guilty at sleeping with two females at the same time, but did not know how to stop doing so without offending either one. I need not have worried because, on the Tuesday, while I was lying in Sandy's arms after lovemaking, she told me that she had been offered a new start with friends of her parents, doing reception and bar work at their hotel in Yorkshire, and that the following Tuesday would be the last time we could be together for some time. I asked her, why now, to which she replied, 'You gave me the courage to face a new future with renewed hope, something I will never forget. I also feel that, if I stay, I will fall in love with you and, like Mo, I know there is no future in that but heartache. Mum and Dad are making the Sunday talent contest a farewell party, and we all hope you will be able to come.'

The next three days I spent in London. The sale of the freehold sites was proceeding well and that, coupled with news from our own accountants that profits for the year ended 31 December could top £3,000,000, simply brought the possibility of the Bun takeover nearer. I told Mike I had still not found the right moment to speak to Uncle Edward and Father to ascertain whether they would see our intentions as constructive or hostile. I then promised that as soon as Father returned from his goodwill trip to America, early in March, I would raise the matter.

I also desperately wanted to raise the matter secretly with Angela, to gauge her reaction, but did not want to put in a compromising situation.

On the Friday I travelled back to Colchester and on to Mo's for the weekend. When I arrived at about seven, all the lights in her little house were ablaze. She welcomed me at the door with a kiss, and told me dinner would be in about fifteen minutes. She ushered me into the lounge and into a comfortable chair, next to where a freshly poured lager and lime stood on a side table. Dinner was superb and, after coffee, I offered to help her clear away and wash up, but this was refused. Mo told me that there was not much left to do, and wished me to sit back and enjoy a well-earned rest.

We retired early that night and, after a hectic period of love-making lay side by side. Mo asked me whether I could still remember our first time at the Angel Hotel, and I told her that I remembered the occasion as though it were yesterday. Mo then confessed that she had been so nervous, she had nearly changed her mind and asked to be taken home. She then told me she was glad she didn't change her mind, as what had followed both then and now had been so wonderful, it had changed her whole life for the better.

The next morning, we stayed in bed late, enjoying each other's company. Mo was in a loving mood, reminding me of special incidents and memories. Cuddling up to me, she told me of her growing love, not only for the passion, but friendship, companionship and business guidance. She also said that I continually made her feel the luckiest girl in the world, especially now she was still very much part of my life and living in her dream house. I reminded her that at first she had not wanted the house at all. She confessed that it had been such a shock; she had not known what to do or say and in the end had behaved badly. I laughed and reminded her that she nearly paid the price for her bad manners. She said that when she had made the gesture she had hoped that I would not respond, but afterwards wondered whether I was a mouse or a man, when it came to women.

'And now,' I asked, 'have I come up to standard?'

She coloured up and said, 'Whenever we have had to face a tough decision, you have proved more than a man, especially as now I am reliably informed that crossing you can have painful consequences.'

That lunchtime we visited her local and had a pub lunch of sausages, onions and mash covered in thick gravy, followed by spotted dick and custard. We returned to her house and sat talking in front of her gas log fire. At teatime Mo produced hot buttered crumpets and good Yorkshire tea. As we munched on our crumpets, I told Mo that, had she accepted my proposal the Christmas before last, we would probably be taking tea in the library, an old married couple.

Mo smiled and replied, 'With me heavily pregnant.'

'That wouldn't have been so bad,' I responded.

Seeing that her previous comment had troubled me, she then told me quietly that if I wanted her to, she would have my child like a shot, and might already have had one, but for my Victorian attitude of marriage before having a family. I stood up, drew her to me and gently kissed her, a kiss which she returned, asking me to take her to bed.

Leaving her drive that Sunday afternoon, I realised how much I still loved Mo, and the heartache I would suffer if we continued with an affair.

That night the party was in full swing when I entered the pub. Sandy was the star of the gathering, and welcomed me to her leaving do. When the party finished, and everybody gone, I took her in my arms and wished her all the luck in the world. She asked me if she could write to me once she was settled and whether maybe, if I was in the area, I could go and visit her. I said I would if I could and would miss her terribly. I then turned, leaving Sandy behind and closing another chapter in my life.

Death and Destruction

Those first two weeks in February were extremely busy, as I tried to balance my work with White Gull as well as assisting Suzie and Mo to prepare the large White Gull tender, which was due to be submitted by the last day of March. Once I appreciated the size of the task I had placed before them I realised that the project needed a base. I persuaded Father to let Suzie and Mo use the twin bedroom suite directly above the suite I was using. I had been given one of the new wings of the house, in fact the wing formally occupied by Uncle Cecil's daughter. She had been in the habit of having girl friends stay for the weekend and therefore the two guest rooms in the wing were furnished with twin, rather than double beds. Each guest room had its own sitting room with soft furnishings and a writing table. Two summer tables and chairs borrowed from the garden store soon turned the rooms into a perfect base for the project. Suzie stayed all week, and was joined by Mo for three days a week. I in turn spent three days a week at White Gull, spending the other two days and most evenings, including weekends, costing the mountain of schedules provided by Suzie and Mo after trips to various locations. Sometimes, after supper, Angela would join me in my room and help to cost the various sheets. The team was joined in early February by Julian, a talented young artist Suzie had met in a coffee bar.

Therefore the wing of the house that I had been allocated by my parents became a daily hive of industry.

Meanwhile at White Gull the continuing depressing economic situation dominated most business conversations. Then in early February, in the middle of the worst power restrictions the country had ever known, the miners voted overwhelmingly for an all-out strike, knowing that such action would bring not only the country but the Government to its knees. The Government responded, to everyone's surprise, by announcing a snap general election, to settle just who was running the country: the elected government or the unions.

Business practices were also under intense scrutiny, as those involved in the local authority bribery scandal known as the Poulson affair were finally sent to jail. Mike and I found ourselves busy drafting codes of conduct in respect of the company's dealings, not only with government departments, local authorities and councils, but also customers in general. Because of my father's absence, due to his trip to America, the quarterly board meeting was put back to mid-April, thereby pulling off decisions about new codes of conduct. Mike was concerned at the delay, especially with the news focus on big business, and got me to agree to the issue of the new codes of contact immediately rather than waiting for approval by the board. Mike also reminded me of my promise to sound out the family on the question of the Bun takeover, as soon as my father returned from his trip to the States in early March.

Looking back, the transfer of operations to my parents' house usually meant more people at dinner than normal, which incidentally pleased my mother. I therefore saw more of my parents than would otherwise have been the case, something I would cherish in the dark weeks to come.

Early one morning I met Angela going into breakfast, and noticed that she had been crying. I naturally asked why, to which she replied, 'Have you not listened to the news bulletin this morning?' I told her I had not listened to either the radio or television that morning as I had been late up. She then told me of the carnage on the M62, where a coach load of soldiers and their wives had been blown up with a huge loss of life. I told her that it was a black day, not only for the army, but for everyone in the country.

On the second Thursday in February, Suzie announced that all the costing had now been completed; there were photographs and sketches to be mounted, and an introduction, additional comments and various pages of index still to be written. On current progress, Suzie thought that the completed tender could be delivered to the White Gull offices, at the end of the third week in March. She thanked everyone for their assistance. Later that day I found myself alone with Suzie, and I asked her how she was. She told me that she was fine, especially with the tender. She also went on to say that, from the early press releases, the Bun restoration had been received well, but it would be the glossy magazines, when they appeared in March, that would seal her fate one way or another.

She then told me that she was very hopeful of the tender being accepted, and I asked her why. 'First,' she said, 'the tender is a first-class document, thanks to everybody's help. Second, without your advanced information, we would not have been able to finish the tender on time. That, in my opinion, will exempt the smaller design companies, leaving the big boys left in the race, and they all have large overhead rates.' I told her she was a clever girl and that I was really proud of her. She smiled and squeezed my hand, and asked whether she had been forgiven for her flight from the bedroom, and I told her there was nothing to forgive.

That night I went with my parents to the airport, to see them off to America. I remember the last words I said to them, and they were, 'Look after yourselves.'

I went into White Gull on the Friday to catch up on two days' post. Later that morning I met with Mike, who was interested in hearing my opinion regarding the forthcoming general election, and I told him that I thought that there would be a return to Labour. Mike asked why, and I told him that to ask the British people a question to which they all knew the answer was electoral suicide.

I spent the weekend at the manor, catching up on sleep. I also arranged a meeting with Pauline on the Monday morning to discuss a new project, and with Peter on the Tuesday morning, returning to London on the Wednesday morning, or so I thought. The meeting with Pauline went well. She had been working on a scheme to buy a further nine properties, which she knew were coming up for sale during the middle of March. The houses were former rented units, but as in so many cases the owners could neither afford essential repairs nor under the current restrictions raise the rent. In the end such landlords were forced to sell. Current property prices for new houses of the type Pauline was hoping to buy were around £10,000 per unit. However, the houses had been neglected for many years and needed a lot doing to them. Pauline had visited all the properties and, using the techniques Mo had taught Pauline the previous Christmas, had drawn up a priced specification for both purchase and restoration. I congratulated her on a first-class document and told her that I would give her an answer the following day. Pauline was staying for lunch, so we had some time to talk. Pauline was thrilled to be allowed to have one of the offices at the manor, which would be ready by the end of March. 'I see from your notes that you spend a great deal of time with Mo,' I said.

'She is a good friend and teacher, and I am eager to learn as much as I can about Mo's job. Now that Lily Estates is really organised, I can spend more time out of the office.'

I then asked her how things were between her and her parents to which she replied, 'Dad now calls me her twice a week to see if I am all right, but Mother never speaks to me.'

I could see from her eyes that the subject upset her, and tried to change tack, but she was eager to tell me that she had changed her ways, and had done everything possible to bring about a reconciliation between her and her mum, but to no avail. I told her that many people who joined religious sects were often unwilling to face the truth about themselves or their life, and I was sorry.

Once Pauline had gone I settled down in the library, with a book I had been given the previous Christmas but had not had time to read. I did not get very far, as a combination of a warm fire and a tired body soon meant I was asleep in the chair.

After dinner that night I retired to my study to check Pauline's figures and then make a final decision. I also checked that my normal arrangements to send flowers to all the female directors was with the florist in good time. In addition I arranged for flowers to be sent to Sandy at her place of employment. I heard the doorbell, and wondered who could be calling at such a late hour on a Monday night. I heard Ted speaking to the visitors as they made their way to my study. The door opened and in walked Angela and Uncle Edward. I got up and went round the desk to greet them. However, the look on both Uncle Edward's and Angela's faces told me something was terribly wrong.

'What is it?' I asked, grabbing the collar of Uncle Edward's coat. 'Tell me, please.'

Angela suggested going into my study, where we could be seated comfortably, but I did not hear her or respond. Finally, Uncle Edward spoke, saying that he was the bearer of grave news. My mother and father had both been killed in a road accident and he had come as fast as he could to let me know and say how sorry he was.

I could not or would not believe him and began punching him on the chest, saying, 'No, no!' I felt myself falling.

Then the lights seemed to go out, leaving me in a world of terrifying nightmares, bright lights and people speaking far from me.

Patches of blissful oblivion followed, where any return to life seemed confused and unreal. Then things started to untangle and I found myself in a well-lit room, looking up a white ceiling. My eyesight seemed blurred, but through the shadow I could make out a woman's face. Speaking softly, she welcomed me back to the world, telling me I was in hospital following a serious accident. She also asked me to stay as still as I could.

My first real need I felt was a need to pee, and told her I needed a toilet. I felt a hand placing something between my legs and explaining to my confused brain what was required. More by need rather than instinct I followed her advice, finding immediate relief. Having removed the bed bottle before I could spill the contents, she asked me whether there was anything else I required, to which I replied, 'A drink, please.' Using a cleverly constructed container, she let me have several sips of water. I then drifted back to sleep.

The next time I awoke, the room was in natural daylight, and someone was doing something to my left arm. She apologised for waking me, but had to take my blood pressure. She had not left the room for more than five minutes, when a lady in a dark blue uniform appeared at my bedside. 'Good morning, your Lordship,' she said. 'I am Sister Brierly and I and my nurses will be looking after you. I know you must be uncomfortable and we will try to sort that out later. In the meantime, is there anything you need?'

I immediately replied that a cup of tea would be nice. She

looked at a chart at the end of the bed and told me she would arrange that. Five minutes later, my angel in blue returned with a strange-looking cup, which she said contained tea. Gently she lowered the feeding cup, as she called it, to my mouth. The tea was warm, and the taste delicious. When I had finished, she gently wiped my mouth. I tried to detain her, but she told me that doctors were scheduled to visit me and she wanted to get my notes from a trolley in her office. She was right as, five minutes later, Sister appeared in the wake of two gentlemen in white coats. The first doctor introduced himself, informing me that he was a registrar (a kind of consultant in waiting), and the other doctor was a senior house officer (the guy who does most of the routine work and who gets very little of the credit). The registrar then proceeded to check for any nerve damage, thankfully not finding such damage. He inspected my eyes, before checking first the X-rays and then the charts at the foot of the bed. He then turned to me and told me that I was lucky not to have suffered more damage. However, I did have a serious fracture to my skull, which would take some time to repair. The damage to my cervical spine was less problematic, and with rest and a stiff collar the damage would be healed in about six weeks. He then addressed Sister, telling her that I was still suffering concussion and should be kept lying flat and quiet, and he asked for a continuation of the current medication.

About half an hour later, Sister returned carrying a feeding cup filled with coffee. When I had finished the coffee, I asked sister what the doctor had said to her as they left. She thought for a moment and then said that, had my skull fracture been any bigger, they would have had to operate. He had been on duty the night I was admitted and it was he who had decided not to operate, and he hoped his consultant would concur with the decision. 'Lord Earlswood, you are still very sick, and must try and do as you are asked. For the present you are to remain flat, and keep quiet.'

Then she told me the good news: she and one of her nurses were going to make me more comfortable. Seemingly as soon as she had said it, another nurse appeared with a trolley containing a plastic bowl and other washing equipment. True to her word, I was washed from face to toe, had my undershorts exchanged for a pair of silk pyjama bottoms, and the sheets changed without me having to move my position. Even when they wanted to replace the bottom sheet, another nurse was called to help steady my head. When they had finished I thanked them for really making me feel comfortable. Sister then suggested that I should try to get some sleep, an easy request to comply with, as before leaving I had had a dose of the prescribed medication.

The next time I awoke, I sensed someone was sitting next to my bed, and said hello. As the person rose and leaned over me, I knew instinctively that it was Mary.

I asked whether it really was her; she gently replied that it was. I then asked her what day it was and the date, to which she replied that it was Wednesday, the thirteenth of February, and asked why I had asked. I mumbled that I seemed to have lost a day. 'That is because you were very ill, Mr George, and you now need to rest.'

My brain raced as I asked Mary, 'Is it true that Mother and Father are really dead?'

Mary almost cried out that it was true – whatever would they do? Again, using all my strength, I told her we all had to go on, and that this lord would rule his kingdom from his manor, and that I hoped that they would stay by me for many years, as I now felt very lonely.

My mind then raced to Mike and his proposed takeover. I would not be able to warn Uncle Edward and Angela before he made his move, and my complicity in the matter would be revealed. 'Ted?' I said, and he answered he was there. 'I have betrayed the family honour and must make amends without delay,' I continued, but he bade me rest and said not to worry as everything would be all right. 'No!' I cried, the pain racking through my head and back. 'You must get Uncle Edward and Angela here, without delay, please,' I uttered as I slumped back into oblivion.

Concerned by my sudden change in condition, Mary went outside to call a nurse, while Ted held my limp hand. Sister then came into the room, took one look at me, and ushered Ted and Mary from the room. She bent over me and quietly asked whether the pain had increased, to which I replied, 'Yes, but nothing I cannot take.' She went to the locker at the side of my bed and adjusted the morphine pump.

Ted told me afterwards that, when Sister returned to her office, she immediately asked what had caused the increase in tension, and Ted told her what I had said and asked of him. Sister asked whether he had this uncle's number, which he affirmed, and he gave her the notebook he always carried, open at the page containing the number. She rang the number and, having said that it was the hospital, was immediately put through. Sister told him what had transpired, and asked for an assurance that both he and Angela would visit the following day. That being done, Sister sent for some tea, and while waiting quizzed Mary, on what sort of person I was, what were my likes and dislikes. Mary, being Mary, then gave sister my whole life history, including my problems with both Angela and Mo. When Mary had finished, Sister told Mary that, though I appeared to be a workaholic, I would need to slow down considerably for at least six months if I were to recover from my injuries.

By the time I woke up, Sister had gone off duty, and I had missed supper. A nurse entered the room and, seeing me awake, asked if I would like something to eat. When I asked whether this was possible, I was told that the ward kitchen was stacked high with goodies brought in by Mary. I chose a baked egg custard, and of course some tea.

The next morning, after breakfast, some porters arrived to take me and my bed to X-ray. Though the staff in that department were very careful in moving me to the correct position, by the time I returned to the ward I was in great pain, and sweating profusely. The staff nurse on duty gave me pain relief, as well as making me comfortable. When lunch arrived, the staff nurse suggested I eat some minced beef and mashed potato, as she told me the sooner I began to eat, the sooner they could remove the drip.

Uncle Edward and Angela arrived after lunch, shocked that I still looked very ill. Angela thanked me for her Valentine flowers, which she said were lovely. I then told them of my betrayal in working on a takeover proposal without telling them. I also told them that I had decided to tell them both and my father, when he returned from the States. Uncle Edward told me there had in his opinion been no betrayal, as he and Father had discussed the possibility of such a deal many times during the past year. The bid would therefore be welcomed, and would allow my aunt and uncle to do all the things they wanted to do, spurred on by the recent tragedy.

My uncle then said that he would like some assurance as to Angela's future, in the event of such a takeover. I thought for a moment, feeling my strength ebbing, and told Uncle Edward that I would succeed my father as chairman. I asked him to tell Mike that, as soon as the takeover was completed, Angela would become managing director designate and take over from Mike when he returned to the States.

Satisfied with my decision, and seeing me tired, Angela bent and kissed my cheek, saying she would visit again soon, while Uncle Edward shook my hand and told me to take care of myself.

Friday morning dawned clear and bright. Sister was in early, making sure that her empire was shipshape for the consultant's rounds. When time came for breakfast, sister happened to be in my room, and was displeased when we were both informed that the kitchen had sent no porridge up to the ward. I said that I would have cornflakes and hot milk, something I had not had since my early days in the nursery. Sister agreed to feed me and sat down at my bedside. During breakfast I asked her if she was going to remove my drip before the grand tour arrived and was told yes.

The rest of the morning was spent ensuring that I also was shipshape and my bed tidy.

When the great man came, he was followed by a large group of people from different interests. He explained to them my injuries, and pointed out fractures on the X-ray, without giving me a second glance. Finally he did ask me if I was feeling better, before leaving the room. Left alone, I wondered what fate had been decided, and whether I would be let into the secret. Sister came back some time later and told me that the fractures did not appear to be healing, although it was early days. The consultant had therefore decided on a further week's total bed rest and would view things again on the following Friday.

That afternoon Mo came visiting, and was shocked at both my prone position and the colour in my face. She bent over the bed and kissed me, telling me how worried she had been. I told her not to worry as I was assured that I would make a full recovery. I asked her how things at Gloworm were. She told me that the White Gull tender was finished, but that Suzie being Suzie was continuously changing the pictures and diagrams where she thought improvements could be made. Mo also said that Angela was helping her with the introduction and covering letter. The tender would go out by the middle of March. Mo went on to assure me that all the modifications and alterations to new premises would be completed on time.

Since the February glossies had come out, there had been a lot of interest in the company and its design capability. The Harwich office was dealing with the enquiries, and logging them for Suzie to respond to. One large hotel had already asked Suzie and Mo to draw up ideas for a complete refurbishment in 1975. Peter and Pauline were carrying out all the work arising from small enquiries. Therefore Mo concluded that I had nothing to worry about, and she advised me to concentrate on getting well. She also thanked me for the lovely flowers that had arrived on Valentine's Day. Had I been fit, she would have shown me how much they had meant to her. I asked her to get Pauline to bring me in certain house specifications as soon as possible. She smiled knowingly, and told me that I still wanted to be Father Christmas.

The message must have got through as, during visiting that night. Pauline appeared with the information requested. When I told her what I wanted, she immediately showed me a specification for a new acquisition, currently being refurbished and near to the hospital. The suggested rent, I thought, might be a little high, and I therefore reduced it, much to Pauline's surprise, but she agreed that it was a nice gesture of appreciation. I thanked her for what she had done at such a short notice, and she replied that I was the boss. She then asked how long I would be in hospital, and how long the injury would take to heal. I answered 'no' to both questions, but said I hoped it would not be too long. She assured me that her part of Gloworm was working like clockwork, and I should not worry, but instead concentrate on getting better. As she made ready to leave, she bent over the bed and delivered a kiss on my lips, which told me how worried she had been.

Saturday and Sunday were spent considering the future, as well as talking to Mary, Ted and Mo, who took turns in visiting. The night staff were glad of Mary's visit. Having been told that some nights the nurses were so busy, they could not leave the ward, Mary promptly brought in several of her meat pasties to ensure that the night staff were fed, and that I did not starve either.

Sister appeared at my bedside on the Monday morning to check my progress. She told me that she was not happy about my blood pressure, and asked if I was worrying about anything. I told her that there was something I would like to talk to her about, when she had time. I also told her that she did not need to keep addressing me as 'My Lord', George would suffice. I also asked her if she had another name, except Sister Brierly. She blushed and told me it was Jennifer, but only when her nurses were not present.

When coffee time came, Sister appeared with coffee for both of us, and took a seat beside the bed. 'Now, what did you want to talk to me about?' she said.

I told her that I was worried that she looked tired, and that I knew it was difficult to sleep in a busy nurses' home. I then went on to tell her that, among other things, I managed a property company. I handed her the details of a three-bedroomed house that Pauline had selected. Sister read the specification, smiled and asked if the document was for real, to which I answered yes. I then told her that, if she liked it, the property would be ready at the beginning of April. She bent over the bed, kissed my cheek and told me I was the answer to a prayer, and asked when she could view the property. I told her that workmen were currently working there fitting new central heating and a new kitchen, and that she could see it that very afternoon. She thanked me again and finished giving me my coffee before blowing me another kiss as she left the room.

That afternoon Mike appeared with an enormous box of chocolates, sent by his wife. He first asked how I was, and enquired as to the prognosis. He smiled and said that Lord Bun had called him, announcing that a takeover bid, on the terms explained by me, would be accepted as a friendly bid, provided that the board accepted me as their new chairman and Miss Angela Brown as managing director designate. He even offered to contact members of the board to ensure that the takeover bid was agreed, by the issue of new shares, and the appointments agreed with me were confirmed. He then told me that he thought that the takeover could be agreed by both boards in April and be completed by the end of May. 'Whatever you did, George, obviously did the trick,' he said. He then stopped in midstream, and said that though Sister had told him not to refer to the subject, he wanted to express his family's sorrow at my tragic loss, and said that was echoed by all members of the White Gull organisation. I thanked him, and told him I would not report him to Sister.

The following morning Sister came into my room, looking like the cat that had got the cream. I asked what she thought of the house, to which she replied, 'Absolutely wonderful. I took my two friends with me to see the house yesterday afternoon and we all fell in love with it. I rang Pauline as you suggested, confirmed that we would love to rent the house as soon as it was finished. She said that, since painting had not started, we could choose our own colour scheme, and she would get the colour charts to us as soon as possible. George,' she then said, 'you do not know how happy you have made three hard-working sisters,' and she squeezed my hand with great affection. She told me that her friend Mickey wanted to come and thank me herself, 'but I need to keep your blood pressure in check.'

Just before lunch on that Tuesday, Sister entered my room with a man in tow. She told me that I had a visit from the police about my parents' death and asked if I was up to seeing them. I said yes, but asked her to stay in case the constant headache suddenly became worse.

The then told me he was Inspector Ward from police liaison, and he had been approached by his American counterparts to see how soon I could fly to the States to identify the bodies, sign official criminal complaint forms and arrange repatriation. Sister nearly jumped out of her skin, telling the poor Inspector that, here was her patient, extremely ill and unable to move, and he was asking him to fly round the world.

I asked the inspector what timescale the American police had in mind, and he told me three weeks at the maximum. I said that that since today was 20 February, I would need to be in the States at the latest by 12 March. He said, 'Hopefully, yes.' I told him that, if at all possible, I would make that date, and would inform him as soon as arrangements could be made. He left his business card on the locker, took his leave from Sister, and then left the room.

Sister was dumbstruck, and said that I must be mad. I quietly told her that I had realised early in the conversation that I had a duty to bring my father and mother home without delay. What would she do if it were her mother and father? Our conversation was ended prematurely, as the strain brought back one of those terrible headaches that needed urgent medicinal intervention.

The next few days the nursing staff gently brought me back to the stage where I could sit fairly comfortably, albeit with a hard neck collar on. I continued with my conversations, at break times, with Jennifer. Finally, on the Tuesday before my discharge, I said to Jennifer that, if she was so concerned about my trip to America, why didn't she come with me as my nurse? Having ascertained that I was serious, she told me that the hospital authority would probably not sanction such a trip at such short notice. I told her that, nevertheless, I would like her at least to ask. Later that afternoon she returned to say that, to her amazement, the powers that be had not only agreed, but in recognition of my mother's services had granted her three days' compassionate leave. She had also been told that White Gull would pay the cost of seven days. This meant with her days off she would have two weeks away, if needed.

I was finally discharged on the last Thursday of the month – election day, not that I was in any fit state to go to the village polling station to vote. Ted collected me from the hospital, and was handed by Jennifer a complete care plan, she had drawn up at the request of Mary and Mo, together with various pills and a letter to my doctor. Ted gave her in return a large tin of chocolates I had asked him to buy on my behalf as a thank you present.

When I returned home, both Mary and Mo were there to welcome me, and on Jennifer's orders immediately sent me to bed. However, I was home, and ready for the difficult job that lay ahead.

The following morning I awoke to the news that there had been a hung election, with the Liberals holding the balance of power. Edward Heath was holding talks with Jeremy Thorpe about an alliance, against a threat that the unions would bring down any government they did not approve of. The country was still in the grips of a power shortage and nobody wanted to see the union action intensified.

Within days the miners' strike was called off, though a large pay award being promised. Once the picket lines at the coal yards were lifted, power stations regained full capacity, and the three day week, which had caused major disruptions to industry, was called off to everyone's relief.

Since being discharged from hospital, I had been on a strict regime of regular painkillers and lots of rest, as had been prescribed by Jennifer. In spite of this, I still suffered from bad headaches.

Jennifer arrived on Saturday afternoon, as she had two days off. She immediately came to my room to see whether I was resting, as laid down in her care plan. I told her how lovely it was to see her, and how I had really missed her. She smiled, and said how good it was to find me behaving myself. Dinner that night was a real family affair, and I was surprised how soon Jennifer had been welcomed into the household.

On Sunday morning, Jennifer and I had a long conversation about many things – her upbringing, her likes and dislikes and her wishes for the future. She told me that, following one nasty experience with a doctor, she had given up on men and was now married to her career. Like many dedicated nurses before her, she would remain unmarried and become an old maid on her retirement. This, she told me, would not please her mother, who desperately wanted a grandchild. I told her that I knew the feeling well, and that when my mother was alive she wanted not only grandchildren but an heir to the family name. That was something my mother would never see, god rest her soul.

Jennifer confided in me that Mary had told her about my unsuccessful relationships with Mo and Angela, and she asked how it was that we all remained firm friends. I told her that each had good reasons for refusing my proposal, which in no way had interfered with our friendship. Jennifer then asked me about my plans following the funeral and I told her I intended to get fit and then return to my various responsibilities, which would keep me fully occupied. Jennifer asked about an heir, to which I replied that I didn't know, but in any case I could never marry someone who was not my soulmate and friend. I told her of Mo's offer to bear me a child out of wedlock, but that would be against all my principles on children needing to be brought up secure in the knowledge that they had a loving mother and father. Jennifer listened carefully and said that I was a born optimist.

The next four days' newspapers and news bulletins were taken over by a debate as to which bed the Liberal leader, Jeremy Thorpe, would opt for, Labour or Conservatives. Three days later he announced that his party would form an alliance with Labour, with a hope that the country could soon return to normality.

Jennifer left on the Monday morning, arranging to be picked up from the nurses' home on the following Thursday afternoon. During dinner that night, Mary told me that, if Jennifer were to accompany me to all the events listed in the itinerary I had been sent, the poor girl would need some appropriate clothes. Could she take Jennifer shopping, on that Thursday afternoon? Mary saw me smile and knew that I had agreed wholeheartedly with her suggestion.

Therefore when Jennifer arrived at the manor early on Thursday evening she was weighed down with bags and parcels, but looked very happy. She mildly scolded me for agreeing to the shopping trip, but said that she now felt like a princess.

On Saturday morning Mo asked Jennifer to go with her into town, only to find Mo pulling into a hairdressing salon's parking bay, and into the shop where both were booked in for a full hairdressing and manicure experience. During dinner that night Jennifer remarked that, with all her new clothes, hair do and manicure, she felt like a new member of a harem being prepared for her first night with her master. Everybody laughed, and I saw Mo and Mary exchange winks.

Ted delivered us both outside the departures hall at Heathrow airport, shortly before midday on Sunday, 12 March. Jennifer was smartly dressed in her sister's outfit, and looked both smart and efficient. I was dressed in a grey pinstriped suit, covered by a camel-hair coat. The arrival of a shiny black Rolls-Royce outside the departures hall drew the attention of a young policeman patrolling the area. Ted went to seek a trolley, while Jennifer sat waiting to alight with the rear car door open. The interest of the young policeman coincided with the return of Ted, complete with trolley. The young policeman helped Jennifer from the car, and then assisted me to alight also. Jennifer introduced me, then herself, and told the policeman of her mission. Ted had by this time loaded the luggage on to the trolley. The young policeman told Ted he would look after the vehicle while Ted took the luggage into the departure hall. We all thanked him, and were rewarded by a salute.

Once we were checked in, we were taken through the various departure procedures before being shown to the first-class lounge. Jennifer arranged two large orange juices before giving me my four-hour medication. The flight was uneventful.

Unlike the British system, the American one required one to collect one's luggage before passing through customs and immigration control. When our turn came, I presented both passports to the officer at the desk. When asked my business in the United States, I told him my name, rank and that I was entering America for urgent talks with the British Ambassador and the police. This seemed to annoy him and he remarked that lords had no favour in his eyes. He then looked at Jennifer and said, 'Why the broad?' This caused Jennifer to tell him her rank and her position to his lordship. The man seemed to ignore her, looking away. She then asked him whether he had a supervisor and if she could see him. The officer scowled and rang a bell. When the supervisor arrived, Jennifer told the supervisor not only who we were, but that the matter would be reported to the Ambassador the next day. Jennifer then completed her complaint by pointing out that the man was unshaven and his uniform a total disgrace.

The supervisor immediately apologised and let us on our way. Thinking about things after, I realised that the combination of Jennifer's uniform and her totally professional approach seemed to ensure total respect everywhere we went.

We found our driver in the arrivals hall, a young man of about twenty-five, slim, fair-haired, with a winning smile. He told us his name was Jerry and he was to be our driver for the whole of our stay. He then drove us to a very fashionable hotel situated in the centre of the city, called the Sheraton City Squire. Jerry told us that it had been chosen because of its nearness to theatres and restaurants, should we have any spare time. Jerry took our luggage to reception, reminding the clerk that the rooms had been booked by White Gull Enterprises, to which all accounts must be sent. A young bell boy took our cases up to our room, while Jerry escorted us up in the lift. Opening the door to my room, he reminded us that the rooms were booked until the following Saturday morning, and that when we travelled to Philadelphia overnight we could take only the things we needed. The time was still only five o'clock, local time, and Jerry wanted to know whether we would need him any more that day. Jennifer told him that both of us had had a long day, and would not be needing his services. He advised that he would collect us at ten thirty the next day to attend two meetings and a lunch.

Once Jerry had departed, Jennifer suggested that I should take a rest, and began to help me to undress, putting away my clothes. Once I was in bed, she handed me my four-hour medication. She remarked that it would have to be taken with water from the tap, and did I know whether this was safe. I took the keys and showed her the small key to the minibar, which was in the corner of the room. I asked for a lemonade, which I would use to take my tablets with. I reminded her that there was the same facility in her room, if the air conditioning made her thirsty. While I dozed, Jennifer hung up or put away my clothes, before creeping out of the room to attend to her own unpacking and to rest.

Jennifer woke me at ten o'clock, telling me that we should have something to eat before turning in for the night. We ordered from room service a plate of chicken sandwiches, orange juice and coffee, which we ate at the small table, at one end of the room. When we had finished and Jennifer had put the supper remains on to the trolley and placed it outside in the corridor, I took my pyjamas and went to the bathroom to prepare for the night. When I came out I immediately collected my dirty clothes and put them in a laundry bag, completed the slip, sealed the bag, and asked Jennifer to put them outside the door. When she returned, in an attempt to be helpful, I asked her whether her dress was washable or needed dry cleaning. Dry cleaning, I told her went into a different coloured bag. Jennifer seemed lost for words, and I reminded her that she would have the clothes laundered and returned by the following evening.

At the end of the bed was a large television set, and on it a plasticised sign informing guests that they could request adult films after ten o'clock. I innocently asked Jennifer what 'adult films' were, only to be told that she would explain things when I was older. She then gave me my sleeping pill, wished me goodnight and left, switching off the light.

The following morning, I was awakened at eight o'clock by Jennifer, who was immaculately dressed in her blue sister's uniform. She handed me two tablets and a glass of juice. She then enquired how my constant headache was and I told her I was fine. The coffee shop was not crowded when we entered it at nine o'clock. We both ordered breakfast, and were soon being served with ice water and coffee as we waited for our breakfasts to arrive. Jennifer had ordered scrambled eggs on rye bread and I had chosen sausages, eggs and a pile of American pancakes and maple syrup. Jennifer was curious about mixing a cooked breakfast with sweet pancakes. I put two pancakes on her plate and offered her the maple syrup. Suspicious of this new world, Jennifer carefully placed the first piece in her mouth. She then admitted that they were very nice and not as sweet as she had thought. Jerry joined us in the coffee shop at about ten past ten and, knowing we had plenty of time, joined us for coffee.

The meeting with the Ambassador was in the boardroom of White Gull. The acting chief executive officer was already in the boardroom studying some papers. He rose to greet us and shook my hand warmly. I introduced Jennifer, telling him how good a nurse she was. Charles Jefferson was about five-foot-six tall, overweight, with thinning hair. I judged him as being about fifty-five years of age. He began by offering me his sympathies for my sad loss. 'I knew your father well,' he continued, 'and I will miss his visits both to White Gull and my home.' I thanked him, and then took a seat at the large table.

I then heard the door open and I stood up to greet the new arrivals. The two men were both in their forties and both attired in dark grey suits. The senior of the two men came forward to shake hands. He immediately apologised for the fact that the Ambassador had been called out of town, and had entrusted the mission to him. 'I understand your father and my chief went back some,' he said. 'His sad and untimely death, caused much pain to the Ambassador, and he sends you a message of sympathy.'

I thanked him, and then turned to the second embassy man, who was an assistant in the overseas office.

Once we had all been served coffee the meeting began. The embassy officials explained the formalities that needed to be observed and the timescales involved. Once I had carried out identification and signed various documents, the medical examiner would release the bodies for repatriation. Once that formality was completed, the embassy would arrange the rest. Jennifer, who had been silent for the meeting, asked for clarification on the timescale. She was told that the bodies would be in the hands of our chosen local undertaker by Friday, 31 March. I thanked the two embassy men for their assistance, telling them I hoped to meet the Ambassador on my next visit.

I then asked whether the manpower services manager could join us. He soon entered the room, seemingly scared like a chased-after cat. He was introduced as Mr Hilary. I began by stating that whatever I said was very confidential and should not leave the room. I confirmed that the Oregon Motels had been sold, and would be transferred on 31 March. There was an intention to use most of the proceeds on American developments. The two projects notified to Mike in England had both received preliminary approval. The smaller of the two projects would fit in well with our current operations. The company had a very good management team, and achieved a good return on capital employed. 'With this in mind,' I said, 'if we do buy the company, we must try to preserve their management structure as far as possible. The larger project is less clear. Checking back, I find that their board comprises family members only. The company produces a very low return indeed. In recent years they have revalued assets to cover their downturn, and it may be that assets are currently overvalued. They also have a poor cash flow record, which probably has hampered growth. With this in mind, if we do decide to buy the company, we pay only $750,000 as tops, and no family members will be taken over.

'My policy is largely the same as my grandfather's, and I want no redundancies or problems with the unions. White Gull will provide a management team to run this second project, drawn from existing staff.' I then told them that White Gull were in the process of launching a takeover bid for a company with substantial interests in the USA. I told them that I could not tell them the name of the target as the board would not be consulted till April. However, many of the business interests dovetailed with our own. They also appeared to have a strong management team and, once the takeover was completed, probably at the end of June, White Gull would leave them to run things until the vacation period was finished. I would then return, probably with the new managing director designated to oversee the merging of departments.

I then turned to the human resources manager and told him that, by Friday, I wanted a list of all staff reaching retirement age within the next twelve months, as well as a list of junior executives being made ready for the challenges ahead.

Over lunch that day, the chief executive told me that he had been totally unaware of planned changes, which would make White Gull a dominant force in the market.

After lunch, the CEO escorted us to our waiting car, where I presented him with a bottle of Haig Dimple Scotch whisky I had bought on the plane coming over. I thanked him for a most constructive morning, and said that I looked forward to meeting the rest of the managers on Friday morning.

On the way back to the hotel, Jerry asked us what plans we

had for supper. We told him none, to which he replied that, in that case, would we like to join his wife and him at a little family restaurant, near to their home? We both agreed, and looked forward to meeting his wife.

Jennifer wore a pretty blue day dress, which fitted her perfectly. The dress was simple but stylish, indicating attention to detail. She carried a blue clutch bag, slightly paler than the dress, with matching shoes. The dress, if anything, made her look both younger and more relaxed than I had ever seen her.

Jerry picked us up from our hotel at seven thirty, accompanied by Wanda, his wife. She was a small creature, with long, golden flowing hair and a good figure. Jennifer and Wanda seemed to take to each other immediately, and both chose to ride in the back of the car on the way to the restaurant. The meal was very nice and the conversation friendly. However, once the girls had left the table and gone to the powder room, Jerry said, 'Whatever you said this morning has caused C J lots of worry, and he called me in and asked me to notify him of any visits to either industrial or commercial buildings.' I told Jerry not to worry, as I had no intentions of visiting such places this trip.

We arrived back at the hotel at about ten thirty. As we left the car we were presented by Jerry with a small case and suit carrier bearing the White Gull logo. 'They are for tomorrow's journey,' he told me. 'I would like to leave at eight o'clock if possible and stop for breakfast once we are free of city traffic.' We agreed and, as we said good night, I handed Jerry the other bottle of Chivas Regal we had bought on the plane. He was surprised at the gesture, and shook my hand warmly, telling me he would see us at eight sharp the next morning.

When we reached my room, and Jennifer began helping me undress, she suddenly said that Wanda had suggested that I should take her out to dinner, while in New York, to Pharoahs' Restaurant. The restaurant had recently opened and anyone who was anyone now dined there. 'Apparently,' Jennifer went on, 'it is very chic and expensive, and way above Jerry and Wanda's budget. Wouldn't it be wonderful if we could take them there on Wednesday evening?' She smiled.

I immediately went to the phone and rang down to the bell

captain, whose acquaintance I had made when we had first arrived on Sunday. I told him it was Lord Earlswood speaking from room 444, and asked if he could check whether he could arrange a booking for four at Pharoahs Restaurant on Wednesday evening, about eight o'clock. I looked at my watch and saw it was still only ten thirty, early for a restaurant in New York.

The bell captain rang back ten minutes later, telling me that the restaurant had confirmed my booking. I thanked him and told him I would catch up with him later in the week. I turned to Jennifer and told her Cinderella would go to the ball, upon which she suddenly kissed me on the cheek, telling me I was the most caring, considerate and generous man she had ever met. She then told me to hurry up in the bathroom so I could get to bed, where she gave me my sleeping tablet and a drink. She wished me good night and reminded me she would wake me at seven o'clock.

Drifting off to sleep, I thought back on the day, realising how Jennifer seemed to command respect wherever she went, and yet could be the charming friend next door, as she was with Jerry and Wanda. The problem was that her authority seemed to spring both from her professionalism and uniform, and I wondered whether she would ever be willing to give up the profession she so obviously loved.

Jennifer woke me at seven and, while I was getting ready in the bathroom, she was packing my overnight bag and suit carrier. She had also laid out my clothes on the bed. When I appeared from the bathroom in my jockey shorts, with my pyjamas clasped in my hand, she reached out and took them from me. 'I will get these laundered while we are away,' she said with a smile.

We left promptly at eight, stopping for breakfast at a roadside diner at about ten. We then drove on down the freeway, arriving at the outskirts of Philadelphia shortly after two o'clock in the afternoon. Jerry drove into another diner, telling us that the facility we needed was this side of the city, and we had time to eat. The importance and fearfulness of what lay ahead sapped my appetite and I ordered just a sandwich and coffee. Jennifer realised my fears and gently said, 'It will soon be over.'

We arrived at the facility shortly after three and were shown up to a Dr Firth's office on the fourth floor. As we entered the room, a man in a white coat rose and introduced himself as the medical examiner. I shook his hand as he introduced a uniformed policeman as Captain Philips of City Traffic. I in turn introduced Jennifer. Dr Firth began by saying how sorry he was at my terrible loss, a sentiment echoed by the policeman. Dr Firth then thanked us for coming, remarking that he knew I had still not recovered fully from a serious accident. He paused and asked me whether I was ready for the identification, and I nodded. He rose from his desk and bade me follow him. Jennifer went to follow, but a look from the policeman made her understand that she was not required. He gently told her that the doc would look after me and she need not worry.

I was in the viewing room with Dr Firth. My mother's body was brought out first and, as they uncovered her face, I was surprised how serene she looked, as though enjoying a blameless sleep. I was asked if this was my mother and I nodded. I then identified my father's body. Again, he looked as if he had simply fallen asleep. I was asked if this was my father and I nodded again. When the viewing curtains closed, I turned to Dr Firth and asked whether they had suffered much. The good doctor then told me my mother had died instantly, and in my father's case he would not have known much at all. Relieved, I thanked him and he rose to show me out.

Suddenly it hit me that my parents were both dead and I would not see them alive again. I asked Dr Firth if I could have five minutes alone, to which he nodded and left the room. My emotions were suddenly mixed as I wanted to cry, yet my upbringing would not allow me to. I was now Lord Earlswood and must finish this mission in a truly gentlemanly manner.

When I eventually entered the office again, there was a sombre mood prevailing. The medical examiner produced various documents for my signature, and I signed them blindly. The policeman then produced another set of forms, explaining their need, but little went in and I signed them where required. I asked the policeman whether I would have to attend court, to which he replied, no, unless I wanted to. I nodded, and got up to leave. The good doctor said again how sorry he was and handed Jennifer a form. I asked what it was and was told it was the death certificate, which I would need to register the death when I got home. The rest of the documentation would be sent to the British Embassy. I turned, shook hands with both men and left.

I said very little on the way to our hotel and there was a strained silence. When we arrived at the Four Seasons hotel, Jerry checked us in and Jennifer escorted me to my room. She immediately found the minibar and got out an orange juice, which she handed me together with two painkillers. She helped me off with my jacket and trousers, rolling back the bed and helping me in. She asked if I wanted to talk and I said no. I just wanted to sleep. She then hung my suit in the closet and left me alone.

When I awoke it was just after seven and Jennifer was getting out my clothes for the evening. She was dressed in a dark blue dress and jacket, piped in red at the neck and down the jacket. She had matching shoes and a red handbag which lay on the table. The outfit fitted her perfectly and again screamed of style and taste, making her look every bit the lady. I got out of bed and made my way to the bathroom to get ready. When I returned Jennifer looked at me and asked if I was all right. I told her that I still had a headache, but that had been the case since we landed. We met Jerry downstairs and made our way to Bookbinders, probably the most famous restaurant in the whole of the USA. The food was excellent as was the service and we dined on clam chowder, then steak, finishing with their world-famous carrot cake, washed down by a good bottle of Californian red wine. My headache was getting worse by the minute and I was glad when it was time to leave. Jerry had sent for the car from the valet parking desk, but as we walked out into the cold night air my legs began to buckle. I fell into the back of the car, closely followed by Jennifer.

Jerry drove as quickly as he was allowed and arrived at the hotel in no time. He parked outside the door and assisted Jennifer to get me to the lift. By the time we reached my room, Jerry already had the door open, and was helping Jennifer to guide me towards the bed. As they removed my jacket, I suddenly struggled up and made my way to the bathroom where I was very sick into the bowl. By this time I was on my knees, gasping for air as waves of pain hit me. Jennifer passed me a glass of water and told me to rinse out my mouth. Jennifer then began to help me to my feet, when I realised I had a sudden but urgent need to pee. I therefore pulled down my zip, aimed down the pan and urinated, not caring that a woman was standing there holding me up and watching every movement.

Jerry had returned from parking the car and helped Jennifer put me to bed. Jerry was worried and offered to call a doctor, but was stopped by Jennifer. She returned five minutes later with her medical bag and pulled out a phial. She flipped off the top and drew the contents into a syringe, which she then administered into my leg. She turned to Jerry, telling him that that should do the trick. Jerry asked whether I would be fit to travel in the morning, to which Jennifer replied yes, if it killed me. The two agreed to meet in the coffee shop at eight the next morning for breakfast. Jennifer then came back to the bed, checked that I was all right, then turned, switched out the lights and left.

The next morning, Jennifer woke me at seven thirty and asked if I was all right. I told her that, apart from the usual headache and uneasy stomach, I was fine. I then apologised for the previous evening's behaviour and said I hoped that it had not spoilt her evening. She said that that was not necessary, as all last night had proved was that I was still very ill.

The journey back to New York was uneventful, and we reached our hotel at about five thirty. Jerry told us that he had rung his wife again and she was overjoyed at the thought of dining at such a wellknown restaurant.

We met Jerry and his wife in the hotel foyer at seven thirty. Jennifer was wearing the same dress and jacket as she had worn the previous evening, whist Jerry's wife wore a dress of emerald green, the pattern on the bodice marked out by tiny beads. The ladies looked quite wonderful. The restaurant was painted out in gold and blue with Egyptian-type logos on the wall, a tribute, I thought, to the treasures unearthed by Harold Carter, and currently on display at the Metropolitan Museum.

The head waiter showed us to our table, placing the starched white napkin on the ladies' laps. He then turned to me and said how sorry he was to learn of my sad loss, and told me that my parents had dined at the restaurant two days before the accident. He then asked if, as a mark of respect to my parents, I would accept a complimentary bottle of champagne. I thanked him warmly and with a flick of his fingers a waiter appeared with the champagne and four glasses.

While we enjoyed the bubbly, Wanda pointed out various local celebrities and TV stars dining in the restaurant. However, she was a bit embarrassed when the menu arrived and was all in French. Jerry too, I guessed, would be unable to read it. To my surprise Jennifer then began to tell Wanda the various dishes on offer and, taking her lead, did the same for Jerry. When the waiter arrived to take our order Jennifer spoke to him in perfect French, even discussing the wine. I did the same for Jerry. The only difference was that Jerry declined wine as he was driving, and ordered a soda. I also, on Jennifer's instructions, ordered a large orange juice.

The meal was extremely good and we all had a really great time. We were finishing our coffee when a gentleman approached our table. He apologised for disturbing us, but wanted to tell me of his grief at my sad loss. He introduced himself as Walter J Gossman, enterprise executive at the mayor's office. He had known my father well and offered any assistance the mayor's office could offer in my current mission. I thanked him but said that everything was being taken care of by the British Embassy. He said that he was pleased to make my acquaintance and hoped that I would call on him on my next visit.

Reaching the hotel, Wanda remarked that it had been one of the best nights of the year, a sentiment echoed by Jerry. The girls then excused themselves, leaving me alone with Jerry. 'I expect that CJ will want to know where I have been and who I have spoken too,' I said.

'Tomorrow we are free and the company has arranged a sightseeing trip round the city,' said Jerry. I then asked Jerry where we would be taken and he told me in detail our route. I asked him who our biggest competitor was and whether we would pass their building. Jerry told me that we would, as it was in the main business area, not far from the Twin Towers. I handed him the business card from the mayor's office, and said to

Jerry, 'Tell CJ that I met this man, and went to the two buildings I have just been told that I will see, but I haven't said why.'

Jerry said, 'That will keep him guessing and extremely worried.' Jerry then said, 'Can I have the bills you paid last night and tonight, as White Gull wishes to use them as part of a claim for expenses, made necessary by the death of your parents.'

I liked Jerry and therefore handed over the bills as requested. When the girls returned, Jerry reminded us that a tour guide would meet us at the hotel at ten o'clock. Wanda said that she would see Jennifer again on Friday for a shopping trip, and me at the farewell dinner on Friday. The girls then hugged each other and Jennifer went with her back to the car. Jerry and I followed on, during which time I gave Jerry a thousand dollars, and told him that I did not want Jennifer to spend any of her own money on presents and to buy something really nice for herself.

Drifting off to sleep that night, my thoughts were all of Jennifer, how stunning she had looked and how superbly she had dealt with the waiter in his own language. I wondered how many other talents she had, yet to be discovered.

Jennifer woke me at eight o'clock the next morning with my medication, orange juice and coffee. She asked how I felt and I answered that I was feeling fine, spurred on by the fact that instead of her blue sister's uniform she was sporting well-cut cream trousers and a bright red woollen top. I asked her why the change of trim, only to be told that this was a day for playing hooky and enjoying ourselves. I leapt out of the bed making straight for the bathroom. When I returned Jennifer had laid out my corduroy trousers and denim shirt.

We were just finishing breakfast when a thick-set middle-aged woman came in search of us. She introduced herself as Maggie, and said she would be our guide for the day. Picking up our zipper jackets and of course Jennifer's medical bag, we followed Maggie outside to her vehicle. There was a converted van with windows in the side. Behind the driver were two rows of seats, each comprising two comfortable armchairs. Set between our seats was a coolbox containing various types of soda.

The tour began by showing us the main theatres on Broadway, and Fifth Avenue with its expensive and exclusive shops. We then moved to Times Square, Radio City and two large museums. We visited Central Park before leaving the city for the pleasant suburbs. Lunchtime arrived and we drew up at a diner saying, 'All You Can Eat for Three Dollars.' Maggie slid open the doors and told us it was time for us to eat. Jennifer asked whether she was coming too, to which Maggie replied that she did not normally eat with clients. I said 'What's normal about us, anyway?' and asked her to join us. I led the way, buying an additional ticket.

Lunch was both plentiful and surprisingly good. We were just finishing our coffee when a gentleman in a raincoat and felt hat stopped at our table. 'Lord Earlswood?' he said. I got up to find the reason for the intrusion when he told me his name was Jim Webb, and he was a reporter from the *New York Times*. He told me he recognised me from my picture in the paper, and had just come to say how sorry he was at my sad loss. I told him that my visit was to arrange the repatriation of my parents and would appreciate no publicity. The man assured me that he had no intention of writing anything, but just wanted to express his sadness. I shook his hand and told him that I would be back later in the year and that, if he left his business card, I would contact him with a real story. He reached into his pocket and gave me his card before walking away.

Maggie had been transfixed by the conversation and, once the stranger had left, said, 'Are you really a lord?'

I told her that, following my father's death in a road accident, I had indeed become a lord.

She then looked at Jennifer and said, 'You must be Lady Earlswood.' Jennifer smiled and did not answer.

During the afternoon we were taken to a viewing platform to watch large liners coming and going, then on to the business centre to visit the Twin Towers exhibition. Jennifer had asked Maggie where we could eat that night that would be unforgettable, to which Maggie said she would let us know at the end of the tour.

We found it strange that, while we viewed the Twin Towers exhibition on the ground floor, Maggie excused herself and disappeared. We both thought that, having royalty in her cab, as she viewed the peerage, had had an adverse effect on her tummy. Ten minutes later she was back with a broad smile on her face. She asked Jennifer if she knew that right at the top of the Trade Center there was a restaurant. Jennifer shook her head, Maggie said, 'In that case you will be pleased to know you have a reservation for two at eight o'clock.' She went on to say that normally it was difficult to get a reservation at short notice, but when she explained who she had in her cab downstairs, there had been no problem. Maggie took us back to the hotel and I tipped her well. She thanked me and said that she was the proudest tour guide in New York, and all future clients would be told who had ridden in her bus.

Jennifer came to wake me up at seven thirty and gave me a real shock. She was dressed in an elegant black velvet dress which, as with all the clothes Mary had had an influence in buying, fitted perfectly. The dress showed sufficient cleavage to indicate two firm, milky breasts. She had done what I asked and visited the hotel hairdresser while I had rested and now looked wonderful. I lay there admiring the view when Jennifer said, 'I thought that you were taking me to dinner.' With me dressed in my velvet jacket and black trousers, we looked in the mirror like a pair of film stars. Then I remembered that Mary had told me that in the pocket of my briefcase was the finishing part of Jennifer's outfit. I walked over to my briefcase and found a small box. Inside was a large, solid gold pendant, which I placed round Jennifer's neck. She gasped at what I had given her and started to protest, but I simply said, 'Now Cinders can go to the ball.' She fell into my arms and kissed my cheek.

I hardly noticed dinner as I could not believe how pretty Jennifer was out of her uniform. Everyone, including the waiters, was charmed by her, and I noticed envious looks from gentleman at other tables. When we arrived back at our hotel, Jennifer followed me into my room to help me get ready for bed. She had just removed my jacket, when we found ourselves kissing each other. Jennifer returned my kisses and together we were exploring the contours of each others bodies. She sighed as I stroked her bottom and back, and I sought to continue. However, as I began to undo the zip of the dress, she suddenly pulled away. She told me to stop and, as a gentleman, I apologised if I had upset her. She told me there was no need and that she had enjoyed the experience. She then reminded me that, in the morning, I would still be her employer and she my nurse, both of us with professional standards to maintain.

Jennifer began to put my clothes away, when I remembered that Dr Firth had also given me a package. I had barely even acknowledged this at the time but now I asked Jennifer to get it for me from my grey suit pocket. I emptied the packet out on the bed and out fell six rings. The two larger rings were my father's signet rings bearing the family crest, and his wedding ring. The other four rings were my mother's wedding and engagement rings, together with a ring of sapphire and diamonds, and the last the Earlswood ring, worn by every Lady Earlswood for 200 years. The ring was an enormous white diamond set in white diamonds.

Jennifer said, 'We must put them into our room safe for the night.' As she attempted to put them back into the packet I reached over and stopped her, taking out the family ring and trying it on her finger. The ring was far too big, but I hoped to convey the way I was feeling. She took it off, and placed it back into the packet and put the packet into the small safe hidden in the wardrobe.

As I made for the bathroom in my undershorts, there was no disguising the effect that she was having on me, an effect that would last throughout the night.

The next morning Jennifer appeared ready for her shopping trip, dressed in a dark grey Welsh wool two-piece suit. Underneath the jacket she wore a light grey Botany wool jumper. As with all the clothing Mary had persuaded her to buy, it screamed elegance, fashion and style.

When I arrived back from the bathroom Jennifer had got out my clothes and was sitting on the bed. She was clearly deep in thought, and coming back to the present began to speak. She told me that she was sorry about the previous night. She explained that it was not that she wasn't fond of me or attracted to me as a man, but she had not made up her mind about whether she could give up her other love, nursing. Additionally she was concerned that she could not fulfil the role as wife, mother and society person.

She asked me not to rush her, and in any case violent movement was at the time bad for my health.

We were both collected from the coffee shop, Jennifer for shopping and me to a meeting with all the senior managers. The meeting began sharp at eleven o'clock and I began by thanking them all for their loyalty to both my grandfather and my father. I outlined the plans that I had discussed with CJ on the Monday. I also explained the reasoning behind the short-term vacancy freeze. I ended by answering questions as far as I could. We all then moved to a large room where a buffet had been laid out. I sat at a small table at the end of the room and asked those present to come and talk to me if they had worries or concerns. This was extremely successful and I learnt a lot about the current management of White Gull (America).

My last visitor was an older man who introduced himself as head of legal affairs. He had been with the company over forty years and would retire in August. He told me how he had taught my grandfather to play horseshoes when he had first arrived in America, and about the wild parties and drinking sessions they had enjoyed. He told me that, whenever my father was in America, he would always have a meal with him. There were tears in his eyes as he described his feelings on hearing of the accident.

I said to him that I deeply appreciated our short conversation and I would have lunch with him the next time I came to town.

Jerry took me back to the hotel just after three, reminding me that he would pick Jennifer and me up at seven.

I was sleeping when Jennifer appeared, weighed down with packages. She told me I was a naughty but lovable man, and that she had had a wonderful day. I told her that we needed to be ready by seven, and she still had time for a rest.

The executive dinner party was held in CJ's club, and all eyes quickly focused on Jennifer and her black velvet dress. I deliberately kept the conversation off work, but was happy to tell the wives about the Bun House restoration project, which had been featured in one of the American magazines.

The party finished just after ten, and it was only ten thirty when we arrived back at our hotel. I went and sat on the bed and Jennifer pulled up a chair. She was anxious to tell me about her day and the purchases she had made. I asked if she had bought something special for herself and I watched her face turn scarlet. 'Wanda took us to this shop specialising in very sexy garments and persuaded me to buy two sets of underwear, so skimpy I am not sure I will ever wear them.'

'Might catch a cold,' I said, 'better stick to woollen drawers.'

'The girls wanted to know what you were like in bed and when I told them I did not know they both laughed. Wanda then said that, if she had not been married, she would be found outside your door, with her knickers in her handbag.' Jennifer then became serious and asked me whether the last few days had been a dream or reality, and, if it was a dream, she said she did not want to wake up.

The next morning Jerry picked us up at ten to drive to the airport. He had brought Wanda with him and all the way the girls chatted and laughed. Jerry told me of a meeting he had had with CJ the previous afternoon. CJ asked him who he thought would be the new managing director when Mike came home. But instead Jerry told him that he already had a super executive in his own company, a woman named Maureen. CJ then flipped his lid saying not only would she be an outsider but a woman.

We said our goodbyes and went into flight side, visiting the duty-free shop. I handed Jennifer the envelope Wanda had given me containing $500 change from the previous day and told her to buy whatever she liked.

The flight was smooth and comfortable, but the air pressure seemed to worsen my headache. Ted picked us up in the Rolls and I told Jennifer I did not feel well and just wanted to sleep. Ted told her it was probably jet lag and sleep would do me good. However, when we arrived at the manor, I was in pain and sweating. Jennifer and Ted helped me to my room, where at the bedroom door I passed out. Jennifer took charge and had Ted help her to get me undressed and into bed. She then administered one of her injections which relieved the agony I was suffering. She turned to Mary and said that she would sit with me, but was overruled by Mary, who told her she looked exhausted and should go to bed herself. Jennifer did not protest and immediately went to bed. Ted was laughing at Mary's stern order, until he too was told to go and get some sleep.

New Horizons, New Challenges

Dinner that night was a happy occasion. I had been allowed to come downstairs for two hours, dressed in pyjamas and dressing gown. Jennifer had put back on her sister's dress, and looked remarkably refreshed after her long sleep. She then distributed the gifts she had bought in America, fancy tops for the ladies, a padded plaid lumberjack jacket for Ted and a bright red jacket bearing the word 'Redskins' for me. I followed up with large bottles of favourite perfumes for Mary, Mo and Jennifer, and a large bottle of Ted's favourite brandy. Over dinner Jennifer related the high points of the trip, like dinner at Bookbinders, Pharoahs, and our visit to the top floor of the Twin Towers. She also told the girls of the experience of shopping on Fifth Avenue and of the expensive things on display. The mood was so gay that I did not want to disturb it, but knew I must. I told them briefly of the timetable for the return of my parents and told them that I thought that the funeral should be on Friday, 7 April. We then talked about the arrangements that needed to be made, and who was doing what and when.

Dinner was just breaking up when Jennifer told us that she had deeply felt my loss and that had reminded her that it was some months since she had seen her parents. She therefore wondered if I would let her take the next three days off, in order that she could visit them in Birmingham. Mary said that of course she must, and that she and Mo could look after me. Jennifer reminded everyone that my recovery was not yet complete and if they allowed me to overdo things there would be a recurrence of what had transpired early that morning.

Jennifer then asked Ted to drive her back to the nursing home the next morning to collect her car, he but suggested as an alternative that she use the Rover, returned by Tiny, which he had had serviced, polished and valeted. I agreed it was good idea and told Ted where to find a copy of the fleet motor insurance cover note that each driver had to carry in case of accident.

Jennifer came to see how I was at eight o'clock the next morning. Satisfied that I could indeed be left in Mary and Mo's care, she took her leave and kissed me goodbye. Breakfast was brought up on a tray at nine thirty, and only then was I allowed to get up and venture downstairs. I had just got seated in the library when the telephone rang. The call was from Mike, asking me how I was and whether things had been arranged. I told him yes on both points. He then told me he had had a strange telex over the weekend from CJ, accusing me of undermining his authority, talking business with both rivals and the press, as well as intending to appoint a managing director who knew little about the business, was young and inexperienced, was Irish and worst of all a woman.

I told Mike that all I did was to suggest freezing vacancies till the end of September, until all the moves were completed, and to ask for a list of all those people retiring in the next twelve months. The first suggestion was common sense and would reduce the risks of compulsory redundancies later on, and the second was prompted by something one of the old timers had said about working for both my grandfather and father. I had therefore decided to send my personal greetings on the occasion of their retirement.

I then explained that our driver had been told to report everywhere I went and whom I spoke to. The gentlemen from both the press and the mayor's office had introduced themselves in various restaurants to tell me how sorry they were at my sad loss and, as far as competitors were concerned, I had visited both the Ziegler building and the Trade Center as part of my sightseeing tour. I had merely picked up a couple of business cards from reception desks for future reference, and I must have left them in the glovebox.

Mike laughed and told me that it served the old fox right for spying on me. I addressed his concerns about the next managing director, and told him that Jennifer, my nurse, had become friends with Jerry's wife, Wanda. 'Naturally they were very interested in Gloworm and the Bun project, which had been covered in many American house magazines. I can only guess that

Jennifer told them of my reliance on Mo, who you met last summer.'

Mike laughed again, and said that it seemed that it was not only the driver who had faced the third degree treatment. Mike said he would write back to CJ and explain things, but I told him that he could tell him face to face as, 'He intends to take up your wife's offer to come and stay with you and to attend the funeral on 7 April. I detected a small groan as he offered any help I needed with the arrangements.

I then rang Angela and told her the date of the funeral. She told me that Uncle Edward had asked her to take on all the arrangements when a date for the funeral had been fixed. She told me that she had already started preparing a list of people who needed to be informed and would go over it the following weekend. My next call was to the vicar, to make sure the church and graveyard were free that day, and I was told it was. The vicar then made an appointment to see me to discuss the funeral the following Friday morning. The next call was to the undertaker, to update him and ask him whether the date I had selected was convenient, to which he also replied yes. I told him that I or Miss O'Shea would visit him the next week to discuss the arrangements. Mary then arrived with coffee, and was surprised and pleased to see me sitting quietly in my chair.

Meanwhile, as Jennifer later described to me, she was driving into the large drive of her father's five-bedroomed house in Edgbaston. She had not rung to tell her mother she was coming and hoped, as she rang the bell, that her mother was in. Her mother opened the door, and the two women fell into each other's arms. Her mother asked Jennifer why she had not rung, to which Jennifer replied that she had flown in from America only the previous day and it was a spur-of-the-moment decision.

'America,' her mother said, 'holiday. I suppose?' and she was surprised when her daughter told her it was strictly work. 'Never mind,' replied her mother, 'it is so good to see you. Go on through to the kitchen and put on the kettle while I make a couple of telephone calls.'

When her mother returned, the tea was made and the serious

gossip started, beginning with Jennifer's recent trip, her moving out of the nurse's home and her life in general. Her mother then updated Jennifer on the comings and goings of her mother's social set and what her father had been up to. The talking lasted right through a light lunch and afternoon tea, which they took in the lounge.

At just after four, they heard Jennifer's father's key turn in the lock, and her mother went to greet him. He asked who this unexpected house guest was – someone important, judging from the smart Rover parked in the drive. He entered the lounge to find his precious daughter standing in front of him, and the two fell into each other's arms and embraced. Jennifer's father told her how wonderful it was to see her after so many months away.

Her mother then entered the room with a fresh tray of tea. 'Jennifer has only returned from America yesterday,' she said, 'she has been working over there.'

Her father's brow creased, hoping against hope that his little girl had not succumbed to the brain drain of nurses attracted to high salaries and a more exciting life. Jennifer noticed the worried look on her father's face and quickly told him that she had only been escorting a very important patient. Her father asked the circumstances and Jennifer told him about her patient, his condition, the doctor's advice for him not to go and then a compromise, which required him to be escorted by a qualified and experienced orthopaedic nurse.

Her father nodded wisely and asked what was so important that the trip could not be postponed. Jennifer shrugged and told her father that her patient was required for urgent talks with both the British Ambassador and the American police. He whistled and asked Jennifer what the name of this important personage was, but she told him that it was confidential.

They talked together till well past five, when her mother reminded them both that the table at Captain Hook's, a new restaurant that had recently opened in Birmingham, was booked for seven fifteen. Jennifer excused herself and went upstairs for a long hot bath. While she lay totally relaxed in the soapy water, her thoughts went to George, the times they had shared together and the growing fondness she felt for him. Should she tell her mother that she had at last found a man whose smile made life perfect, whose embrace left her weak at the knees and whose kiss set her on fire? No, she thought, patients often fell for their nurse and once she returned to work and out of his life, he would soon forget her.

She waited in her bedroom till she heard her parents both go downstairs. She heard her mother call that it was already seven o'clock and that she should get a move on. That was the moment she chose to make a grand appearance, dressed in her black velvet dress and accessories. Her father gazed in amazement wondering whether this beautiful woman sweeping down the stairs really was his beloved daughter. He told her how beautiful she was as he helped her down the bottom step. Her mother then murmured that her dress must have cost a month's salary, to which Jennifer replied that it was one of the outfits bought for her so that she could accompany her patient to various receptions and dinners.

Leaving the house, Jennifer asked her father if he would like to drive the Rover, an offer which he instantly accepted. Jennifer and her mother sat in the back, her mother marvelling at the soft hide upholstery and the polished wooden dashboard shown up by the courtesy light. Her father stated as he drove to the restaurant how smoothly the car handled, much belter than his Ford.

Dinner with her parents was always a happy occasion, but Jennifer found herself comparing the decor, atmosphere, food and service with the elegant restaurants I had taken her to.

Getting out of the car in her father's driveway she remembered the presents she had brought, which were still in the boot. There had been so much to catch up on that there had been no time to deal with her gifts. She quickly removed the duty-free carrier bag from the boot as her father locked the car and went inside. When they were all in the lounge, Jennifer handed her parents the presents she had brought, a lacy top from one of the top shops in New York, and a large bottle of her mother's favourite perfume. Her father unwrapped a golfing jacket, bearing the name of the best-known courses in America, together with a box of his favourite King Edward cigars. Her mother told her she should not have spent so much money on presents, to which Jennifer replied that they were worth it. She hated lying to her parents, but to tell them George had paid for them would raise too many questions.

The next morning Jennifer and her mother went into Birmingham to do some shopping. Jennifer wore her dark grey two-piece with a woolly jumper. Her mother, having admired the outfit, asked if this was part of the wardrobe bought for her to use on the trip. Jennifer nodded.

Over lunch that day, her mother had asked about boyfriends and was told there was no one. Her mother reminded her that Jennifer would be twenty-six the following May, and by that age her mother was married and Jennifer at school. Jennifer laughed off the mild reprimand, knowing how much her parents wanted grandchildren while they were still young enough to enjoy them.

At three thirty Jennifer parked in the car park in the hospital near to her father's office. His secretary was obviously expecting them and had already prepared a tray ready to make tea. Jennifer greeted her warmly, as she had known her father's secretary for many years. Once tea was finished, Jennifer was directed to the new orthopaedic wing, which had been open for only a few months. Jennifer knocked at sister's door before entering.

The sister had been in charge many years and Jennifer had worked on her ward as a staff nurse. Sister greeted Jennifer like a long-lost relative, looking her up and down, admiring how well Jennifer looked. 'The south must be suiting you, you look marvellous,' the sister said, 'and I do like your suit, it really does look good on you.' Jennifer thanked her, and the sister led the way into the new department. Jennifer enjoyed seeing some of the new high-tech equipment, and asked her friend many questions. As they made their way down the corridor, Jennifer asked Sister if she was still single, to which her friend told her, yes, and at thirty-five years of age there was a shortage of eligible men. Sister then asked about Jennifer's love life, only to be told that, like her, Jennifer was also wedded to the job. Her friend told her that if she wanted to settle down and have children she could not wait too long.

Jennifer spent the next half hour talking to both staff and patients about the new facilities, finding it easy to converse with all. As she took her leave and walked back to her father's office, she found herself thinking that what she had just done was the sort of thing she would be required to undertake if she became Lady Earlswood.

She then was taken for an early meal at the restaurant of the main theatre, where they had tickets for the musical *West Side Story*. While she generally enjoyed anything they did as a family, she found her mind wandering to the terrible decision she would need to make should I ask her to marry me. That night, she tossed and turned as she tried to think things out, quickly realising the pressures Mo had found herself under, which had led to her turning me down, in spite of her deep love for me. Next morning she left for home mid-morning, promising her mother that she would visit again soon.

Back at the manor, things were busy. The basic arrangements for the funeral had been made, but there were still the visits of the vicar and undertaker to face on Thursday afternoon and Friday morning. Mike had sent his first draft on the paper that would put to the board on acquisitions and the takeover. The paper, although short and factual, needed substance, and I had spent the past three mornings and two afternoons knocking the document into shape. The previous evening, when Ted and Mary had left and the house was quiet, I had worked on the paper and was now satisfied with the outcome. I would take it down to the office my secretary used and mark it urgent.

The enforced periods of rest imposed by Jennifer's strategy had given me time to think about the future. I did not need the very large house in London, I decided, but did need somewhere to stay in the capital in order to carry out my duties as chairman of White Gull. I then began to think that the flat currently being finished might not be adequate for my needs, and anyway might give the impression that I was watching over the management of the new branch of Gloworm. I wrote down all the advantages and disadvantages of the various solutions, eventually coming up with a positive plan of action. What I decided was to try to let the big London house furnished, if a suitable tenant could be found. Before the house was let, I would put a fence at its former boundaries, thereby giving the large house used as staff quarters some rear garden. I would then have Suzie and Mo completely refurbish the house as a gentleman's residence, employing a housekeeper-cum-cook.

On the Wednesday morning, I consulted Suzie and Mo on my plan, which received total agreement. Suzie would start on designs straight away, and get estimates as soon as possible. Suzie said that she would like to use the same people as had refurbished the Bun residence. She explained that, although they were a little bit more expensive, and had not been chosen for the White Gull tender, their workmanship in dealing with period properties was of the best. She also suggested discussing the details of her initial designs with Mo the weekend after the funeral, when Suzie would be staying with Pauline in Colchester.

I then rang Angela to tell her of my decision. She agreed that it was probably the best solution, and she would seek out a letting agency specialising in the leasing of such properties. She also confirmed that she would be arriving at the manor on Sunday afternoon to assist me with the funeral arrangements. She had already contacted those people she felt needed to be informed, and would contact during the following week anybody I considered needing telling.

It was just after two o'clock when Jennifer pulled up outside the manor steps. Ted appeared to welcome her back, and began unloading the car. She attempted to assist him, but was told that her things would be taken up to her room and that she should not stand in the cold but go inside. She was greeted by Mary, who immediately asked her whether she had stopped for lunch. When Jennifer replied no, and that she was not hungry, Mary would not accept it. She took Jennifer into the kitchen for a fry-up washed down by mugfuls of tea.

Over the meal Jennifer asked Mary how I had been, and was told fine. She then asked where I was, only to be told that I was in my room resting, as per her instructions. Mary asked Jennifer about her parents; had they enjoyed seeing her after so long? Jennifer described the two days she had spent in Birmingham, much to Mary's pleasure. At three o'clock I entered the kitchen, where both women were still talking. Happy to see Jennifer again I warmly embraced her and told her how much she had been missed. She asked how I was and whether I still had constant headaches. I told her I was just fine, but that the headaches persisted. She reminded me that I had a hospital check up the next day and that if, I agreed, she would like to accompany me.

Over dinner that night Ted asked Jennifer how the car had behaved. Jennifer told him that it was a really nice car to drive, especially as the fifty mile per hour speed limit had been removed as part of the measures restoring normality to the country – 'But I am afraid that I did open her out coming down the motorway.' Ted told her that it had probably done the car good. She smiled and said that she could easily get used to driving a car like that.

The next morning we left the manor fairly early, in the Rolls, for our journey to the hospital. Jennifer managed to persuade her friends to help us through X-rays, weigh in, etc, until by ten thirty we were sitting in front of the consultant. He looked up and, seeing Jennifer, stood and warmly greeted us. He began by asking whether the American trip had been successful, to which I replied that I thought so. He asked if there had been any medical problems, and Jennifer detailed the two incidents that had taken place and the treatment she had given. He then asked me whether I still suffered headaches, and I replied in the affirmative. He put the new X-rays on a screen and studied them carefully, allowing Jennifer to see them also. He told me that the fractures were healing well, but if I overdid things I would probably suffer another attack.

Jennifer then explained the regime she had been using, and was congratulated. He suggested that we stick to the regime for another three weeks, then gradually step things up until I felt fully recovered. 'Unfortunately,' he said, 'I cannot guarantee that the headaches will cease immediately. In some patients they do and in others last for many weeks.' He told me that he would write to my doctor advising continuance of my current medication for as long as I needed it. He then rose, shook my hand and told me that I need not see him again unless I was worried.

I thanked him and we left his consulting room very much relieved.

Now, a Rolls-Royce outside a nurses' home, with the driver assisting one of its occupants to carry her bags in, would cause a stir in normal circumstances, but when it was seen Jennifer was also accompanied by a young man, then gossip was inevitable. Having delivered all her gear to her small room, Jennifer accompanied us back to the car, planting a kiss on the cheeks of both of us, reminding us to take care. She then turned to me and told me she would ring as soon as she saw the new duty rotas.

We arrived back in good time for lunch, and I was reminded that at three o'clock the vicar was arriving. Another death had occurred in the village, and he was anxious not to spend too long discussing the funeral service. I handed him an outline of what I wanted, the hymns I had chosen and explained that I and my Uncle Edward would be paying tribute to my parents. He nodded, and said that he would sort it out and if required get it printed by a local firm. I thanked him warmly, and he was on his way before Mary had had time to serve tea. Secretly I was relieved, as I dreaded the day I would have to lay both my parents to rest in our small village churchyard.

The next day, when the undertaker arrived, I nearly lost my nerve and feigned sickness. Ted sensed this and asked Miss Maureen, as he called her, to come upstairs and to sit in at the meeting. Grieving is bad enough, but at the very time you want peace you have to choose a coffin, the lining, handles, etc. Luckily Mo took charge, helping me make the right decisions. The undertaker asked how many cars we needed for mourners, and I told him I did not know, but four at least. The cortege would be led by a horsedrawn hearse, bearing my father's body. The coffin would be draped in the Union Jack, and on top would be his army cap and medals. My mother's coffin should be topped with flowers, as she had loved her garden. Floral tributes would be sent to the undertaker.

Mary broke the tension by suddenly appearing with coffee for all. The undertaker then asked Mo if he could have a quiet word, informing her that with the coffins would be two suitcases of my parents' clothes and possessions recovered from their hotel room and sealed by the police, together with a canvas bag containing the clothes they had been wearing at the accident. Mo thanked him for his concern, and told him that as soon as they arrived at his premises, she would arrange a driver to collect them. The undertaker wished me well and left.

Suddenly the pain and sorrow of the past weeks burst their banks and I broke down sobbing. Mo took me upstairs, and stayed till my grief subsided. I told her I felt so all alone, and could not face the funeral. She gently said that I must and would be able to get through the funeral, and that I needed to be brave. She suggested that I had a lie down before lunch.

I went up to rest after lunch, which had been a sombre affair. I had not lain down long when I heard my bedroom door open. There stood Mo, looking concerned. 'What is it?' I asked Mo, and she replied, 'You're the problem.' She sat down on the bed and softly told me that, while everybody understood what I was going through, they felt unable to help. However, Mary and Ted wanted me to know that they would never desert me, and that I had good friends that cared.

Then Mo reminded me that I had promised always to be there for her and she still needed to know I was not going to give up. I pulled her to me and told her that she would always be my best friend, no matter what, and I would try to live up to my promise. I told her that I really did rely on her support as I had no one else who loved and understood me. She then asked me about Jennifer: she cared, didn't she? I told her Jennifer was just my nurse and now I had been discharged, I would probably never see her again, and I began to cry. Mo held me tight, like a mother comforting a child, telling me that things would be all right. She persuaded me to try to get some sleep, which I did, now being totally exhausted.

The next morning Angela phoned to enquire how I was, how the basic arrangements for the funeral were proceeding, and to confirm that she would be arriving at the manor the Monday before the funeral to help co-ordinate the arrangements. She then announced that there was something she had to tell me that I might find distressing. Then there was a click and Uncle Edward came on the line. 'What Angela is attempting to say,' he told me, 'is that your Aunt Flossie has contacted the prison authorities to get permission for her brother to attend the funeral. I am very sorry.'

I told him that I was not distressed by the news, and that I recognised Auntie Flossie's need to have her brother near at the funeral of her sister. 'Tell Aunt Flossie, that he will be welcome to attend.' I then asked Uncle how my aunt was bearing up, and he said, 'Badly.' I told him that I knew loneliness and the need for family probably better than most, and what my aunt needed was understanding rather than anger and condemnation. Uncle Edward thanked me for being so compassionate and said he would take my advice to heart.

On the Monday Mo came to tell me that Rosie, one of the sisters who would be moving into the house with Angela, had contacted Peter to ask him where they could purchase cheap furniture from, as all three lived in the nurses' home, had no personal furniture, and were therefore starting from scratch. Peter had told her that he would make enquiries and ring her back later that week. I smiled and said that Lily Estates would help out and I would leave it to Peter's discretion what he purchased. 'Good,' said Mo, 'that is what I told him to do.' I laughed and patted her bottom, telling her that one day I would surprise her with a decision she did not expect.

I asked her to stay for some coffee so that we might talk. I told her that the London premises were nearly finished and that Suzie would be moving in the following week. Then we would need to decide our future management strategy. She nodded in agreement and said that Peter had now taken over full control of Gloworm locally. Suzie was starting to build a new branch, and for the present did not need her help. Purchasing and accounts for the local Gloworm had now been sorted and, quite frankly, she wondered what she would be doing in the future.

I told her not to worry, that I had an executive plan which I would reveal after the White Gull board meeting at the end of April. Meanwhile I needed her with me at least till after the funeral. Mo asked me if things were still bad, and I confessed that they were. She then asked whether I had discussed matters with Jennifer while in America, and I told her no. She asked whether there was a romantic relationship blossoming, to which again I said no, and explained that Jennifer was already married to her career and profession. Mo told me she was sorry, as she and Mary had done their best to bring the two of us together. I told her I had already worked that out, and the plan had failed.

On the following Monday Mike rang, to say he had received my draft paper for the board and was really impressed by it. He had decided not to make any last-minute alterations and to submit the paper as it was. He asked if I was well enough to read through some documents and give him my opinion, to which I readily agreed.

The week passed swiftly and, before I knew it, it was the Monday before the funeral. My parents' remains had arrived as expected on the Friday, and the undertaker rang to say that everything was now ready for the funeral the following Friday. Angela had arrived and taken over my study as the centre of operations. I retreated to my private sitting room, out of the way of the rush and bustle that had enveloped the house since Angela's arrival.

Those first few days in April before the funeral were taken up with arrangements for both the funeral itself and the dinner that Angela had arranged for the Friday evening for our house guests. Uncle and Aunt had planned to stay for the Friday night only, as had Mike, his wife and daughter, as well as CJ and his wife. Ted's son Tom had also decided to attend, but would be staying at the bungalow with his parents. Catering for the day was based on 150 people coming back, and three ladies from the village had been employed to cater. Two more would arrive at four o'clock to cook dinner and a further two ladies would arrive later to help serve the meal and clear away. Mary and Ted were banned from the kitchen, and would also attend the dinner as honoured guests. I had not heard from Jennifer, who had said that she would attend the funeral if she could get away. Mo had said that she would be with me all through the day, but had arranged to have dinner and a girls' night out, with Pauline and Suzie, who had arranged to attend the funeral.

On Thursday, 6 April I had an appointment with a Mr Mickleson from my parents' solicitors. He had come down from London by train and Ted had gone to meet him from the station. Ted showed him into my study just after ten and told us he would bring in some coffee. I thanked my visitor for taking the trouble to come and see me, rather than my going to London to see him. He began by saying how sorry he was at my recent loss, and that Mr Andrew, the senior partner, would be attending the funeral to represent the firm.

Once coffee was served, he opened his case and took out a bundle of papers. He began by telling me that, normally, wills were read after the funeral, but as I was the main beneficiary Angela had thought it best to get it over with the day before. He began by telling me that my mother had been deemed to have passed away before my father. Using this he had provisionally calculated the inheritance duty payable. He began to explain his assumptions and calculations, but I asked him just to tell me the bottom line. He looked dismayed that I did not wish to know his detailed assessment, but agreed to proceed on the basis of my request. Basically, after allowing for debts and funeral expenses, small bequests, etc, I would inherit ten per cent of Bun Industries stock, five per cent White Gull stock and approximately £250,000, duty paid. 'In addition,' he said, 'I have applied to the insurance company, on your behalf, for two life insurance policies, both with a double indemnity clause in the event of sudden, violent death. I estimate that they will produce a further £200,000.'

Turning to the other bequests, he said that he would pay them direct, apart from two. 'Your parents left £25,000 each to Ted and Mary. I have taken the liberty of drawing two cheques, which I will leave you to tell them about. That only leaves me to ask you to let me have the bills for any debts your father left and a full statement of funeral expenses. I will then submit my figures to the Inland Revenue for agreement, but I do not expect any problems.'

I rang for Ted, and asked him to take Mr Mickleson back to the station. I stood up, thanked him for his time and shook hands just as Ted re-entered the room.

Once lunch had been cleared away, I asked Ted and Mary to join me for coffee in my study, as I had something important to tell them. Once they had sat down, I asked Mary whether all was in hand for the next day. She nodded, and said that she would feel awkward sitting down for dinner with the family. I explained that, following my parents death, I considered them as family. That, I told them, brought me on to the matter I needed to discuss with them. 'You will know,' I said, 'that my visitor before lunch was from my parents' solicitors from London. He is acting as executor for my parents' estate, and has told me that my parents had left £25,000 to each of you.'

As they were getting over the shock, I opened my desk drawer and took out the cheques and handed them over. Mary was starting to cry, saying that my parents had always been good to them, but £50,000 was far too much. Ted then said that he would invest it for their old age and it would change an outlook of having to manage on their savings and the old age pension. I suddenly realised that they were unaware of the private pension scheme my mother had set up, and I had continued paying. I told them of it, and explained that it would provide a third to a half of their final salaries when they reached retirement age. They both looked at each other and smiled, neither believing their sudden fortune. I told them I would go and rest, and if they had any questions they could ask me at dinner.

The next morning Mo served me breakfast in bed, as she said that the whole ground floor was in chaos. She asked me how I was, and I confessed I really did not know. She told me not to worry as everything was going to be fine.

I arrived downstairs just after ten, in time to greet Mike and his party. Greetings finished, Mike pulled out an envelope and said, 'Arthur Welsh asked me to give you this.' Arthur had been a great friend of both my grandfather and father as well as being a good friend to me while I tried to learn the property game. I excused myself and took the letter into my study. The main letter apologised for his not being able to attend, with nice things about his long association with the family and wishing me well. The bottom line said that the enclosed envelope contained a copy of a letter that would reach me early the next week. I opened the second small envelope and read the letter, only to find that Gloworm had been awarded the complete contract for the refurbishment of White Gull properties.

I was sat back in my chair when Mo came in. 'Time to go,' she said quietly. I slid over the copy letter. She smiled, and I told her to tell the others after the funeral – 'But remember, officially we still do not know.'

The funeral seemed to go well, although for most of the service it was like looking at a cinema screen, an event in which I had no part other than as an observer. Jennifer was able to attend after all, and now joined Mo, and both of them supported an arm, as we walked to the churchyard for the final rites. Many people accepted the invitation for a sandwich and coffee following the service, and many of them were strangers to me. However, I ensured I circulated, saying thank you to all those who had taken the time to attend.

By three o'clock, most of the mourners had left, leaving my house guests and Gloworm directors. Mike's daughter approached me to ask permission to miss dinner, as she had been invited to join the girls' night out. Mo came over as we talked, guaranteeing to see her back safely. Once the girls disappeared to sort out some overnight things, Mike came over, and said that he appreciated my understanding. I smiled and told him I had been young once.

Gradually people dispersed and Jennifer suggested I take a rest before dinner. Escorting me upstairs, she helped me remove my suit, before I got up on to the bed and lay down. I told her I had missed her, and she told me she had missed me too. She explained that the hospital was battling a winter virus and that many of the staff were off sick. She was covering the work in her ward the best she could. She looked tired and I told her she needed to ease up, or she would be joining the sick list. She then gave me a big kiss, and said that was from her two friends for finding furniture for their new house. 'Not a big kiss from you?' I asked, at which she leaned over and for several minutes we were locked in each other's arms exchanging kisses.

I patted the space on the bed beside me and invited her to climb aboard, as I wanted to talk to her. She agreed and was soon lying next to me. I told her of the strange feelings I had had at the funeral service, and she told me that everyone coped differently with grief. I then confessed that, even though my parents had lived in London and travelled a lot, when I had finally laid them to rest I suddenly felt lonely. Jennifer said nothing, but squeezed my hand to comfort me. I told her that I now needed to face the future, both as Lord of the Manor and chairman of a large corporation, as well as my work with Gloworm and Lily Estates. I told her, that only yesterday, at a meeting with a solicitor, I had been reminded of my duty to produce an heir, in order to safeguard the Earlswood Estate. Jennifer told me that sounded like her mother, who had reminded her that she would be twenty-six in May, and it was high time she produced a grandchild. I told her that sounded like my late mother, who sized up each girl I brought to the house as a future brood mare.

'Jennifer,' I said, 'now that I am no longer your patient, could we see each other socially? You know the sort of thing, dinner, theatres, etc?'

She smiled and told me she would like that, but with extra shifts and moving, the next two weeks would be hectic. I then asked her whether she had any holidays due, to which she replied that seven days were owing from the last financial year, which she could take when the winter virus was over. 'Why?' she then asked.

'I would like you to take some time off, so I can show you some of my world, and we can get to know each other better.'

She hesitated, and then told me that she would see what she could arrange. 'George,' she said, 'can we keep our relationship from my friends and colleagues at the hospital, at least for the time being?' She turned towards me, and we kissed passionately. She seemed to respond and welcome my caresses to her neck, back and bottom, particularly the latter. She suddenly pulled away, and told me that if every male was as passionate as that, no wonder they had just introduced condoms and family planning advice free on the National Health Service. I smiled and told her, I would have to look into the matter. She climbed off the bed, straightened her clothes, and told me to get some rest before dinner.

Angela intercepted me as I walked down the stairs, and told me she had some good news for me. Apparently, she had mentioned my house to a colleague who worked in a Swiss bank based in London. He in turn had told her that the bank were moving a large part of their operation to London, and were looking for somewhere to entertain clients as well as their own visiting directors. The house had been visited by the senior director, who was shown round by the butler, and he had rang Angela's friend to say that, subject to reaching a satisfactory agreement, they would like to rent it furnished for the next three years. I took her face in my hands telling her that she was a clever girl, and that if she was willing she could conclude a deal in my name. She smiled, and I thanked her again for all the help she had given me in the run-up to the funeral. I then asked her if her banking friend was the one who shared her flat, and she nodded. I told her she looked happier now than I had seen her for years. She blushed and whispered that they were in love with each other, and that she could never envisage being touched by another man ever again. I told her I was happy for her but, if ever she needed a friend, she had only to ask. She thanked me and we both strode down the stairs to the dining room.

Aunt Flossie was already in the dining room when we entered. I asked her if her brother had managed to get to the funeral and she nodded. 'I am sorry I missed seeing Uncle Cecil,' I said. 'I did look for him.'

'He was brought to the church by two warders, handcuffed, but they did let me have ten minutes with him in the church after everyone had left, thanks to you.'

'I am glad he could come,' I said, 'and that you could talk.'

'George,' she asked, 'would it be against the family honour for me to visit him, do you think?'

Knowing Uncle Edward's feelings towards his brother-in-law, I told her that it would be quite fitting to visit one's brother, and I would talk to Uncle about it.

Mike, his wife and CJ and his wife, had had a tour of the house and immediate grounds, which they thought was everything an English manor house should be. While they were in London earlier in the week, Mike and his wife had shown them some of London, including my London residence, courtesy of Lady Bun, and they had greatly admired the period furniture, pictures and antiques. The ladies were both keen to know our family history and the history of the house.

Dinner was a grand affair, even though it was the day of the funeral. When Angela had informed Mary of the importance of the house guests, she and Ted had decided to show that I (meaning Ted and Mary) still knew how to entertain royalty. The box room had produced the family silver including candlesticks and they now adorned the table together with the best crystal and porcelain. Ted had used his extensive knowledge of my late father's cellar and had chosen the finest wines to accompany the meal. I sat at one end of the large table regaling them with stories of piracy, slave trading, and helping nobility escape following the French Revolution, as well as the history of the house, while Jennifer was listening intently to the gentlemen talking about the future prospects of the British economy, following the finding of a vast new oil field off the coast. They were cautious because, although things had improved with the state of the country since the election, there was now an expectation on the part of unions of substantial pay rises following the generous miners' settlement. The weakness of the pound during the three day week had made those goods that were produced cheaper abroad, but any rise in the pound plus a cost-push economy could easily spell disaster.

Breakfast the next morning was taken early, and one by one my guests left for home. Jennifer was the last to leave and, as we kissed goodbye, promised to phone me during the following week. Ted and Tom went into the village and I was left alone with Mary. I thanked her for her support and hard work to ensure everything had gone to plan. Mary smiled, thanked me and told me she was glad to get her kitchen back. Two girls from the village arrived to clean rooms and change beds, and Mary took them upstairs to show them what was required. When she returned we sat in the kitchen alone, drinking coffee as we had done when I had been home on holiday from school or college. Mary enquired what plans I had for the future, and I told her how I had rented the London house, but would be maintaining somewhere to stay while in the capital. I told her that the manor would be my business and residential base and that I intended to entertain more, which I hoped would not be a problem to her. I then told her about the new contract, and how in time I would need to make some changes within Gloworm. Mary asked how things stood between me and the two ladies in my life, Miss Maureen and Miss Jennifer. I told her that it appeared that Miss Maureen was attached to her way of life, and the other one attached to her career. Changing the subject, I asked whether everything was in order for the next day's luncheon, and was assured that it was. Ted and Tom joined us in the kitchen looking pleased with themselves, and I left them with Mary, as they clearly wished to talk to her alone.

I went to my study and picked up the newspaper. The news from Northern Ireland was as usual bad, with more sectarian killings and now large-scale robberies, suspected of being carried out by the IRA. I wondered if the Troubles would ever be resolved, and if Tom would now be safer in Civvy Street.

Lunch was my favourite, cottage pie, followed by raspberry pie and custard. Lunch was finished and the plates cleared away. Ted asked whether they could have a serious word with me. Ted began by saying that Tom and he had visited the house I had built on the site of two cottages, and it appeared still to be empty. I told them that, owing to work, the death of my parents and my accident, I had not found time to put it on the market. Tom asked whether it was completely finished, and I told him no, as we had left the choice of the sanitary equipment throughout the house, and the kitchen sink and work top, to be chosen by the new buyers. Tom asked if that would be expensive, and I said about £500. Ted then asked what the property was worth, to which I replied about £28,000. Mary asked whether I would sell it to them. Astonished, I asked them what they wanted it for. Mary explained that, since Tom was leaving the army at the end of May, he and his wife had to vacate married quarters by the end of June. Tom had expressed the wish to move nearer his parents, and Wendy, his wife, had agreed. However, prices in Essex far exceeded those in Lincolnshire, and that had made them reconsider a move south. 'We thought that, if we bought the house for them with our recent inheritance, they could move nearer, and we could watch little Katy grow up.'

Feeling very generous, I told them I would be prepared to sell the property to them for £25,000, just as it stood. They all agreed that this was very generous and they would accept the offer.

Tom immediately went into the hall to ring Wendy and tell her the good news. When he came back, I told him that, as soon as he and Wendy had decided on the colour scheme, they should speak to Peter, who could probably get them a good deal through Gloworm as well as any technical support they might need. Tom shook my hand and thanked me again for my help.

The meeting on the Sunday was a joyous affair, with everyone excited about the new challenges ahead. I agreed that Pauline and Mo could join Suzie in London to set up the new office and begin letting the new contracts attaching to the project. Peter agreed to provide any transport required and to run Gloworm while Mo was away. Pauline told us that, apart from a couple of visits per month, the organisation would run itself. We agreed that all the costs of the new business would be paid by Gloworm, but would be separately accounted for with the intention of changing the structure of the business later on in the year.

Once the meeting was over and we all trooped out for lunch, I handed Pauline a note of what I wanted arranged for Jennifer's birthday dinner party.

The next week seemed unduly quiet, with nobody in the house but Mary, Ted and I. I spent the time trying to get the future of my various interests right, so as to allow me ample time to carry out my duties as chairman of White Gull. Jennifer rang to tell me that they had moved into the house and that it felt wonderful, in spite of the chaos. She told me she had asked for three days off early in May and was waiting for her request to be agreed. I said that was good news, and I hoped that she would be free on the evening of her birthday as well as the day following. Jennifer said that was all in hand, telling me the date of the actual event.

On the Tuesday evening after dinner I asked if Ted and Mary would help clear the London house of my parents' personal effects. They agreed, and I told them that Peter would pick them up in the light van (the bench seat being big enough for three) and take them to London. When they had finished Peter would bring everything back, while Ted would bring either my father's Jaguar or the new Rolls-Royce back to the manor. Both in time would go into the garage and we would have to discuss the future of the spare Rover.

On Friday of the following week, Mary came to see me to tell me that she had now sorted all my parents' possessions and had put the valuable jewellery in the safe. She had brushed and ironed my mother's elegant and expensive dresses and put them away in the wardrobe of the guest room. My mother and father's other clothing could be disposed of through her friend at the Red Cross. I thanked her for all her help and told her to dispose of the clothing as she felt fit. I asked where Ted was and was told that Peter had taken him to the station, and he would be back with the other Rolls-Royce later that day.

The board meeting of White Gull was held at the end of April, where, after my election as company chairman, I presented our joint paper. The paper was approved with little discussion, and was seen as a masterpiece of joint management. Angela was also appointed as managing director designate, with special responsibility for the merging of the two companies. The appointment would take effect from 1 July. Lord Bun, on my recommendation, was appointed as deputy chairman, to be available when the chairman was absent. Never again would White Gull, be left with only one major decision-making executive as had happened in my Uncle Cecil's time, however much we trusted our new managing director. We also agreed to approach two generalists on the Bun board to join us on the board.

That afternoon on my way home, I visited the new offices of Gloworm II. Everything seemed a hive of industry, but remarkably well organised, considering how little time they had had in settling in. I was also shown the upstairs flat, which was now comfortably furnished, and where all the girls were living till things settled down. The top flat was well advanced and would be ready in mid-June.

On the train home I had a deep sense of satisfaction over the day's work, but knew there would be hard work ahead, especially if I did not get my businesses sorted out. Still, it would be May the following week, and I would start the month with a target of sorting things by the end of the month.

A Look to the Future

May had blossomed forth with some nice early warm weather. Jennifer had at last managed to arrange some time off during the first week of May, and would arrive for dinner on the Tuesday evening. She was not on duty again till the following Saturday afternoon. Apart from a dinner taken at a remote country pub, I had not seen Jennifer since the funeral, and was looking forward to being with her again.

I tried to keep occupied that Tuesday morning, thereby making the time go faster. The *Financial Times* was predicting a continued rise in property prices. Since 1971, property prices had doubled in the south of England, and seemed set to continue rising. Prices in other parts of the country had not risen as fast, but nevertheless had shown significant gains. Buying to rent, the newspaper concluded, was a long-term gamble, because rental incomes, especially under the pay and price regulations, had not risen to a level to compensate for interest rates on the new property values. The report maintained that, over the next few years, demand for property to rent would rise, while supply might well fall, and in the long run push up rents.

Bad news continued to come from Northern Ireland, and the government were considering increasing the garrison there. There was also a growing suspicion of corruption in high places, especially over certain property deals. Ever since the Poulson scandal, there had been mistrust, and in April more serious allegations had been made. White Gull was in the property sector and, while I trusted Arthur Welsh completely, I resolved to have a fresh look at the company's policies over gifts and incentives.

Jennifer arrived in time for a shower and a change of clothes before dinner. Once dinner was finished, the two women disappeared upstairs, leaving Ted and me watching television. *Z-Cars*, a popular police drama, was nearing its thousandth episode, and it made me realise how quickly time had flown since I had first watched it.

The girls did not appear till after ten, both of them looking pleased with themselves. Mary did not have time to say why they looked so satisfied as Ted wanted his chocolate drink before locking up for the night. When Mary and Ted had left, I asked Jennifer what they had been scheming all that time upstairs. Jennifer told me that, 'Mary has been showing me your mother's beautiful dresses – and do you know that the majority of them fit me perfectly? Some of them are either old-fashioned or do not fit me, George,' she said, 'would you mind seeing me in one of your mother's dresses? They really are lovely.'

I told her she could have whatever she wanted and to tell Mary to dispose of the rest. She kissed me and then cuddled down beside me on the sofa.

We then told each other of our doings since the funeral, and how quick April had flown. I turned to her and kissed her lips, a kiss which she returned. Passions aroused, we started cuddling, exploring each other's bodies through our clothing. This came to an abrupt halt when my hand wandered inside the back of her trousers, where I was stroking her bottom. I apologised, and she said there was really no need, as she had been enjoying the experience. Just before midnight, we both climbed the stairs to our rooms. Reaching her door, I asked her if she needed help getting undressed, or perhaps tucking up in bed, but she smiled and said that she was a big girl now, and thought she could manage.

The following morning after breakfast we went for a drive, and I headed towards Colchester. Driving up to my Lexden house, I was glad to see the contract gardeners busy cutting the lawn. 'What is this place?' Jennifer asked, and I told her that it had been my pad before I moved back to the manor. She remarked that it was a nice place to have a flat. Using my key I opened the door, revealing the stylish hall. Then took her hand, and showed her first the basement servants' quarters, then the ground floor. All Jennifer said was that the house was out of this world. We then proceeded upstairs where I showed her the two guest bedrooms with their en suite facilities, and then the guest suite with its private sitting room and bathroom. I showed her my quarters with all the richness and splendour of Mo's creativity.

I next showed her the bedroom, with its imposing four-poster bed covered in its gold counterpane. Jennifer asked whether this was the place I brought innocent girls to in order to have my wicked way with them. I told her that I was sorry to disappoint her, but there had been only one, whom she already knew about. I removed my shoes and climbed on the bed, inviting her to join me, which she did. She asked me whether I was still in love with Mo. I told her that Mo would always be one of my best friends, and that I still found her attractive. However, she had indicated her reasons for turning down my proposal, and I respected her decision. I told Jennifer that it was now time to move on and look to the future – I had a duty to provide an heir to the estate. 'Hopefully I can find someone to share my life with,' I said, 'but if that does not happen, I will need to examine other alternatives.'

I then pulled her towards me and kissed her gently, knowing she would respond, which she did.

Our kisses became more intense and she did not seem to worry as I undid the buttons to her blouse, or when I removed her bra. She seemed to increase her passionate kissing as my hands wandered over her lovely breasts, fondling, stroking and caressing, and when I left her lips to kiss and lick where my hands had been, she seemed to sigh with contentment. Meanwhile my hands were busy caressing her bottom. Having advanced so far, with Jennifer actively taking part, I moved my hands down to the waistband of her trousers, and undid the button, and slid down the zip. Jennifer was still returning my kisses, as I gently began sliding her trousers down, revealing a skimpy pair of knickers.

Suddenly, she grabbed my hand and asked me to stop. I apologised, but she told me it was her fault for leading me on. While she thought that she was falling in love with me and welcomed our lovemaking, she did not want to become pregnant before she had decided on her future. She asked for time, and I told her I would wait as long as she liked. She pulled up her trousers, put on her bra and did up her buttons. As she did so, she noticed the bulge in my trousers and asked if I needed to take a cold shower.

We continued to lie side by side, talking. I asked her if she thought that one day she might be the new Lady Earlswood and take over the various duties. Jennifer then told me that, since the funeral, she had worried about nothing else. First she was not sure she loved me enough to spend the rest of her life with me. Second, she had had no training or experience in being a real lady, and worried how she would cope if we decided to marry. And third, could she give up her career, and never look back with envy at those who devoted their lives to the profession? She had fallen in love with me and hoped I felt the same way. She had not yet resolved all her fears and worries, that's why she needed more time.

I kissed her gently and told her again that I loved her and would wait until she had resolved things in her mind.

Once downstairs, I made some coffee and took it to my study. Jennifer was very impressed by the furnishings and comfort of what she saw was only a place to work. I told her it was modelled on an American den, where our American cousins not only worked at their desks but maintained the room as a private sanctuary. She then asked me how often I rode horses. Surprised by the question, I told her never. 'Sorry,' she said, 'but seeing the riding crop behind your desk, I thought…'

I quickly interrupted her conclusion by telling her it was a gift from Mo, explaining its significance to any aristocratic wife should she wander. She smiled and said that was something else she would seriously have to take into account before deciding whether or not to marry into a society that beat their wives when they strayed.

We then left the house and drove to the nearby market town of Braintree, where it was market day. We lunched at the Horn hotel, before touring the market. I left Jennifer looking at the stalls while I popped into an estate agent to see what houses they had on their books in need of repair and renovation, which could show a profit. I left with a dozen possibilities which I would study after Jennifer had gone home.

I joined her at a stall selling fresh fish. 'Do you think Mary would mind if I took some kippers home for breakfast?' she asked. I put my arm round her and bought four large kippers.

Jennifer, I discovered, adored shopping, and as we made our way from the market she stopped at every shop to inspect their windows. On our way home, Jennifer seemed more relaxed and happy, having enjoyed our day out. Tomorrow we were off to London, where I hoped we would have time to shop.

The next morning we left early. Ted took us to Colchester station in the Rolls-Royce, promising that he would meet us the same night and would wait for me to call him and tell him when. Our first stop was the London house previously lived in by my parents. I told Jennifer that it was far too big for my needs, and it was let to a Swiss bank for the next five years. We then walked round the block until we came to what was to be my new residence, where work was going on at a furious pace. I took Jennifer round the house explaining that, since the layout was similar to the Colchester property, when restored it would have the same facilities. I told her that, when it was finished, I would employ a cook-cum-housekeeper to look after me when I had to stay over on business.

We then took a taxi to White Gull offices where I showed her my office and introduced her to my shared secretary, who told me Mike was out of the office. We then took a taxi to Harrods for lunch and shopping. Much as I tried to find something to buy for Jennifer, she seemed not in the mood for shopping, and appeared to be deep in thought. She did however buy gifts for Mary and Ted.

The following morning we went to Clacton for the day. The place was very quiet and many of the seafront amusements had not opened for the season. However we found a nice restaurant not far from the pier and had fish and chips, which we both agreed were exceptionally good.

That night, after Mary and Ted had locked up and retired, we kissed and cuddled, Jennifer allowing nothing in the way of petting below the belt. As we cuddled and fondled each other, Jennifer promised to seriously think things over. I thanked her, but said that even if her answer was yes, I could not pop the question until I had seen her father. 'My father!' she exclaimed. 'What has it got to do with him? I shall soon be twenty-six and quite capable of making up my own mind.'

I gently told her that she was his only daughter, and probably someone really special, and honour told me that he would like to be asked officially.

Saturday soon came round and Jennifer left after breakfast so as to be ready for duty that afternoon.

I had decided to return to work the following Monday and re-establish a routine. I would go into London on a Monday, stay overnight and return home on Tuesday evening. Depending on what was on, I would also work on a Thursday or Friday.

On that first Monday back at work, I dined with the girls, and was updated on the progress achieved in the implementation of the new contract, as well as the new design contract for one of the large hotels in the capital. Things seemed to be going well, and there was a general air of satisfaction. On the Wednesday, I had lunch with the bank manager, who was keen to know of all developments. Over lunch, I asked him where I could get financial advice on my share portfolio, and as usual he gave me a name and telephone number.

During the following week I again had dinner with the girls, and all seemed fine, but on Wednesday morning I had a telephone call from Mo, telling me she needed to speak to me urgently, and asking if she could come for the weekend. I told her she was always welcome and I looked forward to seeing her. Peter rang to tell me that 'Boots', his young assistant, had given him two weeks notice, as he was moving to Ilford and had secured a job as a motorcycle courier. I told Peter that Ted's son Tom was looking for a driving job and held an HGV licence gained while in the army, and that Peter should get Tom's phone number from Ted.

Mo arrived just before dinner on the Friday looking very unhappy. I therefore suggested that we go to my study so we could talk freely. Mo began by telling me that her work in London had nearly finished, and she would be returning at the beginning of June. She continued by saying that Suzie was enjoying the freedom of running the new business, and would be keen for things not to change. Pauline wanted to stay in London, as she had found a technical college nearby where she could continue her accounting studies in the evening. Peter was running Gloworm so efficiently he needed little outside help. So where did it leave her? Probably without a job – and she began crying.

I then revealed my strategy to her, and the important role she would play in it. This, I said, was still under wraps and it must remain that way until all the pieces fell into place. Mo cheered up, and I told her that, while I ran any organisation, there would always be a place for her.

She then asked after my health, and enquired how I was coping following the funeral. I told her I was improving every day, but still suffered from headaches, especially at the end of busy days and travelling. Coping was a different matter. While I was fully occupied, things were not so bad, but when I was alone or could not sleep I realised what a loss I had suffered. She told me that time was a great healer, but that I could always talk and rely on her. I thanked her and told her I had never doubted her capacity for understanding.

She then told me she had met Jennifer in town the previous Saturday. They had had coffee together, and eventually Jennifer had followed her home and spent the night at hers. 'Naturally, being women, we talked a lot as well as finishing a couple bottles of wine.'

I asked her how Jennifer had seemed to her and she told me, 'In a whirlpool of worry and torment. She told me that she was fond of you, but still did not know if it was love. She is concerned that, if it is love, is it strong enough to stand the test of time? She knows the pressures on you to provide an heir, and if she married you and was unable to conceive, how long would the marriage last? Additionally, she has not made up her mind whether she could turn her back on a career she still loves, and wonders what her father would think. Talking about her father, she understands the reason why you want to ask her father's permission to wed his daughter, but at twenty-six, she will make her own decision on the matter. While she feels she could learn the skills required of her in the performance of her duties, she is still worried that people might not accept her. Lastly, she finds your advances difficult to control, especially of late. You see, George, although she is a fully qualified nurse of twenty-six, she is as I was before that first stay in Bury St Edmunds.'

I listened to all Mo had said, thanked her, and then asked what could be done to avert her worries. Mo thought for a moment and told me that the deal on offer was in many ways impossible for anyone not born and bred to it – 'That was her reason for turning down your proposal. Once she makes up her mind, you can help her through the problems she foresees. Until then, your courting must be slowed down until she feels more comfortable with your advances.'

Mary brought in cocoa just before she and Ted locked up and retired for the night, leaving us alone in the house. 'Do you remember,' asked Mo, 'when things were strong between us, we could not wait till we had the place to ourselves so we could retire to bed and make love?'

'I remember well,' I said, 'and the rug in front of the library fire. We have come a long way since then,' I told her, 'and we will continue to do well as long as you are with me.'

'I am afraid that I tried to stall Jennifer's worries about having a baby,' said Mo, 'by telling her that, before she had come on the scene I had offered to have your child, and still would if the need arose. She told me that that was heroic, and the offer of a true friend.'

The atmosphere began to grow tense, both of us knowing where things were leading. I tried to change the subject by asking Mo what else was said during their private drinks party. Mo blushed and said, 'I am afraid I gave her a blow-by-blow account of that first time in the Angel hotel, and the story of the riding crop, which I told her you could not use on me, in spite of me asking you to. However, while you were really a pussycat, one should not push you too far and I told her of Pauline's sad fate. I am sorry, but you know what I am like after a few glasses of wine.'

I pretended to be angry with her, threatening dire consequences. I think she saw through me, smiled and told me it was time for bed.

During the week before Jennifer's party, I worked on only two days, Monday and Tuesday, as I had arranged a meeting with the financial analyst. Paul Wexford was medium height, medium build, with a slight indication of a middle-aged spread. He had a rounded face with friendly brown eyes and a smile that gave confidence. We soon got down to the job of going through my portfolio. When we had finished he declared that, while it was a very balanced set of investments, they were all low risk, and the return was poorer than it might be. I told him that I had been cautious of the stock market over the past twelve months when spectacular falls had taken place. He nodded and said, 'Point taken.' We then talked about him taking on the management of my portfolio, and I asked what his fees would be. We agreed a trial period of a year, with him promising to invest for me another quarter of a million at the end of June. I saw him to the door and watched him drive of in his Rover car.

I went inside and saw Ted standing in the kitchen, listening to the radio. I joined him and he told me that Sir Alf Ramsey, the England manager who had won the World Cup in 1966 had been sacked by the Football Association. Ted remarked that he had been a fine manager, proving himself both at club level and national level. His only fault had been to have a string of bad results to change him from saviour to sinner. I agreed, and told Ted that I had been at the final in 1966, and that afternoon Ramsey could have had the earth.

Jennifer's party was both a surprise for her and a total success as an event. The ladies from the village, under Mary's guidance, had prepared a superb meal, and Ted continued to choose fine wines from the cellar. Jennifer's nursing colleagues loved the venue and the grand table setting. During the meal I told the assembled gathering that the dinner party was not only to mark Jennifer's birthday, but also in gratitude for the way she had cared for me, both on her ward and in America. 'I therefore have much pleasure in proposing a toast to her.'

Everyone stood, raised their glasses and toasted her.

Shortly before we adjourned for coffee I rose again, and asked for quiet. I then recalled that, in America, Jennifer had worn a fob watch on her uniform, but when wearing mufti (a term used by nurses to describe wearing their own clothes rather than uniform) she had relied on a very small clock that she carried in her handbag. 'I would therefore now like to present her with a special birthday present in recognition of a job professionally and superbly done.' I then handed her a long case containing a gold watch.

While the rest of the Gloworm crowd relaxed, Jennifer's guests were taken on a tour of the manor by Mo. When they reached the guest room where Jennifer was to spend the night Mickey, one of her housemates, exclaimed that she would not mind being seduced in such a large four-poster bed. Jennifer blushed and told her that, in her dealings with his lordship, things had been strictly professional. When the ladies returned from their tour of the manor for coffee, the nursing officer buttonholed Suzie regarding her work at the Bun residence, while Mickey, worse for wear for wine, asked if there was a job of wife going begging and if so could she apply. That appeared to be the time everyone decided to depart, Jennifer's colleagues first, driven by the nursing officer, then the Gloworm crowd, who were all reminded that there was a special meeting scheduled for Sunday morning.

By eleven o'clock, all had been cleared away, and the doors locked for the night, leaving Jennifer and me alone. Remembering Mo's advice, I did not attempt to kiss Jennifer, but suggested it would be more comfortable in the family lounge. She began by thanking me for the surprise dinner party, and for keeping our real relationship a secret. She also thanked me for my thoughtful present which she would treasure always. She went on to tell me of her meeting with Mo, and how much she had valued their conversation. Much of what had passed between them indicated that, with help, she could carry out the duties as Lady of the Manor. However, she was not yet sure whether she could give up her nursing career and, if she did, what her father would think.

The other major hurdle was that she was not sure that she wanted to spend her whole life with me, especially if we could not have children. I told her that if she liked, and before she made any commitment, we could both undergo medical checks to establish the state of our health and whether there would be any problems in producing an heir. This seemed to satisfy her.

She then told me that in matters of lovemaking she was a novice and, while she had enjoyed my advances so far, she wanted me to promise not to go all the way until we had decided to marry. I agreed, and pulled her to me in order to hold her and kiss her. She responded eagerly and we enjoyed many minutes of passion before we decided it was time for bed.

The following Sunday morning the Gloworm managers arrived for the meeting. To their surprise, I told them I wanted to see them individually in my office, beginning with Suzie. When we were seated comfortably I began. I first congratulated her on her recent success. I then reminded her that, ever since I had first met her in that little office of hers, she had had a burning ambition to run her own business. 'I have therefore decided,' I continued, 'to give you a chance to take control of one of my businesses.' I then laid out the terms and conditions which would apply to Gloworm II. I handed her a piece of paper with a new suggested salary and profit-sharing scheme, which made her smile. I then told her that, now I had decided to have a new residence in London, I had no need for a flat. The whole building would therefore be handed over to the business, together with £50,000 working capital. I told her that I was setting a £200,000 turnover target for this year and expected a gross ten per cent profit – 'How you achieve this is now in your own hands.'

She rose from her seat, leaned over and kissed me, saying my decision was more than she had hoped for. She went to leave, but I asked her to sit down again. 'I understand,' I said, 'that Pauline wishes to relinquish her job with Lily Estates to come and be your operations manager.' Suzie nodded and said that to agree to such a request would help her in her new role as managing director as well as giving her time to develop new projects. 'Very well,' I told her, 'you had better offer her the job and negotiate a salary.'

Suzie rose again and was about to leave when I asked her to send Pauline in. Pauline followed looking worried, so I asked her to make herself comfortable. 'Suzie tells me that you want a transfer to her new enterprise,' I said. Pauline nodded and told me that she liked London and there were better facilities to help her study for her accountancy examinations. I told her she would no longer be a director and she said she understood. 'Will you need your car in London?' I asked, and she replied no, and explained that she would have use of Suzie's Fiesta. I leaned back in my chair and told her she had come a long way since we had first met and how grateful I was. I then wished her well and advised her to negotiate a good salary with her new boss, as well as asking for help with fees, books and time off for study. She breathed a sigh of relief, and I asked her why. She blushed and told me she thought I would be cross, and that she might be bent over my desk again. I laughed and said, 'I will only be cross if you fail to hand over to Mo properly.' She thanked me and left.

Peter was next in, and he sat upright in his chair. I told him how well he had done during Mo's absence, and said that we had decided now to give him that responsibility on a permanent basis. Of course, I or Mo would be there to advise him if he felt unsure. I told him he would continue to manage all the work currently being undertaken. However, I felt that there was room for expansion of the business, and Mo would assist him in a sales campaign. I also told him that Lily Estates would be spending up to £1,000,000 in buying up derelict houses and refurbishing them using Gloworm. I handed him a piece of paper with his new salary on, and told him in addition he could expect twenty per cent of profits after tax as a bonus. His face burst out in a smile. 'In addition,' I said, 'Jenny who currently works downstairs but lives near the depot, and does all your paperwork, will transfer to the depot on 1 July and will need suitable equipment.' I then remembered that I had not told him the other good news. 'Pauline has handed back her car. As soon as the car has been serviced, cleaned and valeted, Ted will arrange to get it to you.' Peter rose and held out his hand and said, 'Thanks, boss. I will not let you down.'

Mo was the last to come to my office, comfortably sitting down as she had so many times before. I had already told her of her role in the new set-up, which she had agreed to wholeheartedly. I told her of the arrangements I had made that morning. 'We do need to attract someone with bookkeeping and basic accountancy experience, and I will leave that to you. My part-time secretary is looking for full-time employment, and I thought we could share her, which will mean the office is manned always when you are out.' I then told her that, as well as making her managing director of Lily Estates, I wanted to appoint her as estate manager, and as such part of the household. I explained that Mary and Ted had a free hand in household expenditure and that must remain. 'I in turn look after any repair bills. What I do not know is how much it costs to run my various houses. I intend that the new bookkeeper can keep the accounts as well as Lily Estate business, but I want you to speak at the quarterly meetings.' Mo agreed and was about to leave when I remembered that I had not told her of her new salary, which I had written down on a piece of paper that I handed to her.

She looked at it, smiled, and said that I was very generous. 'By the way, she said, 'I am staying tonight, and will go back to London with you in the morning.'

That night as I lay dreaming in my bed, I imagined that a beautiful, warm and willing lady had came to my bed and made very passionate love. However, when I recovered from this vivid experience, there was nobody in my bed but me. I concluded it must have been a wonderful dream.

The Lords and My Ladies

June was an important month for me. During the first week, Uncle Edward introduced me to Their Lordships' House so that I could deliver my maiden speech. Their Lordships were discussing the failing economic state of the country and I made a contribution about the coming global market and the need to embrace the new technology, as well as controlling inflation. My speech appeared to be accepted well, and several members congratulated me during a recess.

The second week was highlighted by His Royal Highness Prince Charles making his maiden speech to the Lords, and I crowded in with my new colleagues to hear him. I did admire his confidence and method of delivery, realising instantly that he was now doing the job he had been trained to do since his birth, and I wondered how Jennifer was feeling about the prospect of one day becoming Lady Earlswood.

The rest of those two hectic weeks was spent in London, closely working with Angela on the amalgamation of the two companies. Much of the time was occupied with assuring staff, meeting unions, and trying to draw up plans for changes in both location and in some cases function. The problem was that, while everyone thought that the takeover made the new company stronger, they felt that any amalgamation should be done on the basis of staying put and not changing individual job descriptions. Meetings with the unions got us nowhere and in some cases made the staff position more entrenched than at the start. Angela came to the conclusion that what we were facing was tribalism, which would take months if not years to break down.

During those first few weeks of June, news broke of a mighty explosion in a chemical plant in Lincolnshire, killing many of the workers. This news showed us what real tragedy was, and in some respects dulled much of the confrontation. Angela nevertheless began to lose heart that we would ever get the staff of the two companies to work together, or make the savings, forecast in our takeover report.

The news from Europe was more encouraging. White Gull's European offices were situated in Paris and Rome, while Bun Industries' were sited in Strasbourg and Brussels, meaning we needed only to change the name over the door.

On that second Friday, I travelled home to Colchester on the six o'clock train from Liverpool Street, due to arrive at Colchester at seven forty-five. However, I was so tired that I fell asleep, and did not wake up until the train arrived at Clacton, which was the end of the line. I then had to ring Ted, tell him where I was and ask him to come and collect me. I slept all the way home, had supper and went straight to bed, feeling totally exhausted.

Jennifer told me that meanwhile, during that second week, her parents were in London themselves, her father attending a medical conference and her mother to do some shopping and see a couple of shows. On the Tuesday, at ten o'clock, Jennifer and her mother met each other under the meeting point at Harrods. Jennifer was to spend the day with her mother, have dinner with her parents that night and then stay over, catching the train after breakfast in order to be back on duty by two.

The women immediately made for the nearest coffee bar, settling down to exchange all the news. Jennifer told her mother about the house move, and how quiet and peaceful it was at night, while her mother told her that her father was rumoured to be in line for a chair in orthopaedics in one of the prestigious universities, and that if it came to pass they would have to move. Jennifer told her it would be a shame to leave her nice house and friends, but was cut short by her mother telling her that it was a wife's duty to move with her husband and not to complain.

The two women then made for the ladies' wear department, where her mother was to buy a new outfit for the closing dinner of the conference on Friday night. The problem was, however, that her mother was not a stock size, and every garment she tried on needed some alteration. Finally her mother selected the outfit, leaving Jennifer to explain that the alterations needed to be carried out by Thursday evening at the latest. This was agreed after much deliberation. The women then made their way to the top floor to the main restaurant.

Sensing her mother was already touchy about the alterations and knowing the news that had to be imparted, Jennifer signalled the waiter and ordered two gin and tonics. Once the drinks had been served and her mother was more composed, Jennifer began telling her that she had met a man. Her mother smiled and asked whether he was a doctor, and was visibly shaken when Jennifer shook her head. 'He is a local businessman,' she told her mother. Her mother then asked her in what sort of business this man was in, and was again clearly alarmed when her daughter told her that his business was renovating old properties. 'A builder!' she shrieked. 'Surely not!'

Jennifer shook her head once more and said, 'He is a businessman.' She could clearly see her mother getting agitated, and in order to calm her down told her that the renovation to Bun House, which was featured in her mother's *House and Garden* magazine, had been carried out by George's company. This seemed to calm things down.

Her mother asked her if she loved this man, to which Jennifer replied that, when she was not with him, she felt all alone; when he held her she felt safe and secure; and when he kissed her knees buckled.

'Does he love you?' her mother enquired, to which Jennifer replied that she thought so. Her mother, seeing a worried look on Jennifer's face, said, 'What's the problem, then?' to which Jennifer replied that, if they got married, he would not want her to work, and she was uncertain whether she could live with that.

Her mother then told her that a husband who expected his wife to be chained to the kitchen sink, to cook and clean for him and be constantly pregnant was not worth having.

Questions then flew thick and fast as to this 'George' man's standing in the community, his parentage and family. Jennifer realised that she couldn't take it any longer and said to her mother to be quiet, and to order another drink, as she was going to need it.

Jennifer leaned forward and asked her mother if she could keep a secret from her father, at least for a couple of months. Her mother, anxious to know more, said yes, leaning right over the table as though she was receiving information of national importance. Then she suddenly realised what her daughter had said and accused Jennifer of already being pregnant, believing that and the two months would buy her daughter time to do something about it. Jennifer told her that she was not pregnant, and that George had always acted as a complete gentleman. 'Then what can your father not hear about?' her mother asked.

Jennifer told her that George obeyed an old-fashioned code of honour and would not ask her to marry till he received her father's permission. Her mother laughed and said that her daughter had twisted her father round her little finger since she was three – what had changed? 'Mummy,' Jennifer said, 'don't you see? If you breathe a word, George will be embarrassed when he eventually asks for my hand in marriage.'

'I am not sure,' her mother retorted, 'that any man wishing to interfere with your career will be accepted by your father.'

Jennifer told her mother that she did not understand, and the man she was courting was Lord George Earlswood – and that if they married she would become Lady Earlswood. Furthermore, if they were lucky enough to have a son, then her mother and father would be grandparents to a future peer of the realm.

The colour in her mother's face suddenly drained, and for once she was lost for words.

Both women chose to have the buffet with its vast array of tempting meats, fish and salads. Once they had been served and were sitting down at their table, Jennifer's mother was full of questions, warning her daughter of the possible perils of marrying above one's status. Jennifer told her George was not like that, as she would be able to see for herself when Jennifer brought him to stay in a couple of weeks. Her mother's face went white again. She said that her daughter must be out of her mind, to think that the house could get ready in time to greet a real lord. Jennifer held her mother's hand and told her not to worry as everything would be all right.

Dinner that night should have been a happy occasion, as Jennifer loved her father, and always enjoyed being in his company. This night he was not his old self, and obviously had something important on his mind. When she told him she had a boyfriend, he hardly seem to take it in, and when she asked his permission to bring him home for his opinion, he showed very little interest. Finally, when she could stand it no more, Jennifer demanded to know what was worrying him. Her father explained that the conference had discussed the new Health Service reforms which had been introduced some weeks before on 1 April. When he and his colleagues had learnt that the new Health Authorities would be the centre of power, they had dismissed the new multi-disciplinary management teams as merely another tier of management. They had come to this conclusion when they found out that part of the membership would come from general practitioners (whom he had always considered to be failed consultants), a community medical officer who no longer practised medicine any more and spent his time pondering the future, and a nurse. Who on earth had decided that, he thought? They were fine as consultants' handmaidens, but management of medical services – never.

The consultant body had therefore appointed an ophthalmologist to be their spokesman on this new management team, rather than waste the time of busy surgeons like himself – after all, everyone knew the proper pecking order among clinicians, and surely if management teams required clinical advice they would come to someone like himself. That was only half the story, he continued: they had a new breed of administrators who did not know their place in the scheme of things, not like the old hospital secretaries and group secretaries whom he had twisted round his finger for years. His greatest worry was the appearance at hospital level of treasurers, who would be setting budgets and closely monitoring them. Whoever heard of a clinician arranging his activity to suit a bean counter? 'No,' he told his daughter, 'these arrangements will severely disrupt the delicate balance of power that has been built up over the past twenty-five years.'

Jennifer did not like to see her father so distressed and told him not to worry, as she was sure that, whatever management arrangements were introduced, he would continue to get his own way.

On the train the next morning she worried about her father's objection to change, and for once she started to question his immortality.

Jennifer was in a good mood when she arrived back at the house after duty. Things were going well and she had worked that afternoon on the July rosters to ensure she had a weekend off early in the month. While she had not fully made up her mind about her relationship with me, it was good to plan ahead in case. Therefore when Mary contacted her concerning worries over my health, she was extremely worried. She knew Mary was not a person to panic, and therefore there must be a problem. She thought about going straight over to the manor, but reasoned that she was very tired and I would probably be asleep. She telephoned Mary asking to stay for lunch the next day and promising to be with her early that morning.

Jennifer arrived at ten o'clock and immediately went to see Mary. She crept into my room, thinking I was still dead to the world, and placed her hand against my forehead to check for any signs of fever. This made me wake up, and I opened my eyes to see Jennifer looking down on me.

'Hello, stranger,' I said, 'I did not expect you today.'

'Sorry about that. I suddenly had a long changeover and needed a good old-fashioned Sunday lunch, so here I am. How are you?' she said, looking worried.

'How do I look?' I replied.

'Ghastly,' she said. 'George, is it the headaches again?' she asked.

I replied that the frequency and intensity had increased and the effectiveness of the painkillers seem to have reduced.

'The doctor did warn you that if you overdid it too soon that would happen, and now it has.'

I told her of the terrible pressure the management of White Gull was under to produce the savings we had promised in our takeover paper. I then had to admit that it was all proving more difficult than we had all imagined. Jennifer picked up a sheet of handwritten papers from beside the bed and asked me whether they were important. I told her that it was a report I had been writing till the wee small hours, and my secretary might have difficulty in reading the last page. Jennifer suggested that I had another hour or so sleep, after which she would wake me for lunch. In the meantime she would read the report and correct my grammar and punctuation ready for typing.

She called me at twelve thirty for lunch. As I crawled out of bed, she was surprised to find I still had my clothes on from the day before. She smiled and merely said that normal people got undressed for bed, but at least I had removed my shoes. As I came out of the shower and dried myself, I remembered I had forgotten clean undershorts from the drawer. Accordingly, when I came out of the bathroom with an armful of clothes, all I had on was a small towel wrapped around my waist. As I dropped the clothes into the linen basket and reached into my underwear drawer, the towel suddenly slipped down leaving me stark naked with just a pair of undershorts dangled in front of me. Jennifer laughed at my antics and said not to worry, in her profession naked men were no longer a novelty.

Showered, shaved and dressed, I began to feel happier, and together we went down for lunch. I realised just how hungry I was. I ate a good lunch, settling back comfortably in my dining room chair. I was just starting to doze off when Jennifer awakened me and ordered me back to bed. I must have been dozing for some time as the bed had been made and was pulled back waiting for me to get in.

'Trousers and shoes off!' she commanded as I lay half in, half out of the bed, and I did as I was told. 'I will wake you at three,' she told me, 'and then we can talk.'

True to her word, she woke me at three with a cup of tea, which she placed on the bedside cabinet. She then removed her shoes and, using the bed steps, climbed on to the other side of my four-poster bed above the bedclothes. She said, 'Before we start kissing and cuddling, I would like to tell you something about that report of yours that I have just corrected. The report is a good one and even I, a mere woman, understood the difficulties you face. However, what you don't say is how you intend to tackle the current impasse.'

'That's because we have not yet identified one,' I replied.

She thought for a moment and asked whether we had some building we could use to free up some additional space, which we would need in order to achieve an amalgamation of duplicated functions. Something clicked in my brain, and I grabbed her to me, telling her how clever she was. Finding me in her arms she responded eagerly, returning my kisses with relish. Wrapped in our embrace we began exploring each other's bodies through our clothes, but when I failed to try to undress her she asked if I was either too tired or had lost interest. I told her that I still felt passionate about her and was kept awake dreaming of her naked in my arms. Should that actually occur then I doubted I could stop myself going all the way. She smiled, kissed me again, and said I must be the most thoughtful man in the world.

I risked asking her if she had yet come to any decision regarding me. She looked at me hard and said that things were becoming clearer, but she still needed a little more time. She told me that she had mentioned me to her parents, and had booked a weekend at the beginning of July when, provided she did want me, I could go up and meet them properly. I told her I looked forward to meeting them. Jennifer had dinner and left, as she was on duty the next day.

I was up early the next day, and had had breakfast and was sitting in my study by nine o'clock. I rang Suzie and was put through to her without delay. She was surprised to receive a call so early and asked what was wrong. 'Nothing,' I told her, 'but, remind me, when I helped cost the tender, wasn't there a two-floor building requiring refurbishment and situated not far from Farringdon underground station?'

'Yes,' she said, 'Brunwin House.'

'Tell me more,' I said.

'The structure is fine and so is the roof, there is no damp and the walls are reasonably solid but badly gouged in parts. The building has had a chequered past and has been a warehouse, shops, market stalls and associated offices, but for the past few years a store for old files. These have now been sent for microfilming.'

'What state is it now in?' I asked.

'Well,' said Suzie, 'the outside has been painted apart from the small fire escape. Inside, we have removed all the old partitions, rewired it and attended to the heating. Next week the telephone engineers will fit phone points on the walls. We have allowed for partitions as a PC sum, so that when a new tenant is found he can determine where he wants them.'

'Suzie,' I said, 'remind me how big the building is.'

She looked at the specification and read the measurements off to me.

'Suzie, can you contact your partition contractors and any one else that is involved and find out when all the work will be finished?'

'No need,' she said, 'it is scheduled for completion in mid-August.'

The next phone call was to Arthur Welsh, head of the property management division of White Gull Enterprises. He, like Suzie, was surprised to receive such an early call from the chairman, and immediately asked what was wrong. 'Nothing,' I told him, 'but I wanted to have a talk with you about an idea my colleague and I have formulated over the past few weeks.'

He said that if it affected him, please could I get on with it, fearing that an early retirement was on the cards.

'Arthur,' I began, 'you have worked for my family ever since I can remember, and have always been highly regarded for your loyalty and efficiency. We therefore feel you are the right person to spearhead the setting up of a joint estate management department, independent from headquarters with a high level of management freedom. We have been searching for a suitable building in which to launch our initiative and think that we have come up with a possible solution.'

'Where?' he asked.

'Brunwin House,' I replied.

'Where's that?' he asked.

'Not far from Farringdon Underground station.'

Then he caught on. 'I remember now, the old file store, hasn't been used for years.'

I reminded him that the building was in that year's refurbishment programme, and according to Suzie had great potential. I asked him to contact his opposite number at Bun Industries and arrange a visit to the site, preferably that day. 'Explain to him what I have just said, and tell him that I am confident that with your experience and expertise, together with his youth and energy, the project must have a really good chance of success.' I also suggested that they arrange to meet Suzie there, so that, provided the building was suitable, they could select the right partitioning, carpets and colour scheme. 'I know that you are all busy people but, if at all possible, I would like your opinion today, so that I can put a report to tomorrow afternoon's management meeting.'

I put the phone down and began to sort through my papers to see what other departments shared the floors with the two estate departments to see if by chance I could find a match. Luckily, the legal departments of both companies occupied the space next to their estate management colleagues. The numbers, compared to both estate departments, were small, and I resolved to suggest that the two legal departments be amalgamated as soon as space became available. I also noticed that there was a large area on the third floor without any reference as to what it was used for or who occupied it. That, I thought, would be my first task tomorrow – to check on who was accommodated in this area.

I then surprised Mary when I told her that I was going to go into the village and have a drink at the pub – something I did only at Christmas and New Year – but that I would be back in time for lunch. I found George, the publican, standing at the bar. The pub had only just opened for business and was therefore, as yet empty. George looked up and, seeing who it was, rushed round the bar to greet me. I asked him if he could spare me a few minutes to discuss possible plans for a function I was thinking of holding later in the year. I outlined my plan for having a buffet for about 200 people in a marquee on the lawn in front of the house. I would want the floor boarded and some heating, as the function would probably be a short time before Christmas. I would need tables and chairs that could be stacked away after the meal so as to allow dancing. 'George,' I asked, 'can it be done?'

George looked interested and told me that he had all the contacts necessary to equip and cater for such an event, if the need arose. I thanked him and told him my committee had not yet approved the idea, but I hoped to have an answer very soon, and told him to keep it a secret as I did not wish to alarm Mary, who would have liked to cater for such a function. George smiled and said, 'Do not worry. If it goes ahead and you use my services, I will give her an important role.'

During lunch, Mary was eager to know whom I had seen in the pub, and whom I had talked to, and was disappointed when I told her no one in particular.

Arthur rang me back at about six thirty that evening to tell me that both Martin Gin and he were very enthusiastic about the project and, yes, the old Brunwin property would be ideal. They had spoken to Suzie on site and had agreed both partitioning and colour schemes. 'The one thing that has been overlooked is how the telephones will operate efficiently. Luckily, the telephone people were measuring up, and the man in charge has said that he can supply a small refurbished automatic switchboard which will meet all our needs. The price seemed very reasonable, and as I have not committed all this year's refurbishment money, I made an instant management decision, which I hope you will approve of. While you are on the telephone, can I ask you to unfreeze one of our two vacancies so that we can appoint an operator receptionist in time for our move at the end of August?' I spent the rest of the time that day writing an addendum to the report my secretary had just typed and handed me back.

The next morning I travelled to London, and made my way to Arthur's office. He rose from his desk to greet me and said that, had I asked, he would have come to me in my office. I asked him what the last quarter of the floor was used for, and why the doors were locked. 'Your grandfather's idea,' he said. 'As you know, he hated throwing anything away, so he set aside a small room where redundant furniture and equipment could be stored. Over the years the store has just got bigger, and your Uncle Cecil would not change the policy.'

I asked Arthur to show me the store which, like a cancer, was gradually creeping along the third floor. The store was stacked from top to bottom with old desks, chairs and rusty filing cabinets. It was so full that it was impossible to see exactly what was in it, leave alone actually being able to remove anything stored at the back. Arthur saw my concern, and told me that people in the offices referred to this room as the graveyard. I shook my head, and told him, 'In that case, look out for the resurrectionists.'

When I returned to the office, I put a call into Angela, who was working in her office at Bun Industries that morning. I briefly brought her up to speed on the new progress, and she seemed very pleased. She asked if we could meet for lunch, as she had something relevant to the afternoon's meeting that she needed to show me. We agreed to meet at twelve o'clock in our favourite City restaurant.

When I arrived she was already there, and she smiled as I entered. Over lunch, Angela showed me a consultant's report on Bun Industries' staffing that had been commissioned before the takeover. It concluded that the systems that had grown up over many years were now outdated, old-fashioned and wasteful. The company had not embraced the new technology concerning computers. While a fuller study would be needed to ascertain exactly what information was required, the study carried out so far suggested a manpower saving of about twenty per cent. I told her that the report only confirmed what I had already suspected during my brief time at White Gull, and I was sure that the same could be said of that company.

I then told her about the graveyard. She laughed, and then confessed that Bun Industries had a similar store, situated in a derelict building in East London. She went on to say, 'At least you have had your old records put on to fiche. The store I have just told you about is half full of files. I keep on meaning to do something about it, but have not found the time.'

The meeting with Mike was very constructive, especially when we discussed the need to introduce computing into the joint company. 'The problem is,' Angela told Mike, 'that many of our managers are comparatively old, and fear these new machines.' Mike agreed, but said we should at least make a start. I reminded them of the estate management amalgamation and suggested that we run a pilot scheme there – after all, the necessary cabling could be put in alongside the telephone cabling. Angela agreed to contact the consultant, and to spearhead the project.

When Angela had gone, I stayed to talk to Mike, who seemed to want a word with me anyway. I first told him about the 'graveyard', and how much valuable space it took up. Once it was cleared and the first two moves were completed it would leave me a complete floor empty, in which to move people around. He nodded, so I continued, 'Have you noticed that, apart from the foyer and your office, the rest of the building has become run down and tatty?' He nodded again, and told me his predecessor did not believe in making staff too comfortable. (Now, where had I heard that before?)

I then asked him if there was any money to gradually redecorate the offices, as and when space became unoccupied. He said, 'Tell Arthur Welsh to negotiate a rolling contract and to clear that store. I know there is a lot to do and we may well have to spend money in the short term, so I have set aside £50,000 to cover the costs of amalgamating the two businesses.' I thanked him, and was about to leave when he asked me to stay and said, 'I know you and Angela are working all the hours God sent to get the job done. However, looking at you both, I suspect that you are both overdoing it, and I want you to slow down. Neither of you are any good to me in hospital or worse. By the way, I and my family accept your kind invitation to stay for the weekend at the end of July, and we are all looking forward to it.'

I left the building that night in high spirits. Because I was staying over, I had arranged to meet Pauline and Suzie for dinner, at a small family restaurant not far from their new offices. I caught the Tube to Whitechapel, leaving the station by the main entrance. I had just started to walk down a narrow alley, when I felt a push in the back. I turned round and found two young teenagers, one with a knife, threatening me and demanding my wallet. Even though I was scared, especially of the knife, I told them to get lost before I called the police. This seemed to anger the smaller of the two men, who landed a misaimed punch on my shoulder. This annoyed me, and I took a defensive stance. The young man with the knife aimed a lunge at me and missed. Instinctively, I grabbed his wrist as tight as I could, while bringing my knee up into his crutch, as I had seen done in many a film. He howled and tried to take his free hand to his injured body, but somehow lost his balance and fell sideways. His fall was so sudden that I failed to let go of his arm, until I heard a sudden cracking sound, followed by a scream of pain.

The second teenager had momentarily been taken off guard, but was now in the process of swinging something towards my face. I ducked and felt a painful blow on my head. I was really angry now, with the adrenalin flowing, and I aimed a punch in the middle of his face with all the strength I could muster and saw a spout of blood. His hands both flew to his face, leaving the rest of his body exposed. Again using techniques I had seen only on television, I brought my knee into contact with his femur, watching him fall into a crying heap. I stood there hoping that someone would come to my aid, but no one appeared.

Not knowing what to do next, I prepared myself for another attack, but none came, and the two boys staggered away. I then made my way to the restaurant feeling tired and sweaty. Perspiration was running down my face, as I thought, and I must have looked very untidy.

The girls were already at the table when I entered the restaurant. Pauline looked up and screamed, while Suzie leapt from her chair and held my arm. I realised then it was not sweat that was running down my face but blood, which now covered my right eye, forehead and face. Pauline found a chair and helped me to sit down. Suzie asked what had happened and I told her I had been mugged. Watching the blood drip on my shirt, Suzie suggested I remove my jacket, which so far had not been stained. The waitress brought the first aid box, found a large pad and applied it to the wound. The manager of the restaurant, having seen my entrance from the kitchen doorway, had already phoned for an ambulance. I have to admit that the service was so effective that, before we knew it, two ambulance men were walking through the door. Pauline told them what had happened and when. The older of the two men told me that they would take me to hospital to be checked over. He offered me his arm. As I tried to rise from my chair my legs turned to jelly and, in spite of the ambulanceman's efforts, I landed on the floor. The other ambulanceman went for a stretcher, while his colleague talked softly to me, telling me I would soon be all right.

I was taken to the Accident and Emergency department of the London Hospital, where I was hastily seen by a doctor, who ordered an X-ray. While this was being done, Suzie rang the manor to tell them what had happened, and where I was. Ted thanked her and said, 'When you know whether they intend to admit him or discharge him, let us know.'

Once I was back in the cubicle, the doctor reappeared. He asked me whether I made a habit of using my head as a target. I said not really. He then told me that the blow had landed on the site of the old fracture, causing a crack to appear at one edge. He said, 'Now, Mr Earlswood,' to which Suzie said, 'It's Lord Earlswood.' The young doctor looked confused for a moment and then apologised for not realising who I was. 'Now, your lordship,' he began again, 'the opening of the fracture is not good news, but I am afraid that only time can heal it. As far as the scalp wound is concerned, I will send in a nurse who can sort it out, but it may require stitching. I will give you some painkillers and a letter to your doctor, to take home with you.' He smiled as I thanked him and we shook hands.

While I was waiting for the nurse a policeman appeared, and asked if it was convenient for me to make a statement. I agreed and I was able to give him a full description of the two men who had attacked me. He asked me what had happened to the knife, and I told him it was probably still in the grass verge where I had kicked it. He commented that they had probably already gone back for it, but I told him that they probably had not, as one had a suspected broken arm and a painful crutch, while his mate might have a broken nose and an injured leg. The policeman then asked if I was a professional street fighter, as the two boys had got more than they expected. He left and a nurse dressed the wound on my head, declaring that it did not require stitching. I suddenly realised that it was now gone eleven and the girls had not eaten. The nurse informed them that there was an all-night cafe that did hot food just across the road opposite the main entrance. I gave Suzie some money and told them both to have a meal and take a taxi home, after Ted had collected me.

The time was after twelve when I got home and into bed. My head still ached, making sleep difficult, and I found myself thinking back over my day which, in spite of the attempted mugging, could be classed as successful.

Mo appeared the next morning with breakfast on a tray, together with her newspaper. 'You are in all the papers this morning,' she said, 'and according to an MP interviewed on the news, questions are to be raised in the house this afternoon.'

While I was eating, Mo told me who had been told and about their reaction. Mike had sent his regards and said not to return to work until I was fully recovered. Jennifer told Mo I was stay in bed and that she would come over as soon as her shift ended. Angela had rung to wish me well, along with many other well-wishers, who had either heard of my attack on the radio or seen it in their newspapers. 'Suzie checked to see how you are and said that the fry-up was delicious.' I asked Mo to send flowers to Pauline and Suzie as a thank you for the previous night.

Jennifer arrived just after three and came straight up to see me. 'How are you?' she asked, looking into my face.

'I have a bad headache, but other than that I feel a fraud.'

'What did the doctor say?' she replied, and I told her I had mild concussion and had opened up the old fracture at the end. She frowned and said that I could have been killed and asked why I didn't just hand over my wallet to them. I told her that they would then have probably still assaulted me.

She stood and thought for a minute, then told me that I could obviously not be trusted to stay out of trouble and that I needed a good wife to look after me. I asked her if that meant she had now made a decision, to which she smiled and said, 'Yes – although my final fate will be in the hands of my father.'

Jennifer had gone back that evening, leaving me to think about what she had said. Mo came up to see me and to show me four promising specifications for purchase and renovation. We agreed to make offers on all ten and I congratulated her on her prompt start to the job. Business finished, I turned to her and told her she would always be special, and that I had never stopped loving her. I then told her that I realised she would never marry me, and in my position, I had to move on. I said that I was thinking of asking Jennifer to marry me, and asked how she felt. She asked whether

Jennifer and I really loved each other and were prepared to spend the rest of our lives together. I said that I thought so, but that it was still early days in our relationship.

'You two are still not an item,' she said.

I knew what she meant and said, 'No.'

Perhaps that's something you two need to discuss. Other than that I am pleased for you and now I am to be based here, we will eventually have another girl in the house.' She thought for a moment and said, 'You know, George, that if you and Jennifer cannot have kids,' I would still bear children for you.' I kissed her and she left.

The following week I continued with my work with Angela on the amalgamation of the two companies, albeit at a slower pace. On that last Friday before our visit to Jennifer's parents, I did not go into London, but instead planned what I needed to say to Jennifer's father the following weekend.

Planning and Promises

The following weekend Jennifer and I motored up to Birmingham in my Jaguar, which had been serviced, valeted and polished for the occasion. We arrived at the time appointed for luncheon. We were greeted at the door by Jennifer's father, and ushered into the lounge. Jennifer made the introductions before scuttling off to the kitchen to help her mother finish the preparations. Jennifer's father offered me a sherry which I accepted. He asked whether we had had a good journey, and if there had been much traffic. I told him we had had a very good journey and had made good time. He then remarked that we should have done in such a fine car something he hoped to have in the future.

Lunch was a happy affair, but short on conversation. Once lunch was cleared away, the women suggested that we men should retire to the lounge, and they would follow shortly with coffee. Jennifer's father offered me a brandy, which I refused, but I urged him to have one himself.

I had been rehearsing for some hours what I was going to say, but when it came to it, words seem to fail me. I therefore decided to stick to the point of our visit, and told him that I had known his daughter for some time, and was now thinking of asking her to marry me. He looked up and smiled and told me that now he knew why we men had been left alone to talk. I continued by telling him that honour made it necessary for me to obtain his permission before actually popping the question, so to speak. 'George,' he replied, 'what on earth makes you think that Jennifer will take any notice of what her dear old dad thinks? She is, after all, twenty-six and able to make her own decisions. I do however appreciate the courtesy of you asking, and if Jennifer loves you enough to marry you, then you both have my best wishes.' He then rose and shook my hand, offering his congratulations.

The girls had still not appeared, so he told me that he was not prying, but would like to know something about his future son-in-law. I told him that I was a businessman and was chairman of several companies. I said that most of the names of these companies he would probably not recognise, but that he might have heard of White Gull Enterprises. His face lit up and he said, 'Isn't that one of the big international multiples?' I answered that it was. He remarked that I seemed very young to be a captain of industry. 'The fault of my parents,' I replied. 'You see my parents died recently in a car crash, and I found myself heir to the company and my father's title.'

This made him sit up and ask, 'Did you say "title"?'

'Yes,' I replied, 'I am now Lord Earlswood and if Jennifer agrees to marry me, she will become Lady Earlswood.'

The colour seemed to drain from his face as he sat back in his chair. I waited while he regained his composure and explained the main reason why I had come to ask his permission first: if we had a son, he and his lady wife would become grandparents to a future peer of the realm.

Just at that minute the girls arrived with coffee. He took the tray, placed it on the table, took his wife's hand and sat her on the sofa, opposite where we were sitting. He began by saying to his wife that the George Jennifer had brought home was in fact a lord, and that he had been asked and given permission for George to ask Jennifer for her hand in marriage. Jennifer's smiled and replied that she already knew, hence the late arrival of the coffee.

The rest of the afternoon was spent by Jennifer telling them that, although she would be a lady, she still intended, with George's permission, to nurse part-time. However, later on she hoped to give up nursing to concentrate on caring for their grandchild. I also invited her parents to the weekend house party at the end of the month when the official engagement would be announced, but I asked them not to tell anyone until that time.

That evening we dined at one of the top hotels in Birmingham, toasting the future in champagne. Soon our visit was over and we were on our way home, leaving Jennifer's mother and father shell-shocked but very happy. Jennifer knew both of her friends were on duty, and therefore invited me in for coffee, telling me she wanted me to go before they returned. 'I do not know how I am going to keep a secret to the end of the month,' she said, 'let alone what to say if they find us smooching on the sofa.'

'We can always go upstairs,' I suggested, pulling her to me and kissing her. She would not be persuaded and I was soon on my way home.

I travelled to London the next day for a meeting with Angela. She reported that Arthur and Martin were thrilled at being chosen for the computer experiment, and had already arranged to meet the computer consultant the following week to discuss what information they currently kept and what information they would like to receive. I congratulated her on fast work, and asked her who would be the second candidate for computerisation. She smiled and said, 'Salaries and wages. I was talking to our computer consultant, who carried out the study on our accounts department. He told me that eighty per cent of our employees are white-collar workers on a single pay spine. The other twenty per cent are ancillary workers, cleaners, doormen, drivers, etc. They are pre-paid weekly. Half of them have their wages drawn up off site, and the remainder here. The amazing thing is that some years ago your father and your uncle agreed that they would not compete for the same staff, and agreed to use the same pay spine and rates of pay. This means amalgamation will be much easier than I had envisaged. They can all be accommodated in the space left by your estate management department, legal department and the graveyard.'

'Good,' I said, but I was soon interrupted by Angela, who told me that, when I had visited the third floor, I had assumed that the estates and legal boys occupied both sides of the corridor, but that was not strictly true. 'The other side of the corridor comprises two large meeting rooms, a coffee lounge, a smoking lounge and a dead file store, none of which is strictly needed. I have therefore decided to utilise that side of the corridor as a joint accounts payable and receivable department, who will be the third tranche for putting on the computer. That only leaves the management and financial control departments, who can be accommodated on half of the second floor, thereby leaving half a floor in your building clear, and a floor in Bun House.'

'Well done,' I said, shaking her by the hand.

That evening I had dinner with Pauline and Suzie, only this time going there and back to my hotel by taxi. During the meal Suzie reported that Mr Arthur Welsh had offered her a rolling contract to refurbish White Gull House, spread over the following two years, but that she needed to ask me what exactly was required.

I explained the amalgamation to her, as far as we had got, telling her that the first floor of the contract would begin early in September, finishing at the end of the same month, and that she would shortly be getting details of telephone, computer and electric points required. In the same specification there would be details of changes in partitions to suit the different functions of the new office.

Pauline then said that he had a furniture store that needed clearing, which she would pass over to Peter. There were at least three large lorry loads that would take three days to shift. Some of the items might be suitable for refurbishment, but most only fit for the dump.

The following morning I had a meeting with Mike to finalise my papers on training across both countries as well as my paper of gifts and financial inducements, both papers having received his wholehearted support. I updated him on our amalgamation progress, which again he liked. He then said that perhaps he should not go on vacation, in case his office was removed to Bun House, and we laughed. Over coffee he asked me what I thought about this new Social Contract, which had been signed the month before by the TUC and the new government. 'Not much,' I replied, 'it seems very much like the pay and prices legislation they have just scrapped. Individual unions know how much the miners got in their pay deal and realise that inflation is topping fifteen per cent. Do you think their members will settle for any less, no matter by whom or why the new social contract is signed? I think we are in for a winter of discontent. Furthermore, the fools in the government are watering down the Industrial Relations Act in favour of a strikers' charter.'

The subject then changed when Mike, not used to the sport of association football, asked me who I thought the new England manager would be, and I told him Don Revie of Leeds United, then the dominant force in the first division. I reminded him that he was coming to the country weekend at the end of the month, and he said that they were all looking forward to it. I then confided my secret to him, knowing how discreet he could be. He shook my hand in congratulations telling me that it was wonderful news. 'Keep the first weekend free,' I told him, 'I might need a best man,' and I smiled.

I left London early that day as Jennifer was coming for dinner, and would stay the night as she had the following day off. Dinner had been delayed till eight thirty to allow Jennifer time after finishing duty at seven.

Dinner with Ted and Mary was as always a real family occasion, with everyone very relaxed. Once dinner was over and while we were still at the table, I decided to tell Mary and Ted our secret before Jennifer burst. I told them that, as they were the nearest people to being my parents, we wanted to let them into a secret. Mary moved forward, not wishing to miss a word. 'Last Saturday,' I continued, 'we went to see Jennifer's parents, in order for me to ask her father for permission to wed his daughter, a request he welcomed and agreed to. Therefore, Jennifer and I will announce our engagement first in confidence at the family dinner party on the Saturday before the village fete, making it official during the opening ceremony.'

Mary was beaming with delight and now understood why she had been asked to the family dinner as a guest. She rose from her seat and went over to Jennifer, took her in her arms and told her again how pleased she was, not only at the news but also that we had shared it with them before the day of the dinner. Ted shook hands and told me I would be marrying a lovely girl, of whom he approved.

We left Mary and Ted to clear away, and no doubt discuss our news, while we went upstairs to my private sitting room. Jennifer told me she was glad I had decided to tell them, as she was dying to have another woman to talk to about engagement and in the longer term marriage.

'When did you have in mind for the wedding?' I asked innocently.

'Probably next spring or summer,' she replied.

'How do you feel about a December wedding?' I asked.

'You mean next year? It seems a bit of a long time to wait, but if that's what you want, December will be fine.'

I told her that what I had in mind was this year, not next. She told me that that was impossible, and there was simply not time to make all the arrangements.

'Supposing we could make all the arrangements, what then?' I asked.

Jennifer smiled and told me in that case she would marry me. The next hour was spent deciding the exact date and the venue for the wedding. We would get married on the first Saturday of December, there at the hall. We would have a giant marquee sited on the large lawn, which would seat at least 150 guests. The marquee would have a proper floor and would be heated. Dress would be formal and Jennifer would have at least three bridesmaids.

She then asked how much a wedding of that size would cost, so she could warn her father. I asked her not to tell her parents anything about costs as I would have a quiet word with her father during the weekend.

Mary brought up our late-night drink, and was greeted by Jennifer, who could not wait to tell Mary the date we had chosen. Mary laughed at the excitement on Jennifer's face but added that December weddings meant carrying your baby all through the summer. Jennifer laughed and said, 'We will see what we see.'

Hearing Ted lock up and the crunch of their feet on the pathway leading to their bungalow meant we were all alone. Jennifer came immediately into my arms and kissed me. I responded and we decided to go into my bedroom. Once we were on the bed, the kissing, cuddling and caressing began in earnest until we were both naked except for our underwear. We continued our love-making until all Jennifer was wearing was a small pair of briefs. I urged her to go on, but she begged me to stop, which I did. 'I am sorry,' she told me, 'but when we do make love I want it to be when we have time together afterwards, like a long weekend away.' I told her that was a good idea, and that I knew a splendid hotel in Bury St Edmunds, and smiled.

The next day we were up bright and early to drive to Manor

Park, just outside Romford. We had been invited to the home of the family jeweller, who was to alter both the family diamond ring as well as the family engagement ring, which Jennifer told me she would be proud to wear. He welcomed us to his home and led us into the dining room, where the table had already been arranged for proper inspection. I took the envelope I had been given in America, and emptied the two rings out on the table. He lovingly picked up the diamond ring, with its huge stone ringed in matched diamonds. He smiled and said, 'I was in the army when I last saw this. Your dear, departed father brought a sweet young girl who he said would wear the ring as soon as the war was over. I remember your dear mother was so nervous, she kept popping out to the toilet. I was home on leave and I still remember my father taking out this ring from the safe and showing it to me. "This," he said, "is one of the most famous diamonds outside the crown jewels, and is known as the Earlswood diamond." '

The jeweller told me proudly how his father had boasted that, out of all the jewellers in the capital, he was the one chosen to alter it. 'The diamond appeared out of the East at the beginning of the eighteenth century. The setting is Indian, and of the highest workmanship. The ring was probably made for a great ruler, even before the Raj.' Turning to Jennifer, he said, 'The first Earlswood to wear this ring was George's great great grandmother at the end of the seventeen hundreds, and it has been worn by successive Lady Earlswoods.' He gently took Jennifer's finger and measured her finger on her right hand. He nodded and told us the ring needed taking in, a very simple job. He asked me whether the ring was insured separately and I said yes. I handed him the last insurance valuation, dated late in 1959. 'Must be worth, at today's values, a great deal more,' he said, so he arrived at a figure that he considered appropriate, wrote it on a piece of paper and handed it to me. I nodded and handed it to Jennifer, whose eyes nearly popped out of their sockets.

Then came the engagement ring, worn by Earlswood brides for at least 150 years. The old man examined them with his glass, declaring that the four large matched sapphires were some of the finest he had ever seen, and the smaller diamonds that formed the side settings were also exquisite. He measured Jennifer's other hand carefully, declaring that the ring needed only a small reduction. I produced the current valuation certificates which again were well out of date and again the old man revalued them. 'You have to insure them while in our care,' he said, 'that is why we need to ascertain their value. Now, young sir, what ring will you be wearing at the wedding?'

I produced my father's gold ring, bearing the Earlswood crest. He smiled and said that he should have known. 'The ring is made from Cornish gold and was made for your great grandfather in 1915 when his only child was born, happy that it was a boy, who one day would wear the family ring.

'Now, young lady, what did you have in mind for a wedding ring? He handed her a book of designs. 'Cornish gold, I suggest, and fairly plain.' Jennifer agreed, handing him back the book often at a very plain but attractive design. Turning to me he said, 'Did you wish for a separate wedding ring to go with the family ring?'

Taking up my father's ring and looking hard at it, I said no, one ring would suffice. He inspected the ring under his glass and declared that he would return it as good as new.

He measured my finger, writing down the measurements in his book. 'When did you want the rings?' he asked, and I told him two weeks for the engagement ring and two months for the other.

His wife then brought in coffee and the jeweller proudly introduced Jennifer and me.

On the way home Jennifer told me that she could never wear anything quite so precious, and I told her to forget the value and wear it as a reminder of my love for her.

We had lunch out and arrived back at the manor for dinner. Mo was at the manor and was staying the night. Once supper was finished, Mo asked to see me in my office, and I agreed. I asked her what the problem was, and she told me that Gloworm had been asked by an old and satisfied customer to quote for the refurbishment of a small country house hotel in Suffolk, and she asked if she could help Peter with the tender. I smiled and asked what she had said to Peter, and she said, 'When do we start?'

I frowned and told her I was still the boss and I must

remember to bring one of the things that graced my study in the town house, to help me keep order. She smiled and said that it was time she left. I stopped Mo from leaving and told her my secret, and asked what she thought. She kissed me and said she was very happy. Mo followed me out of the study and into the lounge where Jennifer was sitting. I told her that I had confided in Mo, who could in my absence help her with any arrangements.

The following day I travelled back to London, knowing the time for Mike to leave on vacation was soon be upon us and there were still a few ends to clear up before he went. I entered his office, only to find him reading the *Financial Times*. 'Have you seen this,' he said, motioning to a headline. Before I had time to speak, he told me that apparently a consortium of oil-rich Arabs was buying up property all over London. Did we need to act? I told him no, what the Arabs were doing was buying up valuable sites while property prices were being restrained by legislation. They would wait till restrictions were removed and prices started to rise again, then sell them at a profit. I declared that, while it was a good short-term policy, it had no part in our business plan at that moment, although their actions might push prices of our assets up in the long term. He told me that my forecast as to who would be the new England manager was correct, and Don Revie had got the job.

That night Jennifer rang, telling me that she had booked a week off at the end of August. She asked if we could go away, but not to Bury St Edmunds. Matters for the next two weeks seemed to fall into place. At White Gull the integration was going well, and both the Gloworm concerns were working at full stretch. Arrangements for the weekend were also going well, as well as the preparations for the village fete.

Mo had made offers on twenty properties, ten of them in the nearby market town of Braintree, which was suffering from the gradual closedown of its industries. The stockbrokers report had also been received and, compared with the current level of inflation, was disappointing, but nevertheless showed good potential for growth. From a long-term perspective no industrial country could sustain higher than normal inflation for long, and whoever was in power would be forced to act. Therefore, as I approached the weekend of my engagement, I felt very satisfied with life.

During that third week, Tom and Wendy moved into their new house in the village, now that Katy had finished school. Ted and Mary had achieved their dream of having their granddaughter nearby and could watch her grow up.

I and the Village Celebrate

The Friday before August bank holiday dawned dull and grey, but the forecast for the remainder of the weekend was for the weather to improve. The house was full of activity as I came down to breakfast. Mary had two girls from the village getting rooms ready and Mary was busy in the kitchen ensuring that the additional helpers she had employed for the weekend were kept busy. I and Mo were the only people in for lunch and so we dined with Ted and Mary. I went over the times of arrival for the guests, reminding Ted that he was meeting the three ten train to Colchester, with Mike, his wife and daughter from London. Lord and Lady Bun would not arrive till six and Jennifer's parents about four. There would be only eight for dinner unless Ted and Mary wished to join us, as Mike's daughter was being taken by Mo to join Suzie and Pauline on a girls' night out. The girls were all going to stay at my Lexden house for the duration of the weekend.

Apart from the Saturday night dinner and of course the fete, the girls had planned a programme all of their own. Jennifer wanted to show her parents where she lived and where she worked, as well as shopping and sightseeing in Colchester itself. I asked Tom if he would drive the second Rolls-Royce, giving them lunch at the George, and ensuring they were not back till after five. The Buns and Angela were taking the opportunity to visit long-lost friends in nearby Sudbury and would be away most of the day, returning in time to change for dinner. Ted would drive Mike and his wife with me as guide to Clacton to see a British seaside resort, walk along the pier and have a fish and chip lunch, before driving along the coast to nearby Harwich, where we would pick up our surprise guest from the ferry from Holland.

Mary, Wendy and Katy would ensure everything was ready for the big dinner. I had also agreed with Mary that Monday lunch would be a buffet and the twelve members of the organising committee could have lunch with my house guests. Dinner on Monday would be as normal with all the guests plus the usual Gloworm crew, Mary then asked about my requirements for Sunday, and I told her that I had asked everybody to attend church. Afterwards all the guests would be taken to nearby Colchester to visit the many antique shops and an antique fair. I had arranged lunch for them all at the White Hart hotel. Sunday dinner would be a family affair with just our guests and Mary and Ted if they wanted as, after all, I considered them as family and would be announcing details of the wedding. I knew that that would do the trick and that they would both attend as guests.

Jennifer was the first to arrive, at three thirty in time to meet and greet her parents who arrived just after four. They were immediately impressed by the manor and its grounds, and were even more surprised when Jennifer took them to their suite complete with four-poster bed. Mike, his wife and daughter were next to arrive at four thirty, suitably impressed at being transported in a Rolls-Royce. Mo went to meet them, taking Mike's daughter's weekend case from her and putting it by the door ready to go in her boot. When she was shown to their suite, Mike's wife said that she was looking forward to sleeping in a four-poster bed. The Buns were last to arrive at six o'clock and were immediately shown to what had always been my mother's room, where they always stayed when they came to visit. Jennifer had opted to give up her suite to her parents, taking a room upstairs.

Dinner was a getting-to-know-you affair, as well as part business meeting as Angela told me the latest moves in her task to unite the accounting department.

Saturday morning saw an early breakfast with my guests embarking on their various planned excursions. Jennifer's parents were particularly impressed when Tom arrived at the front door driving the second Rolls-Royce. The Buns soon followed in their Rolls Royce en route to Sudbury. We were the last to leave for Clacton and eventually for Harwich. Mike was just like a small child gambling on the slot machines and games, trying both cockles and candy floss. He even bought a kiss-me-quick cowboy hat and a stick of Clacton rock. The fish and chips we ate at a restaurant right on the main road from the front were very good, especially washed down with a glass of English beer.

At just after three we met the Hook of Holland ferry down on the Harwich quay. Using a large piece of cardboard with Marie Therese's name clearly shown, I waited for her to appear. When she did, I was surprised to find a very short but very attractive young lady with a captivating smile. I took her case and led her to the car, which Ted had parked near by. I made the necessary introductions and Marie Therese got into the back of the car, next to Mike and his wife.

When we arrived at the manor, just before four, Mary showed our guest to her room to freshen up. When she was ready, shortly before five, I showed her into my study where coffee was already brewing. I learnt that she was a long-time pen pal of Jennifer's and that they had not seen each other for several years.

The Brierlys arrived just after five, and immediately went to the kitchen for some tea. Mary told Jennifer that I was in my study and had something important to tell her. She immediately left her tea and went to see what I wanted. 'Come in, my love,' I said, as she appeared at the doorway. 'There is someone here waiting to see you.' She looked to the far end of the study and saw her friend. Jennifer raced to her friend's arms, telling her how unexpected her visit was. I then quietly left the room, leaving the two friends alone.

Just before dinner, I went upstairs and knocked on Jennifer's bedroom door. She opened the door and asked me in. She was wearing one of my late mother's formal gowns and looked every bit a lady. I reached in my pocket and pulled out the sapphire and diamond ring that had come back from the jeweller the previous week. 'Your hand, my darling,' I said and slipped the ring on her finger. Jennifer looked lovingly at the ring, and said quietly that, if my mother was up there, she hoped she would approve. I told her that to have at long last someone who could ensure the Earlswood line would make her very happy indeed. We then kissed passionately until Jennifer reminded me we had guests downstairs who needed entertaining.

The dinner party began on an excited note, with an air of

suspense as to the reason for such a splendid gathering. Uncle Edward, as senior member, said grace and everybody sat down. I rose from my seat, tapped my glass and asked for their attention. I began by thanking them all for attending, complimenting the ladies on their breathtaking appearance. I thanked them all for the help, comfort and support they had extended to me following the tragic loss of my parents. I then told them that it was now time for me to move on, and that I was happy to announce that Jennifer had consented to become my wife and the future Lady Earlswood.

There was a momentary hush, followed by an outburst of sheer pleasure, as many of the girls left their seats to congratulate Jennifer and admire the ring that she had kept hidden till now. Peace restored, the maids began serving the soup, and then the fish course. Before the main course was served Uncle Edward proposed a toast to the happy couple, remarking that Jennifer was probably too good for his nephew, but he still wished them every happiness. Once the main course was finished, Jennifer's father gave a short speech, thanking me for my hospitality and for making his wife and himself the proudest parents in the world.

When it was time for the coffee to be served, the ladies retired to the lounge, leaving the gentlemen with their coffee, port and brandy, with cigars for those who smoked. Conversation was on the ups and downs of governments over the past four years and the perceived damage that had been done to business confidence. At the other end of the table Ted, Tom and the Buns' driver discussed the falling quality of workmanship on the modern Rolls-Royce, and how their vehicles were far superior to current models.

Eventually we all joined the ladies, whose talk had been upon the forthcoming wedding and babies. Mo was first to congratulate me, telling me she would support Jennifer as much as she could in her new role. Angela was next, telling me I had done the right thing. The other ladies followed with their good wishes, including Mickey, her housemate, who whispered an enquiry as to what my technique was for getting into Jennifer's knickers. I gently smiled, patted her bottom and said that she should ask her. The party broke up at about eleven, leaving the maids to clear away.

The next day's excursion, after church, to nearby Coggeshall was a complete success and everybody came away with something. Dinner that night was a very relaxed affair, with everybody looking forward to the fete and the official announcement.

The next morning began well with the sun burning through the morning mist. I was up early and was in my study reading the morning newspapers. More trouble in Northern Ireland, and a full account of the bombing of Westminster Hall the previous week. Then there was a knock on the door and Jennifer's father peeped round. I ushered him in and offered him coffee, which he gladly accepted. He told me that he wished to speak to me about the forthcoming wedding. I put up my hand in a gesture that he recognised as my wishing to speak. I told him that as a proud father he wanted to give his daughter a memorable wedding, but that the reception was also the first time that the new Lord and Lady Earlswood had of welcoming their friends to their home. While I realised that he would wish to see his daughter and her attendants dressed appropriately, as well as toasting the bride and groom in champagne, the rest of the arrangements would be part of a homewarming I wished to give. He smiled, shook my hand and told me I was a wonderful and generous man whom he would be proud to call son.

Jennifer followed him into my study, shortly after her dad had left. She put her arms around me and told me how thoughtful, understanding and tactful I was, in taking over the major cost of the wedding. I stood and we kissed passionately, with me fondling her bottom, which she told me excited her. We then joined the rest of the house guests for breakfast. The buffet served for lunch for my guests and the fete committee was a resounding success, with everyone mixing freely, talking to one another like friends and neighbours.

At quarter to two the chairman advised me it was time to take to the stage and perform the opening ceremony, not guessing what I was about to announce. I began by welcoming everybody to Alswell Manor and hoped that they would have an enjoyable afternoon and spend lots of money. I reminded them of the tragedy which had befallen me earlier in the year, and thanked all concerned for the help and the many messages of sympathy that I had received. 'Before I open this event, however,' I told them, 'there is something I want to share with you all, and that is that I am proud to announce my engagement to Miss Jennifer Brierly, and promise the village that there will be a lady at the manor before Christmas.' There was a spontaneous applause. Waiting for calm to be resumed, I finally declared the fete open. For many minutes we seemed to be in the middle of a crowd, each person wishing to congratulate us.

We then toured all the stalls and side shows, speaking to each stallholder in turn, until at last we reached the beer tent, where George, the village publican, served us cool drink. Taking George aside, I reminded him of our recent conversation regarding a special event. He told me that he remembered it well, and was pleased when I told him to plan for about 150 guests. I said that the date selected was the first Saturday in December, which would be my wedding day. I told him I would visit the pub the following Friday at about eleven o'clock to discuss the arrangements and to receive from him some menus for Jennifer to study.

Seeing that the time was nearly three fifteen, we began making our way back to the hall for afternoon tea. Although it was only a short walk, it took us nearly twenty minutes, as many people wanted to stop us and congratulate us on our engagement. Jennifer told me she felt like a pop star, being approached by so many kind and interested people, people she had never met and whom she did not know. I told her she would have to get used to such things until people got used to her new position. I also told her that we would be holding a press conference the following afternoon, when I would ask the press to keep intrusion to a minimum, so as to allow her to continue to do her job. When we reached the house, most of my house guests and the Gloworm crowd were already enjoying tea. The girls immediately left what they were doing to go to Jennifer and congratulate her. Mo told me that Mary had arranged for them to stay to dinner, especially as it was Mike's daughter's last night at the manor.

Once tea was over, I and Jennifer retired to my study, to have a brief respite before prize-giving at four thirty. Jennifer sank down in the comfortable chair and took her shoes off. I sat at my desk and told her there were a couple of things I needed to ask her. The first was, where did she want to go on her four days off later in the month? I suggested Paris or Rome, which were just the places for young lovers, but she shook her head. She told me that before she took up her duties as Lady Earlswood, she would like to do something totally mad. When she first came to Essex, she had spent the day with some other nurses at Yarmouth. She had never forgotten the fun she had had, and if I did not mind she would like to go back again.

'Yarmouth it is then,' I told her and she smiled happily. 'The second thing is the Colchester house. If, my love, you find that the pressure on you is too great following our announcement, please use the house,' and I rose and gave her the key.

I was just about to move to my next point when there came a knock at the door from Ted, reminding us that it was nearly time for prize-giving. Jennifer presented prizes to the children, and I was pleased to see how well children responded to her and how easy she was with them. I then did my share of the prize-giving, before once again we made our way back to the house, shaking well-wishers' hands as we went. We went to join our guests once more and to have another cup of tea Mary had just brewed. Sitting comfortably on a sofa, Jennifer quietly asked me what the other thing was. I leaned closer to her and quietly told her that, although I knew that her old Ford Escort had been a gift from her parents when she qualified, it was getting to the point where one either had to start spending a lot of money on it or have a newer model. With this in mind, I wanted her to have the Rover she had driven to Birmingham in and to let Ted dispose of the car at a second-hand auction. She thought for a moment, kissed me and accepted the proposition, telling me that she intended to thank me properly later.

The last-night dinner was a really happy affair, where the girls told us all of what they had got up to during the weekend, and said they were looking forward to the next one, which they thought might be in December. I also realised in conversation that, as well as Mike being on vacation for the remainder of August, Angela was joining my uncle and aunt on their annual holiday to Scotland, leaving me in sole charge of White Gull. Jennifer spent the rest of the evening with Marie Therese and her own parents, all of whom were leaving the next morning. I in turn, chatted with the Gloworm gang until they left, just before ten. Mary then served hot drinks, asking people to leave their dirty cups in the kitchen. Shortly afterwards the ladies hired to assist Mary during the day left, as did Ted and Mary. People started to drift off to their rooms to pack and to sleep. I also retired to my room, where I decided to read a little before turning in.

As I settled down, I heard a gentle knock at the door, saw the handle turn and in walked Jennifer, dressed in a matching nightdress and negligee. 'I had to come and say goodnight,' she said. I smiled and told her to come nearer, which she did. My arms went round her as our lips met. Our lovemaking went on for some time as we explored each other's bodies through our clothes. I invited her into the bedroom, but she refused, telling me that her parents would be next door and her mother was a light sleeper. I told her that I thought she was the most lovely creature in the world, to which she told me that flattery would get me just about anywhere. I took her in my arms again, kissing her and holding her close. She told me she knew how hard it was for me, and that she wanted to make love, but not here and not now. I told her that I understood, but roll on Yarmouth. She blushed, took a step back, and after a moment's hesitation suddenly removed all her clothes, standing there so beautiful and tempting. 'You might as well see what you now have as a future wife,' she said, then came forward and kissed me. She finally bent down, picked up her nightdress and put it back on, smiled, kissed me again and left.

The next morning everyone was up early, the Buns and Angela being the first to leave after breakfast. Tom arrived at ten, to take Mike and his family to the station. I stood at the door, and wished them a good vacation. Mike shook my hand and thanked me for a weekend they would never forget. Ted appeared and reminded me of the time, as he was to take Marie Therese and Jennifer to the boat. Once they had all departed, the ladies hired by Mary began making beds, and restoring the manor to its normal perfect condition. I went to the kitchen in search of coffee, and found Mary busy preparing lunch. As I entered she left what she was doing and came to give me a great big hug, telling me that she had wanted to do that all weekend. She then told me what a fine Lady Earlswood Jennifer would make.

The press conference went extremely well and Jennifer handled it like a professional, and not showing the nerves she felt. As we neared the end of the conference, I asked the press not to interfere in any way, as she went along with her professional duties as a busy ward sister.

Dinner that night was a small family affair. After dinner, Jennifer left for home after thanking Mary and Ted for all their hard work. We lingered in the doorway, exchanging kisses. I told her I would ring her later the following afternoon to find out how she had got on on her first day back.

The house then seemed quiet and empty, so I took myself up to my sitting room to prepare for London the next day.

That night I could not sleep, running hopes and fears through my mind. Would Jennifer be put off by all the interest and publicity that would focus on us both, and would she be willing to give up the full-time career she had been wedded to for so long? How would Mo react in the long term, watching another woman enjoying the lifestyle she had turned her back on? I was aware that she still loved me and would always be a close friend, but working so close to her, how would I resist the comfort which she told me would always be on offer? Would Peter continue to grow in the job as with Mo's help his part of the business grew and prospered? How long would Suzie be prepared to use her considerable talents on a business she did not own – and would I one day be faced with a management buyout? Lastly, how good would I be as the chairman of a multinational company and how long would my raw enthusiasm hold up? The answer was that only time would tell, and of course that is another story...

Lightning Source UK Ltd.
Milton Keynes UK
UKOW051600100512

192309UK00001B/1/P

9 781847 485885